The Heavens Are Telling

Child of Deliverance Series - Book Two

B.D. Riehl

The Heavens Are Telling
By B.D. Riehl

Copyright © 2014 B.D. Riehl

All rights reserved as permitted under the U.S. Copyright Act of 1976, no part of this publication may be reproduced, distributed, or transmitted in any form or by any means, or stored in a database or retrieval system, without the prior written permission of the publisher. The characters and events portrayed in this book are fictitious. Any similarity to a real person, living or dead is coincidental and not intended by the author.

First Edition eBook: 2014
First Edition Paperback: 2014

ISBN (ePub): 978-1-938596-25-4
ISBN (Paperback): 978-1-938596-26-1

Published in the United States of America
NCC Publishing
Meridian, Idaho 83642
www.nccpublishing.com

Cover Copyright © 2014 by NCC Publishing

Cover images by:
   Krivosheev Vitaly
   Teerawat Sumrantin
   Patrick Foto

Author image Copyright © 2014 by Michael E. Sloane

Typeface: Imperator – Copyright © by Paul Loyd Fonts (http://moorstation.org/typoasis/designers/lloyd/index.htm)
Typeface: Blokletters Balpen - Copyright © by LeFly Fonts (http://lefly.vepar.nl)
Typeface: Architects Daughter - Copyright © 2010, Kimberly Geswein (http://kimberlygeswein.com)

Many of the designations used by manufacturers and sellers to distinguish their products are claimed as trademarks. Product names, brands, and other trademarks referred to within this book are the property of their respective trademark holders. No association between the author and any trademark holder is expressed or implied.

20140907

Dedication

To Gran and Grandpa Brown

Summers spent at your ranch shaped me more than I can express. To this day, the sound of wind chimes takes me back to my happy place on your back patio. Thank you for sharing those times with me and for all of your love. I love you both so very much.

And to my grandpa "The Great Mr. Davis," I'll miss you forever. And I promise to share the ice cream from now on.

"The heavens are telling the glory of God;
 and the firmament proclaims his handiwork.
Day to day pours forth speech,
 and night to night declares knowledge.
There is no speech, nor are there words;
 their voice is not heard;
yet their voice goes out through all the earth,
 and their words to the end of the world."

> Psalm 19:1-4 NRSV

Chapter One

August – Pattaya, Thailand

Gage Easton's breath came slow and deliberate. He practiced the breathing technique that he'd been using for years to keep himself under control.

He had planned his trip down to every detail. He told Nataya that he would come back for her, that she should wait for him.

And she would be his forever.

Gage had not cleared the trip with his contacts and did not have permission from them to be in Thailand again so soon, but he didn't care. He siphoned money out of foreign accounts to buy the plane ticket and found a cheap motel in Pattaya; one *they* didn't use.

But Nataya wasn't waiting for him. Not like she was supposed to be.

He had been antsy as he readied himself earlier in the evening. He combed his hair, parted on the side and slicked down, just like Nataya had said she liked. He wore khaki shorts, his tropical print silk shirt—the one she had admired just a month ago—tucked in at the waist. Gage strode down Walking Street, passing girls calling out to him, smiling at him. They all wanted him.

But he only wanted Nataya.

He found the karaoke club where he had first met her. He knew that she would be in the back, waiting at the bar for him, just like before. Other men wanted her, but she would wait for Gage.

Only for him.

His heart pounded with memories of her. The way she danced, her eyes on his, begging for him to pick her. Nataya *knew* he could have any girl that he wanted. He had taken a seat at the bar in the back and watched; he liked making her wait. The room was reserved for special clients; those the owners knew were more sophisticated, more adapted to the special tourism opportunities of Thailand.

He was one of the special ones.

Gage had waited before he gave into the longing in her eyes.

Her longing for him.

He had enjoyed making her work for his attention. When he finally waved her over, she came running, anxious to be with him. They left quickly, and after their night together, she smiled at him and asked if he would come back to the bar.

He had fidgeted through meetings all day in anticipation of meeting her. Again and again for the next week of his business trip he had returned and taken her with him. She had waited for him, been as anxious for him as he was for her.

He had asked her to go home with him, but she said she would need time to prepare. Gage had promised to return and now he had.

There was a large crowd in the back this time.

A party maybe?

He didn't like when others thought they were as important as he. Maybe the karaoke manager, Lok Lee, was running a special.

Gage didn't like it.

He spotted Nataya instantly. Her beautiful dark hair, streaked with blond and red highlights; her lovely figure encased in the tight dress he had asked her to buy. It physically hurt to look upon her beauty; his body reacted instantly. He needed her. Gage took a trembling step toward Nataya, but stopped cold.

Nataya wasn't waiting for him. She was standing close to another man, nodding as he spoke with her.

Who does he think he is, talking to my girl?

Gage shook with rage when the man grasped her elbow. He hated the thought of another man's hands on her and watched in fury as she was led to Lok Lee. The manager accepted a wad of bills that was stuffed in his hands and waved Nataya and the other man away.

The slut!

Gage's lips tightened, his cheeks burned. His anger had always blurred his vision red, and now the bar patrons blended together in a dizzying whir of disjointed activity.

Gage tried to follow Nataya and the man, but the crowd was thick; the music was pounding so loudly it seemed to form an impenetrable wall around him. Helpless to catch up, he watched as they slipped out through a back door and onto the street.

Gone.

Gage waited for them all night. At the bar where girls he didn't care about tried to join him, he sat and stewed, swirling whiskey—at least he thought it was whiskey—round and round in his glass. Girl after girl approached him, asked him to play a game, offered to join him in a drink or dance for him.

Couldn't they see that he didn't want them? He only wanted Nataya—his beautiful Nataya. His eyes blurred with angry tears as he imagined her in his bed.

Slut.

How he hated her.

How he wanted her.

She had played him for a fool.

No. It couldn't be true.

She had wanted him; he knew it. She begged for him to come back for her, hadn't she? His mind grew fuzzy, and he shoved the glass across the sticky bar, pressing the heels of his hands into his eyes. The music pulsated around him, loud and intrusive. He felt a hand on his back, knew it had to be Nataya, and turned excitedly.

But it was only one of the barmaids, an ugly one with crooked teeth and large, awkward breasts. He preferred Nataya's delicate frame and straight, white teeth.

The girl leaned close—*why did they all want to be so close?*—and asked if he was having fun. He shook his head at her; he didn't want her. She looked to someone behind him, uncertain, and pressed against him. Annoyed, he stood and shoved her away, terrified that Nataya would return and see him with another woman. She would be jealous.

"Hey, hey, hey!" Lok Lee ran up to him and yelled something in Thai to the girl before he turned back to Gage.

The girl scurried away.

"You want to get rough, that extra!" Lok Lee shouted. The small manager held out his hand, expecting Gage to pay.

Gage shoved his hand away, ready to fight the man who had let his girl go, the one who had sent her away. When Lok Lee only snapped his fingers, Gage scoffed at him and turned to leave, ignoring his bill on the counter behind him. He wasn't paying for that lousy drink. The only way he would pay is if Nataya were returned to him. He whirled to face the manager, ready to squeeze Lok Lee's wiry throat until he told Gage where Nataya was.

He paused when the crowd around him cleared away and three large men that he hadn't noticed before surrounded him. Two grasped his elbows on each side while the other led the way out the back door.

Gage instantly sobered and began to babble. "Listen, guys, I've just had too much to drink. My girl left with someone else. She was supposed to wait for me. You can understand. No harm done. Right? Nothing wrong. I'll just pay my tab and leave."

The men led him through a maze of halls and doors until they came to the alley behind the bar. One of them stepped forward and fumbled for Gage's wallet in his pants.

"That's right. Right there's my wallet, take it and pay my tab and I'll be on my way. No more trouble."

The man located his wallet and pocketed it in his own jeans. Gage opened his mouth to protest, but an explosion of pain ricocheted off of the side of his head. His body fell forward into a rivulet of sewer water next to the board that had just been cracked across his skull. They kicked at his ribs, stomped on his legs. One of them kicked his face. Darkness swirled in front of Gage's eyes while the men silently and meticulously searched his pockets, finding his hidden stash of pre-paid credit cards and cash. They stripped him of his expensive watch and pocketed it while Gage weakly twitched his fingers in pathetic protest.

"Just another night in paradise, mister. Next time, don't try to leave without paying your bill."

※ ※ ※

Simon Russell rubbed the back of his neck, wincing as he hit a pinched nerve. He dropped his hand to his side and rolled his neck slowly in circles, hoping to ease the tension in his head and back. For five months Simon had been on staff in Pattaya, Thailand with Deliverance, an organization that rescued child slaves from Walking Street and placed them in safe homes to give them an education, a future—hope.

He was in charge of maintenance and grounds for the Pattaya volunteer and staff dorms and worked long hours during the day to keep things running smoothly. For the last few weeks he had volunteered in the evenings for a separate humanitarian group that acted as a sort of ambulance service for the tired, dirty nightlife of downtown Pattaya. Dozens of calls, from beat up prostitutes to passed-out drunks to foolish tourists that wandered into the wrong alley, came throughout the night. Simon kept busy.

But he gleaned valuable information from those that appreciated his help. He knew more people and had gathered more names and addresses of possible pimps and girls in slavery than Deliverance had been able to do in months of research. Simon had a way with people, and they easily opened up to him.

Tonight the radios were mostly quiet. He sat with another volunteer, Tori, a med student from Washington that worked in

Thailand in the summer as an English teacher to help pay for college. When the teams weren't out on calls, they sat in a small area on the edge of Walking Street, collecting donations for the gas they used to pick up patients.

They also collected money for coffins.

Simple pine boxes were stacked on top of one another against the building behind their table. Simon hated the sight of them, hated more the reality that the dozens of coffins stacked behind him would go fast over the next week. There was such poverty and despair that when they found a dead body and no one claimed it, they had to dispose of it themselves without knowing anything about the person that once lived.

Simon desperately wanted everyone—even the pimps and traffickers—to know about God and His saving grace. How different the world would be if everyone knew; if everyone believed. He knew that laws were easily broken; morals could not be legislated. The answer was to cut sin off at the source; to show the lost and weary and angry and bitter and broken that they needed the Lord. The desire to tell everyone burned in his chest so tight that he had moved to Thailand to face sin head on. To bring the light of Christ to the darkest place he could think of: the hub of sexual tourism.

But that night the fire felt cold inside him.

He worked and lost sleep and posted to social media sites and sent out letters. Still, Western Christians very rarely understood how deep the pit that he faced each day. They could feed the homeless, host Vacation Bible School, and attend Bible studies—all important. But where was the life-changing passion that the world needed? Where was the sacrificial love that they preached about? Simon ran his hands through his hair. He was tired—irritable.

He knew that in his exhaustion he was being unfair, that followers of God did their best; not everyone felt the intense passion he did for the world around them. He knew believers that cared and did the best they could to love on neighbors and co-workers in the ways that God had called them to.

He watched people passing him on Walking Street in droves: partiers, vacationers, countless men that had come to be part of the tourism that Thailand was famous for. Lost. All lost. Some days the lack of sleep and the never-ending need to do *something* got to him.

Lord, how can I reach them all? You tell us to go, to tell. I'm here, Lord. I'm here and I'm telling. Please drown me out with Your words, Your voice; not mine. Please open their ears to hear.

Tori's radio crackled and they both sat up to listen. It was Tori's last night before she flew home for fall semester, and she was anxious to go out with a bang.

They stood as an address was given and raced for the worn pickup truck that acted as their ambulance. Lance, another volunteer that drove the truck, met them there and briefed them. "Pretty bad head injury. Sounds like paradise got a little too rough for this American perv," he said, climbing into the driver's seat.

Tori and Simon shared a humorless laugh. When they located the man, passed out and bleeding from a gash on his head, Simon winced at the tropical print shirt and the package of condoms that had apparently fallen from the man's pocket when he had been attacked and robbed. The cut on his head was bad, but would only require a few stitches. Tori would be disappointed; they didn't dare patch up Americans for fear of being sued. No matter that this guy would only need a few stitches and some serious aspirin, the Thai hospital would have to take care of him.

Simon shook his head, leaning to help Lance lift the man into the bed of the truck. "Sure makes you proud to be an American, doesn't it, Tori?" Simon said. "Come on. Let's get this loverboy patched up and on a one-way flight back to the Land of the Free."

Chapter Two

Nataya gripped Donny's hand. Her heart pounded in her ears. She longed to look back, to see who followed, see if she would recognize one of Lok Lee's bouncers in the crowded street behind them, but she didn't dare. Donny squeezed her hand and wiped his glistening brow with his other hand. They looked like any other couple strolling through Walking Street: a young, scantily clad Thai woman with long black-and-blond-streaked hair on the arm of an older man with a slight pooch in his middle and a nervous twitch to his eye. She observed girls with downcast eyes, men with eyes averted; dozens of them marched up and down the wide-paved street.

Could it be true that she would never again be one of those girls pretending to enjoy the affections of paying men because her life depended on it?

Flashing neon lights and bass-heavy music pulsated around them. Donny glanced at her once, eyes reassuring, before he shoved her without warning into a narrow alley.

Nataya gasped in fear and shock, trembling. *Had they seen? Would they follow? Why wasn't this man running?*

Donny causally pulled her around a man who was passed out against the side of the building. Nataya's lips curled as they stepped around a pool of vomit and up a flight of creaky wooden stairs. Her spiked heels slipped through a broken stair, and she bit her lip to keep from crying out. Donny roughly yanked her foot free, his gruff manner frightening her further.

Was he really sent to rescue me?

She'd thought she could trust Moree and Dugan, but now she wasn't sure. At the top of the stairs, Donny stopped before a green metal door and fumbled in his pocket.

Nataya chanced a look toward the opening of the alley. *There. Near the sleeping man, was that the glow of a cigarette in the shadows behind the dumpster?* Or was she imagining it? Her belly quaked and rolled. She was going to be sick.

Donny found his key and opened the door. Nataya stumbled over the threshold behind him. The door slammed shut behind her, echoing through a cavernous room. Too dark for her to see, she let Donny lead her across the room.

The click-clack-click of her heels on the floor rang in her ears. *Too loud. They would hear! Too loud.*

Donny ushered her through another set of doors, down another flight of stairs, into another alley. Nataya blinked. A motorbike purred next to the building, the rider's face covered with a dark helmet, his arms taut, gripping the handles. He didn't look at them.

Donny dug in his pocket again and handed Nataya a hairband, waving his hand wildly to indicate she should put her hair up. Shaky and terrified, Nataya obeyed and gathered her long hair into a crude bun. Donny reached behind a large dumpster in the alley and retrieved another dark helmet and a pair of men's pants.

Reading Donny's gestures, she drew on the pants but her heel caught again. Fear escaped her throat in a strangled, desperate gasp. Donny, grim and impatient, ripped off her heels and shoved them behind the metal box. A pair of men's boots was tossed back from the rider, and Nataya pulled them on her feet while Donny lifted the helmet in the air above her. He plunked it onto her head and quickly snapped the straps into place before he finally scooped Nataya onto the back of the bike. A man's jacket was thrown over her shoulders. She shoved her arms into the holes; the tips of her long nails barely broke through the opening of the long sleeves. Her head throbbed from the rough placement of the helmet.

The bike revved once. Instinct shot Nataya forward onto the seat; her arms grasped around the rider's middle as he sped off. She closed her eyes tight against the blur of city lights. Heart in her throat, the moto rumbled through her belly and down to her toes, churning in sync with her frazzled nerves.

The bike rushed on.

Nataya hoped she could remain conscious, even as she felt the blood drain from her face. Her limbs went numb from gripping the driver to remain on the bike through each violent, slanted turn. The helmet blocked out the street noise and her breath traveled the circumference of the interior to land back in her face; a stilted, wheezing, fearful series of groans and gasps. The scene changed every time she chanced a look.

A crowded street full of karaoke bars.

A quiet dirt road.

A closed marketplace.

When they pulled in front of a bus station, her fear settled into indifference.

Too late to turn back now.

Chapter Three

Cannon Beach, Orgeon

"Five minutes to go." An electronic female voice echoed from the phone clipped onto Jakobi's waistband, and she grunted in a mixture of relief and frustration. *Five more minutes…you can do this!*

She swiped an arm across her damp forehead and concentrated on the landscape before her. The sun shone, but barely. The fog on the beach created a glowing haze that engulfed her in its sweet and salty grip. As much as Jakobi hated running, she knew she would never tire of mornings on the Oregon coast.

Cannon Beach had been her home for the majority of her life, and she knew she would soon ache with a longing for every corner of it. Not that there was much to miss. The quaint town had one main street that housed the typical coastal tourist shops: a candy store that boasted the finest salt-water taffy, coffee houses and restaurants, an art gallery that sold seashells and glass bottles filled with ships and beach scenes. Seasoned locals frequented the more convenient shops located twelve miles away in Seaside, a larger town with a theater, chain grocery store, and outlet mall. But Jakobi preferred the subdued streets and eclectic shops of Cannon Beach. She always had.

She spotted the set of concrete stairs that led from the beach to the town and curved to her left, the soft sand pulling her legs down into its divots with surprising strength. Jakobi gritted her teeth and clenched her fists, determined to finish strong.

The voice blared at her as she reached the bottom step, "Run Complete. Congratulations."

Instead of slowing her pace, Jakobi took a deep breath and pursed her lips together, determined to charge up the steps. It was a bad decision. She forgot to breathe and halfway up the stairs her foot slipped, and she came down hard on the sharp edge of a step. She cried out in frustration and pain as her shin hit the cement with a crack. Heart pounding, her limbs shaking and glistening with sweat, she rotated and sat down hard. She steadied herself with her hands on the step behind her as spots bubbled before her eyes.

Jakobi carefully stretched out her leg, sharp pain pulsating from just below her knee down to her toes. The fall had left a cut on her leg and blood dripped down her shin. *Fabulous.*

Tears of frustration pooled in Jakobi's eyes. She had always been thin, but never because of any commitment to exercise. She had received papers a month ago, finally informing her that she would be placed in Cambodia for her term with the Peace Corps. The papers warned that she would need to ride a bicycle from place to place as the Peace Corps banned their volunteers from riding motos.

There was also a possibility that she would be assigned to an area that flooded six months out of the year, forcing residents to get by on canoes. *Lovely. So what you're saying is I should be prepared to run a triathlon to get to my work site.*

She had given her Peace Corps papers a sarcastic thumbs up before loading a training app on her phone that promised to whip her into shape before she left for Cambodia.

Jakobi owned neither a bike nor a canoe. *Go figure*, she thought. She certainly didn't want to adjust her lungs and limbs to strenuous exercise in front of the Khmer people.

One week away from her departure and she could run three miles, but her legs were always rubber by the end, and she was sure she would die after each run. And now she had an open wound to heal before she left.

Jakobi pursed her lips in annoyance and self-mockery while she dabbed at her leg. She gave up and leaned back, trying again to stretch out her leg. The sun continued to rise on the horizon; its warmth finally broke through the mist that blanketed the beach. For a Sunday morning, it was surprisingly empty and quiet. It was the last official weekend of summer, and Jakobi knew that the tourists would soon be out in droves, most descending the very set of stairs she now felt trapped on. She had to finish climbing them and get home.

Jakobi took a deep breath and hoisted herself to her feet, crying out at the sharp pain that radiated down her leg. She clung to the metal railing. The fine sand that coated her hands from the steps caused her hand to slip on the smooth metal. She took one excruciating step at a time and finally made it to the top.

Jakobi was halfway through town and still a mile away from home when a deep voice called out to her. "Well, you're certainly not going to get anywhere on that leg, now are you?"

She winced and turned to face the voice, surprised that he was still in town. Surprised more at how much his voice made her skin crawl. Jakobi drew in a deep breath and looked directly at him. *Yup. Still handsome as all get out.*

Blond hair, perfectly gelled, tall, broad shoulders, narrow waist, clean-cut—the man could model for a fashion magazine. He was too religious for that, however.

"Well, Brad, still trolling Cannon Beach, I see." Jakobi gave him a tight-lipped smile, resting her leg on a low planter bed near the sidewalk.

Brad, ignorant of her disgust, twirled his car keys around his finger and ignored the statement. "Hop in." He gestured to his black sports car.

Jakobi's glance swung from his blue eyes to the car. "Are you serious?"

He laughed out loud, long and deep, at the look of scrutiny on her face. "I'm not going to bite you, Jakobi. Get in."

She rolled her eyes and turned to walk away with as much attitude as she could muster. Attitude didn't necessarily ooze, she realized, when one was bogged down with a limp. Jakobi heard the low snarl of his car engine turning over, shook her head as gravel crunched beside her under Brad's car tires. She glanced over when the passenger window rolled down, but Brad didn't speak, just watched the road and coasted next to her. He draped one wrist casually over the top of the steering wheel, rested his other hand on the passenger seat, calm, yet in control. His laughing eyes had hardened into that look she knew. The one that made it clear he was in charge and would not let up until she admitted defeat.

She hobbled along for a few minutes, her jaw set stubbornly. If she clung to her anger, she could forget her embarrassment over being caught limping through town. *So much for asserting my independence.*

Would she ever forget the memories that slammed through her as his spicy cologne tainted the air around him? Would she always feel the need to prove herself in this town?

Finally, Jakobi's leg ached more than she could bear and cancelled out her turbulent emotions. She let out a gusty sigh, turned, and yanked open the passenger door.

"That's my girl." He winked at her and stepped on the gas before she could change her mind. She gritted her teeth and sat as far away from him as possible, back rigid.

They rode in silence while Brad followed the road past town and further into the hills surrounding it. The car snaked beneath a canopy of mixed trees; pine and spruce, western hemlock and Douglas fir. Jakobi, jaw set, watched the patches of shimmering blue as the ocean played peek-a-boo through the forest. The peace, invoked by the lush green contrasted against the vibrant blue ocean, almost relaxed her. She kept the window down to temper the strong cologne in the car, and the smell of sea salt and pine, kissed by almost constant drizzling rain, entranced her.

"Turn just after the bridge, to your right," Jakobi instructed.

Brad looked askance at her, annoyed. *I know.*

Dirt crunched beneath the car as Brad turned off of the paved road to the private lane that led to Jakobi's family home. She stiffened involuntarily as a torrent of memories flooded her when he easily parked in "his" spot and turned off the engine. Jakobi mumbled a "thank you" and pushed open the door, eager to escape him—his cologne cloud, his assault on her memories.

Brad was faster and appeared at her side of the car, offering a hand to help her out. Jakobi was repulsed by the feel of her hand in his, annoyed at the warmth of his grip. He helped her up the stairs and across the wide porch to the front door. Jakobi opened her mouth to bid him "So long and don't come back" when they both heard tires on the gravel. Brad smiled triumphantly while Jakobi groaned.

"Wow, I haven't seen your sister in forever," Brad said to Jakobi as her fifteen-year-old sister, Ava, waved enthusiastically from the backseat of her parents' white sedan.

Jakobi barely noticed; her eyes were trained on the hopeful look on her mother's face.

❖ ❖ ❖

"Molly, would you like me to set the table?" Brad asked Jakobi's mother as Jakobi turned to go upstairs for a quick shower.

"Thank you, Brad. You have always been so helpful. You remember where the plates are?"

Jakobi rolled her eyes at the sickeningly sweet tone in her mother's voice. *What are you doing here, Brad?*

She resisted the urge to take her time in the shower, torn between wanting to hide from the expectant group downstairs and the need to get the uncomfortable afternoon over and done with as soon as possible.

Her gash had stopped bleeding, and she applied ointment and a bandage to the scrape. She noticed the cut wasn't nearly as bad as the bruise forming around it.

"Good thing I have a week for that to heal before I fly out," she murmured to herself.

The deep rumble of her father and Brad talking in the living room directly below the small Jack-and-Jill bathroom that connected her room to Ava's room made her wish she was leaving that day. Or even better, that minute. *My, how times have changed.*

Jakobi wiped the lingering steam from the mirror and saw a trace of the girl that used to primp there. The one that relished the sounds she now loathed. She saw the long, thick red hair, loose and wavy, the love-glow that stained her freckled cheeks; the light of hope—similar to her mother's—in her eyes. No make-up, of course. Dad hadn't allowed it, and Brad liked his girls fresh faced.

Jakobi shook her head. *Why did it still hurt so much?*

A light knock on the door startled Jakobi out of her reverie.

"Jakobi?" Her sister's muffled voice called through the door connected to Ava's room. "We're waiting on you to pray."

Of course they were. Every minute together was spent trying to suck Jakobi back in. Annoyed, Jakobi yanked open a drawer and pulled out her make-up bag. She twirled the mascara wand against her long lashes in defiance. "Be right there."

Jakobi ran a pick through her curly shoulder-length hair and drew it into a messy bun. She entered her room to yank on a pair of jeans and a blue cotton shirt. At the top of the stairs, she sucked in a breath and held it a beat before she exhaled in rhythm with her descent to the dining room.

Her parents and Ava and Brad were seated at the table, a steaming plate of roast surrounded by potatoes, carrots, and celery set in the middle of them. Brad's gaze flickered over her appreciatively, stopping cold at her bun and make-up. His hard eyes matched her father's, and she raised her chin at them both as she took her seat next to Brad, across from Ava and her mother.

Her mother reached out her hands, indicating the start of prayer. Jakobi held her hands in her lap when Brad opened his palm toward her. Ava reached across the table for Jakobi's left hand and a tense pause filled the room. Her mother, face pinched and pale, shifted her eyes imploringly at Jakobi. Her father's face tightened from his place at the head of the table. Satisfied that she'd regained a small measure of independence, Jakobi grasped Ava's hand. Eyes never leaving her mother's, Jakobi held out her other hand, palm down, wrist slack, toward Brad. Her fingers lay unresponsive in his grip while her father spoke the blessing. When Brad tried to squeeze her fingers at the "Amen" she twisted her hand free. He eyed her, blue eyes hollow, spots of red blooming on his cheeks. Jakobi faced his glare. *What did you expect?*

Jakobi's father quietly ate his dinner while her mother and Ava did their best to keep the stilted conversation light. Jakobi took the offered platter of roast and chose the vegetables farthest from the meat and passed the plate to her sister. Her father's fork clattered to his plate, startling everyone.

"So not only is our faith not good enough for you," her father commented, "our meat is beneath you as well?" He leaned his elbows on the table and clasped his hands together loosely, fingers entwined. His tongue moved inside his mouth to dislodge a piece of roast from the back of his teeth.

"Hal, please…" Molly's soft voice was barely heard above the deafening roar of disapproval emanating from the head of the table.

For the months that Jakobi had been home, she and her father had fallen into an awkward but necessary rhythm of casual conversation and non-committal nods. The dam holding her father's disdain over Jakobi's choices at bay had been cracking; now it burst forth.

Jakobi sighed. "Dad, you know that's not it. I explained this all before. I try not to eat very much meat, and when I do, I only eat organic, grass-fed—"

"Expensive hippie meat. I know." Hal picked up his utensil and forked a hunk of roast and popped it into his mouth, effectively silencing her. "Delicious roast, Molly," Hal spoke, his gaze never leaving Jakobi's.

Jakobi grasped the sides of her chair, toes curling and uncurling in the carpet beneath the table. "Dad, I'm only here another week. Let's not do this. Please."

A pregnant pause settled on the table. For once, Brad didn't try to step in to charm either side. Ava stared at her hands, clasped tightly in her lap. Molly glanced nervously between Jakobi and Hal, who stared down the table at each other. Hal poked his tongue inside his cheek a few times, a twitch Jakobi knew well. He was either about to explode or tuck his anger away for another time. Jakobi, face open, straightened her shoulders. Her father had a quick tongue, but he had never been violent, and he no longer scared her. Hal's pupils shrunk and Jakobi took pity on his pride.

Jakobi broke eye contact and turned aside to address her mother. "Mom, could you pass the rolls, please."

Molly blinked at her oldest daughter, brow wrinkled. Her fingers fluttered near her collar.

"Rolls? Yes, rolls." Molly straightened and passed the breadbasket to Jakobi. The occupants of the table shook loose the chains of exposed emotion and came alive. Forks scraped against plates, delivering bites of pot roast and vegetables to mouths anxious to be busy. Meaningless observations of the coastal weather passed through them before Brad, never one to appreciate public confrontation, found the appropriate moment to make his escape.

He paused at the door, waiting for Jakobi to walk him out as she always had. She gathered a few plates from the table and ran her gaze down his form, making sure that he knew it was only an afterthought, and bid him good-bye before she walked into the kitchen.

Jakobi scraped leftovers into the trash while her mother whispered apologies and excuses to the man Jakobi had once planned to spend her life with.

The door closed and Jakobi snapped on the kitchen faucet, the hot water mixing with fiery tears and memories she'd rather forget.

"Jakobi! I do not understand what has gotten into you!" Jakobi turned to face her mother who stood, fists planted indignantly on her hips, in the doorway.

Jakobi shook her head. *No, you wouldn't.* Aloud she said, "I'm sorry I hurt you, Mom. I'm sorry that you're embarrassed." She held her mother's gaze for another moment, her tone bearing witness to her sincerity, her eyes assuring that she would not back down, before she returned to scrubbing the dishes. Jakobi felt her mother's disappointment. She might have withered and given in if the memories weren't pelting her. Wounds, long ago scarred over and calloused, protected her from the arrows of her mother's guilt. How many years had it been since they stood in that kitchen in the same way; Jakobi doing the dishes, her mother disappointed in her...

"*Jakobi, when are you going to understand that Brad doesn't like you to wear make-up?*"

Her mother had been disappointed then as well.

Jakobi had cried then, the mascara streaking her face, staining the soapy water like little drops of poison. Unlike now, at that time her mother's disappointment had been unbearable.

"I ju-ust wanted to l-look nice for him," Jakobi sobbed.

She had spent hours preparing for her date with Brad. She purchased a new dress with money she'd saved, showered with expensive body soap, carefully pinned back her unruly hair. Jakobi remembered how meticulously she had applied and cleaned off and re-applied the appropriate amount of make-up so as not to be overdone, but to delicately brighten her features. She felt pretty when she descended the stairs to greet Brad for their one-year anniversary date.

He stared at her without speaking, red creeping up his neck, settling into spots on his cheeks. Jakobi had hesitated on the last step. Was he angry?

She had been completely unaware of the full range of Brad's emotions. When she returned home, she tried to talk to her mother about the evening, tried to make sense of all that had transpired.

"Jakobi"—Molly had been exasperated with her—"I've told you what you have to do to keep a man: don't argue, compliment him, do what he wants, please him. Make him happy. This is important, Jakobi. How else will you get a husband?"

Standing at the sink so many years later, Jakobi's stomach clenched. Would she ever forget that night and others that followed? Probably not, although she hoped moving across the world would at least soften the blow. She thought the last five years in college had helped. The awkward lunch with Brad and the accusing tone of her mother proved her wrong.

No, the pain was still deep, the wound raw and open. One thing had changed over the years, however. Jakobi had a backbone. She understood her strength as a woman and could proudly stand firm in that. And if that became too difficult, there was always the promise of two years in Cambodia in just seven days.

Chapter Four

Pattaya, Thailand

Gage struggled to open his eyes. Pain ricocheted through what must be a cracked skull. He licked parched lips and called out for water. Slowly, a cacophony of sounds buzzed around him, mocking his torment: ringing phones, beeps, moaning, shouts, and sandals slapping against linoleum floors. He inched one eye open, wincing at the blinding light from the ceiling.

A hospital ceiling.

An intake of breath sent a feeling like shards of glass ripping through his lungs. The last thing Gage remembered was watching Nataya betray him. Pain that had nothing to do with his stinging ribs sliced through him.

Nataya. How could she do that to me?

His head pounded in rhythm with a sluggish heartbeat. *I need to get up*, he thought, slowly rolling to one side. His eyes followed the roll, tracing the ceiling, then a wall and the floor. He was in a hospital hallway, in a bed against the wall. The other side of the hall was also lined with beds, mostly empty. *Why am I here?*

The memory of the men in the alley rushed back at him, hitting him full-force like another slam to his head. Their fists— the bleak darkness that followed the final blow.

He eased an elbow under his body and rose slowly.

A nurse rushed at him, jabbering—scolding.

I don't understand Thai. He was unable to force the words out through his lips. He was unreasonably annoyed with her. *Why couldn't she hear the words that pounded in my skull?*

She grabbed his arm and pushed him back on the bed. He shook her off. He didn't want another woman to touch him, only his Nataya. The nurse tried again and he shoved her weakly. She placed indignant hands on her hips, her eyes and mouth stern.

Gage obliged and laid back. He groped for his pockets. *Where is my wallet?*

The nurse rattled something. Her voice sounded like Nataya. He hated her for reminding him. He tried to shove her again when a tall male dressed in a white coat placed himself between the nurse and Gage.

"You speak English, mister?"

Gage settled his head on the pillow. *Finally.* He nodded feebly.

"Okay. Brought in last night. Beaten badly. We found nothing in pockets, no money, no wallet. Bandaged your head. As soon as you feel ready to stand, you need to pay. Then may go."

Gage felt his pants again.

Empty.

The light faded to black...

Hours later, Gage woke with a start. The pain in his eyes was still sharp against the blinding light, but much less than before. The halls were empty and much quieter now. Sunlight filtered through a window above the bed that he hadn't noticed earlier, dulling the fluorescent lights overhead. He rolled, stomach lurching, and slowly rose to a seated position, legs dangling over the side of the bed. He waited a few minutes, then stood, testing his strength. He felt like a truck had hit him. He walked shakily toward the exit, ignoring sharp shouts behind him.

An orderly stopped him before he exited and led him to the payment desk. He spread his hands. "I don't have a wallet. They stole my money! How can I pay?"

A middle-aged Thai woman seated at the desk smiled at him, although he didn't think she meant it.

Only Nataya meant it.

"Sir, the ambulance service that brought you here reported that you had been robbed and knocked out. You can contact insurance or bank." The phone rang at her desk. Gage winced, barely hearing the rest of her heavily accented English. "There are phones right over there so that you can work something out. But you cannot leave without paying." She waved a hand toward a bank of phones against the opposite wall and picked up the ringing phone.

Gage wanted to spit on her. *What am I supposed to do? I can't call insurance, I can't have traces of this trip. I'm not supposed to be here now.*

He had come for Nataya. He had promised to come for her. He couldn't call the credit card company; he couldn't risk a paper trail. He thought of the cash he'd used to buy plane tickets.

One for Nataya.

He knew whom to call, but it was dangerous. Gage stood with a hand on the receiver, knees shaking. *I don't have a choice.* He tried to raise the phone to his ear; his clammy hand slipped, and the receiver clattered against the phone base.

Gage gritted his teeth, grimacing against the pain that radiated across his forehead. He wiped his palm on his shirt and tried again, dialing the number that he had memorized, knowing he could never write it down.

The answer was curt—annoyed. Gage licked his lips and whispered his situation. His eyes darted across the busy hospital. A doctor, eyes down on the chart in his hand, walked over to the woman at the desk. Her smile for the doctor was real, Gage observed. He gripped the phone, mouth pinched at the obscenities growled at him from the voice on the other line.

"I know. I understand. But it doesn't work for you if I'm stuck here. It doesn't work for you if I call my insurance…my bank—"

"Is that a threat?" It was a mocking statement more than a question.

"Of course not." Gage cleared his throat. "I just wanted to remind you I'm no good to you here. I have more products that I was able to obtain; they are in my hotel room. I just hope the room hasn't been cleaned. You could go there, I guess, but then—"

"You fool," the voice hissed.

Gage hung up the phone and waited. An hour later the phone rang at the desk. The front desk woman listened for a moment, then glanced around the room, waving Gage over when her eyes met his. This time she didn't try to smile, just handed him a sheet to sign.

"You're free to go."

✤ ✤ ✤

A blanket was settled around Nataya's shoulders. She was not cold, although her body trembled violently. Her abdomen ached from her efforts to press down each wave of nausea.

True to their word, Moree and Dugan had sent help. They employed a well-practiced plan the moment she agreed to go with them; to say yes to freedom. They met Nataya and the rider at the bus station and had quickly ushered her aboard a large bus. Moree bribed the ticket agent, the guard, and the driver. All agreed to forget that they had seen the young girl dressed in baggy pants and a leather jacket.

Nataya was led to a bench seat where she let her head fall against the window, cracked open slightly to let in a slight breeze. She said nothing, only stared into the night as the bus chugged away from Pattaya. She didn't ask where they were going. *It doesn't matter.*

Hours later, still in Thailand but obviously in a smaller city, they pulled into a bus station. Moree supported Nataya down the stairs into a small truck, sandwiched between her and Dugan. The truck rumbled through quiet streets and turned into a wide driveway. The headlights shone on a closed gate. Dugan jumped out of the truck and ran to it, jangling the chains free with a key. Nataya took note of the barbed wire swirled across the top of the fence. She pulled her bottom lip in with her teeth.

Moree followed Nataya's gaze. She tenderly took the young girl's cold, damp hand. "To keep you safe. See how the wire is on the outside? Not to keep you in, but to keep danger out."

Nataya nodded, uncertain.

Dugan opened the gate and jumped back into the truck. He pulled through, parked the truck just inside, and hopped out to lock it again. The chain link rattled as the gate slammed shut, a puny sound that reverberated in Nataya's swirling mind.

Chains. She hated when men brought chains.

Moree led Nataya down a moonlit hall to a small room and offered her the chance to shower, but Nataya shook her head. Nataya wrapped the jacket closer around her shoulders. Moree then led her to a small bed in the corner and sat beside her on the flowery blanket. "Nataya, try to get some sleep. We will take you to the doctor tomorrow, but for now, sleep. It's been a very long night." Moree rose.

Fear of being left alone in the strange room shot through Nataya. She cried out and clung to Moree's arm.

"Hush, sweetie, hush. I'm not leaving. I'll be right there, all night if you need me." Moree pointed to a cushioned chair in the corner. "Right here. I will sit here all night. You rest."

Nataya didn't think it was possible. She leaned back onto the bed, drew her knees up under her chin. The trembling started in her spine, worked its way through her core. Nataya gripped her arms tighter around her abdomen. The soft dip in the mattress pulled her into an exhausted, fitful sleep.

The next morning the trembling remained and her muscles ached as Nataya sat in the small clean medical clinic, surrounded by smiling nurses and sympathetic doctors. Moree, true to her word, stayed by her side. Nataya slouched further down in the chair. Her arms were sore where they'd drawn blood. Moree had tried to explain why, that they were testing her for sickness that might have been passed to her. Nataya worried her bottom lip. What if the tests came back positive? Would she be returned to Lok Lee? Her right knee bounced up and down. Moree watched with concern, but left Nataya to her troubled thoughts.

Daylight streamed through the open windows in the hall. Crisp, clean, country air rippled through Nataya's disheveled hair. It had been so long since she'd seen the sun—so long since she'd taken a breath without the smell of fried foods and smoke and sour beer filling her senses.

They would know she was gone by now. Lok Lee would furiously pick over the girls, checking the numbers, the money. As everyone filed in from their last visits of the night, they would huddle in the cramped hot room, too broken to look anyone in the eye, each would retreat into their own tortured thoughts. Suchin would crawl close—

Nataya's eyes widened, her teeth bit down hard enough to draw blood from her lips.

Suchin!

She had been so focused on being rescued, so desperate for release from that dark and shattered place, she had forsaken her friend. Nataya felt as if she'd swallowed a hot rock; fire and pain spread across her chest. Would Suchin know that Nataya had abandoned her? *No, of course not.*

She would worry and live in fear. Rescue wasn't an option known to them. There was only one other way out. The rock settled into her chest.

Sweet little Suchin, I'm sorry, so sorry. Nataya leaned forward, rocking back and forth.

"Nataya." A brisk, but gentle voice called to her from an open door. The woman held a clipboard and an expression Nataya couldn't decipher. Moree helped her up, gathering the blankets that fell at Nataya's feet. Within minutes of the results being read, thoughts of Suchin were crowded out, replaced by swirling confusion and terror.

Pregnant.

Nataya was pregnant.

❁ ❁ ❁

Nataya waited for Moree to tell her that they were going to cut the baby out. Like last time...and the time before. She waited through the drive back to the house—a different one this time—and through lunch, barely able to keep the meal down. The home-cooked food was delicious, and Nataya wished she could enjoy it. She couldn't remember a time that she had eaten indoors at a table. Nataya chewed her food slowly, glancing around the new house. It was smaller than the last one, with only a few rooms; a large main area, a kitchen, and stairs that led to the roof. It was quiet when they entered, and Nataya wondered if this was where they would cut her belly open. Would she go back to the other much larger home when her wounds were healed? Or was she ruined, destined to go back to the streets of Pattaya?

Moree watched Nataya's pale face through lunch and wished she could ease her fear. They had so much work to do. Such a long journey ahead with different challenges than other rescued girls. Maybe it would help if she saw the other housemates.

When Nataya at last pushed the bowl away from her, a grimace of apology in her eyes, Moree took her to the rooftop. Tables were set up in two rows in one corner, facing a desk in front that was turned toward the rest, a whiteboard set up behind it. The other side of the roof housed boxes of vegetables—a rooftop garden. Nataya had never seen one.

The desks were filled with young girls. Nataya eyed the backs of their heads with a tinge of jealousy. These must be girls whose rescues would work out; girls that did not have the mark of rape growing in them, girls who would not become more of a burden than they'd already been. She crossed her arms over her stomach, wondering why Moree brought her to the roof. A light breeze carried the sweet aroma of fresh vegetation from the garden boxes. Nataya longed to dig her fingers into the soil, to tickle the roots of the plants, to feel life, waxy and real beneath her fingers. The woman in front—the teacher, Nataya assumed—said something to the class and they all stood next to their desks and bowed at the waist toward the woman, hands placed as in prayer in front of their faces, showing her honor, before they turned toward Nataya. Her mouth dropped open.

Every one of them sported a rounded belly, some more pronounced than others.

"They're pregnant," Nataya whispered, staring.

Moree smiled at Nataya's profile and brushed her long hair back over her shoulder. "At Deliverance, Nataya, we are in the business of rescuing and restoring, of giving you hope and a life and a future. There is so much I can't wait to tell you about why we do what we do. For now, I will say that God cherishes you, each and every one of you, and the babies you carry inside. With His help and for His glory, we will provide and make a way for you and for the baby. Both of you are important. Both of you have purpose. At Deliverance, we believe in, and fight for life. Abundant, wonderful, joy-filled life."

For the first time since she'd dared to walk out of the bar with Donny, Nataya felt a flutter of hope bloom in her breast.

Life.

Chapter Five

October – Cambodia

Pchum Ben – Ancestor's Day

Vireak dreaded the holiday every year. Memories that would serve well to remain hidden and forgotten charged before him, haunting his every moment, blackening each step. *Would he ever forget?*

Vireak rose early before the other monks. Soon they would be in prayer all night before the people would come with offerings. For now, he only needed to be away; away from the festival, the offerings—everything.

Six months out of the year, during the wet season, his small village flooded as the Tonle Sap Lake grew in size. The *wat* was set above the town just slightly at the base of a steep incline and free from flooding, but the monks took canoes to navigate through the small village and markets. The floating town was unique and wonderfully complicated.

He stood outside the *wat*, looking down on the quiet morning market, interrupted only by the shuffling of scattered shopkeepers opening their humble booths for the day. A few canoes traveled through the channels of the town, stopping at docks to purchase breakfast and items for the day. It was hauntingly peaceful, but Vireak needed to be away—separate.

He turned to hike up the mountain, away from the village and into the trees. He climbed deeper into the mangrove trees on higher ground to the large tree that stood apart from the forest. Buddha was enlightened beneath a tree.

"Let it be so for me," Vireak whispered. He lowered himself to the ground, eyes closed, mindful of his breathing.

Peace would not come...

"Vireak! Hurry! We must hurry, my son!"

The journey through thick forest walls and underbrush had been arduous. Vireak had struggled to keep up with his father, fought against the fear that swelled when he glanced at his father's tense features.

"Pa, where are we going?"

"I will explain there. We must go, now!"

The huts were different; hidden, private. Only a handful of families. Vireak trembled. "Pa, what about *Mae*?"

"Your mother is here; don't worry."

Vireak's limbs shook as his mother—face pinched with worry—stepped through the front door and waved.

"Where are *Yiey* and *Taa*?"

His father's jaw clenched and he shook his head. "Your grandparents are not coming."

Vireak swallowed hard. "Pa, why are the houses on stilts? The flooding doesn't come this far—"

"Hush, Vireak, hush. No more questions for now..."

They ate a simple meal of steamed rice and fruit from their packs that had been picked from the family orchard. Would he ever see it again? The food soured in Vireak's stomach. His parents were quiet, watchful. His father rested a strong hand on Vireak's head, pulled him close under his chin.

"Vireak, we know the Lord is with us. What have we to fear when He goes before us?"

The words settled like a balm, although they were new. For that night they were together. They had peace and comfort. But not for long...

Fire danced across his memories, white-hot angry flames that licked up all of the peace and comfort he had known. Flames that destroyed everyone in his family. Except him.

His Uncle Kosal had said he was spared, that the ancestors had understood that his heart remained true; Vireak had not fully turned to the strange religion his parents claimed. *But hadn't he?* He remembered such joy when his father told him all that he'd learned about Jesus.

He spent so many years wishing that he had been eliminated by the flames with the rest of his family—Father, Mother, his brother. According to the things that had been spoken in hushed, happy tones in their little hut, his family was with Jesus. Vireak wished he could believe it, but as a Buddhist monk, he knew better.

According to his uncle, their deeds had been so deplorable, so evil, that they had been unworthy to be born again, even to something as lowly as a dog. "Their souls will wander in torment and sorrow for all time, Vireak. You may choose now whether you will have such a fate…"

Orphaned at ten, confused and alone, Vireak knew the choices he must make. He spent two months in his uncle's home, listening to the scathing assessment of Vireak's family. He endured the bitter looks his uncle cast on him whenever Vireak was served his share of the rice meal. Kosal had little patience for his brother's son eating their food. And Vireak couldn't blame him. Kosal had enough children of his own to feed, and his karaoke bar had suffered greatly when Vireak's father had pulled out of the business. Vireak was slightly relieved when he dressed for the celebratory parade given in his honor when his uncle took him to serve in the monastery.

He remembered when Kosal shaved his head in preparation for service. "Make us proud, Vireak. Your father brought such dishonor to us all." He had finished shaving Vireak's thick black hair and leaned down to grab his face in his strong, calloused hands. "I will know how you do; I will know where your allegiance lies. If you dishonor us, I fear your fate could be the same as your father's." His eyes held Vireak's, and the young boy had felt a shiver of understanding…

Vireak didn't realize that he was crying until a tear fell onto his wrist. Embarrassed, he wiped his face with the back of his hand and straightened the orange robe. He hadn't thought of his family in the years while he'd lived as a monk, except during *Pchum Ben*: the festival that honored dead relatives.

This was the only time of year since he was ten—thirteen long years—that he saw his uncle, aunt, cousins, and grandparents together. They came with the rest of the surrounding village to throw flowers and food into the sacred place that Vireak ate, slept, and studied, for their dead relatives. To show mercy.

Each year Vireak would lock eyes with his uncle, knowing what was expected of him, knowing the shame of what his parents had done—the life they had chosen.

The most important day of the festival would start tomorrow. His Uncle Kosal would place a dish of carefully prepared food before him, and Vireak would be expected to eat it, to absorb the nutrients to pass on to his dead family; to appease their angry souls, to pass good karma on to his uncle and the rest of his living family. Then it would all be over until the next year…and the next.

Would his penance ever be enough? He rose from his place and returned to the *wat*, heart heavy, soul aching.

For all of the knowledge and wisdom bestowed on him through the years, he still could not forget the gentle rhythm of his father's voice as he repeated verses he had learned about what he had called, the One True God.

A God that would not share glory or honor with anyone—or anything else.

Vireak shuddered.

Chapter Six

Chaya and her family participated in *Pchum Ben* each year. Although they lived high on the mountain above town, they remained close to the village where their family had been established for generations. Others from their clan had moved away over time, and each year their home was filled to the brim with visitors for the holiday. Chaya and her mother rose early to prepare meals each morning of the fifteen-day festival. They quietly wove their way through uncles, aunts, and cousins. The snores of uncles, who had imbibed overly much the night before, brought Chaya and her mother, Kolab's, eyes together in amusement. They delighted in the full house, remembering a time when their house was empty for the holiday; a time when their family would not come to visit or have contact with them.

Thank You, Lord, for restoring relationships with our family. Please let Your light and love be reflected in our lives that they may not only accept us, but also embrace You.

The mother and daughter shared verses they remembered throughout the morning as they prepared sticky rice and sliced fruit. They also shared memories of Vireak and his family. "When Nuon and I were pregnant with you and Vireak, we would go to market together. We were often a spectacle, sharing all the strange things that were happing to our bodies with each other. We would whisper something to make the other laugh, then turn to merchants at their booths and calmly barter with them. The other woman would be forced to hold down her giggles; it was a challenge to out-shock each other." Kolab's lips trembled. "Nuon was the first friend I had in life; the one to tell me the Good News of Jesus."

Kolab tsk-tsked and selected another apple. "I didn't speak to her for weeks. Enraged at the things she said to me, offended when she said I needed a Savior. Frightened. I was so frightened that I had lost my friend, even more frightened that she might be right."

Chaya leaned into her mother, a slight nudge from her shoulder to Kolab's.

Kolab continued, "Sov had better luck with your father. Heng believed almost immediately. Our souls cry out for the Lord from the beginning, Chaya. Some of us just take longer to listen to the answer to our own desperate cries. Some of us never answer the call at all."

Kolab and Chaya continued to prepare and whisper together, sharing memories of their friends. They prepared meals they remembered the family had enjoyed: crab and green peppers for Sov and Kolab. Their boys, Vireak and Viseth, had been more basic in their favorite: a rice vermicelli and noodle dish. They knew their deceased friends were alive with Christ, that they would see them again. That they walked with the Lord in life and now saw Him in death. Death had not been the end, and they would not eat this food. But Vireak might and they were desperate to connect with him.

The rest of the family rose and joined Chaya and her mother, Kolab, around the cook fire in the middle of the room. The men played with the smaller children. Women bustled together with the final preparations. They all dressed in white and carried their bowls of food—offerings to be placed before the monks who would eat the meal to pass on to the ghosts of deceased ancestors—and marched with the rest of the village toward the *wat*.

When they entered the large, busy space, the cloying fragrance of incense hovered in a haze around Chaya's knees. A committee collected crisp *riel* notes in a basket; they took note of donations, counting busily while an *Achar* with a microphone announced, in rapid-fire succession, the donations of those in the community. The monks had not yet entered the room, and villagers grabbed empty bowls and divided food in a carefully controlled frenzy of activity.

Chaya, along with her mother and father, lit incense and shared names of dead relatives, then turned to arrange the bowls in front of a line of large pillows set out for the monks to sit on.

Where would Vireak sit? *Lord, could you direct us?* Chaya joined the circle her family had made near the pillows, heart fluttering in expectation. The overpowering incense snaked through her hair. The *Achar's* announcements vibrated around her; a headache left in its wake.

The family collected bits of the meal to add to a large bowl, set aside for ghosts that could not partake of the monks' meal. Chaya glanced around the room, and her eyes crinkled in a smile at Jakobi, who walked in with her host family.

Jakobi taught with Chaya at the school, and the American's help had proven invaluable. When Jakobi learned Chaya was a Christian, she'd been surprised.

"I thought Khmer were Buddhist?" Jakobi had wiped a hand across her glistening forehead and averted her eyes.

Chaya nodded. "Primarily, yes, and my parents were."

She explained about their friends that had met with missionaries on a bus to Phnom Penh many years ago, then returned to share with Chaya's parents what they had learned.

Jakobi scoffed slightly, "Let me guess, they told you all about *Jesus* and how He died for you?"

"Well yes—"

Jakobi spoke over Chaya's response. "And I'm sure they immediately gave you a list of do's and don'ts for your new life. They changed every bit of your natural way of life; am I right? Of course I'm right. Missionaries from America love to do that. They really just want to Americanize everyone. Didn't you know the Christian way is the *American* way?" Her voice dripped with sarcastic disdain.

Chaya tilted her head at Jakobi. "The missionaries were not American. And no, not a new list to follow. They gave our friend, Sov, a Bible and he read it to us when our families would gather together. Our lives changed from within because of God's Word, but we are still Khmer."

Jakobi had looked ashamed, her freckled face flushed with anger and embarrassment. She plopped into a nearby chair, a strand of her wild red hair fell into her face, and she impatiently pushed it away.

"I apologize, Chaya. Where I come from, *Christian* can mean one hundred different things, and my experience has not been a pleasant one."

Chaya also took a seat. "Want to share?"

Jakobi shrugged and shook her head. "Nah, not this time."

Instead, Jakobi had stood and continued to put the room in order. Chaya had not met a volunteer as passionate as Jakobi, although the Peace Corps had sent a steady stream to their village over the last decade. World changers and explorers, they all found a special place in Chaya's heart. Her family often invited volunteers to their home for dinner, delighted that every person had such a different story to tell about the part of America that they were from.

Somehow, Jakobi affected her more than the rest. They were immediately comfortable with one another, able to push past their barriers of culture and language. Jakobi was a hard worker that picked up the language quickly because she practiced as often as she could, making an effort not to speak much English, even though Chaya was fluent.

The women planned events for the school together, forged lesson plans, discussed ways to make things better. Jakobi was consistently frustrated at the Khmer school system, and Chaya couldn't blame her. Cheating was overlooked, students that didn't have money didn't have access to the same amount of schooling, and students were rarely given the opportunity to continue past elementary school.

"It will come along," Chaya assured her.

Jakobi would only snort in response, which amused Chaya.

The American was a sponge, anxious to soak up as much information about the ways of their village and country as she could in her short time there. Chaya became exhausted at times from all of the questions.

The Heavens Are Telling

The weeks leading up to *Pchum Ben* had been full of lessons and questions between the women.

"Help me understand, Chaya," Jakobi asked. "Everyone is reincarnated. The dogs that wander the village are believed to be someone who was very bad in life reincarnated; that's a low position, right? But some aren't worthy even of that? Some are so bad in life that they're left to just...wander? And what would be so bad that your fate is to wander as a ghost for all time?"

Chaya grimaced, thinking of what Vireak must believe about his own family. "Yes, that's what they believe, and the latter could be a number of things. It's better not to speak of it."

"Do you go to the festival, Chaya?"

"I am Khmer, aren't I?"

"So I will see you there?" Jakobi asked.

Chaya knew Jakobi's host family would be there in mourning and desperation for their son, Narith's, poor deceased wife. Chaya shuddered when she thought of the young woman's end in life. She had filled her pockets with stones and walked into the Tonlé Sap Lake. Her body had been recovered a week after she went missing, just a month before Jakobi came to live in the village.

"Yes, I'll be there."

"I know Dara will be busy with preparations; do I offer to assist her?" Jakobi wanted to be a help to her very overwhelmed host sister.

"Yes, you can offer to help. She will make her daughter-in-law's favorite meal. The belief is the monks will eat it and pass it on to her, so that she will be satisfied. Otherwise, they believe that her ghost will inflict evil on the house."

Jakobi flinched, eyes narrowed at her friend. "Lovely."

Jakobi smiled back at Chaya now, through the haze of incense, careful to keep her head down, eyes reverent. She walked close to her host-sister, Dara, whose face was ashen, her steps unsteady. Chaya knew the tragic death of their son's wife had left Dara raw and shaken for months. Her health was poor; she also missed her only daughter who had gone to work in Phnom Penh years ago.

A shuffled hush fell over the room as the monks began to file in. Chaya craned her neck to catch a glimpse of Vireak. The incense twisted around her, a long forgotten memory unraveling as the monks' bare feet slapped against the floor...

"Come on, Chaya, don't you want to see it?"

Vireak tugged on her hand, pulling her deeper into the trees. The sun dipped close to the edge of the earth, pulling its light down with it.

"No, Vireak, I don't. I want to go back." Chaya dug her heels into the mud, wishing the rain would return to deter her friend from his mission.

"Big baby," he hissed at her, releasing her hand. He stuck his tongue out at her and continued to trudge through the mud toward the site.

There had been reports of a man that had fallen out of a tree and broke his neck. Vireak said the boys at school told him the body was still there; that if you went close you could see the ghost of the man.

Vireak's family had come to Chaya's house for dinner and communion, something they chose to do once a month after sunset.

"Vireak, they told us we could play until sunset. The sun is setting; we need to go back. My mother made the rice and noodles you like." Chaya called after him, but remained rooted in place as he walked further away; her high voice implored him to stop.

He dodged around a tree, out of sight, his voice wafting back to her. "Not until I see this. I'm tired of being the freak at school, living off by ourselves. I want to be the one to find him."

The silence settled around Chaya. She wrapped her arms around her middle in apprehension.

One minute.

Two.

Three.

A shift in the air pricked across Chaya's skin. Although it was after sunset and birds had fallen quiet, even the chirp and buzz of tropical insects had dissipated.

The empty silence vibrated around her.

"Vireak?" she whispered, voice cracked and frightened. One small shuffle behind her spun Chaya on her heel and into a broad male chest.

"Well, what have we here?" The voice was familiar: Vireak's Uncle Kosal.

Violent tingles worked across Chaya's cheeks, through her spine, down the back of her legs. Kosal. Chaya had never felt comfortable in his presence; his dark eyes watched too closely. He was silent, his demeanor domineering.

Vireak had shared numerous times that he'd heard his father and uncle argue when they thought no one could hear. Kosal hated that his brother had converted to Christianity and left him alone in the karaoke ownership, called him a deserter, said he was worse than a murderer. Chaya had heard her own parents share whispers of run-ins they'd had with Kosal.

"What is a pretty girl like you doing out here in the dark…alone?" Kosal gripped her upper right arm, his thumb spread across her flat chest with an unnerving tap-tap-tap.

She remained silent, pleading inwardly for Vireak to return.

"Chaya. Little Chaya."

She couldn't see his face; only felt his warm breath on her cheek.

"I hear your father can't find work. I've told him I would be glad to loan him money until more work comes. You could work for me until the debt is paid…" His other hand slipped into her hair, playing with the silky strands.

Chaya held her breath, the moisture sucked from her mouth, her tongue felt swollen. *Lord, oh, Lord*…the prayer pounded through her head, fear hissing through her ears in a chaotic rush.

The hiss grew louder. Kosal's hand paused, still clutching the ends of her hair. As if he could hear the desperate prayer screaming through her heart.

"Scweeeeeee! Scweeeeee!" The noise was not a prayer or plea, but an echo of rage, high pitched and menacing, from nearby in the trees.

Chaya found her voice, and a scream pummeled out of her throat into Kosal's face. His hands dropped from her side and hair; her trembling knees pulled her to the muddy ground. A recession of sucks and slaps followed as Kosal retreated, then silence.

Chaya shook, her knees sinking further into the thick sludge. The frightening noise echoed again, slightly farther away, its call haunting, threatening.

Minutes passed in horrifying silence. Chaya, too shaken to rise or run home, waited. Where was Vireak?

Suck-slap-suck-slap-suck-slap.

Chaya sprang to action, another scream rising in her throat, only to be cut off by a small hand slapped across her mouth.

"Chaya, it's me," Vireak whispered brokenly through halting breaths. "I think I scared him away."

Fright flared into fury. She shoved him—hard—satisfied at the thud of his frame hitting the ground. "You foolish, foolish boy!" she sobbed at him. She kicked toward him, satisfied when her small foot made contact with his shin and he howled in pain.

Chaya smiled at the memory, though the night had been close to ruining her. Kosal's offer of a job was still one that crept into conversation in the marketplace. Or it had until recently.

What if Vireak had not frightened him off that night? She watched her childhood friend—head shaved, hands clasped reverently in front of his abdomen, accentuating his sinewy forearms—come closer and closer, stopping at the pillow directly across from her family.

❖ ❖ ❖

Jakobi took in her surroundings, engrossed. She had been in Cambodia only a couple months and knew there would be no end to the discovery of different people and cultures, worlds away from her own.

She had always been interested in the ways other people saw life, how they really lived. She took pages of notes in her social studies classes throughout junior high, scribbling down more questions than answers. Her mother had been alarmed by her constant desire to check out *National Geographic* magazines from the library.

"Jakobi, wouldn't you rather read this?" she would ask, handing her a Christian teen romance novel.

The implication that Jakobi should concern herself with dreams of marriage and motherhood were clear. When she made honor roll year after year, her father had been proud. When she and Brad began to date, it was her mother's turn to bust buttons.

When Jakobi announced that she'd earned college scholarships and received grants to pay for college, her parents had been devastated. They believed that if they didn't pay for college, she simply wouldn't go.

"Jakobi, good grades are fine in high school, and you know I've been impressed with your hard work," her father had spoken slowly, as if she were dimwitted, "but now is the time to get serious. Get a good job at the bank or even a preschool and support Brad while he goes to school."

Her mother could barely look at her the day she moved out. "You're throwing your future away, Jakobi. Brad won't wait around while you play the liberal." Her parents could not understand that her desire to go to college had nothing to do with being rebellious and everything to do with wanting to take charge of her life and be equipped to make a difference in the world.

Her first semester at Portland State University, after a brief stint at Bible College, was spent behind closed doors in her dorm room while the rest of the floor, including her roommate, lived life to the fullest. Countless nights she'd come home from the library to find a sign on the whiteboard that had been fastened to the door: "Don't come a knockin'!" with a wink face drawn next to it. If she tried the handle, the door was locked.

She carried books with her everywhere and studied harder than she ever had in high school. In her anthropology class she finally had answers to great mysteries of the world and human history. Each visit home for holidays and sporadic weekends erupted into arguments. The logic she gleaned in college pitted against her parents' homespun, old-fashioned faith. Her father could barely look at her without disappointment creasing the lines in his forehead. She and Brad had less in common than she and her parents did, and she stopped answering his emails and phone calls.

Her family had come to her graduation, much to her surprise. Her parents' faces were pinched, their manner stoic, while Ava was just happy to see her big sister. The small family posed for pictures, and Jakobi hoped that her parents had finally accepted her for who she was.

Her father turned to her before they left the graduation and his words sliced through Jakobi's heart. "Now that this nonsense is behind you, you can come home where you belong."

Her heart in her throat, Jakobi shared that she had applied for the Peace Corps and that she would move to Cambodia at the end of the summer. Her mother fled to the car in tears. Her parents viewed her independence as direct defiance against God. The more they fought to keep her close and bring her "back to the faith" the more she resisted and pulled away. They imagined that her life in the Peace Corps would lead to a life of demon worship. She could not explain that she wasn't against God, or at least not the idea of a god; she just didn't agree with organized religion. As Christians, shouldn't her family be proud that she wanted to give these years of her life to make life better for people around the world?

What would my family think of this? Jakobi thought, as she placed a bowl of sticky rice before the line of monks and shared the name of her deceased grandmother. She lit an incense stick and placed it with the others, wishing she had thought to bring her camera.

Her family was heavy on her heart the rest of the day. She followed her host family as they left the *wat* for the boats. Her lungs filled with muggy air, and she lightheartedly followed the path of steps down the mountain to the base of the water *road*.

She helped Dara, her host sister—a woman old enough to be her mother—into the boat and took the place beside her as the rest of the family climbed in. Her host brother, Dara's husband, Phirun, handed the oars to their grown son, Narith. Narith gave curt instructions to his three children to climb in and settle down. The boat pushed off from the dock, lazily meandering toward their home. Jakobi leaned back, wide straw hat in place, and gazed upon majestic mountains covered in thick, undisturbed foliage.

Jakobi knew that soon the water would recede, and the streets of the village would be revealed, creating a completely different atmosphere. The boats would be stored until June; motos and bikes would be brought out. She could not imagine that in just a few weeks she would ride a bicycle everywhere instead of traveling by boat.

When she had first arrived in Cambodia, she had spent the first month in the capital city of Phnom Penh with other Peace Corps trainees. They learned basic skills from how to use a squatty potty, to how to successfully bargain, to the many ways they could expect to contract stomach issues. They'd been welcomed in a Buddhist ceremony with two monks chanting over them while sprinkling the trainees with water and flowers. Jakobi had shoved thoughts of her parents aside and embraced the kindness of the holy men.

Training had come to an end all too soon for Jakobi, and she was given her placement: a small village near Pursat in the Kampong Luong commune Krakor district. The experience of living on a river, stepping onto a dock each morning, the sheets of rain that came in dramatic spurts throughout each day—every bit of her new life—was surreal.

The boat sliced through the water and Jakobi watched her reflection in the murky water. She looked like her mother. *Why can't you just be proud of me? Why can't you see the world beyond your religion and fear?*

The flat eyes stared back at her, silent.

Chapter Seven

Vireak had become an expert at observation from beneath downcast eyes. His peripheral vision became honed over the years. Because of this, he was able to watch out for his uncle—and catch glimpses of Chaya.

His childhood friend had grown into a beautiful woman. He noticed her from afar in the village, her black hair bouncing against her shoulders, shimmering beneath the warm Cambodian sun. She carried herself with dignity and grace. He was proud of the smile she always wore; genuine, sincere and full of kindness.

Although she had been feisty when they were kids together, she had always harbored a tender side. She honored her parents, not only in word and action, but truly honored and obeyed from the depths of her being. Where Vireak had rebelled inwardly when their families were driven from the heart of the village, higher on the mountains around them, Chaya had encouraged and did what she could to make their situation better. She served without complaint. She prayed for the families that had rejected them; Vireak had called down insults on them in the raging recesses of his mind.

He remembered how her family had offered to take him in after the fire. But knowing he was the cause, he couldn't risk bringing evil into their house. Not Heng and Kolab and Chaya. He adored them and cared for them even now. He had noticed through the years that they lit incense for his family. He knew as

Christians that their reasons varied greatly from those of his uncle.

Uncle Kosal. He was sure to bring the balls of sticky rice, sure to say the names of his family to Vireak. Vireak would nod slightly, rage filling his heart, even though he knew it was wrong for a monk to feel that way.

He felt a lot of ways that a monk shouldn't, had a lot of thoughts about things his father had spoken over him in the quiet of the night; things that went against everything he had been taught in his years at the *wat*.

His heart beat heavily in his chest when his aunt and cousins, all grown now, walked in and gave their offerings. Vireak was confused when they sat down without his uncle. His aunt sat near Vireak, pushed a plate of fish stuffed with peppers and vegetables toward the monks, his uncle's favorite. The realization coursed through him, hardening his stomach. *No…it couldn't be.*

His aunt whispered, "Kosal," and her eyes flickered toward her nephew. Vireak felt lightheaded. Thoughts of Chaya and her family dissipated in the wake of that name.

Kosal.

Kosal; the mean-spirited uncle whose eyes held a challenge whenever he saw Vireak on the street.

Kosal; who might have molested Chaya or worse if Vireak hadn't intervened all those years ago.

Kosal; the man that drove Vireak and his family away from the village that was their home, deeper into the rainforest, up the mountain.

Kosal; who appeared by Vireak's side when his family died in the fire. Who took Vireak in. Fed him. Prepared him to enter into service to the *wat*. To reconcile for his parents' misdeeds.

Kosal; who ran the karaoke bar in their quiet village and was rumored to have half of the town indebted to him.

Kosal; the only reason Vireak had remained in service as a monk for so many years into adulthood.

Kosal. *Dead.*

And now Vireak was expected to eat of Kosal's favorite meal for him. To absorb the nutrients so that his uncle would not cast evil upon the house of his aunt or his cousins—so that his uncle would not wander in hunger or torment.

Vireak reached for the fish, fingers trembling, scarcely able to deliver the flaky bits of meat to his mouth. His lips parted and he hesitated. A memory snaked through the open pagoda, alighting on him, gripping Vireak with fear and trembling. *Not now. Not with everyone watching...*

His father's voice had carried such authority when he read the Scriptures.

"While they were eating, Jesus took some bread, and after a blessing, He broke it and gave it to the disciples, and said, 'Take, eat, this is My body.' And when He had taken a cup and given thanks, He gave it to them, saying 'Drink from it, all of you; for this is My blood of the covenant, which is poured out for many for forgiveness of sins.'

You see, my family, it is only by the blood of Christ and by His sacrifice that we are made clean. Only He can absolve our sin and give new life."

His father had read to them by candlelight when they settled on their woven pallets for the night. Vireak had not understood it all, had not embraced the change as Chaya did, but he'd felt a deep purpose drum in his chest, like a warrior called to action, when his father read Jesus' words...

Not now.

Vireak shoved the fish in his mouth, choking back a cough as it turned to sawdust on his tongue. He swallowed the bite. It cemented itself deep in his gut.

For Kosal.

Although, Vireak thought as his stomach turned over, *I'm not sure what Kosal will receive if I vomit the meal when the day is done.*

Vireak left the *wat* after the ceremonies, barefoot and empty handed. He hesitated for one moment, foot or boat? He opted for the woods again, climbing through vines, brush, and low trees. It was not uncommon for a monk to walk out into nature, seeking answers and enlightenment, following their own urges and inner self for direction. They could be gone for hours or days, meditating, fasting. Vireak put no thought into his trek, only stumbled through numbly.

Kosal was dead.

Dead.

Why hadn't Vireak been notified before? When a person died, the body was washed and dressed and laid in the home for a week while monks came and performed prayers to guide the confused soul in the right direction. Vireak should have been there.

If his aunt had lit incense for Kosal, had come to Vireak with his favorite foods, could Kosal be a wanderer? A ghost spinning in void because of bad karma? Vireak stopped; the trees blurred around him as he sunk to his knees on the lush forest floor. *Why hadn't they called him?*

Vireak needed answers and was desperate for them. Heng, Chaya, they would know. They were the only ones he could seek for answers without questions stirring up against him in return.

Determined, Vireak rose and took in the trees and landscape around him. From high in the trees, vines draped low across the branches and raised roots, offering a curtained sanctuary for pelicans, storks, and a wide variety of other tropical birds. He recognized where he was and set off for Heng's house.

※ ※ ※

Chaya stepped outside for some air. The family had crowded in and around for most of the day after the ceremony. By that evening, all had departed for their own homes in surrounding villages, some by bus, others by boat. Her cousins had left early enough to make the trip back to Battambang before the day was over. Chaya had worked alongside her mother the remainder of the day to restore order to their hut until the older woman had smiled and ushered her out.

"Take some *nom* with you!" her mother called after her.

Chaya chuckled to herself. They had outdone themselves with snacks, mostly sticky rice balls filled with pork for the guests; her mother was famous in the family for them. They had sent many home in baskets with the family, but would most definitely be eating *nom* for days.

She stepped onto the deck, high above the ground. No water or river would flow here, but when they'd been driven from the community, her parents and those with them felt the stilts would keep them safe. Her gaze traveled across the field to the still blackened pile of rubble that had once been her friend's home.

The stilts had not been enough to keep Vireak's family safe.

Her heart fluttered.

Vireak had looked so pale at the ceremony today, so shaken. Could he have been unaware of Kosal and the manner in which he died? Selfishly, she wondered if he had taken notice of their preparation of his favorite meal and of his family's. She longed to look into his eyes, to ask how long he planned to remain a monk. Most men and boys in their culture spent a short period of time in service. Her father had even spent three months in the *wat* as a boy. Families saw the service as a credit toward the family of good karma. It was also a benefit for the family in other ways; a chance for young men to receive a high education at the *wat* for free. But for how long did Vireak think he must stay? When would he remember the truths his father had taught him?

When she had seen his troubled eyes and slumped shoulders, it was as if he physically bore what he considered to be the sins of his family on his own shoulders. When would he realize that Christ bore the weight of the world, once for all?

The air tingled as the sun set. Chaya rubbed her arms despite the moist heat that enveloped her. She caught movement from the corner of her eye, someone near the edge of the small clearing in the trees. She dropped her arms to her sides and leaned forward on the railing. A flash of orange. Chaya's mouth went dry as Vireak stepped from the shadows and into the fading sunlight.

"Chaya."

She hadn't heard his voice in years; a deep baritone replaced the soprano pitch of his youth. Her knees felt weak as he stepped closer.

"Vireak." Her voice was strained.

"I need to speak to your father, Chaya," he implored and glanced around, anxious. His eyes avoided the burnt rubble that had been his home.

"Of course." Chaya turned and fled, praying that her father would be able to show Vireak that he was no longer enslaved to the *wat*, or Kosal…or himself.

Within seconds after Chaya disappeared in the house, Heng appeared on the stairs. He stopped, locking his gaze with Vireak's before he slowly walked down the steps. When he reached the bottom, he stood face to face with his deceased friend's boy. Vireak was as tall as Heng, if not an inch taller. His features were tight, conflicted. A muscle worked in Vireak's broad jaw. His eyes met Heng's, communicating more than words could.

Heng, not intimidated by the orange robe or shaved head, saw only the boy he knew and reached to clap a hand on his shoulder. "I'm glad you've come, Vireak."

They turned and walked away from the house, into the forest. Chaya watched from the doorway, her heart in her throat, as her father and Vireak faded into the trees.

The men continued on in silence for several minutes before Vireak stopped and stared into the twisted and mangled tree branches all around them. His throat convulsed. Then he said, "Kosal."

Heng nodded. "I heard."

Vireak's hands twitched.

Heng watched the storm rage across Vireak's carefully controlled features; years of practice at being passive and peaceful coming into play.

"I didn't hear. No one said anything. Not until today." Vireak faced Heng, eyes searching. "When?"

"A few weeks ago."

"Weeks?" Vireak brought his palms on top of his shaved head, the skin on his skull bunching beneath taut fingers. "How? Why wasn't I called? Why wasn't anyone called?"

Heng leaned back against a close tree trunk, arms folded across his chest. He considered the darkening sky for a moment. "Vireak, your uncle was…confident. His bar was doing quite wel. He acquired more money than anyone in the village, was even revered as a leader of sorts after…" Heng faltered. "Well, after we were sent away. Everyone looked up to him. Or so Kosal thought. Really, I think everyone was simply afraid of him—"

Vireak shook his head, interrupting. "Afraid of him. Why?"

But that was a foolish question. Vireak of all people understood why. No matter how many years he had been at the *wat*, no matter how much time he had spent in service as a monk, still, his uncle's fierce gaze could freeze Vireak's blood in his veins.

Heng didn't answer, but continued. "Your uncle had once threatened your aunt that he didn't need a bunch of guides after he'd passed. He had reached enough enlightenment on his own. He threatened that he would come back to torment her unless she let him die quietly. So she did. And his death was so sudden; it wasn't difficult to follow Kosal's orders."

Vireak's frown deepened. "Why was she offering incense and food for him today?"

"Vireak, your aunt is heavily rooted in her faith. No matter how much she loved or feared Kosal, don't you believe that she would do what she could to honor him in death, do what she could to appease his spirit? She was too afraid to go against his wishes when he died, was probably in shock. But the weeks on her own have given her strength she didn't know she had. She has continued to run the karaoke bar, but I suspect part of her motive for coming to you during the ceremony today was to indirectly ask you to leave the *wat* and come care for her."

Vireak felt as if Heng slapped him. *Leave?* He'd never considered it.

Heng could read his thoughts. "You can, Vireak." His voice was quiet, assuring. "Men dedicate seasons of their life as monks, then move on. It's normal and natural to leave after a while. And Lord knows you've been there a long time."

Vireak felt weighted down, cemented in place. He ran a hand over his shaved head, unable to remember what it had felt like to have hair on his head.

Lord knows…

"*Vireak, I don't know the answer to all your questions, my son.*" His father had laughed at him in mock exasperation and tousled his thick black hair. "I don't know how long we will live out here. I don't know if they will ever accept us as Christians. I don't know, my son. The Lord knows. We need only to trust in Him that holds all of us in His care…"

Heng watched the battle rage within Vireak, knew that only the Lord could draw him out. They walked together a bit longer, and then circled back to the house. Vireak stopped at the rubble that had once been his home. The fragments of charred wood had become sparse, broken down by the elements where grass grew high around them. Vireak reached out to lift a piece of wood but quickly pulled back as if he was burned. His throat convulsed. "Heng…"

It was a plea, an ache. The little boy that had survived the fire that destroyed his family cried out after years of suppressing his grief. Heng squeezed the back of Vireak's neck and pulled the young man close. Vireak wept, openly, without restraint or shame. Years of seeking enlightenment and living with the understanding that all of life is sorrow, couldn't absolve his pain.

In the house, Chaya sat in silence with her mother. Tears flowed silently down their cheeks, over their lips, dropping from their chins and into their hair as they listened to the desperate mourning across the clearing.

Chapter Eight

Cherished, not hidden away in shame.
Beloved, not lusted after.
Chosen, not taken.
Valued.
Purchased—not for pleasure—but for salvation with the sacrificial blood of Christ.
Treasured. Adored. A delight to her Creator.
Nataya, so hesitant and timid her first weeks in the rescue home, began to smile. Then laugh.
Moree found new adoration and amazement each time she witnessed the transformation of rescued children. Like ice and snow crusted on a river in the winter months, the girls began to thaw when the spring of restoration shed light on their lives. The warmth of the Son slowly melted away the fear, resentment, and filth of their former life. Counseling and prayers and games and school helped bring to life the flowing rivers of promise, hope, and innocence in their young souls. Souls that had been hidden beneath the frigid captivity of fear, abuse, and isolation.
Nataya, for the most part, was no exception, but she held one regret close, and it impeded her ability to accept Christ's love for her completely: Suchin.
"I left her." She would weep to the counselor. "I just abandoned her. I should have brought her with me, should have offered her what had been offered to me."

The counselor, broken at the sheer volume of enslaved children, ached over the personal knowledge of one more. She agonized over Nataya's guilt, knew that she needed a chance to make it right.

Moree often dropped in on the girls that she had worked to rescue. Their exuberance was catching in a vocation filled with raw confrontations of humanity's darkest secrets.

After checking with the counselor on Nataya's progress, Moree sought the young girl in her room. She found Nataya lounging on her bed, listening to music, a sight common of teens the world over. Music had become a great source of release for many of the girls. Nataya relaxed on her back, eyes trained on the ceiling, thoughtful. Her stomach was slightly rounded. Her pregnancy, they'd determined through an ultrasound, was just entering the second trimester. It was a miracle that the baby hadn't been detected by Lok Lee earlier. Nataya turned when Moree lightly tapped on the open door.

"What's this I hear about your friend, Suchin?" Moree asked.

Nataya told of her regret and fear at leaving her young friend behind. Moree's heart broke as she held Nataya, who convulsed with sobs of terror. Moree imagined Nataya felt much like a person on solid ground, watching a friend drown in the ocean without any way of saving her. Moree let the young woman cry, understanding the need. She held Nataya close and patted her back gently. When the sobs melted into soft whimpers, Moree whispered against Nataya's hair.

"Nataya, was Suchin in the same bar that you were with Lok Lee?"

A nod.

"What if we went to her, Nataya? Could you describe her to us well enough that we could go get her, too?" Moree smiled, biting her lower lip when Nataya's whimpering ceased, and she sat up abruptly, turning a splotchy, wet face toward Moree.

Nataya wiped a hand under her nose, her eyes round. "You can do that?" Nataya choked out. Moree laughed as Nataya lunged forward on the bed, squeezing her around the neck.

It took very little time to find Suchin, to purchase her, bring her to a hotel and offer her freedom. As it had with many girls before Suchin, her fear of the unknown trumped the lure of escape, and with heavy hearts, they watched her leave, back to a life of slavery and bondage, dark rooms and evil and abuse no child—no human being—should have to endure.

Nataya watched for Moree every day, raced to meet her, eyes searching, hoping.

Moree pursed her lips and slowly shook her head. "Not yet, Nataya."

Nataya's fear and regret pressed her closer to the Lord. Her counselor explained that God cared so deeply for her, cared just as much for Suchin, and that He was capable of saving them both. That He was big enough. When Nataya imagined Jesus seeking her out as Moree and Dugan and so many others had done, she believed. The transformation was remarkable. His love was apparent in the actions of teachers, dorm mothers, and counselors. His love was obvious in the protection of the life blooming within her. If she were in the bar, Lok Lee would have eventually discovered the pregnancy and scraped her body clean of the baby. She ached for Suchin, prayed for her constantly, not knowing what to say, but assured that God heard and understood. And that He cared.

When Moree suggested that Nataya make a video for Suchin, a message straight from her to ensure Suchin that she could trust Moree and Dugan and enter into freedom, she eagerly agreed. Nataya chose her words carefully, hoping Suchin would see the light in her eyes and know that Nataya had not only found freedom and hope, but had sent her rescuers back for Suchin.

When Moree came to visit a few days after they'd made the video, her expression made Nataya's knees go weak with despair.

Suchin had refused.

Chapter Nine

November – Cambodia

The Peace Corps experience was nothing like Jakobi had imagined it would be—and in some ways everything she had imagined. Her trips to Phnom Penh for training had become less frequent, for which she was thankful. Riding on cramped buses with dozens of other people was something she could use a break from. The stink, the noise, the close air, the time she'd been seated next to a woman with a parcel of dead chickens, the time she had been next to a man with a cage of live chickens—all were interesting fodder for her blog that she was able to update periodically. But, in reality, she had plenty to say to the World Wide Web without being covered in chicken poop by the end of a bus trip.

Her bike bumped awkwardly as she dodged a seemingly small puddle. Last week she had misjudged a puddle in the road, thinking it would be fun to splash through it. Instead, she'd found herself in a small-scale sinkhole. She groaned when the bike stuck fast in the thick mud, embarrassed when some locals had called out to her from their homes. Every one of them had some trick or idea of how she could get unstuck, but the air of mockery in their voices made her cringe. She'd hopped off the bike and struggled to tug it free, but the hot sun baked the muddied roads into hard clay. She had dozens of eyes looking down on her from crooked stilt houses, enjoying the entertaining tussle between the American, her bike, and the mud. With a heave and a disturbing "schlluuup" she'd finally released the bike, brushed off her sampot and collared shirt, hopped onto the bike again, and peddled out of sight, back straight, an air of indifference exuding from her easy glide.

Jakobi had been amazed when the waters receded, finally revealing the foundation of the home she lived in. The bamboo sticks, roped together in a variety of positions, all much taller than the house itself, created a cartoon affect. Jakobi was thankful she'd moved to this village before the waters beat against the homes. No matter how unstable they appeared, she had personally experienced their staying power.

The thatched roofs and bamboo foundations were something Jakobi had expected when she'd applied to be a Peace Corps Volunteer; pictures of houses just like the ones that lined the road on her way to the school were plastered all over the Peace Corps website. She'd expected awkwardness with her host family, had expected to have stomach issues while her body adjusted to the new cuisine. She had even expected the homesickness she often felt, regardless of her disconnect with her family.

Jakobi had not, however, expected to meet and befriend a Christian Cambodian woman her own age. She hadn't expected the poor community to be so full of laughter and friendship. She certainly hadn't expected the village to talk about her so freely.

"Jakobi was stuck in the mud yesterday..."

"Does Jakobi look thinner to you?"

"Jakobi certainly likes coffee, doesn't she?"

She hadn't expected the home she lived in to be so dark and secret, to feel as if she were always walking in on a private conversation. Earlier in the week her host brother, Phirun, and host sister, Dara, had gone out of town without explanation. Jakobi was uncomfortable to have been left alone with their son, Narith, and his children. She confided in Chaya, who suggested she stay with her family until Phirun and Dara returned.

"Won't that be insulting to Narith?" Jakobi worried.

"Just tell him we've asked you to stay with us," Chaya said. "That's all that you need to say."

And it was.

Jakobi enjoyed her time with Chaya and her parents. They engaged her as a member of their small family.

"Jakobi, let me show you how to make rice," Kolab had said to her, patting her arm lovingly.

"Would you like to come with us to set out seed and watch for birds, Jakobi?" Chaya had asked as she and her parents led her to their favorite place in the woods.

The water didn't rise nearly as high in their area, although they still needed boats during the rainy months; they left them close to the edge of the woods and stored them under the house during the dry season.

Jakobi learned, through the week with the family, that Chaya and her mother cleaned an old church near their home; one that they explained had never been used, but they were paid to maintain.

"We go once a month to clear out dust, make sure no animals have taken up a permanent residence inside, that sort of thing," Chaya explained.

There was a bit of excitement in the home one evening during dinner when Chaya's father, Heng, came home from fishing with two announcements.

"Jakobi, I saw Phirun in town today; he and Dara returned in the night. I told them we would send you back tomorrow."

Jakobi fought to hide her disappointment. Her eyes searched the mat between them for nothing in particular.

Heng then turned to address Kolab. "I was contacted by the pastor today."

Jakobi, not knowing the Khmer word for pastor, was left in the dark. She focused on her bowl, interested in the way this family discussed everything but was careful to not appear nosy.

"It seems that they have a tenant coming to rent the church soon," Heng announced.

"A tenant?" Kolab's voice raised an octave in surprise. "In that big place? Is it a group? A family?" She nudged the rice bowl closer to Jakobi, who still had plenty.

Heng finished chewing, a smile in his eyes. "They didn't say, Kolab. We're just the caretakers, remember? But they did say if you were willing to clean the church for the tenant twice a week, they would give you first chance at it. They would increase your pay, of course."

Chaya and Kolab rounded their eyes at him, mouths twitching in astonishment.

"Oh, Pa," Chaya breathed. "God is so good to us."

Jakobi shifted her eyes around their small home. Chaya had shared with her that they used to live in a bigger, nicer home by Khmer standards before her parents became Christians. Jakobi had watched Heng load a moto with what seemed to her an awfully dangerous load of gear to pile on a bike each day to go fishing, and then watched him return with two full coolers added to the morning's load, strapped to either side of him on the bike. If they lived closer, or even out on the lake, he would be free to fish right from his home.

When Jakobi asked why they had chosen to live so far out of town, Chaya answered cryptically, "Our family and another were driven out."

Jakobi's chin tilted up slightly, not understanding. "Because of your religion?"

Chaya, eyes trained beyond their home to a barren place in the woods just across the clearing, swallowed once, her voice husky when she spoke. "Because of our faith, Jakobi."

Jakobi, not understanding the difference, mentally shrugged, sure that their native languages stood in the way of clear communication. She now looked at the small but comfortable home, set apart from town, and wondered at their assessment of a good God. If they were His faithful followers, why would He have them driven out, set to live alone and somewhat detached from their community?

That evening, Chaya and Kolab agreed to show Jakobi the church.

"We've been cleaning it all these years, but haven't had expectation of guests living there. I want to see what it needs," Kolab explained to Jakobi.

Mother and daughter climbed on their moto and waited for Jakobi to line up behind them on her bicycle. She groaned good-naturedly when Kolab told her she would go slowly enough for Jakobi to keep up.

"See, this is when I wish the Peace Corps didn't have some of their rules," Jakobi said dryly.

From what Jakobi had heard, the Peace Corps used to issue motorbikes to their volunteers. When a report showed that the leading cause of death for Peace Corps volunteers in Southeast Asia was from moto accidents, the volunteers were banned from even riding them. Jakobi was glad they provided the bike for her, but wished she could ignore the moto rule at times like these. After all, a short drive on a dirt path through the mountainous woods was certainly not where volunteers had been killed in the past. The busy, hectic city streets were the real culprits.

Resigned, Jakobi waved to Kolab that she was ready and pushed off with her right foot, doing her best to ride quickly so they wouldn't have to slow down too much. "Well, at least I can say I've biked through Cambodia," she mumbled to herself, wondering if anyone at home would truly care.

The women stopped the moto in front of the building, smiling to Jakobi as she pedaled up next to them, sucking in air dramatically. "Thanks for the warning about the hills," she gasped.

Chaya and Kolab laughed at her expression, unashamed. "It is not our fault you don't know how to drive a moto," Chaya teased.

Jakobi bit back a laugh at the way Khmers assessed situations. Instead of not being permitted to, it was thought that she didn't know how. They were the same about her efforts to be mostly vegetarian.

Chaya would be in the kitchen preparing a meal with her mother, say something under her breath, and call out to Jakobi, "Do you know how to eat eggs?"

Jakobi, brow wrinkled would return, "Yes, I know how to eat eggs."

She clapped a hand over her mouth and snorted through her nose when Chaya spoke to her mother again. "Okay, she knows how to eat eggs. But she doesn't know how to eat chicken."

The laugh caught in Jakobi's throat at the memory when she looked beyond the pair to the church. Simple and unassuming, the building was white, with a steeple and double doors at the top of wooden stairs. "Just like the church on Little House on the Prairie," she whispered to herself. The familiarity of the building sent a shiver through her.

"It looks so…American." Jakobi observed.

She followed Kolab and Chaya up the stairs, feeling out of place. Or maybe she felt too acquainted. It had been years since she'd been in a church, but before college, she had practically lived there during her childhood: Bible studies, youth group activities, clean-up service, choir practice, Sunday school, Sunday service, potlucks.

"Where did the wood come from?" she asked, running her hand along the smooth rail.

"They brought it with them," Kolab answered from the top of the stairs in front of the doors, fumbling with a heavy chain and lock looped through two iron handles. She eased the door on the right open, the chain dangling on the left handle.

They stepped into the dark space. Jakobi marveled at how similar the structure was to small churches she'd seen around Oregon and in pictures across America. They walked through a small foyer and then pushed double swinging doors open into the sanctuary. Wooden pews lined either side. A cross was displayed in front, even stained glass windows along each wall. Chaya told her there was a small kitchen in the back, similar to theirs.

"Where is this tenant supposed to sleep?" Jakobi asked.

"There is a small office that is empty. The tenant can set it up how they want," Kolab answered, gesturing toward the back.

After a pause, Jakobi scratched the side of her face and squeezed her eyes shut. "I'm confused," she said. "Why is this place sitting here empty? I mean, you guys are Christians, why didn't they stay here with you?"

Kolab and Chaya exchanged a look. "It's like what you first thought of those that told us about Christ, Jakobi," Chaya answered. "They meant well, but essentially they barged in, built this church, and told the community how to live."

Chaya lifted one shoulder, sad. "It just didn't work well. It was a bad time in our village, which created a lot of distrust toward believers. The missionaries were asked to leave and, frustrated with us, they gladly obliged. I don't know why they've kept up on this property. Maybe it's a pride issue for them. I'm not sure. But God has used the money we earn cleaning the building to bless us, and in turn, we've been able to bless others."

Chaya glanced around the empty space, completely unaware of how familiar the room was to Jakobi.

"It would make sense that they wanted it to serve as a reminder, to absolve their pride at being rejected," Jakobi mumbled more to herself. Wouldn't surprise her.

Kolab rubbed her hands together. "Well, either way, we have work to do."

Jakobi helped the women to air out the church, tidy things up, clean the rust hued dust that settled so easily and quickly on anything and everything. Her throat closed when Kolab retrieved a bag of rice from the moto and placed it in the kitchen. They had so little and shared so freely.

When they finished and locked up for the night, Jakobi pedaled back to Chaya's home, sad that tomorrow she would return to her host family. They were kind and giving as well, but it was simply different.

The next morning when Jakobi entered the chaotic house of her host family, she discovered two more children, an infant boy and young girl with mournful eyes, had come to live in the home as well. She was confused and concerned. The baby looked so frail, the young girl so quiet and dejected.

Where had they come from?

Chapter Ten

Thailand

The sunrise used to signify the end of her day. Nataya had once worked in darkness, locked away in a muggy, windowless room during normal waking hours. Light had never existed to her unless it was manmade. Now as beams of sunshine filtered through the windows into her room, Nataya smiled and turned her face toward the warmth. She would never grow tired of the feel of the sun on her face.

Her heart responded in a similar way to her Savior, the Creator and Embodiment of Light.

"Good morning, Jesus," she whispered.

Nataya curled in around her belly. She rested a hand on her abdomen. *Good morning, baby.* She lay for a moment, enjoying the feel of the sun on her face and the knowledge of fullness within her.

Light and life. Would she ever get used to her new surroundings, to the fullness of life in her heart and body? She hoped not.

Her hopeful mood soured when she thought of Suchin, of her young friend's refusal of freedom, even after she'd seen the video Nataya made for her. She understood; it had taken weeks and numerous visits before Nataya was convinced that the hope of freedom and life was worth the risk that it all might be a lie.

Still, she'd been so sure her words would convince Suchin to trust and flee.

Nataya stayed in bed a moment longer, not wanting to wake her roommates. Finally, the pressure on her bladder propelled her out of bed, and she shuffled into the bathroom down the hall. When she returned to her room, the other three girls, each at different stages of pregnancy, were also awake and readying for the day. As had become routine for them all, they made their beds, got dressed, and brushed their hair, then walked together to breakfast.

The rest of the day passed, blissfully ordinary: breakfast, school, lunch, a few hours laughing together while they made jewelry to sell, prayer, and a Bible reading after dinner. Most of the rescued girls of Deliverance could not get enough of having the Bible read to them. As they learned, some of the more advanced girls would practice reading the holy words aloud. No matter how they paused or stuttered, the group listened intently to the beautiful rhythm of the Word of Life.

The Gospels about Jesus were Nataya's favorite.

Her father had been the first to use her, before he anxiously sold her to his cousin, who sold her to Lok Lee once he was tired of her. She had known men all of her life—mostly in the last twelve years—in a way that she never wanted to. She knew their moods, their desires, their thoughts. She thought all men were the same, until Dugan and Moree found her and offered her a different life—until they introduced her to Jesus.

Few men frequented the house. But those that did shamelessly looked them in the eyes, chucked them under the chins like big brothers or gave them side hugs like fathers. When she learned of Jesus and His sacrifice and pursuit of her, she knew that she wanted to put her faith in Him and serve Him wholeheartedly. She knew she had a lot to work through, but with Christ going before her, couldn't anything be accomplished? He was not like man, ruled by passions, commandeering, or deceitful. His followers, in turn, were honorable, trustworthy, patient men.

Nataya sat in a chair that night during the readings, her hand absentmindedly resting on her stomach as Dao-Ming, their

Chinese housemother, read about Jesus turning water into wine. What a miracle to take something without taste or color, something as common as water, and transform it to rich full wine. She thought of the meeting she had the next morning with someone that would explain the adoption process. She knew they would also present her with packets from couples hoping to be the parents to her baby.

Could God work a miracle even there? Even in the hopeless way she felt at the thought of giving her baby over to strangers, when she already loved it so much? How could she describe to anyone that this baby was part of *her*? Certainly, it had been put in her against her will, but she didn't count it against the baby. She was the first to want to protect it, first to want it, no matter what.

Tears pooled in her eyes as Dao-Ming read, "'Now there were six stone waterpots set there for the Jewish custom of purification, containing twenty or thirty gallons each. Jesus said to them, "Fill the waterpots with water." So they filled them up to the brim…'"

Just like that, water turned to wine—from the purest vats. Nataya was slowly learning that the deeds done to her were not held against her. That she was pure in the eyes of God. But still, weeks of freedom did not vanquish years of slavery. She doubted if any good could come from a body as defiled as hers.

Lord, I know You delivered me from the pit. You called to me and saved me. You know my heart; know how I love this child. Is there a miracle left for me? Do I dare ask?

Before bed, Dao-Ming pulled Nataya aside and shared that Moree and Dugan had gone back for Suchin. "This time, she said, 'yes.'" They were on a plane, fleeing with Suchin, carrying her to safety.

Nataya went to bed, full of promise and assurance, and slept peacefully for the first time since her own rescue.

God had heard her pleas for Suchin and accomplished what she thought was impossible.

Chapter Eleven

It had only been a day since Lydia, a young American volunteer with Deliverance, was kidnapped from Pattaya. Simon had been horrified, along with everyone else, when he heard of the way the men had crashed into her motel room and taken her, leaving her friend behind, alone and terrified. Rescuers with their organization had certainly faced threats and danger in the past; but never had a guest of Deliverance been confronted or in any real danger.

The Pattaya team was a flurry of activity and determination. Waves of shock and panic rolled over them again and again as they did their best to contact the young woman's family and notify the proper authorities—ones they could trust. Simon had been prepared to poke around the city, looking for old contacts to extract what information he could. Instead, Titus, a Deliverance placement manager, had asked if he would hunker down in a small village in Cambodia to keep an eye on two small children.

Simon agreed, mostly out of curiosity, and was immediately placed on a bus for Phnom Penh.

Megan, the manager for the Cambodia Deliverance campus, met him at the station and explained about an orphaned baby and his preschool-aged sister that had been in the care of volunteers with Deliverance and the prevention care program.

"A few days ago," Megan explained, "the grandparents were located and came to retrieve the children. Something about their manner and the exchange gave all of us a bad feeling. I did everything I could to offer them help and support, and they flatly refused. We are concerned for their safety and want to set you up in their village to keep an eye on them and be available if and when they need our help."

Simon set his feet to a wider stance and crossed his arms. "Do we now follow anyone that doesn't want to take part in our programs, Megan? Don't get me wrong, I'm all for tracking these kids all over Cambodia if I have to, but not every person we come into contact with needs Deliverance. Is there a chance you're over thinking this? Maybe the kidnapping of that volunteer has everyone on edge," he suggested.

Megan glanced quickly around the crowded station and ran a finger across her lips, subtly shushing him. "Let's get back to campus. We'll talk there," she suggested.

He followed Megan to her moto outside, relieved when she dangled the keys from her hand and asked if he would like to drive. He wouldn't have made a very good passenger. She held his shoulders and tapped directions on them as he weaved in and out of the busy streets. The campus wasn't far from the station and soon they were parked and walking through the building to Megan's office.

"I know it sounds strange, and absolutely, we're on edge about Lydia. Everyone with Deliverance is. We're getting demands from the girl's captors and are praying through the next step. But even before that happened, we knew we had to have something in place for these children. Something just doesn't sit right with this family. We know that grandma and grandpa have a widowed son and other kids to support. The son is a fisherman, but it sounds like he's been out of work for a few months. We're not entirely sure how they're supporting the kids. We can only assume it's a matter of time before they're desperate."

She opened an office door and flipped on the light as she walked in. Megan walked to the chair behind the desk and took a seat. She cleared her throat and swept a hand toward the other chair in the room. Simon sat, elbows resting on his knees, his hands loosely clasped together in front of his legs.

"There's a story that I want you to know about this baby. The girl that was kidnapped—well, her sister was on this trip with her…"

❖ ❖ ❖

Simon spent the next two days at the Deliverance campus in Phnom Penh skyping with his parents and the pastor of his home church in Portland, Oregon. He also contacted supporters of Deliverance that had connections with travel book publishers with pitches for articles and book contributions. He was hired on a temporary basis with an online travel magazine and would receive $50 per published article.

Praise God.

Fifty dollars a month would be play money in America; in Cambodia the small wage would cover all of his monthly expenses and then some.

Simon boarded a bus and settled in the back for the four-hour ride to Pursat. From there he would hire a moto to take him deeper into the lakeside villages. If he were traveling one month earlier, he would have needed a boat to take him to his new assignment.

He shifted around in his pack and found a leaf of papers Megan had printed for him. Pictures and tourist accounts of the area were sparse, but she had found enough to give Simon an idea of what was in store. Megan had given Simon instructions to find Heng and Kolab, the caretakers of the church he would live in, when he arrived in the village. He disembarked from the moto, thanked the driver with a healthy tip, and walked through the center of the village. He found the merchants at the market to be kind, but their smiles in response to his inquiries verified that he had a long road ahead of him. Frustrated at the language barrier, he looked around, praying for God to show him a way.

He noticed a monk sitting at the edge of town under a large tree where the rust-colored road forked. He'd heard somewhere that monks knew English and hoped he was able to ask his questions respectfully. Simon didn't follow Buddhism, didn't believe that any one man could be holier than another, but this was not his country, nor his culture; he could be respectful without betraying Christ.

He approached the monk slowly, surprised to find a man nearly his age. The man sensed Simon's approach and met his gaze. He sported a shaved head; Simon knew that monks shaved out of reverence, a sign of piety. The monk's eyes were a deep brown, his mouth curved slightly, as though, if given good reason, he would smile easily. He watched Simon expectantly, seemingly not surprised to see an American man standing before him.

"Good afternoon," Simon began in English, although he bowed his head with his palms placed together under his chin, as Megan had taught him to do.

The monk's eyes lit up. "Good afternoon," he answered. His accent was thick and his voice was deeper than Simon had expected.

Simon took a step closer and squatted, one knee in the dirt, his arm resting casually on the other. "I wonder if you could show me the right way to go." He gestured behind him. "I don't think the villagers understand me."

The monk gave a slow grin. "Not many have reason to speak English. We don't see many English speakers outside of the Peace Corps volunteers, and they speak Khmer."

"Right." Simon pulled a piece of paper out of his back pocket. "Well, I don't know if you can help me. I'm not sure if you know many people in the village."

"I've lived here my entire life. I should be able to help." The monk leaned forward to see the papers. Simon held them out and located the names of the caretakers.

"I'm looking for a married couple, Heng and Kolab? I'm told they take care of the old missionary building."

A shadow passed across the monk's face. Simon glanced at the cloudless sky, wincing into the bright sun, then back to the man. The monk wiped his hand over his shaved head, and then dropped his hand against his chest.

"Yes, I know this Heng and Kolab." The monk pointed a shaky finger toward the village. "Past the end of the market, up through the trees. They are on higher ground. The road will break off to the right and there should be a small trail." His voice wavered, his eyes closed in memory. "There will be a row of trees that have low branches in a line. At the end of them is a large sign. Their home is in the clearing just beyond it."

Simon, sure he could find it, rose. He thanked the monk and turned toward the market. After a step, he turned back. "A large sign. What does it say?"

The monk opened his eyes, staring down the road with flat eyes. "It says, 'No Christians Allowed'."

Once Simon located Heng and Kolab, they'd given him a ride on their moto to his home for the duration of his assignment. He'd been astonished by Heng's ability to speak English as well. Heng brushed off the compliments on his accent. "I learned as a boy and have found ways to practice. I enjoy the language."

Simon noticed the sign the monk had spoken of. Although Simon didn't know Khmer, the letters looked bold, unswerving in their statement. Still, he felt compelled, as Kolab and Heng made ready to leave, to tell them one phrase Megan had taught him, the one thing he'd insisted on knowing more than how best to negotiate and bargain in the market:

"Preah Yeasu srolein neak." Jesus loves you.

Tears had pooled in Kolab's eyes and she laughed out loud, grabbing his face with exuberance. Heng bobbed his head in agreement, a smile lighting up his face. "Yes, yes, Simon, yes. *Preah Yeasu srolein neak!"*

After they left, Simon spent hours on the front steps of the building. He held his small Bible, the leather so worn that it curved into the outline of his hand, open to Psalm 19.

The sign weighed heavy on his mind, as did the empty church behind him. Here was a large, empty building with a kitchen, a great space to host festivals and to feed many people. What had happened to the people that brought in expensive materials, stone and solid wood to construct a building? Why did they abandon it?

"Lord, may my time here be spent as You wish. May I offer them not an empty building, a heavy load of rules and expectations, but the fullness of who You are. May I show them You, just You, in all of Your grace and power. Please lead me to these children; I pray that I will find them safe, cared for, and happy."

Chapter Twelve

Boise, Idaho

Gage told his clients that he'd been robbed in Thailand. "Just walking down the street at the market and some guys pulled me into an alley." He pretended to punch his own face. "They got me good, took all of my money."

His clients were impressed with his adventure; he could tell.

"What were you doing in Thailand?" some asked.

Thoughts of Nataya and the man she'd left with flashed through his mind; anger coursed through his veins.

Whore.

He rubbed his thumb and two fingers against his forehead, squeezing the image away. "Uh"—he licked his lips—"humanitarian work…for the firm."

They would nod politely and change the subject back to tax questions or investment inquiries. They would point to the papers they wanted him to look at, effectively taking the attention away from him.

He watched the tops of their heads, angry.

Trust me, lady, he thought as one of his clients talked his ear off about her budget, *if you knew about me, if you knew what my Nataya knew, you would be begging to hear more stories, be begging for me to meet you someplace quiet where your husband would never know—begging me.*

American women were uptight. He needed to go back to Thailand. He sought dark, private corners on the Internet to placate his desires. He also waited impatiently for *them* to contact him, to call him back, tell him he was free to return.

To find Nataya.

Surely by now they saw how much they needed him. Months went by.

Nothing.

Anticipation increased. Desire mounted. He woke in the night twisted in sheets, soaked in sweat, aching all over.

Nataya.

He spent hours online. Sometimes he went to special clubs, but nothing satiated.

Nataya

There was a locked trunk in the corner of his room, filled with magazines and pictures he'd collected since his tenth birthday. He rarely opened it, just liked to know it was there.

Gage remembered the way his father, stumbling drunk, had woken him the night of his birthday party and led him to the basement...

"Shh...son, this place will be our secret."

Gage had been miserable at his party with kids that didn't want to be there, but whose mothers had made them go to be polite. Gage had snuck into his parents' closet when he saw Mary go into the bathroom. There was a small hole in the wall between the closet and the bathroom—a hole that would show him what Mary was really like.

But he hadn't counted on Mary seeing him through the hole, or her screaming like a banshee and blabbering to everyone. Her mother had decided to stay for the party and when she discovered what Gage had done, she stood in front of everyone and yelled at Gage's father, poking him in the chest.

"You sick creep! I knew better than to bring Mary to this trash heap. Just wait until your wife and the rest of the parents hear about this." She'd grabbed Mary—who was still blubbering like a freak—and tugged her outside.

Gage's mother came home from her shift at the restaurant, tired and embarrassed. True to her word, Mary's mother had called her at work.

"Dillon, you have got to stop this. You are going to get yourself arrested. It's bad enough that I work three jobs to scrape by, while you sit at home making movies or whatever it is you say you're doing." She'd lowered her voice, but barely. "Our son is a little creep, and it's all your fault."

Gage sat in his room drawing pictures, red swirls, black figures, painting a story of his anger and desires. Desires bigger than he would ever understand.

His father had never let him—or his mother—into his film studio in the basement. He led Gage down that night. "I'm sorry your party was a bust, Son. Here's your real present."

Gage had been shown pictures, many taken from the hole in the bathroom. He saw the films his father made. Was given his first magazine to keep, with pictures of his friends on the playground, pictures they hadn't known his father was taking, tucked inside.

"Happy Birthday, Son."

Gage only opened the trunk when he felt the same strong yearning that had been aroused that first night, looking at pictures with his dad.

His father had been sloppy. A poor drunk that didn't know how to be discreet or careful.

When his father was arrested, his mother sent Gage to live with her relatives in Boise. Rich relatives that knew how to clean Gage up—educate him—get him into good schools—beat the trash out of him. But he never lost the feeling he got when he looked at those pictures his father took of his friends. Until he met Nataya, until he walked through Walking Street and young girls were brought to him at the snap of his fingers. They fell over him, loved him, *adored* him.

When would they call him back to Thailand?

Gage needed release.

After another month passed, Gage decided to make things happen his way. He began to prep his basement.

But, unlike Dad, I have stealth and imagination.

I won't get caught.

Chapter Thirteen

Cambodia

Jakobi felt the tension immediately.

Her host family had been kind and gracious to her, but from the beginning she had felt the strain on their family. She couldn't understand why they had agreed to host a Peace Corps volunteer when the home was so full.

Jakobi lived in a fairly typical Khmer home: two stories constructed from wood and bamboo, a thatched roof and, due to the close proximity to the burgeoning lake, high stilts. Her room was in the front, closest to her older "brother and sister." Narith and his children took the room in the back. She rarely saw Narith. He was silent, broken and brooding the loss of his wife. Narith's sons were wild, as most boys were. Jakobi enjoyed their antics in class, but somehow when they were home, the unspoken conflict in the family held them silent.

The boys spent their days during the monsoon season swimming between the houses in the village. Now that it was dry, they charged through the forests, dancing across low tree branches, jumping and grasping at swinging vines. Jakobi ate most of her meals in town, desperate to ease the strain on the family. Or maybe just to avoid them.

Her days spent with Chaya's family, laughing and talking together, joking and teasing, were a sharp contrast. She wished there was a way to request a different host family without insulting anyone but knew that wasn't possible.

When Phirun and Dara returned from their trip with two small children, a young girl and a frail baby, Jakobi wondered where everyone would fit. *And where had the children come from?*

The baby cried throughout the first day and night; Jakobi worried that he would make himself sick. The young girl looked frightened and would not eat. She sat quietly, legs drawn up, a worn Minnie Mouse doll tucked into her folded arms. She leaned her little face against the stuffed animal and drenched it with silent tears. When her grandfather or uncle looked to her disapprovingly, her throat convulsed, desperate to swallow her tears. Jakobi, aching to relieve her distress, crouched next to the young girl and patted Minnie on the head.

"I once had a doll like this." She hoped she had chosen the right Khmer words. She was catching on to the language, but still struggled. The young girl's eyes, focused on Jakobi's face, turned to trace her braid. Sensing she wanted to touch her red hair like most of the children in the village had done, Jakobi yanked the band off the end and fluffed her hair out, laughing at the wide eyes of the girl.

Jakobi turned to Dara, who was busy bouncing the whimpering baby.

"What are their names?" She had been hoping they would offer them, but found the need to ask.

Dara passed a look between Phirun and Narith. She looked to the young girl and instructed the girl to answer.

"Maly."

Jakobi softened her eyes at the shy voice. "And your younger?" Jakobi asked as she ran a hand over Maly's shiny black hair.

"Noah."

"Kiri."

Jakobi looked between Maly and Dara, her eyebrows gathered together. Dara shook her head at Maly as if she were dimwitted.

"His name is Kiri," Dara stated and left the room.

Jakobi turned her attention back to Maly, tickling her nose with a wisp of her frizzy hair. The humidity mocked any sense of style Jakobi hoped to have during her stay in Cambodia.

That night, when the house was settled and the baby was finally quiet, Jakobi heard light, hesitant footsteps along the main floor between the rooms. A small shadow filled the bottom of her doorway. Jakobi had been provided a mat from the Peace Corps, although she hadn't needed it. As uncomfortable as the people she lived with were, there was no end to their hospitality. They had furnished her room, the best one in the hut, with a real mattress decorated with balloon themed sheets and a matching comforter. Jakobi sat up when Maly stepped into the room, clutching her Minnie. The moon fell across the girl's bare feet and lit up the fear on Maly's face.

"Sleep here, Jakobi?" the young voice whispered.

Jakobi hesitated for a few seconds before she scooted backwards to make room. "Of course, little one."

Once Maly was tucked in close, Jakobi marveled at the softness of her thin arms, drank in her earthy fragrance. Maly clutched Jakobi's hair in both of her fists, holding tight, as if she wanted to be sure that Jakobi would stay close. Eventually, Maly's breaths fell into a steady pattern of peaceful sleep. Jakobi stared at the ceiling and rubbed a chunk of Maly's hair between two fingers. Where had this small girl and her little brother come from?

And what had Maly called her brother? A most un-Khmer name. A Biblical name. *Where would he have been called Noah?*

✤ ✤ ✤

Simon lounged at a white plastic table in the shade beneath the dock-turned-awning of a small café. He sipped his coffee sweetened with a spoonful of condensed milk, enjoying that it cost him the equivalent of 25 cents. It had taken a bit of time to explain to the smiling grandmother behind the counter that he wanted coffee with milk, and he was surprised when it came iced, but given the warm, humid weather, the cold drink and jolt of caffeine was just the refreshment he'd needed.

His eyes scanned the horizon, appreciating the lush tropics penetrated by wide, packed, rust-colored paths. The café was at the edge of the small village, and behind it, a small but colorful day market had come to life. Buildings high on stilts lined each side of the wide street; some empty beneath, but most converted to booths at street level with the top level acting as a private residence.

At the end of the road, the ornately carved golden eaves of the *wat* rose above the stilted houses and businesses from its foundation high on the side of a mountain. The early morning chant of the monks at the *wat* droned steady and constant, an underlying baseline to the chaotic, varying notes of conversation in the village below. The sun warmed the earth, the early morning air thick and moist. Simon inhaled the spicy soil, his hands itching to dig something or build something. The country stretched before him: otherworldly in its simplicity. The acres of farms and lush forests—dotted with thatched roof huts and crumbling stone buildings—churned something primitive deep in his gut.

I could get used to this.

Simon noticed a group of school children clustered together around something on the side of the road. The girls stood close together, but separate from the boys, some of whom were picking up sticks to poke whatever it was. Suddenly the group erupted in squeals of surprise and laughter as the boys with the sticks jumped back. Simon saw a flash of brown matted fur before the group closed the circle again. A low growl raised the hair on his arms.

"Oh, man," he muttered.

Simon rose and paused for a minute, choosing to leave his laptop on the table. "Please still be here when I get back," he said, and strode toward the children. The tallest boy had lifted a baseball shaped rock above his head, and Simon caught the boy's arm as it came down to drop on the dog.

The animal, brown and gray, fur matted in patches over its body, curled a wiry tail between its legs, white teeth bared at the boys; what was left of the fur down the ridge of his back stood high in defense. Simon plucked the rock from the young boy who turned with narrowed eyes to see who had taken it. The dog bolted through the distracted children, taking the opportunity for escape. A dozen pairs of eyes rounded at Simon.

The lean American knew enough about Cambodian culture from his crash course with Megan that he understood he needed to help the boy with the rock save face.

Simon tossed the stone from one hand to the other slowly and began to juggle it. With his eyes and chin, he motioned for the boy to hand him another one. Anxious to see what would happen next, the children all searched the ground excitedly. The tallest tried to hand another rock to Simon, who shook his head. *How can I communicate this?*

He stuck his foot out and nodded his head backwards a few times to indicate that the boy should toss it to him. The boy glanced at his friends quizzically. Simon stopped tossing the first rock and held his hand up, catcher-style, and tapped his fingers against his thumb a few times. The boy caught on and tossed him the rock. Simon winked at the group and began to juggle the first stone, then the second. The girls squealed while the boys made appreciative nods and noises. Each took turns tossing in rocks. Simon dropped some and successfully worked a few others into the rotation.

Nailed it, he thought, proud of how quickly he'd averted the children's attention. They watched in fascination as he juggled the remaining three rocks. Simon wondered how long they would wait; his arms burned from the weight. From the corner of his eye, he noticed another adult standing behind the kids.

He glanced over to see a young woman with fiery red hair, set ablaze by the early morning sun, straddling a bike, one arm draped across the handlebars, her chin propped in the other, an amused smile curling her lips. *How long has she been there?*

Simon missed the next rotation and jumped from foot to foot as the rocks thudded around his feet into the rust-colored earth. The children giggled as the woman spoke to them in Khmer. With groans and grins, they scattered.

Simon smiled at them as they retreated. He wiped a hand on his jeans and reached out to the woman. "Simon Russell."

She remained on the bike and walked it forward a few steps, her long brown skirt tickling her calves, and stretched her hand to take his in a surprisingly strong grip. "Jakobi McNamara."

They shook once and dropped hands to their sides in awkward silence. Simon knew that the Peace Corps had volunteers in this village and had expected to run into them but wanted her to start the conversation.

Jakobi crinkled her brow at his silence. "I'm a Peace Corps volunteer," she finally offered. "I teach at the school and live with a host family just outside of town."

"I thought Peace Corps volunteers were given monthly stipends to live on their own," he said.

Jakobi gave a small, airy laugh. "Well, things are very different in Cambodia, including the living arrangements. When I first applied for the Peace Corps, I envisioned a mud hut somewhere in the jungle, cooking over a campfire, alone with my thoughts, fighting off tigers…" She rolled her eyes heavenward, a dreamy expression on her face.

"And the reality?" Simon's brows rose, his mouth curved to one side.

Jakobi flattened her mouth and began to tick off the fingers on her hand. "Let's see. I have a host brother and sister, who are old enough to be my parents, but they want me to call them 'brother' and 'sister', their son—also to be called 'brother'—who is a widower. From what I have gathered, his wife passed away in some horrific way and they believe her ghost is all around the house." Jakobi flinched. "That makes for restful sleep, let me tell you. Uh, let's see"—she fanned out her hand and held up three fingers on the other hand—"the widower has a few kids—you just juggled for them—aaaannnd brother and sister just returned from a trip to Phnom Penh where they brought back two more kids, because apparently our house wasn't full enough." Jakobi let out a gusty sigh.

Adrenaline shot through Simon at the mention of two new children from the city of Phnom Penh. *Lord, would You lead me to them so quickly?*

"Well, I better get to school. If I hurry, I can catch up with everyone." Jakobi pushed off with a friendly wave.

Simon stood watching her, conflicted about what to do. Should he confide to Jakobi, tell her why he was there?

No. The answer was clear.

She was the only other American in the place; surely it would be easy to forge a friendship without suspicion. He thought of her face, the light brush of freckles across the bridge of her nose, her wavy red hair pulled back in a braid but most likely a wild mess in the humidity if she let it down. Her brown eyes and narrow chin. Her slim ankles beneath toned calves. Spending time with an attractive woman like Jakobi certainly wouldn't hurt…unless she became too distracting.

"Careful there, Simon," he muttered to himself. "First things first, you need to find out if those are the kids you're looking for. Don't forget that you're here on a mission."

❖ ❖ ❖

Simon gathered that Jakobi took the same route to school each day. He rose early and rode the moto, he had purchased the day before, to the market. He bought his coffee—iced with a tablespoon or two of condensed milk—as well as one for Jakobi, and waited underneath the makeshift awning. While he knew a friendship between them was necessary to be close to who he assumed were the Deliverance children, he still felt leery of rejection, which would be a slam to his own personal pride.

While he waited, Simon closed his eyes to concentrate on the sounds around him.

A faint rat-a-tap-a-rat-a-tap-a down the street grew stronger, and he opened his eyes to see Jakobi on her bike and a young girl on the handlebars bump over a small hill, giggling in innocent fun.

His heart leapt. *Could this be the girl, Lord?* Simon schooled his features and stood to wave Jakobi down. "Well this either looks like great fun or a great mess waiting to happen," he teased.

Jakobi laughed, easing the bike to a stop and walking it close to him, still straddling the bar. The front of the bike twisted under the awkward load, and Simon caught the young girl as she fell.

"Whoa, princess!" He took pity on her frightened face and set her down. She fled to Jakobi's side and hid her embarrassment in the long, heavy skirt Jakobi wore.

Jakobi disembarked and leaned down, her features concerned, to comfort the girl. Simon wished he understood Khmer as Jakobi's words came fast and her face lit up in animation. The young girl laughed, and Jakobi rose to thank Simon.

"Although," she added with a glimmer in her eye, "she wouldn't have fallen off if you would have just let us ride on by. I can balance much better the faster we go."

Simon shrugged. "I just wanted to offer you some coffee." He turned to pick up the iced cup on the table behind him.

Jakobi rewarded him with a dazzling smile. "My hero," she uttered, sipping the sweetened brew. She made a noise in her throat and rolled her eyes heavenward before she said something to the young girl, wiggling her eyebrows up and down. The girl giggled and looked up at Simon through long, dark lashes.

"What did you say?" Simon twisted his lips in suspicion.

Jakobi laughed and took another sip. "I told Maly, here, that coffee is the way to an American girl's heart, and that she can trust a man that buys her a cup."

Simon's breath caught at the name Maly. He quickly recovered and winked at them both. He nodded at Maly with exaggerated charm.

"She's right, kid," he said, pleased at the smile on Maly's face when Jakobi translated.

"Simon, you never did tell me yesterday why you are in this remote village in Cambodia or where you're staying," Jakobi commented, sipping the coffee again.

Simon scratched the scruff on his chin. "You're right, I didn't." He waited a beat then chuckled at her expectant expression. "I'm staying further up, past the *wat*, in a church if you can believe that."

The laughter fell from Jakobi's expression, her features flattening. "Oh, you're the one." Her dry tone matched her appearance. Simon was astonished at the change in her.

She handed the coffee back and turned toward the bike, her hand waving for Maly to follow.

"So you're a missionary." It was a statement. An accusation.

Whoa. What did I step into there? Simon cleared his throat. "No, I'm here on assignment to write a few chapters for a Cambodian tourist book and to send articles to a travel magazine. There is very little first-hand experience written about these remote villages."

Jakobi eyed him, the tension still radiating across the few feet that separated them. "Hm. Okay. So what's with the church?"

"It's a building my employer was able to rent." He crossed his arms, unimpressed with her anger toward him over living in a church building. He glanced at Maly and felt a nudge in his spirit. He relented. *Oh, Lord, guide me. I can't mess this up.* "You can come check it out if you want; I'm not exactly holding church service there."

Jakobi snorted, "Yeah, no thanks. But thank you for the coffee." She sat on the bike seat and clapped her hands, then held them out for Maly.

Simon plucked her up around the waist and steadied her on the bike. "Jakobi, I would really like to get to know you"—he ducked to look in her eyes—"if for nothing more than to have an American friend to talk to while we're experiencing culture shock."

Her pupils throbbed slightly. "Sorry, Simon. It was a long night." Her gaze traveled over Maly's head. "We better get to school. But I do think it would be nice to get together sometime." She offered him an apologetic smile before she pushed off.

He watched Jakobi pedal away, Maly giggling from the front of the bike as Jakobi spoke words that he didn't understand in a light, silly tone.

He'd wanted to tell Maly that Jesus loved her, sure she would recognize the meaning of those words. But Jakobi's hostility at the mention of a church building told him he needed to tread lightly.

Lord, Lord; maybe you've sent me here for more than just Maly and Noah. "Don't screw it up, Simon," he muttered and went back to his coffee.

Chapter Fourteen

"Okay, Jakobi, that was a little uncalled for," Jakobi murmured as the bike hit another series of bumps, and Maly squealed in delight from the handlebars. Jakobi smiled at the little girl's exuberance and, at the same moment, felt curious about it.

Maly had arrived in the home scared, shy—quiet. When Jakobi reached out to her, she'd lit up from the stranger's attention. If her host brother and sister were Maly and Kiri's grandparents, why wasn't there more of a connection? Why would Maly connect with a redheaded, freckle-faced American over her kin?

Jakobi turned toward the small school building and eased the bike to a stop on the cement sidewalk between the elementary building and the one for older grades. She carefully helped Maly jump down from the bike and leaned it against the wall before she reached for Maly's hand, happy to have the girl's company, wondering how Dara fared at home with Kiri.

The baby had kept most of the family up with his cries; whimpers so woeful and pitiful it seemed the baby was calling out for someone. Jakobi suspected he sensed the absence of his mother, despite his young age. Dara was so worn; she'd almost collapsed in relief when Jakobi held Kiri for the morning rice meal. A large hammock had been strung in the middle of the room, and Jakobi sat in it with Kiri, pushing her legs to create a rocking motion to soothe him. His cries had intensified until

Jakobi began to hum. To her annoyance, the only song she could think of at that moment was "God Is So Good." A song she had learned in Sunday school long ago. Kiri's cries were almost immediately extinguished, and he'd swung his head toward Jakobi's voice, mouth open in a circle, eyes trained on her face. Within minutes, he was asleep. Jakobi placed him gently in the hammock with a tug on the side to keep up the swinging motion. Dara, fatigue traced across her worn features, looked like she would fall asleep right with him.

On impulse, Jakobi had said, "Dara, I would love to take Maly to school with me today; would that be all right?"

Relief washed across the older woman's face. "Yes, Jakobi. Thank you." Dara looked Maly over, her face indiscernible, before she turned away.

Jakobi turned excitedly to Maly and explained that the girl could go to school with her. She laughed at Maly's exuberant squeal of delight.

The day passed quickly. Chaya and Jakobi had arranged for an "Introduction to Proper Hygiene" day with another Peace Corps volunteer, a nurse from California. When the day was through, Jakobi asked the nurse, Sara, if she would mind giving Maly a check-up.

"Sure, Jakobi," she agreed. She was animated with Maly, who had Sara and Jakobi in stitches of laughter with her funny faces and gestures.

After a quick checkup, Sara set Maly on her feet and sent her to play with the other kids. An impromptu game of soccer had formed; boys on one side, girls on the other. Jakobi had noticed right away upon her arrival in Cambodia how naturally boys and girls split up for play. She noticed other things as well: the tattered ball that was in dire need of air and the dirty, bare feet that kicked the ball around in the red dust.

"She looks great, Jakobi." Sara leaned back against the small table that had been used for exams in the schoolroom. She wiped an arm across her forehead, the warmth of the day finally permeating the air indoors.

"That's what I thought, Sara. Thank you. I don't know why I feel so funny about her and her little brother. Something just feels off there."

Jakobi crossed her arms and leaned against the table with Sara, envying the other woman's khaki capris. All Peace Corps women volunteers were expected to wear collared shirts, but teachers were expected to wear a *sampot*—an ankle length skirt made of heavy material—when out in the community. Because Jakobi lived with some of her students, she was careful to dress in her sampot at all times. Rivulets of sweat worked down her legs and she lifted the bottom of her skirt up and down to create a slight breeze to dry off.

"Have you heard what happened to their parents?" Sara asked.

"I understand that their mother died, but there has been no mention of the father."

"Didn't you say that their other son's wife died before you got here?"

Jakobi gave a short, humorless laugh. "Yeah. And from what I can tell, she committed suicide, and now she haunts the place."

"Yikes." Sara widened her eyes at Jakobi, her mouth twisting in mock terror.

"Tell me about it." Jakobi saw Maly run past the open window, laughing as another girl chased her. "I just…there's something off," she said again.

They sat together in silence for a moment. "Well," Sara ventured, "I guess, keep an eye out and report anything you see to your superior next time we have training. If anything, they can probably arrange to move you to a different host family."

Jakobi watched the children play soccer through the open window after Sara had left. The school day had long ended, but the kids were enjoying their play, and she had no desire to send them home. It seemed they all had enough worries of their own. Her lips curled as she watched them laughing and joking with one another, pondering what Sara had said about changing families.

"Right," she mumbled, "but then what would happen to Maly?" As if she knew she had been the subject of Jakobi's thoughts, Maly bounced into the room, hair tousled, face moist. Jakobi grinned at her, hoping her concern didn't show.

Jakobi finished straightening the classroom with Maly's help. She wrote a few lessons on the board for the next morning. To Maly's delight, Jakobi could not help but come away from the task covered in white chalk. Jakobi bent down, fists teasingly planted on her hips and scowled at Maly for making fun. She reached out to snatch Maly in a bear hug, startled by the roar of a moto outside of the school and a loud cheer from the remaining soccer players, all boys. She set Maly down, grabbed her hand, and walked out of the building, her hand in salute against her forehead, shielding her eyes from the sun.

Simon killed the engine on the moto, yanked the helmet off of his head, and turned to look behind him. Jakobi followed his gaze to see what the children were all pointing and laughing at.

The mangy mutt, from the first day they met, followed Simon at an easy pace, tail high and wagging. He strutted past the children and collapsed in the shadow of Simon's bike, obviously believing that he belonged there. Simon turned back to the crowd of boys and held his hands out toward the dog. Though they wouldn't understand, his face expressed the words Jakobi heard him say over the teasing calls. "What did I ever do to make him think he's mine?"

Jakobi hid a smile behind her hand as he turned to face her, his own smile confident.

"Hello, ladies." He winked at Maly while Jakobi translated, although she substituted "girls" for ladies. His swagger was enough to show the little girl what he meant. Maly waved.

The boys circled around Simon, talking to him all at once. He climbed off the moto, pushing the dog down as it danced excitedly at his feet. Everyone chattered at him and Simon looked questioningly to Jakobi.

"They want you to play soccer," she translated.

The tallest boy in the center nodded and held the ball up for show. Simon readily agreed, and Jakobi sat on the sidewalk to watch, her legs tucked to the side and Maly in her lap.

Simon moved with the agility and grace of a natural athlete. Jakobi appreciated that he played with careful restrained competitiveness, allowing shots to slide when a boy wasn't paying attention, cautious with their bare feet up against his boots. The dog continued to hop around Simon, chasing down the ball with the others, growling when it came near him. He was in his prime, tongue lolling out of his mouth in happy anticipation of Simon's every move.

Twenty minutes later Simon bent over, hands on his knees, gasping for air, his shirt moistened with sweat. He watched, still breathing heavy, as the boys waved good-bye and walked down the rust-colored road, passing the ball between them as they rounded the corner and out of sight.

"You okay?" Jakobi called, stifling a giggle.

Simon let out an exaggerated groan. "I just forgot how old I am." He locked eyes with the dog, which sat at his feet, tail sweeping back and forth across the earth. Simon sneezed and waved the dog away. The mutt, encouraged by the attention, leapt up and licked Simon's cheek.

Jakobi and Maly laughed at the happy, goofy-faced dog and Simon's grand production of disgust. Jakobi saw the twinkle in his eye and knew the dog had found a master, whether Simon liked it or not.

Simon feigned annoyance at their giggles and stuck his nose in the air. "To think I came to invite you ladies to dinner," he sniffed.

"Aw, what a shame," Jakobi retorted sarcastically.

Simon cocked his head at her. "Now, why don't you sound more impressed, Miss McNamara?" He strode to where he had parked his moto. "I just bought this baby this morning, and she was anxious to act as chariot to two lovely young women."

Jakobi rolled her eyes at Maly, who watched them both with curiosity.

"Well," Jakobi sighed, "I'm sorry, but you'll have to let her know I can't ride her. The Peace Corps forbids it."

Simon sobered, "Really? Why?"

"Too many accidents. Apparently they like to keep their volunteers alive during their service. Go figure."

"Ah." Simon tapped his lips with a finger. "Well, perhaps we can arrange something else?"

Jakobi chewed her lip, thinking. *It would be kind of nice to talk with another American for a while, especially one that isn't part of the Peace Corps.* She finally shrugged. "We can still have dinner." *What harm could it do?* "I need to check in with Maly's family first," she hedged.

Simon pumped his fist into the air triumphantly, making the dog at his feet yip excitedly, and Simon roughly scruffed the dog's ears. "Hear that, pup? She said yes. Must be my charming disposition."

Jakobi blushed and mumbled something about meeting Simon at the market in an hour. Simon smiled at Jakobi, his eyes trained on hers. Jakobi's stomach fluttered and she turned to retrieve her bike.

As he had that morning, Simon gave special attention to Maly and hoisted her into his arms, holding her there while Jakobi walked her bike to them. The little girl looked completely at ease, rubbing her hands along Simon's sculpted biceps. She noticed a tattoo just under the rim of his shirtsleeve and lifted the fabric to get a better look. Jakobi watched a look pass between Simon and Maly as the little girl traced the image; a large hand with a fish—the Ichthys or "Jesus Fish" design across the palm. A look passed between Simon and Maly before he, noticing Jakobi's watchful gaze, averted his eyes and set Maly on the handlebars. He held her steady until Jakobi was in place. Jakobi settled on the bike and looked up to let Simon know she was ready.

Her breath caught at the expression of both tenderness and despondency that rippled through his blue-green eyes as he again locked eyes with Maly. Simon looked away for a moment, as if to collect himself.

"All right, Jakobi," he said when he met her confused stare, "I'll see you in a bit." He pressed a kiss to the top of Maly's head and jogged toward the moto whistling for the dog, who immediately followed. Jakobi pushed off, wondering if she would ever put the pieces of that puzzling exchange together.

When she entered the home, Jakobi winced at Kiri's shrieks of protest. Maly, more withdrawn and quiet now that they were with the family, walked beside Jakobi into the main room. Dara desperately mimicked the movements of Jakobi that morning, trying to calm the baby as Jakobi had done. She was humming and swinging back and forth in the hammock, but Kiri continued to wail.

Distressed at the panic on Dara's face and the dark brooding of Phirun, Jakobi reached out to stroke the baby's head. "Let me help, Dara. I'm sorry I stayed so late."

She had asked Sara earlier that day about the baby's incessant cries. Her friend thought the boy might not be getting enough to eat and sent Jakobi home with special formula and bottles. Jakobi went into her room for a water jug and dropped her bags on the bed. She quickly mixed the water and powder and brought the bottle to Dara. The older woman was in tears and clearly at the end of her nerves. Jakobi reached for Kiri, hoping to comfort where needed and not overstep. Dara eagerly relinquished the squalling boy.

Jakobi cradled the infant in her arms and offered him the bottle as she walked the perimeter of the room. She hummed, "Twinkle, Twinkle Little Star," one of the tunes she'd remembered as she racked her brain all day for songs beyond her Sunday school memories. He turned away from the bottle and cried harder. Jakobi bit her lip and tried again, singing, "God Is So Good."

As he had that morning, Kiri quieted and turned to her, entranced. She kept singing, pressing down the desire to roll her eyes at the words, and eased the bottle into his mouth. The room fell quiet except for her singing. When Kiri was again fast asleep in her arms, Dara reached for him.

"Jakobi, you must teach me that song," she said.

Chapter Fifteen

Simon was beginning to wish he had offered to pick Jakobi up at her host home when she rode up on her bike, alone.

"Where is the charming Maly?" he asked, walking to meet her where she leaned the bike against the side of a tree; the same tree where he had met the monk his first day. The dog trailed behind him, and Jakobi patted the mutt's head as she disembarked.

"I thought it would be good for her to share dinner with her family. The baby finally settled in after a good dose of formula, and everyone seemed to relax after that. Maly attached to me so quickly; I don't want to hinder her connection to her family." Jakobi had changed into a fresh sampot and clean olive colored polo shirt. She smoothed her skirt, a hesitant light in her averted eyes. Simon understood her reservation. They didn't know each other, just happened to be the only Americans in a small town that seemed to be frozen in time.

He took her elbow and turned her toward the market. "I greatly suspect that I'm being overcharged at the market. Let's test it." He winked at Jakobi, who relaxed.

The market was small, only a few booths compared to the large wide streets of Pattaya that Simon was used to. The quiet conversations between villagers were charming in contrast to the loud music and frenzied activity of the larger markets.

Simon kept Jakobi laughing as she bargained with shopkeepers in Khmer, ordering rice, fruit, and fish from different vendors. She had a word for everyone and seemed to make an effort to buy one thing from every booth. Most of the villagers indeed had been overcharging him, but Simon knew it was his own lack of familiarity with the language that was to blame. And he didn't really mind paying more; they had to earn a living just as much as he did. In fact, they probably worked harder selling their wares than he did writing for the magazines. Almost everyone gave him strange looks as the dog continued to keep in line with every move he made.

Jakobi led him to a booth he'd been curious about, but hadn't ventured to yet. "This is the baker." She explained that the French invasion of Cambodia years ago had left its mark, both in abandoned French influenced buildings and remarkably delicious baked goods. They ordered warm rolls. Simon's stomach cramped at the aroma as they turned away, only just realizing he had forgotten to eat lunch.

"Where shall we partake of this fine feast?" Simon asked, eyeballing the stand where he bought coffee each morning, thinking they could sit at one of the tables out front.

"This way," Jakobi instructed, walking past the coffee booth and back toward her bike. She unzipped one of the saddlebags secured behind the seat and spread out a brightly colored woven blanket on the ground beside the bike. They set their food out picnic style beneath the mammoth tree.

Simon reclined back on his side, legs out and away from the food, his back to the tree trunk. Jakobi tucked her legs to the side under her skirt and opened a few packages, offering the fish to Simon first. The blanket was scratchy under his arm.

"This blanket reminds me of one my friend bought on a mission trip we took to Mexico," he commented, offering a bite of fish to the dog that had plopped down near Simon's feet.

Jakobi regarded him, head tilted to one side in a disturbingly attractive gesture. "Well, that answers that question," she replied.

He resisted the urge to watch the delicate pulse at the base of her throat. He wished her hair were down instead of twisted into a fat braid, accentuating her slender neck. He cleared his throat. "What's that?"

"Whether you are okay with living in a church," she said.

Simon shook his head, brow furrowed. "Why would my going on a high school mission trip to Mexico affect how I feel about my living situation today?"

Jakobi opened her mouth and closed it. "I guess it wouldn't. I'm sorry, I just…I guess I have religious issues."

I'll say, Simon thought, contemplating her strange reaction that morning. Aloud he asked, "Want to tell me about them?"

Jakobi chuckled. "Smooth. You going to witness to me now?"

Simon, immediately flustered, sat up. "Jakobi, I'm just talking to you here. I have no angle, no agenda. But here, let me lay it out: I am a Christian. Not a religious person, but a man that has surrendered his life to the Lord and is doing his very best to live a life that honors Him."

He held up a hand when she opened her mouth to speak. "I was not raised this way. A friend in junior high invited me to a winter retreat. I went because I had a crush on a girl that I knew went to his church. The girl didn't go, but I met God there and surrendered to Him. Nothing in my life had made sense before then. From that weekend on, I established a habit of reading God's Word for myself. A day has not gone by in the last fifteen years that I haven't started with His word first. Whatever little box you've put Christians and their ideas into"—he spun a finger in her direction—"you can take me right out of it."

Jakobi pursed her lips together and crossed her arms.

They sat in silence, the air between them electric with emotion and pride.

Jakobi felt the first drop; her anger replaced with panic. "The food!" she shouted as sheets of rain pummeled around them.

The shade of the tree offered some amount of shelter, but mostly just pockets of safety between the rivers of rain that poured through the openings in the leaves. In desperation, they huddled side by side and tucked their bags of food in close. The dog whimpered and nuzzled his nose into Simon's back. The rain stopped almost as quickly as it began, the air thick and moist. The fragrance was unlike anything Simon had experienced in the dirty city of Pattaya.

"Whoa, would you take a look at that!" Simon pointed behind Jakobi to the small village.

Streams of sunshine, the kind that lights the end of a day in brilliance, as if to say "I'll be back", fell across the stilted homes. A rainbow arched from one end of the market to the other, overshadowing and dulling the normally brilliant red and gold of the *wat* in the distance with its vibrant colors.

Simon murmured in worshipful awe, "'The heavens are telling of the glory of God; And their expanse is declaring the work of His hands.' The sky, Jakobi, everything around us that is created by Him is bursting to tell of His excellence."

Simon glanced to his side where the magnified light found Jakobi's face, accentuating her freckles and the red tendrils of hair that had escaped from her braid. He looped a brotherly arm around her shoulders. "I don't know what you believe, Jakobi, but that right there makes those scriptures hard to deny."

Jakobi had to admit she was enchanted, romanced by the moment, by the beauty of the rainbow and brilliant sunlight against violet clouds. His words were melodic and something in her yearned to fall into them.

She gently removed his arm. The storm had quenched her anger, but poems could not replace reason. "Until you factor in science and logic," Jakobi answered.

Simon decided not to press it. They surveyed the damp bags, happy to discover that most of the damage had been done to the packaging and not the food. They moved on to easier topics. Both delighted in the discovery of their hometowns, only two hours apart.

"We went to Cannon Beach with my mom's family one week out of every summer," Simon declared.

"You and everyone else," Jakobi snickered. "My friends and I drove to Portland whenever we wanted Red Robin."

Simon slapped a hand on the still-moist blanket. "You drove an hour for Red Robin when you could walk to Bill's Tavern?" He shook his head mockingly. "Man, Jakobi, I thought we could be friends."

Jakobi punched him on the arm. "Easy for you to say. At least at Red Robin no one is listening in on your conversation."

They bantered back and forth, sharing homesick moments and delight over the fluffy rolls, strange encounters on their travels, and their shared sadness over the poverty they faced in their work. Simon almost slipped and shared stories about Deliverance and clamped his mouth shut.

Jakobi noticed, but pretended not to. "You know, Simon, I am sorry for how rude I was about your faith." She fingered the edges of the blanket. "Believe it or not, I was raised in a Christian home, went to church and even a semester of Bible College."

Simon, again in his reclined position, legs out, propped on one elbow, and clasped his hands together. He met her gaze, communicating that he was listening. The dog, full from the bites of food Jakobi and Simon slipped to him, laid down next to Simon. Simon patted his head and both he and the dog turned their eyes toward Jakobi as she shared more.

"I was raised that women become mothers and wives. From the time I was a teen, my mother groomed me to be a good girlfriend. When I was sixteen, there was a boy in the church that asked my dad if he could court me. My parents were thrilled. I had a crush on him, thought he was nice. We dated through high school, although he hated how much time I spent on my studies. He didn't understand my drive for good grades." She shrugged. "Somehow, even though I didn't openly rebel against the idea of being a wife and mother, inside...I just felt I needed an out.

"I rarely wore make-up, but for our one year anniversary, I decided to dress really nice and style my hair. I spent hours primping and fluffing as my dad called it. I walked down the stairs for our date, expecting Brad—my boyfriend—to appreciate the effort. Instead, I spent the evening being told how much I looked like a hooker."

She snorted at the memory, a humorless sound. "No wife of mine is going to paint her face like a street walker," he said. He spent the rest of the night telling me exactly what kind of wife I would be. When I got home, devastated, I told my mom and she was on his side. I determined then and there that I would be no man's property."

For the first time she looked Simon in the eye. "I continued to date him, right up until I left for my first—and only—semester of Bible College. I had a scholarship because of my grades, but I had no backbone. I told him I wanted some school under my belt for when I homeschooled like he had said I would. He wasn't happy, but didn't argue.

"I was so sheltered and protected, Simon. My parents didn't let me entertain any school of thought outside of theirs. I went to a small high school, but didn't have much of a social life. My dad wouldn't even let me take a debate class that the school offered because he didn't think it was necessary for me to know 'how to argue'." She twisted her mouth to one side.

"One night in college, a group of my friends decided to attend an evolution lecture at Portland State to gain talking points to argue for the creation theory, and I tagged along out of curiosity. I was completely captivated by the lecture."

Jakobi turned her face toward the west. The rainbow had long since faded and the retreating sun pulled the dusky remnants of daylight down with it. She waved her hand to encompass the lumpy dirt road they picnicked beside. "To me, that lecture was like discovering a hidden, magnificent, untouched world, one that had been hidden from me. But one that was so real and complex and fascinating that I just couldn't get enough. I was suddenly free to live and explore and *be something*.

"Without telling my parents, I switched to the university the next semester; my credits didn't all transfer, but I found a job on campus and applied for grants. When I explained to my parents that I loved the idea of their God but that I couldn't buy into it all. Then…" She took a deep breath and in the fading light, Simon could see the turmoil drift across her features.

"Then?" he prodded.

"Let's just say our relationship changed dramatically. They no longer knew how to talk with me—relate to me. They acted as if I had committed some horrible sin, when all I wanted was a real education. When I applied for the Peace Corps, you would have thought I had stood in the street burning my bra or something." She laughed and caught her lower lip in her teeth, embarrassed at her words.

Simon chuckled with her, charmed by the spots of pink that curled on her cheeks.

Jakobi sat up, startled to have rambled on for so long. "Oh, Simon, I'm sorry. I got carried away. I really need to get back so I can see my way along the path. My bike has a light, but it's not all that great."

She stood and brushed her hands quickly over her backside before she leaned down to gather their trash. Simon helped her to fold the blanket and pack her saddlebag. She settled onto the bike seat, one foot on the ground and one on the highest pedal, and considered him a moment.

"This friendship might just work out, Simon," she mused.

He gave a short laugh. "I sure hope so, Miss McNamara."

She offered him a shy little wave and pushed off, gracefully gliding down the bumpy lane. The dog yipped and trotted alongside her for a few feet before turning back to sit beside Simon. Simon absentmindedly patted the mutt's head before he shoved his hands in his front pockets and watched until the light and distance folded over the woman and her bike.

"I hope so," he said again.

Chapter Sixteen

It had been one month since Nataya had met with the adoption coordinator. The kind woman had talked with Nataya for an hour about families that were right there in Thailand, ready and willing, to care for her baby. Families that loved the same Jesus that she did and would raise her baby to do the same.

Her baby. *Their* baby if she agreed. And she had to agree, didn't she?

Everyone, it seemed, expected her to sign her baby over in four months. Each day her belly protruded a little bit more, and the little one inside of her became more animated. She loved the feel of kicks and rolls, flutters and pokes. Her heart ached at the thought of looking at her sweet baby's face, only to have another woman step in to care for it and love it.

But how could she, a teenager, a victim of trafficking, a rescued girl of Deliverance, possibly care for a baby? She knew it was impossible to keep the baby—that someone else could give it a better life—but still...

Still, she prayed and cried out to the Lord. She prayed for the ache to go away, but with each passing day, it only grew stronger.

Ratana came to live at the little Deliverance house, a dark and quiet girl. Nataya was enchanted by her beauty: flawless skin, strong jaw—fierce, liquid, brown-black eyes. She wore a determined expression and prominent stomach.

As when others had come, Nataya smiled politely in greeting, but left the girl to her thoughts. Each person came from different situations; all trusted the promises of Deliverance for different reasons. But all had been face to face with darkness and evil unlike most of the world had experienced. Just as someone coming into the bright sunlight after time in a dark cavern, the light of new life and hope could be blinding and difficult to adjust to at first. Deliverance girls understood this and did their best to provide the privacy needed to adjust. Ratana was placed in the bed that became open in Nataya's room when another girl had given birth and moved to another house.

Nataya smiled at her when she entered the room after devotions that night. Ratana had sat silently through dinner and the devotions, her eyes becoming glazed and vacant, then determined and hard.

Ratana looked back at her and asked how old she was.

"Sixteen," Nataya answered.

Ratana responded that she was fourteen, and averted her eyes out of respect for the older Nataya, her eyes instead brushing over Nataya's slightly pregnant belly. Ratana was obviously much further along, but Nataya didn't think now was the time to ask about the baby.

"It gets easier," Nataya spoke quietly.

"It will be much easier after I have the abortion," Ratana answered bluntly.

Unexpectedly, an image of a woman standing over Nataya with a knife flashed through her mind. Her head swam and she sunk down hard onto her own bed to avoid falling over.

Abortion? *Could Deliverance have possibly promised Ratana one?* The word and deed had never been mentioned to Nataya by Deliverance, the option never presented. She'd heard Christians didn't believe in them, assumed the same for Deliverance and had been relieved.

Nataya's memories washed over her. Violent, horrific memories; the tearing and screaming. Hot, searing pain, weeks of agonizing recovery; the great void covered crudely by a jagged scar across her abdomen. *They wouldn't possibly do that to the girls here, would they?* Could that be why they never saw girls once they left to have their babies? But then why would they offer adoption services?

The pain of the past hit Nataya hard in the gut and a wave of nausea spun through her. She gripped the side of the bed and took deep breaths. *Lord, what if I tell them I don't want to give up my baby, and they cut it out of my belly, just like before?*

Chapter Seventeen

Jakobi and Simon fell into an easy friendship. He would greet her in the market some mornings with a cup of coffee. She helped to train him in the Khmer language. He often asked about the children and privately prayed for ways that he could offer assistance to the baby without exposing his purpose to Jakobi. He feared that if she knew of his reasons for being in the village, she would cut off communication with him. As her friend, Simon was able to let her vent about the tension in her host family, all while gaining valuable insight into the well-being of the children.

Jakobi had a blog she liked to update once a week, just in case her parents and sister were checking in. Simon had assignments to send out and receive via the Internet. There was no Internet access in their small village, but a small Internet café was available in the town of Pursat, a little more than an hour away by automobile. Jakobi began to look forward to the cramped van rides into Pursat on her day off now that Simon came along. They would laugh at how many Cambodians saw fit to crush into the vehicle, some carrying live—or dead—chickens, others greatly in need of Jakobi's hygiene class. In Pursat, they would make the most of restaurants and the busy market, exploring, sharing, and laughing. Their banter remained light, only turning serious when they talked of faith. Their attraction went unspoken, but understood.

Understood, too, was the realization that a romantic relationship between their two very different schools of thought would never work. While Simon couldn't deny that he was greatly attracted to Jakobi, that he found his gaze drifting too often to her lips, or that he had strange sensations in his chest region whenever he watched her with Maly or the other children in the village. He wanted her heart to be softened toward things of God for her sake alone.

"Jakobi, it doesn't make any sense!" he had declared on one of their outings. "The earth is held together with such force that if it moved even the slightest bit closer to—or away from—the sun, we would be instant toast or icicles. We are held in place by a force and design greater than any accident could possibly throw together."

She raked her fingers through her hair, exasperated. "Simon! How does a God with no reason for existence and a story that He spoke everything into creation make any more sense than the evolution theory? At least science can explain the layers of rock that indicate that the earth was formed millions of years ago, the way that some animals have remained, while others are extinct. Survival of the fittest makes so much more sense than a universe spinning under some puppet master."

"How do you explain the spiritual element in all of us, Jakobi?" Simon had asked once over iced coffee and a shared mango dish in a quiet café in Pursat.

Jakobi tilted her head to the side, considering him. "I've met plenty of people that have no interest in the spiritual, Simon. I think it's awfully presumptuous of you to say everyone has that element."

"Then how do you explain that humans have a moral code, Jakobi? Each one has knowledge of right and wrong. The Bible says it is written on our hearts from the beginning of life; that all are without excuse."

He glanced around and lowered his voice. "In the country we're in now, there is a drive to be and do better. To do everything just right, to live a right life as a good Buddhist and be elevated in the next life. So why is this place full of corruption and slavery? For that matter, why is America or any other country so full of evil? If we evolve, learning to do better and survive better and our genetics evolve with each generation...why has no one gotten it right? Why is the world decaying? Why is nothing being made new?" He paused, then asked, "Why are we all so blasted evil, right down to our core?"

Jakobi had furrowed her brow at him. "I don't think I'm evil. And I don't think you're evil," she added with a whisper.

Simon swallowed. "Jakobi, in my heart of hearts, I am a man that wants his own way, a man that fights back violent urges, that is easily offended, that would be inclined to shove everyone else out of my way so that I could be successful at their expense." He placed a fist over his heart. "But there is a new Spirit in me, one that stops my selfish thoughts and acts and sets me aside so that He can work and love through me."

Jakobi gave him a sad smile. "So you think I'm evil, Simon?"

Simon's gaze softened. "Nah, not according to the world, Jakobi. You have a soft heart. But do you live *for* Him, to glorify Him? If not, nothing you do is really for anyone but yourself. Although I can't imagine evil in you, I know that the Word of God says all are without excuse." He had tucked a stray spiral of hair behind her ear. "And as much as I think this lovely woman is as close to an angel as they come, that includes you."

Flustered, she had blushed and averted her eyes. Troubled.

On a separate visit to Pursat, Simon and Jakobi sat across from one another at a busy café, laptops open between them. Simon checked the emails from the magazine, glad that they enjoyed his last article, smiling at his newest assignment. He inconspicuously observed Jakobi over the top of his screen, delighted in her look of concentration. He had teased her once that she looked grouchy when she concentrated; a fact she vehemently denied and immediately became self-conscious about. She wore a serious expression as she typed furiously away at her keys, unaware of how she made the table shake.

The corners of Simon's mouth lifted in amusement as he checked his emails from Deliverance. One email from Megan inquired about the children:

> Do they seem to be fed, cared for, in need of anything?

The rest of her message gave Simon cause to let out a shout of praise, drawing curious looks from both Jakobi and the rest of the café. Simon lifted his shoulders, sheepish but unapologetic, and continued to read Megan's email:

```
Kiet was able to tell a great number of people
about the Lord and His work with Deliverance.
Lydia, our kidnapped girl, surprised everyone
when she arrived at a gathering near the river
for the light festival. She had incredible
miracles to tell us about that I will have to
wait to share with you. The Lord was indeed
with everyone, and we are able to rejoice in
her safety and Kiet's victory.
```

Simon answered her questions about the children as best as he could, glancing up every so often to be sure Jakobi was still occupied. When he finished the emails and jotted down a few notes, he closed his computer, intrigued by the small smile that played across Jakobi's freckle dusted lips.

"Well, you must not be concentrating," he teased. "Your face isn't all scrunched."

Jakobi rolled her eyes at him and slapped at his hand on the table. "I'm reading an email from my little sister," she said, typing a few words before she clicked "send" and shut down the laptop.

"It seems she's met some 'dreamy guy' online that went to her school until he moved last year. Apparently, he has had a crush on her for a long time, but was too shy to approach her. She says they talk for hours online, and she's pretty sure he's the one." Jakobi giggled. "Ah, to be young and in love…through social media," she teased, looping her laptop case over her shoulder.

They exited the café, but instead of their usual perusal of the day market, Simon pointed Jakobi in another direction, hailing a *tuk tuk*. Jakobi stood, bewildered, and did not immediately follow Simon's urging to climb into the covered passenger cart.

"Where are you planning to take me that we can't walk to, Simon?" she asked, smiling at the driver.

"First, Jakobi, could you ask the man if he knows where *Koh Thas* is located?" Simon winked at the man as Jakobi questioningly pieced together the Khmer words. The driver bobbed his head up and down, enthusiastic.

"Yes, *Koh Thas*. Yes." The driver pointed for the pair to get in the cart.

Jakobi raised a brow at Simon.

"It's not that far, Jakobi. I've been given an assignment close to Pursat, and I thought it would be fun to bring you along. Do you mind?"

Jakobi, intrigued, climbed into the passenger cart, flashing a good-natured shrug and grin at the driver.

The *tuk tuk* twisted through the streets of Pursat and out onto the highway toward Battambang. The day was warm and Jakobi relaxed against the seat and enjoyed the wind in her face.

It had been a long week in the school, trying to arrange tests and opportunities for the poorer children to attend school. Much of her time at home had been spent with Maly and offering helping hands to Dara, who became increasingly withdrawn and agitated. Jakobi wondered if she battled depression. It would make sense, she reasoned to herself; there was a lot going on in that home.

Phirun, Dara's husband, appeared more unsettled every day and, in fact, stayed away from the hut most nights with his son, Narith. When Jakobi asked Dara where the men were, the answer was always, "They were called to go out"—accompanied by a helpless shrug.

The Khmer language didn't allow for much fault to be placed on anyone for bad behavior and was very non-confrontational in nature. Normally a peacemaker, the rhythm of placing blame elsewhere had made some sense to Jakobi. But the more Dara retreated within herself, the more Jakobi began to wonder how they would ever care for all of the children in the home. She also began to wish she could directly confront Phirun about his frequent absence.

The *tuk tuk* made a turn toward a white gate and then drove through it. Jakobi recognized the area from previous trips she had made on her own before Simon moved to the village. "Oh, are we going to the Oknha Khleang Moeung shrine?" she asked Simon.

She had been intrigued more by the story behind the golden statue than the actual shrine. Legend told that the man, Khleang Moeung, had killed his family then himself in order to build a ghost army to assist the king with reclaiming his throne. Jakobi found the idea horrifying, but the Cambodian people revered the man, seeing his act as completely selfless and patriotic. It was considered respectful and lucky to visit the shrine, and many Khmer annually made the pilgrimage.

Simon only shook his head, and Jakobi watched in bewilderment as the moto sped past the shrine and continued straight on the dirt road. Dust swirled around them, and Jakobi casually placed a hand over her mouth, watching the unfamiliar surroundings. *Why did I let Simon plan a surprise trip?*

Eventually, the *tuk tuk* came to a fork in the road, and the driver turned right, continued on for a while longer and then turned left. Simon watched in delight as Jakobi sat up in her seat, her mouth agape.

A wide river stretched before them, with a tattered, weather-worn bridge stretched from where the *tuk tuk* parked to what looked like a small island on the other side.

"He's not going to drive us across that, is he?" she asked inconspicuously out the side of her mouth, her eyes wide.

Jakobi climbed out of the passenger cart, shielding her eyes against the sun. Simon paid the driver and offered him a curt wave before he turned to sling an arm around Jakobi's neck.

"I figured your childhood in Cannon Beach meant you are okay with swinging bridges," Simon whispered in her ear.

Jakobi guffawed. "Right. Those bridges are minuscule compared to this one," she protested, jabbing her thumb in the direction of the bridge. "Do you see that thing? It's over a-a-a *massive* river, not just a cute little stream!"

Simon smiled and pecked her on the cheek. "Come on, Miss Peace Corps, let's see what you're made of."

Jakobi looked around at the empty countryside and road that led away from the bridge. She couldn't very well just tell him she'd wait. She surveyed the long and narrow bridge, wondering how old it was, nervous about Cambodian standards—or lack thereof—for public safety.

In the large cities she'd visited, she had observed the way electric and phone wires were haphazardly bunched, stretched, and tangled together around poles. The reminder did nothing for her rolling stomach. Simon patiently waited on her decision, his wide grin enigmatic.

Resolved, Jakobi took a deep breath. *Well, Jakobi, you didn't travel across the world to hide.* She dipped her chin at Simon. *Let's go.*

The bridge was surprisingly taut considering its great length across the Pursat River. Simon walked behind Jakobi, allowing a comfortable distance so that he could be assured of her safety, but close enough to talk with her and keep her mind busy.

He told her about the assignment from the magazine. "I was told to visit Koh Thas, a small island resort. Looks like there should be a number of huts with straw roofs along the edge of the river to relax in. We can get authentic Khmer food here and, if you're up for it, there's something like a zip line across the river somewhere."

Jakobi turned her face slightly toward him, incredulous. "You've got to be joking."

"Not at all, why?"

Jakobi snorted. "I like zip lines as much as anyone in the right place; in the woods where I'm not going to drown if I fall off." She took a few delicate steps across a plank of wood that looked questionable and made sure to point it out to Simon before she continued. "I think this is all the adventure across the river I need for today, thank-you-very-much." She could see the point where the bridge met the island beach. *Just a few feet more.*

Simon chuckled, "Fine. Then how do you feel about renting a paddle boat?"

"A paddle boat? What does that mean?" Jakobi eagerly stepped off the bridge onto solid ground, unsure if the quivering in her knees was from the moments of rocking on the bridge or suppressed nerves.

"Just what it sounds like," Simon answered, stepping beside her on the sand, holding his hands in front of him and imitating the doggy paddle. "They have little boats shaped like a swan or duck. I'll give you the honor of choosing which you prefer, and you use your legs like riding a bike to direct it around the river."

Jakobi hid a laugh behind her hand. "Let's just see, shall we?"

They walked toward the center of the island, lush with trees, enjoying the symphony of the tropics; twittering birds, screeching monkeys, humming insects, and clapping trees. After a short walk, the trees cleared away to reveal a wide beach, curved around a small inlet of the river. The huts Simon had described were near the water; a row of charming straw-covered structures, opened toward the river inlet. Simon led the way and chose one in the middle, setting their things on a woven mat placed underneath the cover. They sat side by side, watching the ripples of water lick at the beach.

Jakobi leaned back on her elbows, enjoying the music of the water. "I miss the ocean," she sighed.

"I'll bet." Simon leaned back as well, turning on his side to watch her, sensing she had more to add.

"When I was younger, I used to have this song I would sing at the beach when no one was around." She averted her eyes from Simon's probing stare. "A worship song," she said, feeling his green eyes on her face.

"What song, Jakobi?" he asked, his bass voice lower than usual.

She squinted, staring into the river as if her memory would emerge there. "I don't remember the words," she admitted. "But I know that I would throw my arms up wide, and at the time, I meant it with all of my heart." Her mouth twisted and she rubbed her chin against her right shoulder. "I'm just feeling melancholy; my parents still haven't reached out to me. I got together with friends from the Peace Corps for Thanksgiving and plan to again for Christmas. They talked about the care packages their parents have sent, emails they've received…" her voice trailed off.

"I'm certain your parents care and are thinking of you, Jakobi. If they were as protective as you say, don't you feel they did that out of love? Even if it came out as fear, it was fear that they would lose you," Simon reasoned. "They probably feel that their worst nightmare has come true and might not be sure how to reach out to you. Give it time." He brushed away a tear that had slipped down her cheek.

Embarrassed, Jakobi swiped a hand across her eyes. "I'm sorry. Just tired. I came here to volunteer my time and resources, and I feel like I'm accomplishing nothing. I'm gaining a wonderful experience, but will I have made any difference when I leave in eighteen months? I feel guilty every time I leave Maly for the day. The house is still indescribably tense. What if things aren't better for them by the time I need to go home?"

"Jakobi, right now, you *are* here. You are a comfort to Maly, a help to Dara, a friend to Chaya…to me. God has orchestrated it all. If only you knew how much," Simon said.

"What does that mean, 'If only I knew how much'?" Jakobi asked, confused.

The blood drained from Simon's face, and he sat up, wrapping his arms around his legs with his ankles crossed together in the sand and his knees apart. He cleared his throat. "I just mean, eh, that we never know what the Lord is doing, do we?"

Her brow furrowed, Jakobi sat up as well, her knees together, legs tucked to the side. She had worn khaki capris since she would be out of the village where she taught, but she was in the habit of accommodating her skirt. "Well, I certainly don't. I'm convinced that even if there is a God, He's left us on our own to work things out."

Simon winced, pained at her words. He opened his mouth to reply, but a Khmer woman approached, asking if they would like lunch brought to them. Jakobi translated for Simon and they both agreed. The woman bowed and walked back to a hut where a family was stirring a large pot and dishing food into paper bowls for the visitors dotted across the beach. Minutes later, she returned and Simon paid the amount she quoted to

Jakobi. They accepted steaming bowls filled with rice and fish, vegetables and red curry.

Simon prayed to himself, thankful for a meal, anxious for Jakobi to know how active the Lord was in her life. He took a bite, surprised by the delicious sweetness. "Oh, wow," he muttered, tucking into the rice again. "I thought this was going to be spicy with that red all over it."

"Sweet potato," Jakobi answered. "Dara said Khmer cuisine has a lot of sweet potato to keep it sweet and not spicy. The red is probably from *Kruop kak* seeds, not the curry. It is delicious," she agreed.

They ate in companionable silence. Simon feeling peace settle over him. *She belongs to You, Lord, if not yet in spirit; You created her. You are calling to her. Please keep me out of the way; please break down the barriers she holds around her heart. Please help me to remember that You love her more than I ever could, and You alone can save her. Remind her of that song she would sing to you.*

Simon swallowed his lunch and, reaching for Jakobi's empty bowl, asked if she had decided between a duck or swan paddleboat, not allowing himself to realize he'd just admitted to the Lord that he loved her.

Simon and Jakobi enjoyed the rest of the day on the island, laughing as they haphazardly steered the duck paddleboat through the choppy river. Later they played at the beach, cautiously wading in and out of the water, fully clothed. When they tired, they collapsed on the warm beach, marveling at how quickly the sun dried out their clothes.

When the day was over, Simon hailed another *tuk tuk* back to Pursat, where they met a van that would drop them off in their village. Cramped together with a dozen others in the van, Jakobi leaned her head against Simon's shoulder, the unexpected rendezvous a happy memory that broke through unexpected hurt she had allowed to bubble to the surface. Simon leaned his cheek against her head, relishing the feel of her silky hair against his cheek, wondering how long he had before Deliverance would be assured that Maly and the baby were safe enough for him to go back to Pattaya.

Chapter Eighteen

Simon continued to seek out Jakobi, though a few late nights of prayer were needed to hold his attraction in check. Her spunk spurred him to say things that would easily set her off. As a man that had held God's Word in esteem for most of his life, it was natural to quote Scripture in response to questions about life or even in praise when something wonderful happened. Such as when Jakobi announced that Kiri seemed to be gaining weight and cried much less.

"Praise the Lord!" Simon had exclaimed, genuinely relieved that the boy he'd secretly been sent to keep watch over was thriving.

Jakobi had rolled her eyes at him, the starting bell for a small, spirited debate.

"Is it genuine and authentic if you shout 'Praise the Lord' over everything, Simon?"

"Everything that is good and perfect comes from the Lord; it's natural to want to offer thanks and praise to the hand that blesses."

"But, Simon," she'd countered, "was it necessary to shout 'Praise the Lord" when I brought you a coffee this weekend?"

"Everything good and perfect, Jakobi." He smiled, reaching to tuck an ever-escaping wave of hair behind her ear. She had rolled her eyes, face flushed.

Jakobi took Simon to spend an evening with Chaya and her family, privately hoping for their approval, curious as to how Simon would interact with these Khmer Christians. Would he tell them how to live, how to be better Christians simply because he was from a so-called Christian country?

When they met in front of Chaya's home—Simon on his moto, Jakobi on her bike—they shared an amused smile when the mutt that had attached himself to Simon trotted into the clearing. Simon had finally named the dog "Pest" when he found it on his doorstep each morning. Pest would follow Simon around town and wait for him at the church when Simon went into Pursat. Heng stepped into the doorway, drawn outside by the sound of the moto, and laughed good-naturedly when he saw the dog. Simon instructed Pest to stay, and Pest begrudgingly collapsed onto the ground with a sigh, watching as his master climbed the stairs into the hut.

Simon greeted Chaya's family with respect and appreciativeness of their hospitality. He was both charming and kind, and Jakobi consistently blushed when Chaya caught her staring in admiration at Simon.

Chaya elbowed Jakobi in the ribs, teasing. Jakobi bit her lips and dropped her eyes. *What is happening to me?*

Simon, of course, already knew Heng and Kolab as the caretakers of his temporary home.

Temporary. The word sliced through her heart. *How long will the magazines keep Simon here?* Jakobi worried. He certainly couldn't fill many pages with the adventures of their small village. The thought of Simon leaving filled Jakobi with despair she couldn't define.

When the conversation between Simon and Heng turned to a spiritual discussion, Jakobi held her breath, realizing that she had been waiting for this moment from the time she had asked Simon to dinner. She wanted to test him, to see how he would treat her friends if their Christianity played out different than his.

Simon asked about the sign at the entrance to the village that said: "No Christians Allowed."

"Do they know you're Christians?" Simon asked, taking a drink of the tea that Kolab had placed before him.

Heng nodded at Simon. "Yes, and that sign was placed there after we moved to this clearing." Heng locked eyes with the women in his family before he admitted, "Those were dark times, Simon."

"Can you tell me about them?"

Heng considered Simon for a moment, then let his gaze flicker to Jakobi.

Jakobi had wanted to ask for so long, but was now embarrassed that Simon had been so inquisitive. *Was it their business?*

Heng stared at his hands and then bobbed his head, once. "Simon, we had good friends tell us of the Lord—of Jesus." He smiled at Kolab.

She smiled back, radiant.

"There was hope, such as we'd never known, in Jesus. It was easy for us to believe; everything about Him and the Lord made sense. We were heavy under the weight of expectation our lives and Buddhist faith had put on us. We wondered how we could ever live rightly every day all of the time. We lived in constant fear that we would do the wrong thing and heap such bad karma around us that we would be reincarnated into a dog, like that pal of yours outside, Simon."

The group shared a small laugh. Simon laughed along good-naturedly, but gave Heng his full attention when he continued the story.

"When we were taught of God the Creator, God who sees and hears and understands, everything in our life made sense. All of our fear of reincarnation and not being enough faded away. As if He had been the missing piece all along. We immediately understood that our souls had longed for Him from the beginning. With the knowledge and receiving of Jesus as our Savior came joy. But also came testing."

Heng took a deep breath before he continued, "Our families drove us out of the village. It is highly offensive, in our culture—to the ancestors—to reject the ways of Buddha, to reject reincarnation and karma. We abandoned everything we'd believed for so long for the truth of God. That's a frightening thing to many around us. We were threatened and driven out. Around the same time, a group came in from America—Christian missionaries—here to reform us."

Jakobi's face darkened. Simon leaned back and crossed his arms, listening.

Heng continued, "They told us we could no longer bow to one another in greeting, 'You shall bow to no one but the Lord,' they said. When they discovered that Kolab and I were Christians, they told us we had much to learn. We were told we needed a church to meet in. We couldn't possibly know the Lord if we hadn't read His word daily, couldn't possibly raise our children in the poverty that we were in." Heng scratched his cheek, and then held his hand out, palm up, toward Simon. To Jakobi, the gesture spoke that Heng trusted that Simon would understand what he had to say next.

"Nothing they said went along with what we'd been told of Jesus," Heng said, while Kolab and Chaya nodded in agreement. "Certainly, we had learned of our sin, of our need of Him, that only He is holy. And, yes, Simon, we wanted a Bible more than we could express—still do," he said, his eyes filled with longing. "But Kolab and I felt hesitation in our spirit that we knew was from the Lord. Weren't they just giving us more rules to follow, when we believe that there is no way for man to come by grace with works?"

Simon agreed a slight nod and "hmm." *Exactly.*

"The missionaries were obsessed with building us a church. 'You need a church, need a church!' It was their only concern. Until it was completed and no one came, then they began to tell the people of the town that they had families in America willing, *waiting*, to adopt their children."

Jakobi gasped, appalled. "No!" she whispered, glancing at Simon.

He held his chin in one hand, a finger hooked over his top lip, eyes closed, brow furrowed.

Heng stared in the distance, remembering the events of another time. "After a month or more, additional visitors arrived, offering—demanding—to take our children and give them a better life. Some villagers were confused and agreed, thinking the children would come back. Others sent their sons to serve as monks in the *wat* to protect them from the foreigners. It was chaotic.

The Heavens Are Telling

"During that time a man in our village, Kosal, rose up against them and did a lot of good to keep the children with their families. Or we thought he did good. The sons had a place to go, to the *wat*; they could be monks. But what of the girls? Kosal hid them away in his karaoke bar." Heng's voice had gone soft, sad.

Simon hung his head. *Oh, Lord...*

Jakobi frowned. That didn't sound ideal, but certainly better than strangers taking them away. *Wasn't it?*

Heng watched Simon. "You understand that the girls...they didn't come back, Simon."

Simon, realizing how transparent he had become, met his gaze. His "I understand" was hoarse.

Jakobi looked around the circle of people gathered around the meal on a woven mat on the floor. They held an awareness together that Jakobi had no part in. *What am I missing? Why wouldn't the girls come back from a karaoke bar down the street?*

Heng continued, staring at his hands linked together in his lap. "It was a very chaotic time. Finger pointing; a lot of fear and anger. No one wanted to hear about the peace and love of Christ. No one believed that was what we preached. The family that lived close to us, that had first told us of the Lord..." Heng's voice faltered, pain awash in his features.

Kolab reached for his hand, as did Chaya. Clearly what he had to share next was worse than all the rest. Absentmindedly, Jakobi reached for Simon's hand. He opened his fist and held on to her palm when her delicate fingers brushed against his.

"Kosal was the brother of the man of that home. Our friends were Sov and Nuon, their two sons, Vireak and Viseth, were close with Chaya. Kosal was so angry when his brother turned away from their traditions and to the faith. They had been partners in the karaoke bar, and then Sov turned away, repented of his work there. Kosal was enraged and he stirred up the village against them. The arrival of the missionaries only added to the outrage.

"One night we woke to screaming. Such horrible, awful screams. I ran outside and saw Sov and Nuon's home engulfed in flames. We could see them inside," Heng choked, tears falling in rivulets down his face, into his mouth. "It was too late. We could not save them."

Heng closed his eyes. "I will never forget that. Never. Only Vireak, the oldest boy, survived. Kosal spread stories, terrible lies that the ancestors had set the house on fire as punishment. 'We've let them come among us, live among us, spread their poison among us, and this is how it will be for anyone that believes!' Kosal made the sign for us, and he and others drove the missionaries out. He resented Vireak's survival of the fire, resented his own responsibility to care for the boy. Within months, Vireak was given over to the *wat* to serve as a monk. Kosal said that was the only way the bad karma brought on his family from his brother's betrayal could be credited as good."

They sat in silence for a few minutes, listening to a heavy rain pound against the house.

Heng, overcome with emotion, gestured for Kolab to share the rest. Her soft voice barely rose above the storm outside. "Eventually, the village fervor died down. Our close relatives moved away, but have returned every year for Ancestors Day. In time, when they saw that we weren't anything like the Americans that had come, they began to trust us and to stay with us. The market was an unfriendly place for a long time. But when suspicion died down and their concerns were changed, the fact that we were Christians became less of an issue. The sign is still there, but no longer something that is a threat to us. Instead, it serves as a reminder to pray for the people of our village and Cambodia. We have been able to talk with a lot of friends about Jesus, and there is much interest in the verses that we remember. We wish we had a complete Bible to share, but for now, we share the news that changed our lives; that Jesus saves. He takes our sin away and gives us new life in Him."

Jakobi worried her bottom lip, feeling out of place in the intimate circle of faith her friends had formed. Her stomach quivered with something she couldn't define. Fear? Longing? The conversation moved to Simon's articles and stories of Jakobi and Chaya's students. Eventually, Simon and Jakobi thanked their hosts and bid them goodnight.

When they descended the stairs, Jakobi asked Simon the question that bothered her the most during dinner. "Why didn't the girls come back from the karaoke bar, if they just worked there? I don't understand."

Simon placed his hand against the small of Jakobi's back, guiding her around a large mud puddle at the bottom of the stairs. "That rain we heard must have been pretty intense," he murmured.

Jakobi glanced at her bike and sighed. "I would be better off walking home and coming back for the bike tomorrow. I'm not up for getting stuck in a puddle in the dark."

"I'll walk you and your bike home," Simon said, patting his leg for Pest to follow. He gripped Jakobi's bike seat in his hand, rolling it along beside him as they walked.

"Simon, I asked you a question." She gently elbowed his ribs.

He sighed. "You really don't know, Jakobi? Have you been to the karaoke bar?"

"Yes," she answered. "That's why I don't see what the big deal is. They play loud music, serve alcohol, and play games, which is very similar to bars in the states."

Simon looked askance at her. "And you didn't notice anything strange?"

"Well, they have some really freaky music videos they play to go with the songs. Full of ghosts and strange images, but, other than that, no, not really."

"Were there women there, Jakobi?"

"A lot of women work there; there weren't many female patrons. I get the idea that's not socially accepted here. When I went I was with some Peace Corps friends that came to visit, so we were mostly just laughing at the music videos. What are you getting at, Simon?" She pressed a hand to his arm, stopping him.

"It's a brothel, Jakobi. Something very common in this part of the world. The girls that were sent there to be safe were then used for the pleasure of others. Most likely the families became indebted to Kosal, and he would not let them leave. The women there are slaves, Jakobi. They are not allowed to leave."

"What are you talking about?" she asked, bewildered.

Simon, heartsick and annoyed, turned to her. "Jakobi, how can you know so much and so little? Are you really so naïve?"

Hurt, Jakobi swallowed past a lump in her throat. "I'm sorry you think I'm such a fool," she whispered, pushing past him to walk home.

Simon watched her go, then groaned and jogged to catch up with her. "Jakobi"—he grabbed her arm and turned her to face him—"I'm sorry," he implored. "That was unacceptable of me. I am trying to digest all of the information they gave us back there, and I took it out on you. Will you forgive me?" He ducked to look into her eyes.

Jakobi considered him for a moment, hesitant. Finally, she shrugged. "No, I should apologize. You're right: I am naïve. I knew that kind of thing went on, but I just...I don't know, I guess I didn't really think about it."

"Well, a lot of people don't, Jakobi." Simon twisted his mouth and turned to walk again, leaving Jakobi to wonder at his cryptic tone.

Jakobi and Simon walked to her home in silence, both absorbed with thoughts of the night. Pest scampered in front of them, tail high, pausing periodically to sniff at the air. Jakobi smiled to herself at the dog's protective manner.

They passed the "No Christians Allowed" sign, both sobered at what it represented: Dark times of the small village where so much needless pain was inflicted on unsuspecting people.

When they reached her home just outside the village, Jakobi turned to Simon, the uncharacteristically bright starlight illuminating the shadows of confusion on her face. "See, Simon? Do you understand now why I think people need to be left alone? If it can't be proven that God exists, why needlessly stir up confusion and heartache?" She stamped her foot, voice catching. "I hate Christians! They think they know everything, are so sure that they are the only ones with answers, and they inflict judgment and pain wherever they go. They—"

Simon gently laid her bike down in the dirt. He straightened and faced Jakobi, eyes softening as he placed a finger over her lips, silencing her. She looked full in his face, considered the anguish in his eyes, the grim twist of his mouth. He ran his finger along her lips until his hand cupped her cheek. His other hand came up and enclosed the other side of her face. Pest sat down next to Simon and whimpered up at them, jealous of the attention his master gave to Jakobi.

Simon ignored him. "Jakobi, I want you to listen to me very carefully. I have seen the transforming work of God in the lives of people. I have seen broken, barren, lost, hungry souls restored, reborn, found, and fed. I have watched people who love the Lord risk their lives and give up everything they own to show love to those that society deems 'worthless.' Do not be mistaken for one minute that the folks who came here with an agenda and rules that had no foundation in Scripture were here to transform and share the love of Christ for the sake of those who would hear. People are known by their fruit, Jakobi, and every group has people that claim to be members who are only out to cause trouble." He released her face and stepped back, thrusting his hands in his pockets.

Jakobi resisted the urge to touch her palms to her cheeks, to settle the wild tingles his touch had sent through her. Without thought, Jakobi held her arm out toward Simon, imploring him to come close again. She had never seen him angry and wasn't sure if that was the appropriate word to describe the agitated state he was in. Emotional? No. *Impassioned.*

Simon remained where he was, eyes on the heavens. Jakobi dropped her arm, embarrassed.

The moonless night in the quiet, unplugged Cambodian village afforded a starry tapestry that reminded Jakobi of clear nights on the beach in her hometown. Jakobi followed Simon's gaze, and they watched the sky, seemingly still, yet alive with light and promise and mystery. Hoping to lighten their intense evening, Jakobi gently hooked an arm through Simon's and leaned her head on his shoulder.

"That's incredible, isn't it?" she breathed, enjoying the feel of Simon's arm entwined with hers; warm, solid. Dependable.

Simon spoke into the night, his voice strong and sure, unwavering. "'The heavens declare the glory of God', Jakobi."

He looked down at her. "You say we have no proof, that we can't confidently tell others of the realness and surety of God?" He jutted his chin toward the heavens. "God has an answer for all of our own assurances, Jakobi. He said to Job, 'Where were you when I laid the foundation of the earth? Tell Me, if you have understanding, Who set its measurements? Since you know. Or who stretched the line on it? On what were its bases sunk? Who laid its cornerstone?'"

Simon waved a hand toward the heavens, warming to the passage Jakobi vaguely recognized. "'Where is the way to the dwelling of light? And darkness, where is its place that you may take it into territory and that you may discern its paths to its home? You know, for you were born then, and the number of your days is great! Have you entered the storehouses of the snow, or have you seen the storehouses of the hail...Can you bind the chains of the Pleiades, or loose the cords of Orion? Can you lead forth a constellation in its season, and guide the Bear with her satellites? Do you know the ordinances of the heavens, or fix their rule over the earth?'"

Simon pulled a hand free from his pocket and grasped the hand that Jakobi had curled around his bicep. He looked into her eyes, imploringly. "Do not confuse the wonderful things we learn about our universe through science with a full knowledge of things beyond our understanding. And do not confuse the sins of evil men that say they follow the Bible with the intentions of the Author of that Bible. God is love, Jakobi; there is nothing in nature or His word that refutes that fact."

Pest straightened suddenly, a low growl from deep in his chest causing the hair on Jakobi's arms to rise. She gripped Simon's hand tighter when Phirun emerged on the road in front of the house from the direction of town. He stumbled toward them, stopping to eye their entwined hands. Simon reached down with his other hand to assure Pest, who continued to threateningly growl at Phirun.

"It's okay, boy, it's okay." Simon quieted the defensive dog and offered Phirun an apologetic smile.

Jakobi's host brother only harrumphed and stumbled up the stairs. Pest snorted once and sniffed the trail that Phirun had walked. Jakobi squeezed Simon's hand and Simon turned toward her. "We live in a sinful world, Jakobi. It was never intended to be this way. But we have hope. And it is imperative that you reexamine your reasons for clinging so tightly to a theory that offers no solid proof or hope. You might be the only chance Noah and Maly have at someone showing their family the truth. For their sake, isn't it worth looking past the over-protectiveness of your parents to the faith they cared enough to raise you with? " He glanced pointedly to where Phirun had just been.

Simon pressed a tender kiss to her cheek and bid her goodnight.

Long after Jakobi had tucked herself into bed, with Maly curled into her back, she realized that Simon had called the baby "Noah." The same name Maly had spoken the first day, and that Dara had so quickly covered up.

But she hadn't mentioned that to Simon…had she?

Chapter Nineteen

Portland International Airport

Zack Tanner hated his job.
He hated the bustle followed by hours of inactivity. Loathed the all-important attitudes of businessmen that couldn't be bothered to hang up their phones or take off their shoes. Abhorred the wary looks mothers gave him when he had to pat down their kids.
What did they think? That he was getting some sick pleasure out of it? They didn't know he had kids of his own: a daughter that coped daily with Type 1 diabetes, and a son that drove him and his wife, Tanya, crazy with his dreams of being a soccer star. Soccer was expensive, but they loved him and sacrificed to make him happy.
They sacrificed for their daughter, Emma, too: ballet classes, gymnastics, anything to make her feel like a normal kid. The parts that weren't normal: the test strips, insulin, doctor visits, and a carefully planned diet, were all vexing and expensive, but their daughter was Zack's angel and Tanya's delight. They worked hard. Their kids were happy and well liked in the neighborhood elementary school.
But Zack wanted more for his family. He worked two jobs, his wife one. It had been years since they'd had a vacation or

any real quality down time. And still, they were barely scraping by.

At lunch, Tanya called, crying—hysterical. "Emma's doctor is cutting his practice and going to a new system. If we want to stay with him, we'll have to pay five thousand a year, either at once or quarterly, on top of insurance."

Zack banged a fist on the breakroom table. "We can't afford that, Tanya, no way." He clenched his jaw and stared at the peanut butter and jelly sandwich he had every day for lunch. The guys made fun of him as they brought in food from the airport restaurants.

"Nice lunch, Tanner," they would mock. On payday they talked about things they planned to do, big boy toys they planned to buy.

Zack would do the math in his head to figure how much insulin they could buy, and if he could surprise his family with a pizza. He would sweat at the thought of miscalculating somewhere.

Tanya cried into the phone, making him feel helpless. "Zack, this is the best doctor we've found. Emma loves him. We have to figure it out; we have to make it work."

Zack hung his head, the phone dangling from his hand. He promised he'd figure it out and that she shouldn't worry.

He was stretched out and wound tight, and still it wasn't enough; he was failing his family.

As he checked out that night, he remembered the man that had come through the security checkpoint months ago: portly, about his age. Well dressed, but disheveled somehow. *Slimy.* Zack had immediately felt uneasy around him and searched carefully through his bag. The man had handed him a card and promised that he could raise his wages exponentially. Zack had waved him on, pocketing the card and forgetting about it.

Now he wondered.

He found the card under his seat in the car that night after work:

Gage Easton
Financial Consultant/Accountant

Zack fingered it, speculating what an accountant could have for a TSA agent to do. He pulled out his phone and punched in the numbers from the card before he could change his mind.

A man answered, his voice filling Zack with the same unease he'd experienced in the man's presence. Zack explained who he was, asked about what the job entailed.

Gage paused, seemingly to consider whether he could trust Zack or not. He cleared his throat after a full minute. "Well, Zack, it's very simple, really. I have some, eh…items I will need to take with me the next time I leave the country. Items that are…uh, sensitive in nature, if you will. I just need you to help me get through the airport. I have a connection for my international needs; I just need help getting out of PDX. That's where you come in. I could more than make up for any inconvenience I cause you."

Gage named a figure that raised the hair on Zack's arms.

"This would be one time, no more?" Zack asked, uncertain, but already imagining what he and Tanya could do with that amount of money. They could pay off debt; pay for the doctor…so many things.

"Wait," Zack asked, not sure if he could really go through with it, wanting to know as much as he could. "What kind of items? You're not planning to bomb the plane are you?"

Gage chuckled.

Zack curled his lip at the sardonic tone.

"Goodness, no, Zack," Gage assured him. "I have something much larger than a bomb. I'm taking my niece with me on a business trip to Thailand. Her father is okay with it, but her mother…she's being difficult. You understand. Just help us get through customs and we should be fine."

Zack licked his lips, heart pounding.

"Can I let you know?" he asked.

"Of course, Zack, of course." Gage's voice dripped with charm; charm he couldn't quite pull off.

Two weeks later, when Zack was laid off from his evening security job at the mall, he called Gage back.

"I'll do it."

"Wonderful. When my niece and I are ready, I will call you and make the arrangements."

Zack hung up, feeling heavy and desperate.

Chapter Twenty

Cambodia

Jakobi wrestled all night over Simon's words. About God. About the stars and orchestration of all things.

About his use of the name *Noah*.

Had she told Simon about the name that Maly had shared that first day? No, she knew she hadn't. Had Maly told him? No, Maly couldn't speak English and had never been alone with Simon.

How did he know?

So many incidents swirled in her mind, none of her thoughts connected, but they were related somehow.

Maly's immediate bond with her.

Baby Kiri's colic.

Dara and Phirun's tension, their fervent whispers when they thought no one was listening.

Simon's arrival, seemingly out of nowhere.

Their instant connection; the unbelievable coincidence that they were from the same state, their hometowns merely 90 minutes apart.

The awful story Heng shared with them at dinner.

Simon's presence in the very church building that had caused such chaos in the sleepy village so many years before.

In her exhaustion she found herself praying for the first time in years. *What purpose, Lord? For what purpose are these things happening? Is Simon part of those early missionaries, sent to steal the children?*

She tucked Maly in close to her, absorbing the child's sweet, trusting innocence, wondering who could ever think to rip her from the life she knew. But what life was that? Where had she and the baby come from?

Around and around the thoughts danced, teasing, tormenting, almost connecting, and then blowing away again like leaves twirling in an autumn breeze.

Morning dawned and Jakobi stirred, then propped up on one elbow, running a hand over her face. She was exhausted from her sleepless night, but determined to confront Simon. Through her tormented confusion, she realized that all of her thoughts led back to Simon; he must be the key. She slipped quietly from the bed, careful not to disturb Maly, and pulled on her *sampot*, thankful that the school had a break for the next week. She was amazed and annoyed when she first began at her post and at how many breaks the school afforded, but that morning she counted it as lucky.

No way could I have taught like this, she thought. *I'm exhausted.* She sat back down on the bed and rested her face in her hands for several minutes. *I should just go back to bed.*

Instead of lying back as her body ached to do, she felt a sudden urgency to get to Simon, a drive that she couldn't ignore. Maly awakened and Jakobi assured her that she would be back later and scurried down the steps to her bike. She pedaled hard, soaring over bumps and divots in the road, biting her lip when she landed too hard on a few. When she at last rode up to the little church, she leaped off the bike, abandoning it on its side in the dirt.

Simon didn't answer her first knock. She balled her hand in a fist and pounded on the thick door.

Nothing.

Jakobi bit her lip, her heart thudding in her chest. She dashed down the stairs and leaped over her bike where she'd abandoned it on its side on the forest floor. She walked under the stilted building, unsure of what she was looking for, knowing only that she was desperate to get to Simon. She paused.

What was that? She waited, the birds awakening in the exotic land behind her, trilling and shrieking their morning melody. She tilted her head. There. A low moan and what sounded like rambling. *Simon. But who was he talking to?*

Jakobi ducked out from under the house and darted back up the stairs, pounding incessantly with both fists this time.

No answer.

She let out a desperate sob and ran to her bike. She pedaled hard and fast until she came to Chaya's home. She, again, leapt off of her bike, carelessly dropping it in the field. Where she'd spent the night doubting him and questioning him, now she was completely consumed with worry for Simon's well-being.

"Chaya! Heng! Kolab!" she called out, tears choking her words, blurring her vision. When Chaya arrived at the door, her forehead knit in confusion, Jakobi begged for help getting to Simon, not realizing that she was speaking in English. Chaya could not understand the torrent of slurred, desperate words. She reached to steady Jakobi with strong hands on the frantic girl's shoulders. Heng appeared behind Chaya, also anxious to help if they could just understand her.

Finally, Heng understood the word "Simon" and pushed past Jakobi to his moto. Jakobi raced after him and climbed on behind him, not the least bit concerned with Peace Corps protocol.

Heng made it to Simon's church in a fraction of the time it took Jakobi to pedal from it. She followed him up the stairs and through the door, eyes tearing across the dark interior, past pews and the kitchen to the back room where she'd heard Simon talking. She and Heng found him, drenched in sweat, eyes clenched shut. Jakobi dropped to her knees beside him on his pallet, placing a hand against his fever-hot brow.

She looked to Heng. "What do we do? He's obviously very sick." She brushed a matted shock of chestnut hair from his forehead, leaning in as he mumbled something.

"Noah, I have to get Noah, watch Noah. Maly. Maly knows…"

"Maly knows what, Simon?" Jakobi asked. Heng knelt beside them, also touching a hand to Simon.

"He must be taken to a hospital," he concluded. "His fever is too high. He needs medicine."

"But how will we get him there?" Jakobi asked, consumed with worry.

"There is a man in town that has a truck we can use, but we'll have to pay—"

"I'll pay whatever he wants," Jakobi assured him.

Heng nodded once and glanced at Simon. "Keep him calm. I'll be back with the truck as soon as I can." He turned and raced from the room.

Jakobi watched him go, and then turned back to Simon, cupping his face in her hands, tears clogging her words. "Simon, you are going to be fine. Heng went to get a truck, and we'll get you to the hospital, just hang in there." Her heart clenched when he tried to open his eyes, then slammed them shut as if the light had needled them.

"Jakobi?" His hand searched weakly for hers, barely pressing into her palm when she grabbed on.

"Yes, Simon, I'm right here. What is it?"

"God sent me to watch Noah and Maly."

Jakobi reeled back. *What? He has to be hallucinating*, she thought. "Shhhh…Simon, don't talk. Save your strength. We'll get you to the hospital."

Simon mumbled, "Phnom Penh, Jakobi, you have to take me to Phnom Penh."

Jakobi shook her head. "Simon, no, Phnom Penh is further away than Pursat. We'll take you to Pursat."

His eyes flew open and his face tightened in pain, his eyelids fluttered in obvious agony. "No, Jakobi, please listen. You have to take me to the Deliverance campus in Phnom Penh."

"Where?" Jakobi asked, but he had closed his mouth and eyes tight against the pain and didn't speak again.

When Heng returned with the truck, Simon continued to mumble incoherently through his feverish state. The only clear words that he repeated over and over were, "Deliverance in Phnom Penh. I have to go to Phnom Penh." Heng chose to listen to Simon.

"Jakobi, there has to be a good reason because that's the only clear thing he's spoken. I know he first came from there. We need to trust him," Heng said.

Jakobi crouched low in the bed of the truck for the long ride, doing her best to hold Simon steady as the truck bounced and jostled them around. She breathed a sigh of relief when they pulled onto National Road 5, the paved road that would carry their sick friend to Phnom Penh. Desperate sobs and prayers tore through Jakobi, none of them making sense.

"Please, just please…" she whispered over and over as she touched a soft towel to Simon's face, mopping up his sweat. She thought of all of the *Little House on the Prairie* episodes she'd seen as a child where a feverish patient was placed in bed and covered with layers of ice. She wished she could fill the truck bed with chunks of ice from the Olsen's supply right at that moment.

Only once did she wonder if Simon's sickness might be contagious. Her hand froze in midair, her body stiff against the violent rocking of the truck. *I don't care.* She leaned to kiss his forehead, her hand gently resting on his chest. His heart thundered a rapid staccato beneath her fingers.

They finally entered the clogged streets of Phnom Penh by mid-day. A cacophony of moto beeps and shouts surrounded them as the truck chugged slowly through traffic. Heng did his best to dart through open lanes, but the truck was no match for the quick motos, so they spent more time waiting in traffic than participating in the ebb and flow of commuters. Heng stopped near a market and ascertained directions to Deliverance.

They were close. Heng maneuvered through a maze of side streets, taking one wrong turn and flipping around before they pulled up to a large row of buildings surrounded by beautiful landscaping and a soccer field…and a high fence with a locked gate at the entrance.

Jakobi leapt from the truck and hurried to the gate, stumbling once. She rattled the lock and hollered for someone to let them in, noticing a large mural on the side of the building, the Ichthys on a hand with spread fingers, palm facing out. Just like the tattoo on Simon's arm. A few men came rushing around the side of the building, one holding a shovel in his hand.

"Simon Russell," Jakobi called out to them, pointing to the truck. Although two of the men appeared American, the oldest looked to be Khmer, or even Thai. She spoke Khmer to him, her eyes pleading with his. "I have Simon Russell here and he's very sick."

Recognition dawned on their faces, and the youngest of the three men went running for the building. The Asian man dug in his pocket for a key, his eyes sweeping the street behind Jakobi as if checking for evidence of deceit. He hesitated for a moment to Jakobi's frustration.

"Please hurry!" she shouted, her concern for Simon taking over. "We've driven from the Pursat area, and he asked to come here. Please. We don't know what's wrong with him."

The man looked between Jakobi and Heng before he climbed halfway up the gate to peer into the bed of the truck. He must have recognized Simon in the back. He jumped down and quickly opened the gate, calling out to Jakobi while he fumbled with the lock.

"Tell your driver to pull right up to that last building once I get this gate open." He spoke English in a strong American accent. Jakobi hopped in the cab with Heng, pointing to where he should go as the gate swung open. She heard the door slam shut with a loud clang, the lock back in place as they raced toward the last building. A group of people, all varying in nationalities, rushed out and worked together to carry Simon inside.

Jakobi watched as he disappeared through a door, her elbows tucked close to her ribs, her hands clutched against her arms, unsure if she should follow. She and Heng waited in the bed of the truck for close to an hour before an American woman, who introduced herself as Megan, approached them, speaking in Khmer for Heng's sake.

"Simon appears to have dengue fever," she told them. "Our on-site physician took blood samples, and we should know for sure by tomorrow morning. For now, he's resting and we've given him acetaminophen, and his fever seems to be reducing. You did the right thing to bring him here. Can we offer you a place to stay? We'll pay for a safe motel."

Heng shook his head no. "I have to get the truck back," he answered, looking to Jakobi.

Jakobi looked past Megan to the row of buildings, thinking the grounds looked like a small college. "Can you tell us what this place is?" Jakobi asked, not ready to accept a motel recommendation from a stranger, but not ready to leave Simon.

Megan cocked her head to the side. "First, would you come with me to my office and tell me more about who *you* are?"

Jakobi, her concern for Simon forefront in her mind, chose to trust the American woman, and told Heng she would find a way back to the village once she was sure Simon was all right.

Megan led Jakobi to her office and explained about the work of Deliverance to prevent children from being sold or kidnapped into slavery, their efforts to rescue children that already lived in slavery, and the resulting restoration work for rescued girls.

Jakobi scrunched her eyes shut, pressing shaky fingers against her temples. "What does Simon have to do with all of this?" Jakobi held her hands out, palm up, toward Megan. "If he works here with you, then what was he doing in my village? He said he wrote for a travel magazine; I helped him on assignments." *Was everything he told her a lie?*

Megan leaned forward on her desk, arms folded over one another. "That's true. He does work for a magazine so that we didn't have to take money away from our projects here. Simon was on, or rather, *is* on, a very different task than we normally take on."

Jakobi sat in shock as Megan told her of a young girl that had been part of the prevention program. The girl had arrived at the campus one morning, hysterical, asking volunteers to come to her shack near Rubbish Mountain. The volunteers found the girl's mother dead, a squalling infant boy near her cold body.

Maly and Kiri? she wondered.

Megan shared about the volunteer from America who had been pumping and was asked to nurse the baby when he wouldn't take a bottle. She'd cared for the baby for a week, and a family nearby had cared for Maly until they found the next of kin.

"Something about the behavior of the grandparents gave us cause for concern. It was clear to us that they had a full house with many mouths to feed and not much income. We offered them the aid of our programs and they flatly refused. Obviously, we care greatly for the children in our organization, and I felt it necessary to have someone close by to be sure the children were being well cared for through the transition."

Jakobi swiveled her head from side to side in disbelief of what she was hearing. She pressed a hand to her chest. "I live with that family, Megan. I have fed that baby. Maly, the girl, sleeps with me every night. She has connected with me more than her grandparents, and it never made sense to me until now."

Something else occurred to her. "When the children first came, Maly called the baby 'Noah' but the grandmother calls him 'Kiri'. Last night, Simon also called him 'Noah'. Can you explain that to me?"

Megan smiled gently. "His mother died before she named him," she answered. "We called the baby Noah and, until now, I didn't know what the family called him."

Jakobi nodded, understanding illuminated the foggy corners of time since she'd met Simon. Her mind raced as every strange, disjointed detail from the past few weeks fell into place. The fervent whispers of her host family, Dara's depression, Simon's sudden presence and concern for the children. Her heart ached as she realized something else: Simon only befriended her to get to them.

Megan assured Jakobi that they could point her to a safe motel. "If you're going to stay, we can let you stay on campus just as soon as we run a background check. You understand. We've had a lot of exposure to the public lately, and we have to be careful with the children in our care."

Because of her position with the Peace Corps, Jakobi was cleared the next day and hid away in the dorms for the rest of the week, waiting for Simon to recover enough to accept visitors. Near the end of the week, Megan sought her out and asked if she would like to get out and tour parts of Phnom Penh. Jakobi had spent her first weeks of training with the Peace Corps in the large city and wasn't up to touring the Killing Fields or even Angkor Wat. She'd explored plenty in those first exciting days in the new country.

"Right now, I just need to process the last few weeks," Jakobi answered.

Megan weighed her answer for a moment before she responded. "I understand. Then would you like to tour our prevention and aftercare programs?"

Jakobi agreed and Megan promised to return for her later that afternoon after a few meetings she had scheduled. As she waited for Megan, she grew nervous. How should she behave around girls that had once been sex slaves? Jakobi was so naïve and sheltered that she hadn't been aware that the karaoke bar in her small village had served a darker purpose. What would she face that day and could she handle it?

※ ※ ※

Megan first took Jakobi through classrooms and the daycare program. "Many of the families around here have parents that work long hours in the city to provide just enough to eat each day. The children are left to fend for themselves, and predators take great advantage of that. Our daycare gives parents freedom to work and children a place to play and learn in a safe environment."

They walked through a courtyard where children were busy painting the high stone walls with a happy collage of bright suns and rainbows and flowers. Another group gathered around their teacher beneath the shelter of a large tree, singing a song and clapping together. Jakobi smiled at their enthusiasm, imagining Maly joining in the wild, carefree antics of these children.

Next, Megan took Jakobi on a tour of one of the rescue homes. The girls were busy working in classrooms, and Jakobi watched from the doorway as they listened to the teacher lecture. The home was large and clean. Tables were arranged near a small kitchen. Three bedrooms, each with two sets of bunk beds, were brightly colored and supremely feminine. Artwork, that Megan explained was part of the girls' therapy, covered the walls. The living room, or gathering area near the front of the home, looked cozy and inviting with well-worn couches arranged in a circle. The large wall at the rear of the room had been painted with the words, "She who is in Christ is a new creation!" and was surrounded by paintings of handprints that had been transformed into butterflies. Tears welled in Jakobi's eyes looking at it. No matter her beliefs, that was a beautiful promise that had obviously come true for these young women.

And what of my beliefs? Jakobi couldn't deny that her first thought when Simon was sick was to plead for mercy and guidance from a God she claimed she didn't believe in.

The highlight of the tour came when Megan explained to Jakobi about the vocation training the girls went through at Deliverance. "We want to equip them to care for themselves and their families once they leave our program, so that they never again find themselves in a situation where they have to use their bodies to make money. We have cafés where they are taught not only to cook and bake, but hospitality and management courses. We teach them to make jewelry and pay them monthly to do so. The jewelry is sold worldwide and the money comes right back into the program."

Megan led Jakobi to a small building on campus and offered her a mischievous smile as she opened the door, gesturing for Jakobi to enter before her. "We also have a hair salon."

Hours later, Jakobi relaxed in the private dorm room, with blond streaks in her trimmed and braided hair, smiling at the memories of her day. While she felt her work in the Peace Corps was important, here, she saw results. She saw deliverance for families in poverty, training and hope for girls that might not otherwise have had any hope or future.

She saw the transforming work of selfless love.

Chapter Twenty-One

Vireak spent most of his time in the aftermath of the announcement of Kosal's death in meditation in various places outside of the *wat*. Suddenly, the *wat* felt more like a prison than it ever had, though he had more liberty to leave now that Kosal was gone than he'd ever had before.

He sat on the forest floor face-to-face with a wildly intricate spider web. Suspended between three branches, the layers and patterns swirled in perfection. Vireak focused on its beauty, trying to lose himself in the design.

But he couldn't concentrate. His father's face, his words, rolled over him.

"Jesus, Vireak. Jesus is the only truth. The only constant. He is the way, the truth, and the life. Don't forget my son, don't forget..."

Vireak's body shook with conflict.

Nothing he had learned in his life as a monk aligned with his father's beliefs. Nothing brought him the peace and comfort he'd experienced in his childhood home. He ached for those years; years of joy and delight and love, regardless of the tension and fear that surrounded them. In that home there had been love. A love unlike anything he'd seen or experienced since.

He sat, pensive, feeling that his life spun in circles like the web before him. The sky opened above, drenching Vireak within minutes and closing again; the rain ceasing as quickly as it had begun. Fat droplets clung to the web, like a string of pearls, sparkling, an abstract reflection of light and color. Birds surrounded him and their endless calls and songs vibrated in accord with the brilliant light in the dewdrops.

Vireak watched the world shimmer around him, longing for enlightenment, hearing only the words his father spoke each morning as the family rose to greet the day...

"The earth is the Lord's, dear ones, and all it contains; the world and all who dwell in it."

Unprovoked, the night his family died rushed at him in a blur of confusion and fear. He remembered that at dinner his father had looked pained, distraught. They had specifically prayed for Kosal; Vireak's father had been desperate for Kosal's salvation.

Vireak had heard his father whispering to his mother long after Sov thought his sons had fallen asleep.

"Nuon, I know he is evil and corrupt, but he needs the Lord. I see the lost man inside of him, and I plead with God daily to let me show Kosal the love and forgiveness God has for him."

In the stillness of night, Vireak had woken to a house filled with smoke. Survival instinct propelled him toward the window and onto the deck, choking on the acrid air. He had flung himself over the railing, landing hard on the earth below. He frantically ran the circumference of the house, waiting for his parents and brother to join him. As the minutes passed, and the fire completely engulfed the small hut, Vireak grasped his hair in tight fists of desperation. The heat was like a wall, a force powerful and malevolent, drying the salty tears that drenched his cheeks.

Kosal appeared immediately, jagged shadows and flickers of light shifted across his grim features. "Vireak, the ancestors have spoken." He swept his hand toward the hut, his soot-covered fingers pointing, accusing.

Vireak did not know how to respond. He ignored his uncle and crawled through the mud, sobbing, beating the earth. The horrific screams faded; the silence was deafening.

With a feral grunt, Kosal grabbed Vireak's hair and pulled him to his feet. He screamed in the anguished boy's face. "They're gone, boy. *Dead*. Because of their misdeeds. Because of their choice to turn from all that is right and follow this *Jesus*." He let go of Vireak's hair, shoved him away and turned.

A sinking numbness settled on Vireak, quieting his tears until they hardened into a ball of disbelief that settled in his gut.

"Follow me, boy."

Vireak looked back at his home. Only the outline of wood beams remained, black against the raging orange glow. The frame held for just a second more before it crumbled to the earth with a loud crack. It was then Vireak saw Kolab holding back a screaming Chaya in her arms on their high deck and Heng kneeling in the earth on the other side of the hut, watching the flames in the same numb trance as Vireak. They locked eyes across the fire; Vireak's searching, Heng's pained.

"*Now*, boy!" His uncle had screamed and Vireak had no choice but to follow…

Not until that moment, as an adult, did Vireak realize there was no reason for Kosal to be there at that moment, unless he himself had something to do with the fire. The awareness buzzed in his head, loud and intrusive—so obvious now. The words of his father, the faith of his mother, swirled around him in dizzying intensity. Just as he had the night of the fire, Vireak grasped his head in his hands to still the turbulent thoughts.

He thought he would spin off the earth until he cried out, "Please, enough! I believe!"

Immediately, the darkness faded from his heart and light shot forth, chasing away every hesitation, every doubt, every fear that had burdened him since that terrible night. As the flames had eaten up his family, his faith—his everything—so now the Light ate away the dark, barren years that had followed. Vireak breathed out, long and slow, amazed and humbled.

He rose, hesitating only a moment, before he walked purposefully for Heng's home.

Chapter Twenty-Two

Simon tested his shaky legs, weak from lack of food and too many days in bed. Jakobi had been to see him a few times, after his fever had finally gone down and his eyes had stopped feeling like they were going to explode out of his head every time he moved them. Their conversation had been light and short. Simon could see the questions in her eyes, but she kindly refrained until he felt better. Determined to make a full recovery, Simon stayed in bed an extra day after the sickness seemed to finally wane. Megan came when he asked for her and agreed when he suggested he and Jakobi leave as early as possible the next day.

"Jakobi mentioned that she has experienced a lot of tension in the home since the children arrived. I think it is imperative that you get back and stay close. Now that Jakobi knows about your purpose for being there, she has agreed to work with us as well," Megan explained

Simon ate dinner in the Deliverance kitchen with Jakobi that night, wishing he could satisfy his hunger but knew better than to overload his empty stomach. The conversation between the two friends was stale, uncomfortable. Simon shared their travel plans but fell silent when she merely nodded and concentrated on her food. He watched her downcast eyes, understanding that she must feel betrayed. He noticed her hair and smiled.

"I see you visited the Deliverance Salon." He tugged on a blond strand of hair.

She reached to touch her waves, lips curling slightly. "Yes," she said softly, remembering. "Those girls definitely love what they're doing. They wanted to chop my hair off to give me a glamour look, but I told them I needed to be able to pull it back." She pulled a strand in front of her face and considered the length. "Maybe I should have just let them."

Simon's eyes softened as he looked her over. "Nah, I think it's just right."

Jakobi met his gaze, pain reflecting in the deep pools of her hazel eyes.

Simon reached to cover her hand with his. "Jakobi, nothing is different. I am still who I was before we came here, although a bit feebler." He smiled wryly.

Jakobi shook her head. "How can you say that, Simon? Nothing is the same. I know nothing about you." She pulled her hand away and rested it in her lap. She bit her lip and asked the question that had burned in her heart since Megan had explained why Simon was in her village. "Did you only pursue a friendship with me to get close to the children?"

Simon weighed his words. "Yes," he answered.

Jakobi closed her eyes with a sharp intake of breath. She knew it was the answer, but it hurt more than she'd expected. She opened them again, tears trembling on her lashes before one escaped down her face. She swiped at it, embarrassed. "I feel so foolish," she murmured.

Simon pushed his chair back and leaned toward her, his hands on her knees. "Jakobi, I have to be honest. When I met you and found out in that first conversation that Maly and Noah were with you, I felt compelled to stay close to you so I could watch over the kids, no doubt about that." He ducked his head, trying to capture her gaze. "But, Jakobi, believe me when I say my feelings for you are completely authentic. I struggle with my attraction and affection for you. The absolute only thing holding me back is our differing beliefs, because I know how difficult life would be if we tried to marry our two schools of thought."

Jakobi blinked, surprised. "Marry?" She scrunched her face.

Simon's cheeks reddened. "Well, I mean join our…er, combine the way we—" Simon cleared his throat, flustered. He charged ahead. "Jakobi, what I'm trying to say is that I don't know how long Deliverance will have me watch the kids. We're going back tomorrow, and I plan to live as I've been, and I hope you'll trust me enough to allow our friendship to continue. Just because we can't date, doesn't mean I want you out of my life."

Jakobi nodded, relieved. "I feel the same way, Simon. But"—she shrugged—"what about when you come back here?"

Simon gently squeezed her knees. "We'll cross that bridge when we come to it. Okay?"

❖ ❖ ❖

Jakobi thanked Megan the next morning for showing her around Deliverance. "And thank you for the work you guys do here," Jakobi said. "It's amazing to see the difference you're making."

"The credit and glory belongs to the Lord, Jakobi," Megan answered, squeezing the young woman's hands. "He equips us to do this. He alone is able to transform and renew these children. We are simply His instruments, willing to be used where He's placed us."

On the bus ride to Pursat and then the cramped van ride on to the village, Jakobi worried her lip and pondered what Megan had said in light of the things Jakobi had witnessed at Deliverance. Simon elbowed her as they neared the road that would lead to their temporary homes.

"A *riel* for your thoughts," he said.

Jakobi snorted, "A single *riel* isn't even worth a penny."

"Come on, Jakobi, give."

"Simon, I've been thinking of what you said the night before we left. About how you've seen God's work in the lives of people the world sees as worthless. I get that now. I'm not ready to say I agree with everything you believe, but there is something different about the things I saw this week. Love oozed out of that place. And hope. And peace." She scoffed, "I mean, I work for the Peace Corps, and I don't see anything even remotely close to that in the work that I or the other volunteers do."

Simon nodded. He understood. He also knew that a response wasn't necessary. *Lord, you're at work here. Thank you.*

They disembarked from the cramped van and simultaneously sighed. "I have decided that I am addicted to the simplicity of this place," Jakobi confessed. "I loved Phnom Penh but am so happy to be in this backwards, quiet village."

"Agreed." Simon dipped his chin. He grabbed Jakobi's hand and asked if she wanted to go with him to visit Heng, Kolab, and Chaya. Before they had left, Simon asked Megan if she could supply him with a Khmer Bible for their friends.

Jakobi had choked up when he showed it to her on the bus. "Oh, Simon," she'd breathed, "this will mean more to them than just about anything."

She shook her head. "I really want to check on Maly and Kiri. I know they're fine, but I just have to lay eyes on them."

Simon acquiesced. "I'll be by later," he promised.

He made the trek to the hut hidden away in the clearing in the woods, anticipation rising as he thought about the looks on their faces when he handed them a Bible in their own language.

Chaya opened the door, a surprised smile on her face. "Simon! You are well!" She pulled him into the home. He laughed at her enthusiastic greeting and followed her into the room. He stopped when he noticed the monk sitting in the corner with Heng and Kolab. All were smiling from ear to ear.

Heng jumped up to greet Simon. "Simon, our dear friend, come! Come! Meet our Vireak. This is a day for rejoicing!"

Simon bowed respectfully to Vireak, who in turn extended a hand in greeting. Simon shook it. Vireak looked overwhelmed, and Simon turned to Kolab, hoping he wasn't overstepping, but anxious to share the Bible. He sat the family down and presented them with the wrapped box.

"Thank you for your hospitality, your fellowship, and for rushing me to Phnom Penh. You saved my life," he said.

Heng took the box and then offered it to Kolab, who placed the box in her lap and pulled back the paper, amused by the idea of a gift. She lifted the lid to reveal the Bible and the family froze, staring in disbelief at the treasure. Chaya raised her eyes to Simon's, opening and closing her mouth. Simon glanced at Vireak, who looked on in curiosity.

Heng leaned over Kolab and reverently lifted the Bible from its box in her lap. He lifted it to his trembling lips and kissed it three times. He passed it to Kolab's waiting hands; she touched the book to her chest, her face, her cheek, kissing it over and over. Chaya held shaky hands to her lips, waiting for her turn with the Bible. When it was handed to her, she held it above her head, whispering the same phrase over and over. Simon turned to Vireak whose face contorted in undefined emotion when Heng and Kolab joined Chaya in repeating the phrase.

"What are they saying?" Simon asked.

Vireak cleared his throat, overcome with emotion as he watched the family cherish their gift. "'Holy is our God who hears. Holy is He.' The last time they saw a Bible in their language was the night before my house and family were consumed with fire over a decade ago. A fire I now understand was set by my uncle to rid the community of all of us. But by the grace of God, He kept me safe."

Simon was overcome as he watched the small family of believers immediately sit together and pour over the pages of the Bible. Simon cherished the Word of God, always had, but was completely humbled by the reaction of Heng and his family. Where Bibles in various languages were commonplace and even cheap in America, he saw how greatly it was treasured in this home. *Lord, may I always see Your word as a fortune greater than gold, as this family so obviously does.*

The family gathered around Simon, tears flowing as they thanked him for the priceless gift. Heng fell to his knees and pulled his family down with him as he prayed, thanking the Lord for His living Word, thanking Him for the deliverance of Vireak.

"Amen," Simon agreed when the prayer was over, shooting a questioning look to Vireak. "Now this is a story I must hear!" he said.

Vireak offered a weak smile. "I've only just decided to leave the *wat* and life as a monk," he told Simon, flashing a shy glance toward Chaya, who smiled at him reassuringly. Vireak looked down at his red-orange smock and ran a hand over his shaved head. "I need to go back and officially end my service, but something told me to come here and tell Heng first. Now I'm thankful that I was here to see this. Their joy over this gift, Simon, reminds me of my parents." He took a deep breath, trying to gain composure.

A sudden incessant pounding accompanied by shrieks for help sounded at the front door. The group in the room froze in surprise.

Simon recognized Jakobi's voice and leapt into action. He opened the door and she fell into his arms, sobbing and shaking uncontrollably. "They're gone, Simon. *Gone*. Dara only said they're in a better place, that they are safe. She won't tell me where they went! Her eyes, they were flat and emotionless; I think she's been drinking. I'm so afraid, Simon! What has she done with them?!" she shrieked and pounded on his chest.

Simon grasped her shoulders and tried to steady the torrent of panic. "Jakobi, settle down," Simon shook her.

She fell into him as her knees buckled.

Simon lowered himself to the floor, Jakobi slumping down next to him. "Jakobi," he tried again, "tell us what has happened."

They listened in disbelief as she explained that she'd returned to a home completely turned upside down. "It looked like a tornado had landed in their home; things were turned over, papers and rice everywhere. Dara was in bed, covered in bruises, crying. I asked her where the children were, for her to tell me what happened."

Jakobi took a shuddering breath, desperate to explain so that they could figure out what to do. "I asked her what had happened, where the men were. She would only say that she did good, that she didn't tell. 'Phirun had struck a deal, I had to act quickly, Jakobi,' was all that she would say." Jakobi rubbed her nose, eyes puffy and swollen from her desperate cries. She didn't notice the way Vireak pushed off of the wall where he'd leaned, arms crossed, mouth grim, listening to Jakobi.

But Simon noticed.

"Vireak," Simon implored, "you know where they are, don't you?"

All eyes in the room rounded and turned questioningly to Vireak.

The monk met their gazes, mouth flat. "I have to be sure." He crouched before Jakobi and Simon where they huddled together on the floor of the hut. "I will return after the sun sets. While I'm gone, you need to gather as much money as you can." He rose and turned to Heng. Quietly he spoke, his eyes shifting to Chaya and then to Jakobi and Simon. "If they are where I think they are, I will need you two to come together."

Chapter Twenty-Three

At Vireak's instruction, Jakobi chose to abandon her post in the Peace Corps. She would receive no assistance from the American government in a return flight to the states, but that was the least of her worries. Simon took her on his moto to gather her things and to protect her if anyone in the family caused problems for her. The house was eerily quiet, empty. They found Dara asleep in her bed, curled in on herself. The strong odor of alcohol permeated the air.

Simon led Jakobi through the chaotic mess in the main room of the house to her bedroom and cautioned her to think over her decision carefully. "Jakobi, will your Visa be valid if you are not here with the Peace Corps?"

She knelt on her knees, palms flat against the floor and ducked to see if anything had been kicked under the low bed. Satisfied that the area was clear, she rummaged through the locked trunk the Peace Corps had provided for her to store her things. She held up a mosquito tent. "Do you think this would fit all of us if we need it?"

Chaya had asked if she could come along. She had seen enough of Maly over the last few weeks to be concerned for her well being.

"Well, at least for you and Chaya, I have one for…" Simon began to answer and shook his head. He took a step toward Jakobi and grabbed her shoulders. "Look at me."

Jakobi conceded and brought her hands up to clasp the bend at his elbows.

Simon held her gaze for a moment. "Jakobi, are you sure about this? I don't know what Vireak has in mind, but I do know we are about to enter some dangerous waters."

"Simon, this is in no way how I expected my time with the Peace Corps to end. And I would be lying if I said I'm not scared." Her hands squeezed his elbows with surprising intensity, and she leaned forward, her nose almost touching his. "But please hear me when I say that I have never been more certain of anything in my life." Jakobi's eyes misted over and she dropped her gaze. "Those kids deserve for me to do everything I can to step in and chase after them, no matter what the cost may be to me."

Simon folded his arms around her, pressing her close to his chest. He rested his chin on her head, understanding the emotion dripping from her voice as she mumbled, "No matter the cost to me, I have to give them a fighting chance. If Vireak knows where they are and needs me to help get them, I will not stand by in fear of the unknown."

※ ※ ※

Vireak walked back to the *wat* on adrenaline-charged legs. When his uncle had been alive, he had instructed that a percentage of every offering Vireak received in his years as a monk was to be given right back to Kosal. Vireak began his time in the *wat* as a young boy: confused and orphaned, immediately the scapegoat for his family's so-called discretion against Kosal and the others by becoming Christians. Habits and ideas shaped by his uncle's cruel mind had been nearly impossible to break. Vireak, out of habit, had continued to set a portion aside even after he learned of Kosal's death.

Vireak entered the grounds and walked purposefully to his room where a small bed, simple and unpretentious, stood in the corner. He knelt to retrieve a thick bundle wrapped in an extra robe and quickly stuffed it under his arm, hoping it would be enough. Quietly, heart pounding, he slipped down the hall and knocked lightly on another door; one he had avoided for many years.

The old monk was shorter than Vireak now, although Vireak could remember how small and insignificant he had felt in the man's presence so many years ago.

How helpless and afraid.

Confusion raced in the man's eyes as Vireak stepped past him into the room.

An hour later, Vireak left with more money, and a smartphone programmed with maps, numbers, and the contacts he would need. Bribery seemed to run in the family.

❖ ❖ ❖

Jakobi and Simon met Chaya at her home and waited for Vireak to join them. Simon felt it would be important to locate a van or even a truck, and knew they could do that in Pursat. For the journey there, they would take Simon's moto.

"I'll drive Chaya and Jakobi, you and Vireak share yours," Heng had suggested.

Jakobi smiled in spite of the serious situation. She had observed the numerous things Khmer's were able to pile onto motos. She'd even seen a trailer with a houseboat strapped to it hauled behind one. It seemed that the moto had become the equivalent of an American truck; anything could be hauled with it. She was surprised that Heng hadn't expected the four to just share Simon's moto, strapping on Maly and Noah when they found them.

If we find them. Jakobi's throat closed around her fear.

When Vireak arrived, Jakobi thought he looked pale, and wondered at the disappointment in his voice when he shared his news: "I was right. I know where they are. Or rather, I know how to find them. The only question is: How much money can we pool together?"

Simon had some and promised that they could wire Deliverance for more in Pursat. He then surprised Jakobi by declining Heng's offer of a second moto. "Let's just take mine," Simon said, causing Jakobi's heart to stop. "We will need to sell it in order to get another vehicle, and I don't want to leave you without, just in case we need to call you for help, Heng."

Heng considered Simon and nodded in agreement.

Pest jumped around the group, yapping and panting, excited by the tension and adventure in the air. Simon knelt down and rubbed him behind the ears. "Sorry, buddy, you can't come this time." He glanced up at Heng, who rolled his eyes.

"Fine, we'll watch the mutt," Heng said.

Simon thanked him with a firm handshake.

Vireak placed a hand on Heng's shoulder and looked past him to Kolab, who stood back watching the activity with her arms wrapped around her middle, revealing the mother's anxiety.

"I will bring Chaya back to you," Vireak promised.

Kolab dipped her chin at him, her eyes shimmering with unshed tears

The group piled onto Simon's moto, packed together like sardines in a can. Although Vireak had chosen to leave the *wat* permanently, he explained that it was imperative to their mission that anyone they came into contact with from that moment forward needed to believe he was a devout monk. Monks were not to come into physical contact with women, so Vireak took the driver position, Simon next, then Jakobi, and Chaya—who felt more comfortable balancing precariously on a moto than Jakobi—on the rear.

Jakobi worried her bottom lip as Vireak climbed onto the small bike, watched as Simon tried to settle behind him without feeling out of place pressing up against another man. He seemed to crave Jakobi's touch behind him to balance out the awkwardness and held a hand out to her.

She hesitated.

As soon as she climbed on the moto, she would officially abandon her post. Images of Noah—she no longer thought of him as Kiri—his eyes so watchful as she fed him a bottle, and Maly, face soft and sweetly relaxed as she slept peacefully, swept through her. She shook off her hesitation and climbed aboard the moto. Simon's hands clenched hers reassuringly when she reached around his middle. She leaned her cheek against his broad back, cringing when Chaya climbed on behind her, and the moto started down the bumpy road.

Jakobi clenched her eyes shut and focused on Simon's steady heartbeat, ticking beneath her hands. The awful statistics and stories the Peace Corps had shared about the average number of deaths and injuries that took place on motos each year pressed into her mind. *Don't think about it, Jakobi.*

For what seemed like hours, Vireak guided the moto through the highways of Cambodia, inching closer to a destination that was known only to him. Jakobi's body tensed and stiffened from the smashed quarters and rocky vibrations on roads that were lacking in upkeep.

Just before dawn, Vireak pulled to the side of the road, and the four warily climbed off, groaning simultaneously. Vireak pulled a phone from the folds of his robe and wandered to the middle of the street, where he found a stronger signal.

Jakobi's mouth dropped open, watching Vireak work the phone. She elbowed Simon. "I thought monks weren't allowed to use modern stuff!"

Vireak raised a brow in her direction before he turned his back to them, a hand cupped over his ear as he spoke low into the phone.

Chaya came alongside Jakobi and whispered, "That's how it used to be. And technically, no, they are not supposed to have phones, but many do." She watched Vireak, affection in her voice. "I don't think I've seen Vireak with one in the past; perhaps he got it when he went back to the *wat*."

Simon shifted on the other side of Jakobi and leaned down to whisper past Jakobi's profile to Chaya. "Do you know where we are, Chaya?"

Jakobi felt Chaya's loose hair brush her face as Chaya shook her head. "I have no idea."

Vireak walked back to the small cluster, his phone at his side. "Okay, he's expecting us. Jakobi, Simon, are you ready?"

In the pink hue of the sunrise that broke through clouds overhead, Simon and Jakobi exchanged glances. "Ready for what exactly, Vireak?" Simon asked.

Chapter Twenty-Four

Jakobi's heart thundered so hard she thought it would leap out of her chest. Simon secured an arm around her waist, playing his part.

Husband and wife. It was the only way.

She understood it was pretend—for show—but Jakobi's palms were moist with nerves. Her feelings for Simon were difficult enough without pretending to be his wife. His bride. She gave herself a mental shake. *Get it together, Jakobi. There are far more important matters at hand than your feelings for Simon.*

She, Simon, and Chaya followed Vireak along a path that twisted next to a large grouping of rocks large enough to rival a mountain range. Suddenly, Vireak turned to the right and disappeared. When Simon rounded the corner, he pulled Jakobi with him into what she now saw was a small crack between two boulders. They took two steps in the darkness before a shaft of sunlight scattered the shadows, followed by another and another. Jakobi's breath caught as the underground cave—rather, an underground palace, for that's what it looked like—took shape in broken beams of brilliant light.

"What is this place?" Simon whispered to Vireak, his voice drenched in fascination.

Chaya answered, "I've heard of this place—places like this—but never dreamed how beautiful…"

Vireak turned slightly. "There are many ruins from the rein of the Khmer people. You've visited Angkor Wat?"

Simon and Jakobi nodded.

Vireak gestured to the cavern. "Underground temples and vast areas like this were carved out during that time and have also been abandoned." They stood at the top of a massive stairwell; each step was chiseled stone, the vast room at the bottom broken up by pillars of craggy rock that had been left by stonemasons. "This is considered a holy place, although not many know that it's here."

Jakobi wrapped both hands around Simon's arm as they inched down the stairs. The steps felt sturdy, although the edges crumbled away under their feet. The foursome grew quiet, the crunching of their shoes on ancient stone echoed around them. It smelled damp and musty, but warm and...enchanted, somehow.

Vireak glanced to Chaya, who took each step carefully behind Simon and Jakobi, wishing he could go to her, help her down. Her eyes were trained on the stairs, concentrating. He clenched his fists and turned away, knowing it was imperative he play the role of a monk for just a while longer. There would be plenty of time to talk with Chaya, help her...hold her.

They reached the bottom of the stairs, and the sound of Chaya's astonished gasp tingled in Vireak's head.

"It's beautiful," Chaya exclaimed.

The cave opened into a room of intricate stone carvings; images of daily life were captured in square stones and carved into the pillars and walls. Another column of stairs rose up across the room, curving to the left, opening onto a curved balcony, bathed in sunlight and encircled with intricately engraved railings. Wide cracks in the roof of the cave opened above the balcony and high above them. Shafts of sunlight shimmered through other small openings, catching columns of dust that danced alone in their secret beauty.

"Greetings," a deep voice called out and echoed across the room, jolting Jakobi out of her trance. Her nerves sizzled to the ends of her extremities as they squinted into the shadows toward the baritone voice.

There. On the balcony, close to the rocks, the form of a man took shape among the crags and dents in the rock walls.

"The happy couple has come a long way for a child of their own," the voice spoke again—lilting, mocking—but the man didn't move.

Jakobi opened her mouth to answer, but snapped it shut when Chaya squeezed her elbow. *Right.* Jakobi was not supposed to speak or understand Khmer. She was not a Peace Corps volunteer; Simon was not an employee of a non-profit organization that rescued children from trafficking.

Jakobi and Simon were now a childless, hopelessly barren American couple that had their hearts set on adoption. Adoption that wasn't possible in the States because of medical complications.

After Vireak had explained their roles by the road, Jakobi had wondered aloud, "But don't we need to explain why we are after these two particular children? And why can't we just tell Deliverance where they are?" Jakobi had turned to Simon, including him in her inquiry. "Didn't you tell me, Simon, that because Dara and her husband are the caretakers and they essentially gave up their rights by selling the kids, that Deliverance would automatically be deemed the guardians of Maly and Noah as they were caregivers of sorts when their mother was alive? I don't understand why we can't just alert the authorities to whatever it is that Vireak knows, and get the kids." Her questions ended, strangled with a sob.

Simon opened his mouth to answer, but Jakobi pressed on, composed but still distressed. "Why the pretense and games? If you know where they are, why can't we talk to the authorities and Deliverance and go get them?" she asked again, her hands against her cheeks, tears rolling over her fingers.

Vireak held his hands up, silencing the torrent of questions. "Jakobi, we are all concerned about these children; no one more than I." He glanced at Simon, knowing that he understood the level of danger the kids were in. Vireak lowered his voice. "We have walked onto a precarious and dangerous web that has to be delicately balanced or we will lose them forever. It has to be this way. We have to pay many bribes and play their game." He brought his hands together in front of his chest, palm to palm. "It has to be this way," he repeated.

And so they stood together, now, playing the game for the sake of wicked men. Jakobi hoped her face conveyed a young woman so desperate for children that she was willing to pay any demanded amount and sneak through caves and jump through various hoops to make it happen.

Vireak stepped forward into a beam of light. The skin on his shaved head glinted in the sun, his robe shone bright. Remembering her role and feeling helpless, Jakobi linked her arm with Simon's and leaned into him.

Chaya translated the Khmer words for Simon; Jakobi pretended to listen as well. Simon elbowed Jakobi, and together they bent at the waist toward the man, hands together in a posture of prayer.

Simon spoke in English. "Yes. We have brought the money requested." He patted his shirt pocket as Vireak had instructed. The man waited in the shadows a moment longer, then stepped into the light.

Jakobi winced as the bright sun bounced off of the orange monk robe, blinding her. Simon sucked in a breath and squeezed Jakobi's hand when she gasped. *A monk?*

The man looked like a broader, older version of Vireak. He strode down the stairs, almost majestic in his confident gait. Jakobi's hands shook and her heart thundered as Simon let go of her to join Vireak and the man to hand over the money. They spoke in hushed tones too low for her and Chaya to understand. The women clutched one another's hands and looked around expectantly for someone to present Noah and Maly.

Why can't I hear them? Jakobi wondered.

Vireak bowed to the monk, who turned to Simon. When Simon obliged and also bowed to the monk, he turned toward the stairs and ascended again. Jakobi watched the monk retreat into the shadows, amazed at how the rocks seemed to absorb him.

Vireak and Simon turned and walked back to Jakobi and Chaya, Simon stretching out his hands to usher the women back to the entrance.

"Wait!" Jakobi protested, whispering. "Where are they—?"

"Jakobi" Simon interrupted.

The week at Deliverance and frightening realization that the children were gone, the long night on the moto all worked against her and she sobbed. "No, Simon, where are they?"

Simon wrapped an arm around her shoulders, squeezing her close to him. He pressed his lips against her ear. "That's fine, Jakobi; that's good. You be as desperate and as upset as you like. Just like a woman desperate to be a mother would be. I'll explain everything, but for now, you just cry your eyes out."

And she did.

❖ ❖ ❖

They piled back onto the moto and drove to another town. Vireak weaved the passenger heavy bike through back roads to the *wat* in the center of the town, where he would sleep to keep up the pretense. The *wat* was intricately beautiful; peaks laced in gold, vibrant red roofs, intricate carvings etched the walls around the vast property. Vireak stopped the moto just outside the gate and disembarked, taking his small load with him.

Jakobi felt trepidation squeeze her throat as their connection to the children disappeared within the courtyard. Simon took over driving and found a small market where he and the women could purchase dinner. None of them were very hungry and only nibbled at the rice and curry dish. Each bite tasted metallic on Jakobi's tongue.

With Chaya's help, Simon asked around the market and found someone that had a used truck for sale and was willing to trade for Simon's moto and some money. The travelers gratefully climbed into the cab, still close to one another, and ready to be tighter when Vireak joined them the next morning, but thankful for space and seats.

They spent the night in a motel, knowing they needed to get as much sleep as possible for the journey ahead. Simon took the chair in the corner, his feet propped on the end of the bed where the women slept.

They didn't speak; there was nothing really to say. Vireak had said that he would explain everything as soon as they were back on the road.

They pulled onto the street outside of the *wat* early the next morning and waited for Vireak to appear. He rounded the corner, his features drawn and weary. Simon scooted to the middle, allowing Vireak to climb into the driver's seat to avoid physical contact with the women. Jakobi found it ironic that they had to work so hard to help Vireak maintain an air of holiness when they were using underground connections in the Theravada monk community to find two helpless children that had been sold for profit. Jakobi could only imagine what gain the children could guarantee their captors. She thought of the sinister purpose behind the karaoke bar in the small village. She shuddered now with the realization that she had supported it in a small way with her drink purchase.

The travelers remained silent through town, the windows down to help them breathe through the thick tropical air. Once alone on the highways, Vireak did his best to explain what he knew. "This could be a long process."

"Vireak, what in the world do Buddhist monks have to do with these children?" Jakobi questioned, baffled and exasperated.

Vireak took a deep breath and held it. He kept his eyes on the road, pensive. Quietly he explained that for years he had turned the other way as he noticed monks acting deceitfully. There were memories of hushed conversations, children ushered through halls one day and gone the next, money hidden in robes, passed surreptitiously in shadowed corners of the market.

"I thought monks were holy men." Jakobi jutted her chin toward the windshield, annoyed at her own naiveté. Beginning with her complete ignorance of the vastness of the trafficking issue and how she had supposed that monks were holy, innocent.

"Why did you stay quiet?" Jakobi asked, her tone relaying her irritation with no one but herself.

Vireak worked a muscle in his jaw, his eyes on the road. "Jakobi, I entered the *wat* as a young boy. My family had died in a fire and all that had been told to me was that our ancestors were so outraged at my family's betrayal of Buddha and all of his teachings that they had burned our home to the ground. I had been spared to work off the evil my family brought on the rest of our relatives.

"My uncle reminded me every time he saw me. If anything went wrong for him, he laid the blame at my feet. From the beginning I was taught to keep my head down, be quiet and be a good monk." He shrugged one shoulder and smiled sardonically. "Although, I, myself, was deceitful from the beginning, my uncle insisted I keep back part of my morning offerings for him. I would hold an amount back, not too much that I was questioned when I turned over my offerings from the morning, not too little to incur my uncle's wrath. It was a miserable balance. At first."

The cab grew quiet, but the charge in the air was expectant. "But...Vireak, these men. They aren't just religious men that can go home and live one way after behaving perfect in public. You live in the *wat*, you chant and meditate and pray and absorb the teachings of Buddha. How in the world can there be such corruption?"

Vireak's voice was a low rumble, barely loud enough to be heard above the growling of the old truck engine. He spoke on as if he hadn't heard her. "There is a lot of abuse that can—and does—happen in *wats*."

Chaya sucked in a sharp breath. Jakobi glanced at her friend, not sure she wanted Vireak to continue.

"When I first arrived, an older monk took me in his room one night, thinking he would take advantage of me. But I was not as young as I looked. I fought. Surprised to be deterred, afraid to be caught, he began to make arrangements for me to be transferred. My Uncle Kosal found out and stepped in because he wanted me close. He wanted control over me. Now that I think back, I believe Kosal was involved in the underground trafficking channel; how else would he have known about the attempted abuse or been able to keep me there if he wasn't connected somehow?

"For years I have kept my head down, turned the other way when I saw corruption, and worked hard to do what's expected of me. I thought I was doing good, and not all monks are corrupt. Most of those men feel they are doing right by their family and their faith. When my uncle died, my world was completely rocked. It's like once he died, my chains fell away, but I was too scared to run. Now, I think it was the hand of God holding me back for the sake of these children. The monk that tried to abuse me, that made a deal of some kind with Kosal, is still alive. He is the one that is directing us to the kids, thinking that you two want them, not at all caring why. He might even believe that I've picked up where my uncle dropped off, that I'm supplying children for the back rooms of karaoke bars across the country."

Silence settled again. The truck moaned as it bumped over gaps and cracks in the road. Vireak gripped the steering wheel. He was sure that God's hand was on him, but still full of questions and uncertainty. He shifted in his seat, wondering what Chaya thought of his confession. What must she think of his hypocritical role as a holy man?

Simon sensed Vireak's discomfort and broke the silence. "So what now, Vireak? What's the plan?"

He replied again that they had hoops to jump through. There was a sequence of stops that they needed to make, fees—bribes—that had to be handed over, *wats* to visit just to prove that they were sincere in their venture. They wouldn't know where the next destination was or when the children would be produced until they'd accomplished each task.

"Like a twisted quest or scavenger hunt," Jakobi observed.

"Exactly." Simon understood. He's spent months with Deliverance, had been face-to-face night after night with the heart of corruption in Thailand. "We need to prove that we're not authorities out to catch wrong doing. We need to hang in there, pay what they want, and follow along."

"For how long?" Jakobi asked, worry mounting as she thought of Maly and Noah, vulnerable in the hands of twisted morals.

"For as long as it takes." Simon and Vireak answered in unison.

Chapter Twenty-Five

Thailand

There were a few young women that came each weekend to visit the girls in the Deliverance home. These women were among the first group of slaves to be rescued and restored under the guidance of Deliverance. They had jobs and were hardworking, productive members of Thai society. Some worked in the Deliverance Café, others in hair salons, and others still were seamstresses that sold their wares in the market.

All belonged to the Lord. They loved to spend one day a week loving on girls that had come out of the same situations as they had. A small worship service was held in the gathering room, a short Bible study and then one on one time, the older women encouraging and teaching the younger rescues.

Nataya usually looked forward to the day the restored women came. As kind as their dorm mother was, as understanding as their counselors and teachers were, no one empathized as the mentors did who came to visit each weekend. There was a sacred and beautiful understanding between them.

But that morning Nataya kept to herself, tucked into the corner of the couch, hunkered down around her belly in confusion and fear.

Anong, a plain, petite woman that worked in the café and was studying to be a nurse, sat next to Nataya when the music was over. The rest of the group broke off to play games or practice make-up application with their older friends.

At first Anong sat silently beside Nataya, who stared ahead, hand resting on her slightly extended abdomen. Anong had been rescued around the same age, and after ten years in the program, she had hope unlike anything she'd dared to dream of. The horror of the first sixteen years of life was something she would never completely erase, but her nightmares had waned, and her confidence and assurance grew more each day. Christ had made her new, and she was forever grateful. As a result, Anong longed to help other girls come to the same life-altering place of confidence in God and His power.

She knocked a knuckle lightly on Nataya's knee. "Want to talk about it, young friend?" she asked, watching Nataya's face for the answer.

Nataya shrugged, her eyes desperate to talk, her mouth clenched as if she were afraid it would speak of its own volition.

Anong understood fear and uncertainty. Where Nataya had embraced healing quickly, Anong had held back for years, too afraid to speak or to hope. When she did speak, it was in angry and accusatory tones. After the tricks and abuse of sixteen years, she couldn't help but test the motives of those around her. How would they benefit from her rescue? What would they take away from her schooling or training? It took many nights of screaming until her voice was hoarse, many loving responses to her hatred, and weeks of patience in light of her taxing behavior, for Anong to finally break down and accept that the love they expressed day after day after day was sincere. And that only a loving, all-powerful God would call and equip His people to love as Anong had witnessed.

Nataya had been one to warm to honesty and pure affection from the women around her almost instantly. For the first few weeks she had been quiet, but eventually, Anong looked forward to the high-spirited greeting she would receive from Nataya upon her entrance in the home. To see her so pensive and miserable was heartbreaking, but understanding. Perhaps after the initial joy of rescue, the reality of what she had been rescued from haunted her.

"You can talk to me about anything, Nataya. No matter what you're feeling. No judgment." Anong waved her hand in the air. Safe space.

Nataya bit her bottom lip, the hand on her belly tightening. "Moree said that Deliverance is about giving life. That when I was rescued and they found out about the baby...that we would be safe, no matter what." Nataya glanced at Anong.

Anong raised her brows, face open and expectant.

Nataya's chin trembled and her lips tightened. "Then why would Deliverance promise one of the girls an abortion? And if I don't want to give my baby up for adoption, will you kick me out...or force me to have an abortion, too?" she whispered, terrified now that she'd spoken her fears and desires into the open.

Anong's jaw dropped and she quickly folded Nataya into her arms, holding the young girl as she wept. "Nataya, who in the world told you that she was getting an abortion?"

Nataya went still, silent. Anong recognized her struggle; everyone in this home had come from her own personal life of hell. They were careful with one another, sisters in a way no one else in the world could relate to.

"Never mind." Anong rested her cheek on Nataya's soft hair. "What's really important is that you understand who the people behind Deliverance are. They are people who love the Lord with all of their hearts and who want the very best for you and the others. The Bible is very clear that human life—all human life—is precious and worth protecting and cherishing. That goes for you"—Anong gently poked a finger in Nataya's ribs—"and that baby in there. No one here would ever, ever make you do something to hurt yourself or your baby. I promise." Anong pulled away and held Nataya's chin, locking her gaze on the young girl's tear-filled eyes.

Nataya sniffed and dipped her chin. "But what about Rat—eh, what about the other girl? She wants one. An abortion, I mean."

Anong placed her hands on Nataya's shoulder. "Nataya, I guarantee that this girl is scared and the counselors can handle that and talk with her. We are not going to provide an abortion. We will provide any and every girl in this house with the tools they need to handle their current situation and anything else that may arise."

She pursed her lips together and ducked her eyes to catch Nataya's gaze again. "And, Nataya, that goes for what you just said about wanting to keep your baby, too. We can help you to do that."

Nataya rounded her eyes at Anong, disbelieving. "But I'm so young. I don't know how to care for the baby, can't possibly provide for it…" Nataya's shoulders tightened as she curled in on herself, overwhelmed.

Anong curved her lips upward. "Nataya, this is *your* baby. Yours. If you want to keep your baby, no one will stand in the way of that. Deliverance has equipped many women who have come here pregnant to keep their children. Have you told anyone that you don't want to give the baby up for adoption?"

Nataya shook her head, confirming what Anong had already concluded.

"Well, sweet girl, you better tell them. You are free here. Free to speak, to think, to explore, to question. Just be honest. No one can guess your feelings."

Nataya bit her lips, eyes brimming with joy, head wiggling up and down enthusiastically. "And I can really keep the baby?" she asked.

"Really and truly, Nataya. I think you should pray about it, but this is a place that will do everything to help you and this little one live life to the fullest."

Nataya threw her arms around Anong, overjoyed that God had heard her heart and made a way.

Anong went with Nataya to speak with the housemother, Dao-Ming, who was overjoyed to hear that Nataya wanted to keep her baby.

"This is wonderful, dear girl!" she exclaimed.

When Anong helped Nataya share her concerns about girls that wanted abortions, the housemother also reassured her.

The Heavens Are Telling

"Nataya, we've been rescuing girls for many years, and as can be expected, many that come to us are pregnant or even have young children already. While that certainly changes things, like what house you are assigned to, based on your needs, it is not something we will ever see as a problem. The Bible tells us that children are a gift, a reward. We don't fault anyone for not seeing their baby that way given the circumstances that might have led to the pregnancy," Dao-Ming said.

Nataya took a deep breath. That part of her reality was very dark and confusing. How could she love a baby when it was forced upon her, when the man who put it there had done so against her will?

But God...

Somehow, even in the newness of her faith, Nataya knew that God had nurtured the love she already had for the helpless life inside of her. And perhaps that was why she adored her baby, related to it. The conception was just as much thrust upon the baby as it was upon Nataya. Neither could be blamed and both deserved life.

Her housemother continued, "We try to let you get used to freedom, settle into routine and work through your thoughts and feelings before we ask outright what you would like to do. I'm sorry that by having you meet with the adoption coordinator, you assumed we wanted you to give your baby over to someone against your will."

She rested her hands lightly on Nataya's shoulders, tilting her head at her, smiling. "Now that we know what you want, dear girl, we will begin to make sure you feel ready when this baby comes and to be the absolute best mom you can be; the mom God has created you to be."

Chapter Twenty-Six

Boise, Idaho

Gage needed to have control. Needed to exert his power. He'd been working diligently for months, to prove himself to them. Still, they hadn't called. He was getting anxious to be near Nataya. He knew she must be waiting for him.

His basement was finally in use. Gage had found a purveyor he could trust; a man who didn't ask questions, just set a price and delivered.

Gage spent countless hours on the Internet.

He searched, watched, approached, fooled. He earned trust.

But it wasn't enough.

Thoughts of Nataya tormented him. The memory of her skin on his; the way she said his name.

He knew she missed him. But he couldn't get to her and he was becoming desperate.

He needed release.

He had everything ready to show them he was able to play the big game. He would be invaluable to them. The basement was ready.

He already had his first test subject in mind.

Zanna. The owner of Got Your Back downtown.

He checked his social accounts, snickering at how open and transparent people were online. How trusting and naïve they were.

Zanna announced that she and her staff were going to a local bar for a night of celebration during inventory weekend. He knew it was something she did the first weekend of every month. Now he knew when and where she would be for sure.

"Gotcha," he said to the empty room.

He showered, put on his best shirt, nicest jeans, shaved and slapped aftershave on his face. With one last glance in the mirror, he left the bathroom, checked to be sure the basement door was locked tight and gave his home a quick once over. He cocked his head, listening. If there was movement downstairs, no one would be able to detect it.

Satisfied he'd done all he could to conceal his business, he grabbed his keys and pocketed what he needed from his medicine cabinet before he left the house.

Zanna had scorned his subtle advances for months, but tonight—if everything went as planned—she would be all his.

Chapter Twenty-Seven

Zanna focused on her breathing.

She felt cold wet lips on her bare shoulder, her back. She breathed in slowly, imagined drawing her energy from every corner of her body and holding it in the center of her thoughts. She focused on keeping still, resisting the urge to flinch.

I'm asleep. Please believe I'm asleep.

The kisses stopped, but a clammy hand moved to caress her leg. Her stomach lurched in disgust. She focused the gathered energy into a pool. A tranquil pool, undisturbed. Just breathe.

How did I ever end up in bed with him?

Her headache and the foul taste in her mouth answered the question for her. She had drunk too much again, that's how. How was it that one beer could so easily turn into five? Her stomach churned more and she realized if he didn't get the hint soon, she would be sick all over his bed.

That would probably do it, she thought, biting the inside of her cheek to suppress a snort. *In and out, girl, just keep your breaths real slow and steady.*

At last, he cursed under his breath and roughly exited the bed. *There you go. Point taken.*

"Zanna," his voice was sharp compared with those hungry kisses from a moment before, "unless you're up for more of last night, I have things to do. Get out."

She kept up the pretense of a woman that had been zonked out and stretched slowly, peeking one eye open to glance at the man she'd gone home with the night before.

Gage stood naked beside the bed, hairy and greasy and not at all attractive. She felt sick and dirty with shame that she wished had been more prominent before she slept with him in the first place.

She sat up slowly, the frayed yellow comforter clutched tightly against her chest. Zanna cocked an eyebrow in his direction, her eyes looking just above his left ear. The less she had to make direct eye contact with the object of her shame, the better.

"I'll gladly be on my way if you'll point me toward my clothes." Her voice was cool, noncommittal.

He took the hint and tossed a pile of rumpled clothes at her. She held her breath against the stale smoke smell that emanated from her skin and the pile of clothes as she yanked her shirt over her head.

Zanna left Gage's townhouse, vaguely recognizing the street he lived on. She walked down the street and connected her surroundings, just a few blocks away from the bar. Zanna found her car parked where she left it in the parking lot the night before and drove the short distance home to her small bungalow in downtown Boise. As she followed the front walk that led from the street to her porch steps, she drank in the sight of her place.

Gran's place.

Zanna's grandmother had passed away two years before and had willed her home to Zanna. Despite attempts from family to get the home away from her—from challenging the will, to outright bribing her—Zanna had clung to the unexpected gift. She hadn't seen Gran in years, had only exchanged a few phone calls on birthdays. That her grandmother had left her home to the one member of the family that spit in the face of God was nothing short of astonishing. While the family suspected something sinister, Zanna guessed that her grandmother had made up the will long before Zanna left her conservative home for the real world.

Or perhaps she'd simply been senile.

Either way, Zanna had fond memories of the woman that had never turned her away; no matter what Zanna's father believed about his daughter. Zanna's heart swelled with admiration every time she came home, every time she realized it was really hers. It was the first time since she'd left home as a teen that she had a place to call home. Even more, it was the first time in her life that she'd belonged anywhere.

The small brown bungalow was only 1,118 square feet and every bit of it needed work. The porch stairs sagged in the middle, the windows let in cold air and condensation in the winter; the rooms were stuffy in the summer. The kitchen was outdated and the cabinets squeaked. In the few months since she had moved in, Zanna spent every spare evening, weekend, and rare weekday off sanding the floors, painting rooms, cleaning out cabinets and making Gran's home her own. She owned her own clothing boutique, Got Your Back, in downtown Boise, and felt as if she were constantly fighting to balance the two dreams. She needed the boutique to succeed to have the home she wanted; she needed the home she loved to be liveable so that she could focus on her business.

She climbed the front steps, loving the groans of protest beneath her feet as if she affronted each one. "I know, fellas, I know," she spoke aloud. "You're tired and worn out from people walking all over you while you just lie there and take it." Zanna flattened her mouth and spoke under her breath, "Trust me, I know how you feel."

She fitted her key in the lock of the new scarlet red door—a recent splurge. She had been unable to resist the square of stained glass in the top half of the door, artfully covered in a wrought iron shield. Entering the small foyer, she hung her bag on one of half a dozen old cabinet knobs she'd anchored to the wall to serve as a coatrack and walked straight to the laundry room.

What was once a small sun porch off of the kitchen was now plumbed and wired for a washer and dryer. Zanna had found a used set for a couple hundred dollars in the paper just two weeks before.

"They're in great condition," the weathered man in a plaid shirt and hiked up jeans had assured her when she arranged to check the set out. "I wear the same clothes for a week, and it was just me all of these years."

Zanna had forced a smile when he rambled about a love that had gotten away. Feigning interest in his story, she had lifted the lid to the washer, and then stuck her head into the dryer. Both clean. In fact, she felt as if she were back in the early nineties checking out a brand new set.

"I'm afraid the dark green color has scared other buyers away. I finally had to drop my price."

Zanna gave him a real smile that time. "I think they're perfect."

Once she had them home, Zanna adored how the almost vintage look of the washer and dryer rounded out her enclosed sun porch.

That morning, however, she barely noticed as she lifted the washer lid and peeled off her clothes, ignoring the open windows all around her and the abrasive chill in the room; she was desperate to rid herself of Gage and his scent. She dumped detergent and bleach into the washer, not caring if she ruined her clothes, and pushed the knob in before she turned to walk back through the kitchen to the bathroom.

Her home, while small, felt large with windows high along every wall and an open floor plan with no walls to separate the small space. The living room and kitchen flowed into one another, creating the feel of one big room, with the main bedroom, a much smaller second room, a linen closet, and the bathroom branching off of the living room. Zanna marched for the shower, anxious to feel clean.

The hot spray warmed her but did little to wash her humiliation away. She rolled her head back and let the water pelt her face, while events of the night before, or rather, what she could remember of them, crashed unwelcome through her mind...

She knew she had driven the short distance to the bar in order to keep herself from drinking too much. She had been determined to enjoy the night out with her friends after weeks of working hard at the store and on her new home, while remaining responsible. It started out as a great evening. She

The Heavens Are Telling

remembered dancing with a few of her girlfriends, jumping up and down like fools and singing into each other's faces. She was waiting at the bar for a beer when she saw him.

"Hey Zanna," he shouted above the noise as she leaned against the counter, waving some cash to get the bartender's attention.

She looked at him sidelong, sure that her lip curled at the sight of the flashing lights on his greasy face. *How does he always manage to look greasy?* she wondered.

"Hey, Gage," she mumbled and immediately turned her back to him. "Shane, I'm in serious need of a beer over here!"

She could feel Gage staring at her, and it gave her goose bumps. She couldn't stand these guys that hung around just waiting for someone to get into bed with them. Having a business relationship with Gage didn't help her to feel any less uncomfortable. Movement from the corner of her eye brought her attention back to him as he rounded the corner of the bar and located the beer for her. She glanced at a still busy and oblivious Shane at the far end of the bar and suppressed a smile in spite of herself as Gage dug in the cooler and then turned his back to her as he located an opener and popped the top off of the bottle and spun to hand it to her.

"Milady," he had bowed, obviously trying to be charming. Unfortunately, he stumbled and what would have been charming from someone else came across desperate, and the stench of it sickened Zanna. She rolled her eyes and tossed a five on the counter. She lifted the bottle in a salutation of thanks and danced her way back to her friends...

The water suddenly turned cold, indicating the hot water had kicked on in the washer, and Zanna fumbled for the handles, out of habit twirling the hot and cold spigots together. She stood dripping in the chipped tub for a moment, for the first time not admiring the old claw-foot bath, no matter the shape it was in.

That was only my second beer, she thought, *and that's the last one I remember. Is it possible he had time to slip something into it?* Zanna shook her head. "Get it together, girl. He didn't slip anything in your drink. Accountants don't do that, especially to their own clients."

She groaned, realizing that she had to see him again in just a few weeks for a payroll and tax meeting. "And that's why you don't let yourself get drunk and sleep with everyone that moves, Zanna. Seriously."

The self-chiding didn't help.

It certainly wasn't the first time she had let herself get out of control; wasn't the first time she had woken up in a strange bed. At least this time she knew the guy. Still, her gut told her that something was off. She had taken extra precautions to assure herself she'd stay in line and honestly didn't remember drinking very much. Her accountant had asked her out before, and she'd always found a way to refuse him, citing their work relationship as the excuse.

As she reached for her towel, she realized she was shaking. Had the man finally found a way to get her into bed? A look that had passed over his face when he handed her the beer, like he knew some secret he couldn't wait to share, flashed before her, and she felt nauseated.

The doorbell rang and Zanna quickly wrapped the towel around her shivering frame and shrank behind the door, sinking slowly down to the tiles.

Please don't be him...

The bell rang again, an offense to the quiet of her home. The third ring barked at her like a threat, then silence. Zanna sat in her small bathroom, her bare bottom growing sore and cold from the tiles beneath her, but her heart thundered, afraid of the pairing of thoughts from earlier and an unexpected intrusion on her morning.

She finally shook her head and muttered to herself as she slowly rose to her feet. "This is ridiculous, Zanna."

A sudden rapping at the door outside of the kitchen brought a shriek from her lips that echoed through the sparsely furnished home. She quickly clapped a hand over her mouth, as if that could pull the noise back in.

"Zanna?" a female voice called and the tapping became a more persistent bang.

Recognizing the voice, Zanna rolled her eyes and charged out of the bathroom. "Lydia, what are you doing here scaring me like that?"

Chapter Twenty-Eight

Lydia stood on the steps outside of the sun porch door, balancing two large to-go cups from Cuppa, their favorite coffee shop, in one hand and a brown paper sack in the other. She peered through the windows on the top half of the door, a look of bewilderment on her face.

"What do you mean, what am I doing?" Lydia's breath puffed white before her.

Her high voice hit a nerve that exploded into a headache behind Zanna's eyes. Zanna flipped the deadbolt and yanked open the door. A bitter January wind pulled across her feet. She spun her back on an exasperated Lydia, and tucked the corners of her towel under her arms. Shivering in the kitchen, Zanna reached for a bottle of aspirin on a shelf near the kitchen sink.

Lydia kicked the door shut behind her, and followed Zanna into the kitchen, dropping the bag on the small rolling cart that served as an island. She held up one of the cups of coffee, indicating it was Zanna's before she set it on the cart and repeated her question.

"What do you mean, what am I doing? Why are you in a towel? Didn't you remember I was coming to help you sort jewelry today? And what on earth did you scream for?"

Zanna closed her eyes against the questions that were pounding in her head. She placed the aspirin on her tongue, and then took a sip of coffee to help it down and cover the taste. She held up a finger to Lydia and took a deep breath, enjoying another sip of her favorite coffee while giving herself a mental check. *Deep, slow breaths, Zanna. Think of good things. Breathe in the light, cast out the shadows.*

She tried to concentrate on positive thoughts: her house, her store. But they were immediately choked out by images of bills, walls that needed paint, and accountants that slipped date drugs into their client's drinks. She shook her head. Why couldn't she concentrate? Even quick meditations used to do the trick, but lately…her mind must be too full. She had forgotten Lydia was there until she felt a gentle touch on her shoulder.

"Hey, you okay?" Lydia asked.

Zanna's eyes snapped open, embarrassed. She cleared her throat and turned to retrieve a mug from the cupboard behind her. "You want one?" she asked Lydia, holding up a purple ceramic mug. "I know I hate the feel of a paper cup when I can have a real one."

Lydia eyed her suspiciously. "Sure."

They popped the tops off of their cups and poured the steaming coffee into the purple mugs. Zanna ducked into her room to slip on a faded pair of jeans and a worn but cozy sweatshirt. She found Lydia in the living room eyeing the few posters she'd hung on the walls until she was ready to paint. Lydia took a sip of her coffee and contemplated a map of the world. Zanna cleared her throat and led Lydia to the front room where they sat on the worn sofa placed against the picture window.

Zanna apologized again for not making it to Lydia's presentation at her church the night before. "You know how churches make me sick," Zanna reasoned.

Lydia nodded. "Yeah, I know, Zanna. It's fine. I felt the same way before I left, remember?" Lydia shifted to lean against the edge of the couch and stretched her legs out in front of her, resting them on the old trunk Zanna used as a coffee table. "It's still an adjustment for me, you know? The church experience in Cambodia and Thailand was very different."

Zanna didn't comment. She well remembered how connected she'd felt to her former employee. Though Lydia was thirteen years her junior, Zanna had seen herself in the teenager:

young, rebellious—trapped in a religious world where no one understood her. Then Lydia had gotten herself into trouble and had been sent to Thailand on a mission trip with her church and came back completely different.

Lydia took a long pull on her coffee, thinking back on the talk she gave at the "New Year, Same God" ladies tea at her church. She was glad Zanna hadn't been there to experience Lydia's fumbling attempt to share her conversion and life change to a group of church ladies.

When Lydia had returned from her mission trip to Thailand just a month ago, she was a changed person walking into an unchanged world. Her grades were still low, her teachers had to learn to trust her. In Thailand, God had stripped her bare of comfort and security to show her that He, and only He, could offer her everything she needed. Her Savior knew that she was new and washed clean of her old self, even if not many believed it.

That's not fair, she thought, remembering the stories about how her church body had relentlessly prayed for her safety and return, when she had been kidnapped and trapped in a closet for two weeks. She hadn't known until after she'd been miraculously led out of captivity that a betting ring had kidnapped her to coerce Kiet to fight for her freedom.

Kiet.

His face flashed in her mind and warmth that had nothing to do with the coffee spread through her. They communicated mostly through emails in the time that she had been home. Once, Kiet had been able to call her, his tenor voice rich with friendship and security that both frightened and thrilled her.

He'd encouraged her when she told him she was going to speak at the tea. "Lydia, I think that's a good idea. Just be yourself and tell them about what God accomplished for you."

Lydia could picture his brown eyes focused intently on hers, questioning, communicating his point while making her insides flutter. She'd fumbled through the rest of the conversation. When they said their good-byes and she tapped the off feature on her phone, she'd groaned deep in her throat and dropped face first into her pillow. Why, after what they'd been through, was it so hard to remain composed while she talked to him? She blushed even now, and took another sip of coffee to cover it up.

Lydia looked up at Zanna and all of her warm thoughts about Kiet dissipated.

"Zanna?"

The older woman, face white and pinched, stared blankly at the mug in her hands.

Lydia reached out to touch Zanna's arm and called her name again. She had never seen such a forlorn look on her former boss's face. Zanna was the strong one, the fearless one, the confident one, the one that Lydia could now feel trembling as she reached out to her. Lydia set her coffee on the table and reached for Zanna's mug. Zanna jolted out of her trance and coffee spilled on both of their hands and Zanna's jeans. Zanna cursed under her breath and jumped up for a towel. Lydia walked to the bathroom to wash off her hands and found Zanna in the living room wiping up the spill. When she was finished, Lydia grabbed Zanna's shoulders and told her to sit down. She was surprised when Zanna hung her head and obliged. Lydia knelt in front of her and demanded to know what was going on.

Her heart ached as Zanna's words came out in a rush. "I think he slipped something in my drink. I didn't drink that much. I don't think I would have gone to bed with him on my own. I was going to be good last night because I felt strange getting drunk knowing I would see you today to work on the jewelry—"

Lydia interrupted her, "Wait. You think someone raped you? Zanna! We need to call the police!"

Zanna shook her head, wiped her nose on the back of her hand. "I can't prove it. I can't be sure. I just want to forget about it."

Lydia's jaw clenched as Zanna took a shuddering breath of resolve. "Zanna," Lydia grabbed the solemn woman's shoulders and, with more authority than she felt, said, "I don't know what has happened to you to make you feel so insignificant. To make you believe that a man slipping something in your drink so that he can take advantage of you while you are passed out is okay...but I'll tell you something. It stops now. If it takes all of my energy to show you how significant you are, how irreplaceable and special, then so be it."

Zanna stared at Lydia, stunned by the fire in her eyes.

"You've changed," she said.

Lydia's mouth curled upward slightly. "Yes, I have. Now it's your turn."

Lydia left soon after Zanna's confession. She sensed that Zanna needed some time to work through her feelings, so she promised to come back later to help sort the jewelry.

Feeling numb from the inside out, Zanna wandered into the kitchen to make more coffee, hoping to clear her head, or at least warm her stiff, cold limbs. She had spent many bitterly cold mornings shuffling around Gran's house, but that day she couldn't decide if the numbness was from winter leaking through the old windows or the chill that had grabbed her in the shower.

Zanna noticed the brown sack Lydia had left on the counter, unopened. She peered inside and found two large sticky buns from Cuppa—her favorite. Her belly warmed slightly as she imagined Lydia bringing them to her out of her newfound kindness. Zanna pulled out a china plate from the cupboard above the stove, smiling subconsciously as the door creaked. She loved the sounds of this kitchen. The creaks and groans reminded her of Gran bustling around to make Sunday dinner for Zanna's large extended family. As the sticky bun warmed in the microwave, Zanna wondered if the family still got together on Sundays. If so, who would ever be able to fill Gran's shoes as the hostess?

The roll was delicious; the rich caramel swirled with cinnamon and butter and browned pecans reminded Zanna of something her gran had made for her once. Her heart ached with the memory. What was it about the light she now saw in Lydia's eyes that reminded her of her grandmother?

The roll eaten, Zanna felt slightly better, but jittery and unfocused. *I need a smoke.*

As much as she tried to quit, there were times her limbs twitched in their ache for a cigarette. *Maybe if I have just one*, she thought, *I could clear my mind enough to untangle my memory of what happened last night.*

Before she could remind herself of all of her efforts to quit, Zanna pulled on her boots and wrapped her arms close around her as she pushed open the back door and walked down the stone path to the cottage in the large backyard.

The cottage was truly a shed that Granddad had built and insulated for Gran many years ago so that she could have a place to work on her lessons when she was a schoolteacher. Her grandmother had decorated the shed with a rug, couch, desk, and curtains for the windows Granddad had supplied. When Zanna was young, there had been low shelves inside full of books for her and her cousins. She had spent many sunny afternoons in that cottage, escaping into the worlds of *The Secret Garden, The Chronicles of Narnia, Little House on the Prairie,* and, as long as she didn't tell Mama and Papa, *Junie B. Jones* and *Ramona*.

Gran had anchored flower boxes outside and painted the door red. While time had taken its toll and family members had cleared most of the furniture away, one rocking chair still graced the small front porch that Granddad had built for Gran months before he died. Her desk still sat in the corner of the small space inside, covered in dust. Zanna hadn't brought herself to open the drawers yet to see if any of Gran's things had been left. Zanna used the coat rack Gran had left inside to hang up her "smoking jacket"—a heavy flannel coat—the only one she wore while smoking. She kept a beanie and gloves, as well as a lighter and cigarettes, in the front pockets. Somehow it felt appropriate to keep her smoking things outside in the cottage, out of Gran's house. Since Gran had been the only one that Zanna cared about disappointing, having to go into the cherished space served as a deterrent to smoking.

Usually.

She pulled on the coat and beanie, saving the gloves for after she lit the cigarette and puffed it awake. The rocking chair was cold and hard; it matched Zanna's mood. The roll that had so warmed her and reminded her of her grandmother now weighed her down. Her stomach rolled with thoughts of waking up in Gage's bed. Anger replaced her earlier shame. It hissed with each puff on the cigarette, glowing as hot as the cherry at the end.

How dare he? How dare that slimy, ugly, little weasel feel that he had any right whatsoever to touch her? He was nothing. Nobody. Completely insignificant. She should write it off as a pathetic guy just trying to fulfill his natural urges. Shouldn't she be flattered that he'd wanted her?

But she wasn't.

Years ago, maybe even months ago, this kind of thing wouldn't have bothered her. Why did it bother her so much now? Hadn't she told Lydia last fall that she liked a guy that was a little rough? Wasn't a rapist the epitome of rough?

Tears rolled from her eyes, freezing on her cheeks. She swiped at them, shifting her focus to the yard, seeing the overgrown lawn for what it had once been: a sanctuary for herself and her cousins, a magical playground full of happiness and light. Now it was cold and barren, but for the weeds that snarled beneath the snow, some peeking out to mock her memories of a better time. How often she had played and dreamt and laughed in this space. How many times had she sat beside Gran on this very porch, coloring while Gran served lemonade and told stories of her childhood? Zanna took a long draw on the cigarette, her eyes narrowing against the exhaled smoke, peering into a very different memory from a very different time…

"Zanna, my darling, do you think those tears will help?"

Gran's feet had stopped next to the table. Through wet eyes, nine-year-old Zanna thought the lacy-white tablecloth looked like a long apron against Gran's soft gray slacks. The tablecloth lifted and Gran's warm wrinkled face peered beneath the table where Zanna sat, knees drawn close with small, skinny arms wrapped around them. Zanna buried her face in her arms, ashamed of her discovered tears. Only babies cried.

Gran's small grunts brought wide eyes out of their hiding place, and Zanna's mouth fell slack as she watched her beloved Gran bend and contort herself to fit under the dining room table with Zanna. The young girl could hear the rest of the family in the next room—debating, always debating—and she could smell the Sunday afternoon coffee as it perked in the adjacent kitchen. Normally she loved Sundays at her Gran's home. Her father and his three siblings and their families would converge in the small house, spilling into every corner to talk and laugh and share the Sunday meal.

Her father's voice, as usual, was the loudest. She cringed at the authority his tone carried, even among his older siblings. And they all listened to him: the pastor, the holy one. The one who knew all things.

She winced. What would Papa say if he saw Gran crawling under this table with her? Would Zanna be punished later for this as well? Her stomach growled, and she locked eyes with Gran.

"Well, I'm in a real pickle, Zanna." The older woman had such a smooth, deep voice. Zanna often leaned in against her chest while she talked, just to feel the vibrations of that velvet voice. Here, under the table, Gran's words reverberated around her, pulling Zanna close.

"You see, I made sticky buns for dessert because I knew they were your favorite."

Zanna cringed, her throat burned in shame.

"Want to talk about it?" her grandmother asked.

"Gran, I just—I didn't mean to. I wasn't trying to embarrass Papa or be disrespectful…"

"I know, child." A soft hand on her head, so warm.

She drank in the fragrance of it: cinnamon. Her Gran always smelled of cinnamon.

"I know you didn't mean it. And your Papa doesn't mean to be so harsh." Gran's tone was cloaked in sepia, the color of memories. "When he was little, oh my, the looks I would give him in church! He was a wild one, for sure."

Zanna's throat scratched out a scoff. *Right.*

"No, it's true. And his antics were not such things as a growling tummy. No, he would pull girls' hair. Or he would kick the pew in front of us—right where the pastor's wife sat—

hard. Even belch right in the middle of a prayer, if you can believe it."

Zanna's eyes peeked up from behind her arms, wide, unbelieving. Hoping. If Papa were like that as a young child, surely her growling stomach would be something he could forgive?

Pain sliced through her chest as she remembered how he glared at her from the pulpit that morning as her siblings snickered around her. She hadn't meant to skip breakfast, had been trying to help her mother get her younger sister ready. Mama was sick, much sicker than she'd been with her previous pregnancies, and Zanna knew she needed to help. She hadn't meant to skip a meal and cause a scene in church. She knew how her father hated to be embarrassed. He'd been stony on the ride home, pulled her aside on the porch when Gran opened the door to them.

Gran had welcomed her mother and siblings, flashed a curious smile at Zanna, before she sent a sidelong glance to Papa and shut the door. Papa's hand was heavy on her shoulder, his eyes hard, unforgiving.

"You know better, Zanna—"

"Papa, I..." Her lips trembled, and she clamped them shut at the firm set of his mouth.

"You know better," he repeated. "Scripture says, 'God is not mocked; for whatever a man sows, this he will also reap.' As such, I am ashamed of your mockery during the sermon. You are not welcome to eat with us. Sit in the front room until we are finished."

Her tall broad shouldered Papa disappeared from her blurry sight, into the house. Her stomach cramped with pain as she sat on the couch, fighting her tears. When her cousins and siblings came to tease her with their tales of buttered rolls and roast beef, she sought solitude under the table.

Gran's eyes softened on her, as they always did. Zanna couldn't imagine how this woman mothered her angry Papa. Where she was gentle, he was harsh. Where she sympathized, he took offense. Where Gran emanated grace and love, warmth and laughter, Zanna's father was sullen, serious, cold, and utterly vengeful. Except to his congregation. There, in the presence of people that looked to him for spiritual guidance, his charm dripped like honey. Where Gran was sincere, her father was deceitful.

And where Gran worked as a teacher for the poorest section of town, Papa's one dream was to pastor the largest—and richest—church in the state.

Gran stroked Zanna's hair once more. "Your father is under a lot of stress. It's hard to be pastor and have everyone judge every move you and your children make. Give him time. Soon he'll find his groove and remember that it's only what the Lord thinks that matters."

Zanna's back stiffened. The Lord her Gran talked about and the God her Papa preached of were completely different, as different as the mother and son.

"Oh, child"—Gran gently reached out to lift her chin in her soft hand— "when you feel that bitterness creep in—the kind that puts rods in your back and doubt in your heart—you pray. You pray your heart out."

Zanna broke down then, reaching out to the kindest woman she knew, whispering her anger and hurt in the sacred space of her Gran's arms, beneath the worn kitchen table. When her sobs finally subsided and Gran left her alone, she wiped her face off, willing her cheeks to not be splotchy and red when her father came looking for her. Her stomach growled again, loud and long, and Zanna pulled her legs in close. The tablecloth lifted again, and this time a plate that held a large sticky bun was passed to her.

Grateful, but afraid, Zanna held the plate in her lap for just a moment before hunger won out over fear.

When her father came in, she nearly choked on the third bite of the gooey, warm roll.

"Mother, have you seen Zanna?" His voice was condemning in even the simplest question.

Zanna forced the bite down past the fear that ached in her throat; fear that he would catch her with the forbidden food.

I won't be able to sit down for a week, she thought with a quiver in her belly.

The Heavens Are Telling

"Oh, she's around here somewhere."

Zanna heard dishes being stacked before the kitchen faucet squeaked on. "Dear, would you hand me that stack of bowls?"

More clattering.

"I need to have a serious talk with that girl."

"Why?"

Zanna held her breath at Gran's forward question. She'd never heard anyone question Papa. Ever. Gran's tone held a warning, a challenge.

The water turned off.

"I'm the pastor, Mother. If I don't set an example of righteousness and piety, who will?"

Water gurgled and Zanna imagined the way her Gran would dip a dish in soapy water twice after she'd scrubbed it, before she set it aside to rinse.

"So set that example for your daughter. Show her that grace and love you forget so often to preach about."

"Mother, we serve a righteous—"

Gran interrupted him, "Son, I'm not sure which Bible you're preaching from, but mine says a lot of things about cherishing children and fathers not aggravating their children."

"And what about honoring thy—"

"And I see absolutely nothing..."

The gurgling stopped and Zanna could see Gran's feet rotate toward where Papa stood.

Her voice, that velvety voice, spoke straight and sure. "...*Nothing*, about a child working herself to death to help raise her younger siblings. Nothing about spending so much time on appearances and fancy sermons that a father forgets—or outright ignores—the physical needs of his child. Nothing whatsoever about a young girl being so committed to helping her parents that she misses out on breakfast, is forced to sit through a two hour service while her siblings poke fun at her and her mother pinches her arm as a result, and on top of that, is denied lunch with her family. I see nothing about that in that book you carry around like a hammer instead of the loving Word of God that it is."

An hour later, when they were home and Zanna's bottom was on fire from her father's "rod of discipline" she did her best to pray against the bitterness as Gran had told her to.

But instead, she screamed and raged in her head at a God she had begun to doubt even existed.

Chapter Twenty-Nine

Cambodia

There came a few days where there were no check-ins, as they began to call them, only hours of pensive waiting that grated on everyone's nerves. They waited in a town with no *wat*, and Vireak was relieved to share a room with Simon and let up on the pretense in the evenings. But the children's faces haunted his dreams. Though he didn't know them, he felt knitted to them. Each in the party was desperate for a sign that the children were okay, an assurance that they would get to them in time. Simon almost let the days pass hunkered down in a motel waiting for instructions, but on a whim, he suggested they hike a little.

"Do you think that's all right, Vireak?" Simon checked with the man, who grew more pale and drawn as time dragged on. Simon knew he was ready to shed the orange robe and search out the things of God, but that he felt the weight of Maly and Noah's lives on his shoulders. Without him and his connections, they would be lost.

Vireak thought for a moment, eyes on the sun shining beyond the dingy window in the corner of their shared motel room. "Simon, I think that would be a great help to all of us."

The women were reluctant to leave the safety of the motel. The men assured them that if they were being watched, it would look suspicious that they were hiding out in their motel. After more prodding, the women relented, and the group finally ventured out. Simon, map in his pocket, led them away from the motel and through the quiet streets of a sleepy town.

"Where are we?" Jakobi asked Chaya as they trailed behind the men. Through scattered buildings and hotels on one side of the street, she could see water—the ocean maybe—shimmering, dancing in carefree abandon beneath the sun. Impressive mangrove-covered mountains loomed on the other side of the town, curving around the community. Jakobi couldn't decide if she felt tucked in cozily against the water or cornered by the massive mountains.

"*Krong Hoh Krong*," Simon turned to face the women, walking backwards and answering when Chaya merely shrugged. He jutted his chin toward the mountains. "Those are the Cardamom Mountains." He swept a hand opposite of the peaks to the water. "That's the far side of the peninsula on the west bank of the *Koh Poi* River, or so they told me at the front desk."

Chaya blushed when she caught Vireak's eyes on her face, embarrassed to be so ignorant of her own country. The only reason she had been able to get a job teaching was because of the lack of English speakers in her area and the generosity of the Peace Corps. Vireak had studied geography, math, English, science, philosophy, and many other subjects she could only dream of. What must he think of her lack of knowledge? For years she envisioned and prayed for the day that Vireak would remember the faith of his youth, when he would remember her and walk away from his life as a monk. Dreams had become reality, in part, and now she wondered what she could possibly say that would be of any interest to him.

The sun and air and firm ground beneath their feet were good for the anxious travelers. They chose to have lunch at a French café in the center of the town.

Jakobi still could not adjust to the vision of French cuisine and architecture in such an exotic place. Temples and silk, curry and rice, did not mix with croissants and romantic storybook beams and arches, at least not in her mind. It was at the same time charming and confusing. But the warm, flaky bread and sharp cheese was satisfying; the ice cream refreshing.

"We should go back to that place for coffee before we leave tomorrow; if we leave tomorrow," Jakobi commented as they left. Her face burned with shame immediately after the words left her mouth. Simon watched as she rounded her eyes at him and covered her flushed cheeks with her hands. *How could she think of something as insignificant as coffee at a time like this?*

He gently took one of her hands and interlaced his fingers with hers. "You're only human, Jakobi." His tone was kind, understanding.

They found there were plenty of trails to hike, resounding with the calls and songs of wildlife all around them, high in the trees. They stepped over the complicated web of roots and branches of the trees lowest on the hills before the mountains. Jakobi allowed Simon to help her across, then watched as he hopped back on a high branch to reach a hand to Chaya.

Vireak watched, his eyes betraying the restraints of his position as Chaya clambered up with Simon's help. Vireak made the trek effortlessly, and Jakobi focused on the intricate tangles of the roots, fascinated by the way the trees seemed to have fingers that spread out to grab hold of the earth to anchor them in the ground when water rose around them.

As if they were designed for this climate. She rubbed the back of her neck, pushing aside the thought.

Waterfalls that must be impressive in the wet season trickled down the mountain, lazy and underwhelming in their off-season descent. Simon led the group in and out of tangles of mangrove trees and back down to the empty, wind-swept beach. Shells scattered the chunky sand and Jakobi leaned down to finger a few before dropping them back to the ground. Simon walked alongside Jakobi; Chaya trailed behind. Vireak sat alone near the water, contemplative as always.

Simon reached for Jakobi's hand. "We missed Christmas day, Miss McNamara; did you realize that?" Simon watched the water lap at the beach.

Jakobi's lips parted slightly, surprised. "I didn't even think of it," she answered.

"I almost didn't say anything," Simon admitted. "What does Christmas matter to a woman that anchors herself in evolution, or to a Khmer Christian or a questioning monk?" He worked a muscle in his jaw.

"I still celebrate Christmas, Simon," Jakobi whispered. *Did he think she didn't believe in anything?*

Simon tipped his mouth sardonically. "I'm sorry. I didn't mean to imply that it doesn't matter to you. I should have said: what does Christmas matter when we're trailed along by thieves and kidnappers in hopes that we can make the right moves, pay the right amount of money to rescue two beautiful children, knowing there are probably countless more in need of help?"

Jakobi stopped and turned to face Simon, her eyes searching his. "Are you afraid, Simon?" If he was, she didn't think she could hold herself together.

Simon let go of her hand and looked out to the water again. "The Bible says that the Lord has drawn a line in the sand." Simon crouched low and swept his finger across the sand, leaving a streak in its wake. "The ocean—the waters cannot cross it without His permission."

Jakobi didn't know what to say. She stared at the mark in the sand.

"I'm a man that has to be on the move, Jakobi. I'm a man created to fight and rescue. An adventurer. A provider." He worked his jaw again. "I want to race into every *wat* we stop in and squeeze every neck I can get my hands on until they tell me where those babies are. Every ounce of self-control is exercised when I drive on to the next place with empty hands. I'm frustrated. I'm agitated. I'm tired of *their* way, and I'm ready for things to be done *my* way."

Jakobi made a noise in her throat, brows raised. "Get in line, Simon."

He stood and turned to face her, his hands on her arms. "But hear me, Jakobi, when I say that no, I am not afraid. Whether you believe it or not, those babies, you, Vireak, Chaya, and I are in the capable hands of a God that created these waters and told them how far they can roll. How close they can come."

The Heavens Are Telling

He marched into the waves and scooped water into his hand, clenching his fist as water rolled down his arm. He repeated his bend and scoop and squeeze gesture again. "I can't hold this water, Jakobi, can you?"

She shook her head, confused.

"Try it," Simon demanded.

She wrinkled her brows at him, glanced around to see if anyone was watching his erratic behavior.

"Try it," he ordered again.

"Simon—"

Simon grabbed her hand and led her to the water, pulled her hand down to the waves. "Try it, Jakobi." He spoke as one would to a child that refused to see something important in a lesson.

Annoyed, Jakobi bent at the waist and grabbed a handful of water that, of course, escaped through her closed fingers. "There, Simon." She wiped her now wet hand against her jeans. "Happy?"

"Can you hold the water, Jakobi? Can anyone?"

"No." Jakobi rolled her eyes, wondering what had gotten into him.

He straightened and looked at her with pity. "Right. Except He who made the water and can tell it to come no further." He spread his hands looking at the wavy line of frothy water that licked at the sand, back and forth, back and forth. "What is stopping it from spilling over?"

Simon shoved his hands in his pockets, his tone flat. "How dare I doubt, for even a minute, that those most precious souls belong to Him?"

He moved down the beach, away from Jakobi and the rest and sat on the sand, legs bent up, elbows rested on his knees, his face reflective, similar to Vireak's quiet mood just yards away on the beach.

Jakobi walked the shoreline, bewildered. Again, she bent over, fingering shells. Some swirled around nothing, empty and polished inside, others fanned out, patterns of lines and grooves splayed across the face. Each unique. She fingered a shell curved in on itself like a cinnamon roll, a perfect home for a large snail or crab; iridescent inside, like the face of a pearl. She rubbed a hand along the bumpy surface, tracing the perfectly spaced grooves that swirled red and white together.

She remembered her days as a young woman; she had once been a girl that fully believed in the God of the Bible. Could Simon be right? Every time he spoke of God, she felt her soul soar. Unlike the terrible, choking faith of her parents, the one that said to be a good Christian woman she must stay at home, quiet and obedient, Simon showed her a mighty God that could use her in whatever way He saw fit. To serve in foreign countries. To chase after trafficked children.

For the first time in her adult life, she even thought that if God called a woman to stay home, it wasn't a weak or pitiful position if it was one assigned by Him. She watched the waves, thinking of what Simon had said. Was it true that science could be a way to know God better and not a sign that He didn't exist? Jakobi pocketed the shell and turned back.

Eventually, one by one, the group gathered around Simon, Jakobi was the last one to sit down. There was no pomp or ceremony when he pulled out his Bible and began to read the account of Christ's birth in the gospels from the small Bible he carried in the pocket of his cargo pants, just a steady voice and the soft crinkle of pages rustling in the breeze. But the rhythm of the words as Simon read aloud was enchanting to Jakobi in a way that felt both familiar and terrifying. When Simon was finished, Vireak thanked him.

"My father often recited Scripture," Vireak told Simon and the women. "I used to think there was evil at work in those words. They've haunted me, tormented me all of these years in the *wat*. I would try to meditate on things I was learning, and most of the time, I've been able to. But sometimes..." Vireak stared into the horizon where the afternoon sun crept closer to the edge of the earth. "Sometimes I just couldn't ignore those words spoken over me so many years ago. There is life in those words; they don't die. Now I understand that they are blessed and not cursed."

Simon held his Bible in both hands, working his hands back and forth to bend and release the leather-bound cover. "You're right, Vireak. Hebrews says, 'For the Word of God is living and active and sharper than any two-edged sword, and piercing as far as the division of soul and spirit, of both joints and marrow, and able to judge the thoughts and intentions of the heart.' Even more, the world was created by the Word of God. He spoke, and galaxies were set on their foundations. He breathed, and life was brought to man. He shaped and formed trees, not just their mighty branches and roots and leaves, but with a word He created photosynthesis, oxygen, carbon dioxide, pollen, sap; His words carved out rocks and their layers, caves, mountains, cliffs; the depths of the oceans, creatures—some we're only just discovering—more beautiful and colorful than any paint a person could mix. His words spoke life. His words *speak* life.

"Palaces and the Egyptian pyramids and temples of old, fade and crumble, but the world the Lord has spoken into existence still stands on its axis, spinning just as it was designed to. Abraham is spoken of in the Bible as a man who 'believed God, who gives life to the dead and calls into being that which does not exist.' God created everything, in one breath, out of nothing."

Simon's passionate torrent slowed, but his words still came steady and sure. "God says, 'For as the rain and snow come down from heaven, and do not return there without watering the earth and making it bear and sprout, and furnishing seed to the sower and bread to the eater, so will My word be which goes forth from My mouth; it will not return to me empty, without accomplishing what I desire, and without succeeding in the matter for which I sent it.' Your father was wise to cover you in the words of God, Vireak."

Without shame, tears streaked Vireak's face. To hear the word of God again was a balm after the years of it echoing and resounding in his heart and mind, ricocheting in the confused recesses of his young mind. As Simon spoke, the words rooted themselves further into Vireak's heart and he remembered.

Oh, how he remembered the Way of Salvation, and of Jesus Christ, who offers hope to the sinner.

Vireak trembled in the shame and guilt of his sin. "Simon, I fear that my soul has become frozen from years of neglect and misuse. What can grow from my heart but thistles and thorns?"

Simon clapped a hand on Vireak's shoulder. "In the winter snow piles up, seemingly useless on frozen earth. It's when the soil thaws that the snow melts and soaks in, working its purpose. Don't lose heart, Vireak. The Word of God has been heaped upon you, but it is not dead. You are just beginning to thaw. The crop will come."

Jakobi felt tears welling in her eyes, her heart responding to the hope in those words for the first time in years.

Chapter Thirty

They left the beach before sunset and shared dinner together at Le Phnom, a restaurant with authentic Cambodian cuisine. Chaya ordered *Banh Chev*, assuring Jakobi that she would "know how to eat it." Jakobi suppressed a smile when the dishes were brought out; a bowl of sautéed shrimp, followed by sliced scallions, mushrooms, sweet peppers, and bean sprouts, arranged artfully on shared platters. A plate of savory pancakes was passed around the table, followed by a plate with lettuce leaves. The smiling waitress bowed slightly before she left Chaya and Vireak to explain the meal: fillings of choice rolled up in the pancake, pancake rolled up in the lettuce leaf and the completed combination dipped in a sweet and sour sauce.

Jakobi breathed in the delicious spices and smells, her mouth watering. She tucked into the meal, enjoying the delicate balance of savory and sweet that the chef had mastered, trying to forget the afternoon and recharge for whatever awaited them in the days to come.

Chaya and Vireak, however, excitedly pelted Simon with questions, their appetites whet after his sermon on the beach. Jakobi suppressed a groan. Simon had a scripture answer for everything. She felt tormented by her thoughts on the beach, yet felt as anxious as the others to hear the words Simon spoke.

Simon noticed a change in her, but left Jakobi to her thoughts.

When dinner was finished and they walked back to the motel, Simon accompanied the women to their room. He bid Chaya goodnight, thankful when Jakobi hung back. Vireak walked on to the room he shared with Simon. The door clicked closed and Simon reached for Jakobi's hand.

"Walk with me," he urged.

"Walk where?" Jakobi asked, looking pointedly down the narrow hall.

"I have somewhere in mind." Simon led Jakobi back through town. Where it had been busy during the day, it was eerily empty as they crept through with only the starlight to guide them.

Simon turned toward the water between two buildings that looked like they were yearning to lean into one another for support.

"Simon, where on earth—?" Jakobi's whisper fell short as he pulled her alongside him. At their feet, a staircase carved into a low cliff that wound down to the water, and ended with a rock platform that jutted out toward the waves. Small lamplights were strung across the stone railing, illuminating the path.

"I saw this place earlier and wondered what it would be like at night." Simon breathed into her ear. Jakobi let go of his hand and took two slow steps down toward the water. She placed a hand on the railing and closed her eyes, listening to the waves crash against the rocks at the bottom of the stairs.

Simon followed and stood next to her, waiting.

His presence filled the small space on the step. The scent of ocean air on his skin revived something inside of her. No, his words on the beach had. Something that she had suppressed years ago came alive inside of her spirit.

She felt his nose brush against her ear, her stomach quivered with anticipation at his nearness. The atmosphere was intoxicatingly peaceful. Jakobi drank in the sight, breathed in Simon's scent and relished the feel of his nearness. She took deep breaths, unsure why his comments and scriptures spoken through the day had rattled her. *Why can't I get past those verses?*

All evening she had wrestled with memories. Memories of prayers she had said as a child, songs she had sung worshipfully at church camp. Words and moments, that at one time, she had seen as sacred and special, but that had simply become memories of religious hype during her college years, poured over her. Like the waves below them, the thoughts came, crashing against her resolve, breaking down her arguments. Squashing her so-called logic.

Verse after verse beat against the stone that encased her heart, washing away the rubble. She turned to face Simon, who looked over her head to the ocean; the lamplight peeked over her shoulder to illuminate his face. She watched him for a long time, thinking of the man he had proven himself to be.

Simon was full of life in a way she had never seen before. She had known and been friends with plenty of men that were loud and full of life. But none had been like Simon with his sure and steady demeanor. He exuded joy, even in the midst of their grief and anxiety over the children.

She remembered when he shared his life story with her on the small island near Pursat. His life had been surprisingly bland:

"I was the second son of four boys born to my parents. Dad eventually got bored and left; mom raised us alone. Nothing out of the norm there. I've always been a little off, I guess. My brothers were really into sports; I was into education. I've been a voracious reader for as long as I can remember. And always interested in religion. And music. I remember summers that I would beg the neighbors to take me to Vacation Bible School. I eventually grew out of that and into girls. And I've shared the rest."

So dull and yet so remarkable. This unpretentious man had surrendered all comforts of home and normality to work as a grounds keeper for a place that rescued children from sexual slavery. Even more, he had left there to live alone in a strange village to keep watch over two kids that may or may not have been in trouble. And now he abandoned everything again to follow the directions of the very people and activity he fought against in Thailand to give those same children a chance at life.

Jakobi sucked in her top lip and continued to stare at him. Simon felt her gaze and turned to meet it.

"Simon, I don't..."—her shoulders rose slightly—"I don't know how to say this without it sounding like a wishy-washy woman."

He cocked a brow at her. "Okay."

"I believe it." There, she said it.

Simon stared at her. Jakobi stared back.

"Okaaay." Simon repeated, his chin raised and mouth set in confusion.

Jakobi looked around them, flabbergasted. How else could she explain it? She pointed at the stars. "Those? Your belief in their Maker? I believe that, too."

Simon reeled back as if he'd been slapped. He watched her, uncertain.

"It's not a new thing, Simon. For weeks you've reminded me of things from my childhood. Things I once learned and believed with all of my heart. Things I've walked away from since then." She shook her head, throat tight, and bit her lip.

Simon's heart turned over in his chest as he watched her eyes grow moist. The tears on her lids caught the starlight, but the rest of her face remained mostly in shadow. He cupped her cheek with his hand. "Jakobi," he whispered.

"I don't know why I argued with you so strongly; I don't know why I embraced something so different for so many years." She wiped her nose on her sleeve. "And I don't know why I'm so desperate for Him now. I still think my parents should have given me more opportunities for critical thinking; opportunities to grow faith and trust on my own instead of shielding me from any confrontation at all. But that's not the point." She brought her hand up to hold Simon's against her cheek. She closed her eyes. "I don't want you to think this is a way to get to you because I'm attracted to you. It's just..."

Simon waited, a smile stretched across his face. A smile Jakobi didn't see.

"It's like you told Vireak about the frozen ground in the winter. Only for me, it's like a lake. The surface of my heart is frozen over, but the water is moving just beneath the surface, waiting for the thaw. Does that make sense?"

Simon brought his other hand up to cup her face. He leaned his forehead against hers and took a deep breath. "Yes, Jakobi, it makes sense. You are His, aren't you?"

She leaned into him, her eyes closed, and nodded. "I'm ashamed of how long I've pushed Him away, and I don't exactly know where to go from here. I was walking on the beach today, looking over shells. When my mom was little she took me to the beach and told me to hunt for seashells. I brought her handfuls. She told me the Word of God was like that: a treasure to be sought after and cherished; a treasure that I should never tire of finding. On the beach today, did you notice that you couldn't take one step without stepping on a shell? That and all of your talk about the heavens proclaiming the glory of the Lord...I just sat there as you read the Bible and thought, 'Yes, Lord. Yes!' Over and over."

Simon pulled her to him, his arms locked behind her back, his cheek resting on her head as her arms came up to encircle his waist. They stood that way; two people that had immediately connected and now shared a mutual faith.

Jakobi, embarrassed about her tears and confession, laughed into the crook of his neck. "This is all your fault. All that talk and those verses. You knew just what you were doing, piling snow on a frozen heart."

Simon chuckled as he pulled back to look into her eyes. He wiped a finger across her cheek, catching a stray tear. "Jakobi?"

"Hmmm...?" She looked up at him, heart full to bursting.

He caught her chin in his hand. "What I'm about to do has everything to do with what you just said, and has been on my mind since the first day I met you." His eyes dropped to her mouth as he leaned down and gently brushed his lips against hers. She pressed into him, her lips full on his, absorbing his warmth. The waves crashed their approval below.

Simon deepend his kiss for a brief, intoxicating moment, then pulled away and pressed his lips to her forehead. "Now, my friend, we can pray together—fight for these kids together—in a way we haven't been able to until now."

"Simon," she whispered, leaning back to look at the rocks where the waves crashed against the platform at the bottom of the stairs, "what if we don't get them?"

"We will, Jakobi. We will."

She kissed his chin and leaned back to look at him, embarrassed. "Simon, I have one more thing I need to do. Will you wait for me?"

Simon agreed, confused when she pulled away from him and walked down the stairs to the platform that jutted out over the water. He crossed his arms and leaned against the railing, smiling and praising God when he heard her soft voice rise in a love song for her Savior.

"She's returned to You, God." Simon closed his eyes, absorbing the sweet sound of her voice against the crashing waves.

※ ※ ※

The next day they were contacted and sent to another town, another *wat*, another agonizing wait. Vireak began to dread his nights at the *wat*. There were times that he had to be in service for a few days. He sat in the streets in the mornings to collect his offerings of money and breakfast and rose early to chant with the other monks. He struggled to fit in with his old life, while reserving his heart for the Lord. Through morning chants, Vireak would whisper the Scriptures he could remember under his breath, closing his ears to the lyrical mantra that vibrated around him.

"There is such oppression there," he told the rest as they drove away from a *wat* one afternoon.

They made it a priority during their private times together to read Scripture aloud, memorizing passages together. When Vireak entered a *wat*, Simon, Jakobi, and Chaya would check into a motel nearby and take shifts praying for him all night until they met with him again.

He grew stronger and his anxiety decreased over the weeks. But the routine was taxing.

Jakobi worried over Maly and Noah each morning when they awoke. Were they being cared for? Fed? Protected from the abuse Vireak alluded to? *Lord, watch over them. Oh, Powerful, Watchful God, put a hedge of protection around them. Please, let this next stop produce them.*

She knew she didn't have much longer before the Peace Corps became suspicious of her departure and would notify the authorities, or at the very least, her family. Her Visa wouldn't be valid if she didn't renew it soon. She wondered if she should contact the Peace Corps and get professional help. Clearly this method wasn't working.

One morning, Chaya and Jakobi waited while Simon went to get Vireak from the *wat*. They were challenging one another to memorize Philippians and they sat together while Jakobi could help Chaya read through the English Bible. The men returned and Jakobi felt the shift in their moods. Simon was practically jumping out of his skin.

"What's going on?" Jakobi asked, setting Simon's Bible down.

Simon strode across the room and kissed her soundly on the mouth. "They want us to come to the next place. We're going to get the kids this time!"

Chapter Thirty-One

Thailand

Nataya crumbled in frustration, her head hitting the table in front of her with a loud thud. The dress she'd been trying to sew was in a haphazard mess, tossed to the floor.

"I will never get this right!" Her muffled voice carried across the room to Susanna, a volunteer from Gerogia that taught a sewing class each week. Susanna had a bright, dimpled smile, her teeth pearly white against smooth, ebony skin. Her tone was sweet but no-nonsense, and there was a cadence to her words that was sometimes hard to understand as Nataya struggled with the English language. Susanna was Nataya's favorite teacher, and she hated to disappoint her.

"All right, girl, what's going on over here?" Susanna patted Nataya's back.

Nataya turned her tear-streaked face toward Susanna. "I'm not good at this, Susanna. I can't do this." Her face scrunched closed again. "How will I ever take care of a baby if I can't even sew?" Her hands flew up to cover her face, embarrassed at her outburst, seemingly helpless to stop it.

Supressing a smile, Susanna sucked the insides of her cheeks and cleared her throat before she squatted next to Nataya, ignoring the curious glances of the other girls.

Susanna had been teaching a sewing class and an English class for the last year in Thailand. She mostly worked with the expectant girls because she had a strong and reassuring nature that gave the girls both comfort and bravery. She had experienced numerous meltdowns and had come to learn who had talent and who didn't, who was just tired and who needed to be directed elsewhere.

"Nataya, how are you sleeping lately?"

Nataya sniffed, thinking of her nightly trips to the bathroom, the leg cramps that shot her out of bed, her inability to find a comfortable position. She rubbed her eyes with her palms. "Well...not too good."

Susanna nodded. "Nataya, there is nothing that says you have to be a seamstress; this is one of many vocations we can teach you to earn a living when the time comes. But remember that you have years of school to finish, plenty of time to learn something—anything—you want to learn." Susanna made sure she had Nataya's attention. "But I see a real talent in you. This is a difficult technique that you're learning this week, one that not many pick up right away. Be patient with yourself. There is no rush."

Nataya dropped her hands, frustrated, unfamiliar with her raging emotions. "But, Susanna, I have a baby to care for. I can't rely on Deliverance forever."

Susanna's brows raised. "You're right," she said, not unkindly, but bluntly. "You can't. But you *can* take all the time you need. We want you to succeed and that takes time, Nataya. You are excelling in classes, racing through lessons. You make more jewelry in the afternoons than anyone else; you are a natural in all of your childcare classes; you rarely take a break. Slow down, girl."

Nataya took a deep breath. "But what if no one wants to sponsor me? Who wants to sponsor a pregnant girl?" Nataya fingered the fabric, her hands unable to rest anywhere but her belly.

Susanna leaned her head back as understanding dawned. "Ah."

Sponsorship was a precious thing among the rescues. Two of the older girls in class had been able to meet their sponsors when they came through on a mission trip. The elated teens had been gushing for days and while the rest loved to share in joy with one another, Susanna could see the tension in Nataya's face.

Nataya sniffed, her downcast eyes reflecting her misery.

Susanna cupped Nataya's chin in her slender hand. "Honey, a sponsor will come, you have to believe that. In God's timing, just the right person will come along."

Nataya didn't look convinced.

"Nataya, your baby will be supported either way. The Lord Himself has made this child and will provide for him or her. But, I tell you what, why don't you prepare for a sponsor?"

Nataya scrunched her face at Susanna, confused.

"In faith that God loves you and plans to care for you, as He's already done, why don't you write a letter to your sponsor?"

"But I don't have—"

Susanna placed a finger over Nataya's lips. "Believing that you will get one, write a letter and have it waiting. You can tell your future sponsor why you want to keep your baby and how grateful you are for their support. Then put the letter in an envelope and keep it under your pillow. Pray for your sponsor, that God would show them the love He has shown you, that they will be blessed for their care of you. In faith, Nataya, be prepared to respond when you do have one. Then, when one comes through, you'll be ready to send off the letter thanking them for their care of you and this little one."

"You think that's okay?" Nataya asked, instantly relieved.

"Of course."

Nataya giggled with relief, still so much a young child herself. Susanna gave her a light squeeze around the neck and helped to pick up the dress that had been discarded on the floor.

Lord, I know you have great plans for these girls, I pray You would hold all of their fears and anxieties in Your great hands and let them relish their freedom.

Susanna winked at Nataya and went back to instructing the girls in different sewing techniques, careful to pay close attention to each one, to let them see in her eyes and manner how very special they were.

Chapter Thirty-Two

Boise, Idaho

Zanna finished the cigarette, her heart heavy, soul aching. Her memories threatened to overtake her and she did her best to keep from allowing them to go deeper, where the darkest ones were kept.

The ones that changed everything.

She wanted to hold onto the warmth of her gran, without the shadow her father cast on everything. Lydia had said she would be back and, where earlier Zanna had wanted to be alone, now she anxiously waited for Lydia to return. Lydia—who was now so much like her gran.

Gran.

Zanna could not stop thinking about her. What was this yawning ache to be close to her? Zanna had been in Gran's home for almost a year now and had indeed had moments of missing her, but today was vastly different. The encounter with Gage had rattled her, reminded her of times best left forgotten, times when she so desperately needed her. How would her life be different if she had called her gran that night so many years ago?

Zanna snuffed the cherry out of the cigarette and tossed it into the coffee can she kept on the small porch before she stormed back into the cottage, eyes trained on Gran's desk. She reached out to open the top drawer, but pulled back, biting her lip.

"Screw it."

Before she could change her mind, Zanna yanked the drawer open. Her heart sank: old pens, a box of paperclips, a yellowed stack of blank paper. Where seconds before Zanna was hesitant, now she was desperate and ripped through the remaining drawers. Hope shattered as she found one empty drawer after another. Furious, she reached for the skinny pencil drawer, pulling so hard that it flung out from the desk frame and clattered to the floor. A small leather-bound journal flew out of the drawer and landed with a *thud* across the room. Zanna sank to her knees and her hands flew to cover her lips. They opened and closed—silent gasps of disbelief made her chest rise and fall.

Slowly, she shuffled to the journal—desperate, hoping. With shaking hands, she picked it up and slowly unraveled the two strips of leather that wrapped around and loosely knotted over the front cover. The thin pages crackled as Zanna opened to the middle. Pages covered in scribbles of blue and black and red stared back at her. The words and colors swirled together, blurring.

Zanna's heart quivered—not a journal, but a small Bible with Gran's handwriting all over it. Her shoulders shook with mingled tears of frustration and gratitude. She could filter through the scriptures for the treasure of her gran's words, she was sure.

"Zanna!" Lydia called in the distance.

Zanna choked on her sobs, startled. She quickly rose from the floor and placed the pencil drawer back in the desk. She tucked Gran's Bible under her arm and exited the cottage as Lydia and her sister Charlotte came through the side gate to knock on the laundry room door.

"Here I am." Zanna forced a cough to clear the tremble in her voice.

"Hi, Charlotte," she added, looking askance at Lydia. Great. *So you decided to tell your sister all about my night. Lovely.*

Charlotte smiled and returned the greeting. She held up a small box in her hands. "Lydia told me you two were sorting through jewelry today. I had some to contribute and thought it would be nice to spend some time with adults."

Lydia, looking sheepish, added, "We ordered pizza. Hope that's okay."

Zanna shrugged. What was she going to do now, kick them out? A few months ago she might have. But the changes in Lydia had rattled her. Intrigued her. Shamed her. The fire that used to mock Lydia for her boyfriend problems, the one that gave her the guts to smoke weed in the back room of the store with a high school boy…that fire had gone out. And after her encounter with Gage, she wondered if she would ever be warm inside again.

Zanna led the way inside, and the women gathered in the front room. Zanna opened the trunk in front of the couch and pulled out a few floor pillows to sit on, and jewelry and inventory sheets soon surrounded the three. Despite her dark mood, Zanna found herself intrigued and enchanted by the bantering between sisters. They shared stories of their past as people usually did in mismatched groups. When the conversation turned to Bible studies and some retreat for the women at their church, Zanna mostly tuned them out. When Charlotte went to her car to retrieve a tub of material for a fundraising idea she had, Lydia leaned back with her hands behind her on the floor and tilted her head at Zanna.

"You okay?"

"Why? Are you going to tell your sister if I'm not?" She hadn't meant to be so sharp.

Lydia winced, and blinked open one eye, the other scrunched to match her lips. "Hey, I just care. I want to help you. I wanted her advice."

Zanna felt the blood drain from her face as realization dawned on her. "Wait. The men in your family are cops. Did you guys tell them?" Her voice raised an octave as panic snaked through her.

Lydia reached to touch her shoulder. "No, I promise. I didn't tell my dad at all. I only asked Charlotte what she thought, and she won't tell Sam unless you ask her to. Legally, nothing can be done unless you personally bring charges against him."

Zanna fingered a red and black beaded necklace. "So, what did she say?"

Charlotte's voice broke through, startling Zanna. "I told her that we needed to love on you and take extra care, showing you that you are valuable."

Embarrassed and offended for reasons she didn't understand, Zanna straightened her shoulders. "Well, maybe I do value myself. I'm a believer in women. I know the power I possess. Maybe I am just not so sure that he raped me, and I don't want to cause a big fuss for nothing."

She looked Charlotte in the eye, hoping to shock her off of the subject. "It's not the first time I've woken in bed with a man, not remembering the night before." She forced a laugh and, with a wink toward Lydia, added, "And hopefully it won't be the last."

The statement fell flat, and instead of blushing or turning away, Charlotte met her stare with an expression of sorrow...and pity.

Where Zanna had felt offended just minutes before, now she felt shame that she hadn't in years. Not since that day she walked through a line of people that spat on her as she walked by, scared, hurting; broken. Resolved. *Defiant.*

The doorbell rang, breaking the awkward moment. Charlotte went back out to pay for the pizza, and they changed the subject as they enjoyed the tantalizing cheese and vegetable combo over garlic cream sauce from Idaho Pizza Co.

"Mom and Dad had this pizza the first night I came home from Cambodia," Charlotte reminisced. "I know I wasn't there for long, but after days of mostly rice, pizza was good therapy."

Lydia swallowed her bite and wiped her chin with a napkin. "Is that why you had pizza for me when I got home?" she asked.

The sisters talked about their experiences with the food and the culture of Cambodia and Thailand. Zanna listened with curiosity. She knew Charlotte had nursed a young orphaned baby and had to give him back when his family was found. Lydia had been kidnapped and held ransom so that some guy would fight for her. Zanna was very confused about the details and Lydia didn't like to talk about it, other than to say, "God brought fire for me and for Deliverance girls."

How could these two, who experienced pain and fear in a foreign country where they went—not to explore or relax, but to serve and work—how could they talk about their experiences with joy?

Zanna had never been to Thailand, but had worked with plenty of humanitarian and environmental groups in the past. The work was draining, frustrating. Every time something was accomplished, something more needed to be done. She knew this was true of Deliverance, or they wouldn't have to work so hard to raise support. But somehow, the stories she'd heard had been full of joy and hope. It was baffling.

"So, I came up with an idea," Charlotte told them once they'd eaten their fill and tucked the remaining pizza in the fridge. "I am not much of a seamstress, but Karen from church showed me a few little things, and I was able to make these cloth headbands." She pulled out the tub full of colorful strips of cloth. She held one up and Zanna could see the cloth was the shape of a headband, made complete with an elastic strip. "I got the idea when Michelle said she could never wear headbands because her glasses get in the way. I personally hate how headbands dig in behind your ears after a while. I know I didn't invent the cloth headband, but I thought these would be easy to make and send to girls that are sponsored. Maybe we could package them with the sponsorship cards."

Zanna filtered through the dozen or so headbands, thinking she could easily make some to sell at her store. "Sponsorship cards?"

Charlotte reached for her purse. "Lydia and I signed up for a sponsorship challenge at church. We have fifty girls that need monthly sponsorship." She pulled out a stack of cards in clear plastic covers with pictures of young women and girls on the front. Zanna took them and sorted through them. One picture in the middle of the stack stood out to her. Where many of the girls had hesitant, frightened eyes, this one's expression was hollow. So much like her.

"Can I sponsor her?" Zanna asked, turning the card around to show them.

Lydia nodded. "Definitely! I was going to ask you if you wanted a girl to sponsor, but you've done so much, I just didn't want to bother you."

Zanna barely heard her; she was reading the short paragraph about the girl on the card:

Name: Nataya
Age: 16

Rescued from Walking Street in Pattaya, Thailand before she became a dancing advertisement for the brothel she worked in. Details of her past still unknown

Rescued: August

"August?" Zanna was outraged. "This girl was rescued in August and is still waiting for help? How do they take care of her? Does she have to earn her keep while waiting for sponsorship?" Her skin pricked. "Or do they stop rescuing girls while they wait for money to come in to care for them all?"

Before they could answer, Zanna ruffled through the rest of the stack, gasping at how long many had been waiting for sponsorship, determined to sponsor every last one.

Lydia placed a hand on hers, staying the frantic shuffling. "No, Zanna. They just keep rescuing girls and trusting that God will provide for them all. So far, He has."

Zanna breathed out. "Oh."

Charlotte reached for the rest of the stack, blinking in gratitude as Zanna hurriedly grabbed two more for her pile.

"I think I'm going to take these with us to the retreat in McCall, Dee Dee." She used Lydia's family nickname, and glanced through them. A groan proceeded an exaggerated exhale and Charlotte asked them both, "How on earth am I going to say what I know I have to say?"

Lydia snorted. "Well, you've never had a problem talking before…"

Zanna ducked as a pillow sailed through the air from Charlotte toward her sister.

They laughed and Charlotte turned to Zanna. "Hey, you're welcome to come. I know a lot of the women that know how much you've done for Deliverance and would love to meet you."

Lydia quickly agreed. "Oh, Zanna, you should come!"

It was Zanna's turn to snort. "No offense, ladies, but I can't think of anything I would rather do *less* than attend a church retreat."

The afternoon melted into evening and when Charlotte and Lydia left, Zanna felt lighter than she had that morning. She gathered napkins to throw away and put their water glasses in the sink before she remembered her gran's Bible.

She didn't feel as desperate for Gran as she had earlier, but still anxious to connect with the only member of her family she had ever felt close to. Zanna prepared a cup of herbal tea and settled into a high backed chair in the corner of her bedroom. She reached for the Bible, her hands shaking as she flipped through the pages.

Scattered notes and underlined verses that made no sense to Zanna brought the faint smell of cinnamon, once again, to surround her. A chill raced through her when she found the source of the scent. Not imagined, but real and tangible.

She found the scented, folded sheets of paper in the book of Hebrews.

Chapter Thirty-Three

The knot in his stomach hardened and twisted. Gage relived the moments of the night before over and over, and became increasingly sick. His body ached; he shook with cold sweats.

The bar.

Zanna.

Her look of disdain.

His anger.

His *right* to have her if he wanted her.

The beer.

The small, discreet vial.

The shiver of triumph when she went back to her friends, nursing the beer he'd bought for her. The beer he'd spiked for her.

Because he was a nice guy. A good guy. Didn't she know?

The way her friends briefly flicked their eyes up and down his form when he asked to speak to her privately. Their shrugs of dismissal.

Tramps. What did they know?

If they only knew how Nataya fawned over him; how she couldn't get enough of him. If only they knew how important he was to the higher ups in the exciting and dangerous world of underground activity in Thailand.

Gage knew he could show them all—that he *should* show them.

But first: Zanna.

She had stumbled against him.

He groaned in memory of it. The night before, he'd relished the feel of her, shook with the knowledge of his own power.

Nataya's face flashed before him now—desperate, searching for him, faithfully waiting for him to come back.

He knew she could explain that man away. *"Him? Why, he was just an uncle,"* she would say.

No, she would purr. She purred for him when he told her to. She talked and walked and did just as he liked. Because she loved him and needed him so.

A low groan rumbled in his throat.

But he had touched another. Embraced another.

I needed to show her; she needed to understand. It had nothing to do with Nataya and everything to do with our future—Nataya's and mine—surely Nataya would understand that.

He kept the shades drawn and drank a bottle of pink acid reducer.

Frantic, petrified that somehow Nataya would know, he searched airline tickets for available flights to Bangkok or Pattaya.

Nothing until next week.

He cursed.

He couldn't go anyway, not until he could bring proof with him. Proof that he could roll with the big boys, trade, and buy and sell with the best of them. Live, tangible proof.

But Nataya.

He could feel her slipping through his fingers. How long had it been since he had seen her? After his night in the Pattaya hospital months ago, he had been unable to return to Walking Street to look for her again. He knew she was waiting, but he hadn't been able to put off his business meetings any longer. The consequences would have been too great. And much worse than the blow to his head.

Business.

Gage snapped to present day and dug tense hands back through his hair.

He had chosen to overlook that Zanna was a client. He didn't need her business, certainly didn't need her money.

But now he saw the danger of that thinking.

What if she talked? What if she figured it out?

No, he was certain she was too loose and too dumb to put it together. He's seen her stumble out of the same bar many times with other men. Often, he wished it could be him. She was slight, like Nataya. But brazen and bold, cocky and condescending. He wanted only to show her that he was better than her.

He wanted to show her what Nataya and the others knew.

That he was in control.

Maybe he did want her to know. What was the use of dominating someone that wasn't completely aware of the authority set over her?

The scar above Gage's left eye throbbed. He couldn't change it now; had to stop thinking about it. His remorse had churned until it grew white hot with anger and disgust. Who did Zanna think she was?

And what right would Nataya have to look down on him?

Nataya.

He ached for her. Physically hurt with desire for her, to have her again.

His appetite, satisfied for a time with Zanna, now raged stronger than before.

He shuffled across his house to the small office in the back. Crisp and clean, everything sleek and smooth—the room emanated strength and control.

One good thing I learned watching Dad, he thought, *"Messes lead to arrestes"*

He snickered at his childhood rhyme. How he'd mocked his father, in his head, of course, for years. If his father hadn't been such a slob, if he had paid better attention…

Well, anyway, my office leaves no room for mistakes, that's for sure.

He turned on his laptop, signed onto a social network site. He perused pictures, the rock of ice in his belly melting. His mood transformed as he went through "liking" and "commenting." Not as Gage, the forty-something-year-old-man. Here he was seventeen-year-old Trevor who was into skateboarding and punk garage bands. The girls that accepted friend requests from Trevor were fond of the duck-face mirror poses, many of them leaning over or perched on their beds in provocative positions. His legs tingled as he commented on a few.

No new messages.

He signed out Trevor and signed into another account as Toby.

These girls were fun. Shy in person, he supposed, but their bravery came out online, behind closed doors where only their smartphones and people they never had to meet could see. These girls liked to play sexy in the privacy of their rooms and see how they liked it.

Bloop.

His laptop notified him of a new message:

```
Hi Toby,
Just got back from family dinner. Boring!
My parents are mad at my sister and insist on
making sure I don't turn out like her. So
annoying!
```

Gage smiled to himself. *Little wench. Who cared?* But he better pretend to. There was something about this one. Hesitantly rebellious. He had found her online months ago, and she'd finally begun to trust him more. And she talked a lot about her sister who lived in Cambodia. She might be one worth meeting.

They chatted online for the next ten minutes, him baiting and building, her venting and trusting. They signed off and Gage, calmed, yet aroused, spent another hour online in darker, more deliberate places. It wasn't the same as holding Nataya in his arms, but it would do until he could get back to Thailand.

To her.

They looked like her and, for now, that was enough.

He readied for bed, a frown replacing his assuaged mood.

Zanna.

He knew better than to leave that alone. Women could be emotional—irrational. He wasn't sure how Zanna would react, but was sure he needed to keep things as clean as his office. Women made things so messy.

He remembered Cindy, his college roommate's girlfriend. How she'd looked down on him, warned friends to keep away from him.

Her haughty eyes and tight mouth angered him. Oh, how he had relished the way her face paled and her lips parted in fear when he mentioned the cameras. That he knew her parents' address and could send proof of what their precious daughter was doing with all of her study time.

And all of their money.

It was amazing what a little bribe could do.

Zanna was simple. One well-timed text would do it.

Chapter Thirty-Four

Oh, Lord, how majestic Your name is. How much higher are Your thoughts than my thoughts! I praise You, Lord. May I always know Your grace and peace. Lord, this place is beautiful; this bench is just what these old bones needed. Grace thinks I'm nuts for coming out here each morning and evening, but I am called to this place. This small hill, carpeted with pine needles. The spicy scent of the forest, the sound of the rushing river just beyond those trees; out of sight but mighty in its current. Here, Lord, in this place with these dear friends, I am anchored in assurance; Your word penetrates and runs deep. It's when I go home…

Jesus, You know how I ache for my Zanna. My darling girl. I love all of my grandchildren (and I've been blessed with so many! Praise You!). But Zanna—she is my heart. Her piercing eyes are so watchful. She sees and absorbs everything. When You created her, You must have delighted in the way You designed her mind, her eyes, her heart.

Her heart.

Oh dear God, I fear my son will crush it all together. Smash it to pieces. I see the hardness in her. I see how she closes her ears to anything he says about You. And why shouldn't she? Zanna has not yet been shown the loving, merciful Savior that You are. Indeed, just the opposite. Can't my son understand how he pummels over people with his fire and brimstone sermons? Certainly, God, You are mighty and just and all must stand before You. All must make a choice to surrender to Your will, or be enslaved by their own.

But, God, You are grace and mercy as much as You are wrath and judgment. Such matchless grace and mercy You give to us, Lord. Oh, how my darling Zanna girl needs to know that. I can tell her until I'm blue in the face, but no one can influence like a father can. And my dolt son insists on keeping her meek and broken. Doesn't he see? He's hardening her, pushing her away-destroying her.

I fear for her. I fear once she's pushed over the edge, she'll never come back.

Jesus, Oh Jesus...

Zanna couldn't see through her tears. She could hear her gran's voice; long suppressed memories of songs and verses that Gran would speak and sing over her came rushing back. Zanna trembled beneath the weight of her sorrow. She would give anything to sit with Gran again, even if it meant listening to her rambling about her Jesus.

Jesus.

Zanna still couldn't think of or hear that name without feeling nauseated and violently angry.

"*Jesus would spit on you Himself!*"
"*You insult the name of Jesus!*"
"*Harlot! Sinner! Jesus sees. Jesus knows! God Himself will smite you with His mighty hand!*"

Zanna could hear the voices from so many years ago. She could see eyes filled with fire and hate, lips curled back in snarls of anger, spittle forming in the corners of seething mouths. Mottled cheeks, corded necks stood out, defined enough that they, too, looked ready to take their turn condemning her. Screaming the name of Jesus at her. For her, Jesus had been a curse word, a word that aroused hatred and pain.

But for Gran, Jesus had been a balm. A safe place.

Why?

Zanna's gaze fixed unfocused on the wall opposite of her. Tears burned the back of her throat.

Do I really want to know?

Zanna started and glanced again at the stack of papers in her hand. A letter to God written on some bench in the mountains. Did Gran say where she was?

Zanna riffled through the papers, scanning the rest of the letter, smiling at Gran's description of a roommate snoring in the cabin, keeping the rest of the women awake. A loud laugh escaped when the next page told the story of shoving pinecones in the snorer's sleeping bag. Zanna quickly flipped to the front page to check the date. Gran was close to seventy when she wrote the letter.

That rascal. I can just picture my tiny, sixty-eight-year-old Gran sneaking pinecones into someone's sleeping bag.

The last paragraph gave Zanna the information she sought:

> Lord, thank You. Thank You for a weekend away, to reconnect with my friends. To laugh and fellowship. To smell the pine and breathe deeply of the mist that covers the mountain each morning. McCall, Idaho might not seem like much of a place to the rest of the world, but to me, it's a haven of

revealed truths. I don't need the mountains or time away to know You and love You, Lord. But the times I can sit with You on this bench in Camp Pinewood have stood out through the years. When I return home to life and problems and an empty home; when I face my worry over Zanna and the rest, this place will be an anchor in my heart of times that I've been alone with You. Times I've drunk deeply of Your creation and Your Word and the love of Your people. Thank You, Lord.

One thing I ask, if I may be so bold: someday, would You grant my Zanna a morning here on this bench? Would You open her eyes and heart to Your love and truth?

The papers shook in Zanna's hands, the words blurred on the page.

Camp Pinewood, McCall, Idaho.

Wasn't that where Charlotte and Lydia had invited her to go?

Chapter Thirty-Five

Lydia pulled her Jeep into a parking space at Central Valley Christian School and cut the engine. She let the keys dangle from the ignition, focused on the folksy voice of JJ Heller streaming from the speakers. The song would only play for a moment longer with the engine turned off, but Lydia needed that long to pull her thoughts together.

When she returned from Thailand, her parents and teachers had agreed she should come back to school at the start of spring semester. She'd come to the school once to speak in chapel before the break and before she lost her nerve. She's made up for the work she missed when she had been held captive in Thailand. The work was a balm to her healing heart. She had some of November and all of December to work through the aftershock of her abduction with the steady support of a counselor at her church; the nightmares had begun to subside.

But sitting in the parking lot of her school made her stomach quiver with basic insecurity.

How could I live through something like that and still be afraid to face Ethan and Jay?

She received only one text from Ethan since she had spoken in chapel. Full of mockery and scathing heat, she deleted it and blocked his number. She hadn't had strong feelings for him before; had only appreciated his company and the camaraderie of his hatred for their school. Now she wondered how she could face him.

The music stopped abruptly, but Lydia remained where she was.

Lord, I've been changed. I'm new. It doesn't matter if anyone else agrees or knows, so why am I so nervous?

A series of brisk thumps rang out around her, jolting Lydia upright in the seat. Michelle's face, wearing a satisfied grin, pressed against the driver side window, gloved hands at rest on the window on either side of her face; Luke, in similar fashion, pounded playfully on the passenger window.

Lydia puffed a small laugh and reached for the handle. Michelle backed up with the door, face and hands still planted on the glass. Luke opened the passenger door and retrieved Lydia's book bag for her. Michelle looped an arm through Lydia's before she reached above her to retrieve a warm to-go cup of coffee from the roof of the Jeep. She pressed it into Lydia's free hand.

"Girl, you got this."

Lydia's throat throbbed with an overflow of emotion and gratefulness.

Luke and Michelle met Lydia at her car each morning that first week and walked her into the building, strong and united as friends that had experienced hell together. After the first few days it became obvious that Ethan had every intention of ignoring Lydia, which was perfectly okay in her book. Jay, on the other hand, heaved compliments her direction whenever he got a chance. He called her "sister" and smiled at her with a pat to her shoulder. She withdrew, resisting the urge to hurl her satchel at his head. The rest of the students eyed her with tolerance and curiosity, but it had been too many years of disdain and too little time left in their senior year to bother fixing it.

Lydia no longer cared what anyone thought of her. For once she was not defiant, just aware that this place was a means to an end: a necessary step toward graduation and college, and hopefully, a life of ministry with Deliverance.

The Heavens Are Telling

Friday afternoon Lydia tossed her satchel into the back seat and slid into the Jeep. She heaved a sigh of relief that her first week back was behind her and that she could focus on the women's retreat in the mountains that weekend.

Her phone buzzed at her from the depths of her satchel. With a groan, Lydia twisted around, one arm bent unnaturally behind her. Her tongue stuck out of the corner of her mouth, one eye squinted closed. Her fingers brushed against the phone and she closed them around it, swiping a thumb across the face before she saw who was calling.

"Hello."

"Hey, there." Kiet's tenor voice sent a thrill down her spine. Lydia placed her free hand against her warm cheek, covering what she knew must be a foolish grin.

"Hi, Kiet." *That's great, Lydia, could you sound more excited?* She rolled her eyes heavenward pulling her hand down the front of her throat. "How's it going? Wait—what are you doing up? Isn't it four in the morning there?"

Kiet chuckled softly, "Uh, yeah, it is."

"What in the world are you doing awake?" Lydia asked again.

"Just wanted to catch you before you headed to your retreat. I don't have a roommate yet, so I knew I could get away with setting an alarm and calling you."

"Oh, that was nice..." Lydia bit her lip. Why was it so hard to talk to him on the phone? She could tell Kiet anything in an email, but somehow while talking on the phone their conversation became stilted and awkward.

Kiet cleared his throat, but seemed to be sharing in her difficulty. He asked her about school and her job, filing for a medical clinic. She asked him about Deliverance happenings; there wasn't anything new to report since their last exchange of emails. Lydia felt disappointed that after Kiet had gone through the trouble to wake up early and call her that she couldn't make it worth his while. She glanced at the clock on the dash.

"I'm sorry," she breathed into the phone, "but I need to hang up so I can drive to work."

"Okay, well, have a good day."

Was it her imagination or did Kiet sound relieved? She swallowed hard, her earlier thrill now a disappointed brick in her belly. "Yeah, Kiet, you too." She stared at her phone for a minute, wondering if they were trying too hard for something that only seemed to work on foreign soil.

❈ ❈ ❈

"Babe, what are you doing up?" Sam shuffled into the living room, the soft glow from the lamp illuminating his droopy eyes and disheveled hair. Despite her roiling emotions, Charlotte felt her knees go weak. *He is so handsome.*

Sam sunk into their worn couch beside her and leaned his head back against the wall behind it. He settled a warm hand on Charlotte's knee. Charlotte only shrugged at him.

"Talk to me, Lottie." His fingers squeezed encouragement.

Charlotte fingered the notebook in her lap. "I just couldn't sleep. The retreat is tomorrow and I still don't know what to say. Well"—she rubbed her hands on her cheeks— "that's not true. I know exactly what to say, I just have no idea how to say it."

Sam's breathing deepened, emitting a chuckle from Charlotte. She pushed on his shoulder. "Get out of here; go back to bed."

"Are you sure? I want to be here for you," Sam protested through a yawn.

Charlotte shook her head with a smile. "No offense, Sam, but you're not much use to me this way. I'm fine, just working through my thoughts."

Sam kissed her on the cheek and rose sleepily. She watched him disappear down the hall, slowly taking in her surroundings before she turned back to an old journal she had been flipping through. She had kept a prayer journal for most of her adult life. It was humbling to look back and remember how she'd felt and responded to certain seasons. Her choices in college ashamed her the most and those journals were the hardest to read. But the pages spoke of grace that sheltered her in those times, even though she hadn't seen it then.

Lord, you have changed so much in my life. Ever since I cried out to You and You answered so mightily. Thank You. I am amazed at Your mercy, and so ashamed of what it took for me to finally see You. I know my story is one that You asked me to share. Now please give me the guts to talk about it...

✦✦✦

Zanna couldn't believe what she'd gotten herself into.

When she had finished reading her gran's letter, she called Lydia and asked if she could change her mind and go on the retreat with her and Charlotte. To her credit, Lydia hadn't reacted, only agreed and promised to call the woman in charge and sign her up. When Zanna awoke the next day, she realized what she'd done and decided to call Lydia and cancel.

When Zanna had rolled over in bed to retrieve her phone, she noticed a blinking light, indicating she'd received a text message. Her blood ran cold when she saw it was from Gage. Her finger shook as she swiped it across the phone, unlocking it to reveal the short message:

```
I find it highly unprofessional the way you
came on to me last night. I understand that
life can be lonely at times, and I'll overlook
your behavior. If you wish to maintain your
reputation with my firm and the community, I
highly recommend you keep your behavior last
night to yourself. I, in turn, will consider
all forgotten.
```

She dropped the phone as if she'd been burned, watching the color return to her white knuckles.

Had she been mistaken about everything? Had she been the instigator, the unprofessional one? Suddenly, where she'd felt violated and wronged the day before, now she was mortified.

Not only had she slept with a man that handled her finances, a man she found repulsive, but now this man was *rejecting her*.

Raw and humiliated, she marched into the shower, pulling on the familiar cloak of anger, and continued on with her day. She took inventory, sold shirts, dealt with vendors and customers, all while imagining them laughing about her actions from the weekend.

In the chaos of her emotions, she forgot to cancel with Lydia. And by the end of the very long week, after she'd read Gran's letter a few more times, she was more determined than ever to find that bench. If only to be in the place where Gran had once felt close to her God…so that she could personally bawl him out.

Now Zanna climbed out of Charlotte's car in McCall, her shoes slipping slightly on the tightly packed snow. Zanna met Lydia and Charlotte around the back, ready to unload the trunk. Before Charlotte could unlock it, a woman with a clipboard came out of a large building, her words puffing white in the cold afternoon air. "Hey, ladies. I have your cabin assignments right here."

Charlotte greeted the woman with a little side hug and stood with her arm around her while they looked over the list. Zanna took in the camp, wondering if the bench would be hard to find. The property was smaller than she'd expected. They stood beside one large lodge, and next to it was a small building that she assumed was the chapel.

A path, the width of a car, split through the rest of the camp, snow piled high on either side. Little cabins were scattered throughout the woods beyond the main clearing. Zanna hoped they were assigned to the one farthest from the little chapel.

Women in groups of two and three milled around the cabins and walked toward the lodge. Their serene faces set Zanna's teeth on edge.

"Sorry I couldn't get here earlier to help, Judy," Charlotte said to the woman with the clipboard as she glanced up at Lydia and Zanna with a wink. "I had some working women I was waiting for."

The Heavens Are Telling

Zanna, defensive, opened her mouth to protest, but Judy spoke first, "Lucky dogs. Have you ever tried to set up for a women's retreat? I was hoping all morning that the hospital would need me to come in for an emergency, just to get out of set-up." Judy sighed and rolled her eyes heavenward. "Lord, forgive me for wishing harm on others so that I could get out of cabin check-ins. Amen."

Her tone and expression were so comical that Zanna was caught off-guard. She almost laughed out loud as Charlotte and Lydia did. Instead, she clamped her mouth shut, only nodding slightly when Charlotte introduced her. She was not there to befriend anyone or to be sucked in. She was only there to get out of town, into the quiet snowy mountains, and to find Gran's bench. She shifted from one foot to the other, anxious to unload their things and change into her boots. Why hadn't she thought to wear them for the ride? Again, she opened her mouth to ask if they could get on with things, but Judy and Charlotte were busy cutting it up together.

Zanna resisted the urge to roll her eyes. *Yes, you're two regular comedians; can we get on with it?*

"So, Charlotte, since you're our speaker for the weekend, we put you ladies in a room above the chapel. There's a little loft up there, and it's the quietest place to be in the evening. The only drawback is when the worship team practices each morning, it's right below you."

Charlotte nodded. "That sounds great, Judy. Lydia has been getting up early for school all week, so I'm sure being in bed until six will feel like sleeping in, right?"

Zanna wondered at the pensive shift in Lydia's expression as the younger woman nodded. Zanna found Judy looking at her; her expression questioning. After an awkward pause, Zanna started and cleared her throat. "Oh! I don't mind being up early; I doubt I'll really sleep this weekend anyway."

Charlotte pressed an open hand to her abdomen. "Me neither; I'm just so nervous."

Judy slipped an arm around Charlotte and squeezed her shoulders. "You'll do great."

She smiled at all of them and walked away to greet a van that had just pulled in. Zanna was surprised when women began to pile out, laughing and calling out to each other. The driver dashed around the side of the car and pelted a passenger with a handful of snow as she exited through the side door. The passenger howled before she twisted and knocked the driver on her back, returning a handful of snow to her face. The rest of the women shrieked with laughter, and Judy called out wrestling moves as encouragement.

"Sheesh, what kind of church camp is this, anyway?" Zanna mumbled under her breath as she turned to retrieve her suitcase and sleeping bag from Charlotte's trunk.

Zanna followed a snickering Lydia and Charlotte to the chapel and through a cramped set of doors into a small hallway. Beyond another set of glass doors, she could see the chapel and a chill coursed through her at the familiarity of the set-up. Rows of wood and green-upholstered pews lined either side of the room, all pointed toward the small stage, complete with a rickety pulpit and a simple wooden cross hanging high on the back wall. Three microphone stands stood to the left, a keyboard to the right. She didn't see the projector and screen that would display the song lyrics, but knew they could be tucked out of the way, ready to roll in when worship began.

In the beginning of her life, the churches that her father pastored had looked much like this worn chapel. Only later, when he became well known and attracted the right kind of congregation, did his church building gleam with fancy fixtures, comfortable pews, and expensive equipment for the worship stage.

Charlotte turned before they entered the chapel and ascended a narrow stairway with walls so white they hurt Zanna's eyes. She watched Lydia's black boots ascend the stairs in front of her instead.

Their room was just as Judy had said: a small loft above the chapel: four twin beds, two on either side of the room, a sink with a mirror above it, a door that most likely led to a bathroom, and a small window facing the parking lot. One of the beds had a pillow and sleeping bag spread on top of it, with a Bible resting on the pillow. A bag had been tucked into the space under the bed. Zanna's heart leapt at the thought of sharing the room with anyone beyond Charlotte and Lydia. They knew she was not a Christian, knew she hated the thought of church and God and the Bible. But they never made her feel like church people did. What would their roommate have to say about Zanna?

Lydia and Charlotte each took a bed near the window, leaving the one near the stairs for Zanna. She tucked her bag underneath as the others had done, spread out her sleeping bag and pillow, and plopped on top, wishing she could crawl into her bag instead.

The quiet drive with Lydia staring pensively out the window and Charlotte chattering nervously had been uncomfortable at best. Zanna could only imagine how much her headache would increase as the weekend continued.

Chapter Thirty-Six

McCall, Idaho

Zanna lifted a faded Garfield coffee mug to her lips and hid a yawn behind it. When Lydia and Charlotte had invited her to a weekend retreat, she hadn't expected to be up at dawn and sitting alone at a table in a dining hall.

Well, I expected the alone part, she thought, eyes scanning the women gathering together as they waited for breakfast to be served.

The large room buzzed with the chatter of women. Laughing, gabbing, shouting, hugging, whispering.

Church women.

The buzzing turned to a roar inside her head. Zanna rubbed her ears with open palms, resisting the urge to clamp her hands over them and shout for everyone to shut up. *Breathe Zanna, just breathe. In and out. Nice and slow.*

Although she had been out of the scene for many years, Zanna remembered the way religious women were. They watched and waited for someone, anyone—especially one of their own—to slip and fall so that they could rip them to shreds. Zanna didn't know how she had survived the night; couldn't believe they hadn't picked up on the scent of her lifestyle.

The previous night, after they set up their room, dinner was served buffet style in the dining hall. Zanna had offered to save a table, mostly so that she wouldn't have to stand in line and make small talk with anyone. She had sat, much like she did now, in a corner, watching different interactions and wishing the weekend would go by faster. Charlotte had surprised her when she and Lydia returned to the table with a plate for Zanna and a knowing smile. Was it that obvious that she didn't belong?

Zanna poked her fork around the plate of chicken cordon bleu, a garden salad, roll, and chocolate cake. She ate around the chicken, careful to avoid any lettuce that had touched the meat, surprised by the delicious simplicity of crisp greens, slivered almonds, dried cherries and a creamy peppercorn sauce. She finished the salad, roll, and even the cake. Full but surprised that she had been able to eat, Zanna was relieved when they cleared plates to exit the dining hall. She knew chapel was next on the agenda; a perfect time for her to sneak out and search for Gran's bench. But Lydia linked arms with Zanna and pulled her through the door with the throng of women. Zanna grit her teeth, ready to tell Lydia that there was no way in—

"Thanks for coming, Zanna. I know this isn't your thing. I'm still a little uncertain at these kinds of events myself. I spent so many years angry at church people." Lydia interrupted Zanna's thoughts and nudged her along to a place in a middle row on the right. Lydia plopped down and pulled Zanna down to sit with her on the lumpy bench.

"I know I am a new person here"—Lydia patted her heart—"but it doesn't always translate as quickly here"—she tapped her temple with her fingertips—"and my emotions are a little raw right now. If Charlotte weren't speaking, I don't know if I would have come this weekend."

Zanna sat—back rigid—through the singing, refusing to stand, not caring what anyone thought of her. She watched the women around her with closed eyes and raised hands through the worship, a metallic taste filling her mouth. She realized she was biting the inside of her cheeks hard enough to draw blood and clasped her arms across her middle.

The singing finally stopped and a nervous Charlotte got up to speak. Zanna and Lydia both straightened slightly. No matter how she felt about Christians in general, Zanna couldn't deny a friendly affection for Charlotte. She was mild and boring, completely clueless to what the world was really like, but she had never pushed Zanna and always treated her like a friend.

Charlotte stepped behind the small tilted podium with her Bible and cleared her throat. "While I am so happy to be with you all this weekend, I have to admit I am not sure how much good I will do as the speaker." Charlotte's cheeks flushed as she searched the crowd for someone.

Her eyes lit up in recognition and she pointed a slightly trembling finger at a woman near the front. "All I have to say is, if Patsy Porter ever calls you in the weeks before Women's Retreat, do yourself a favor and let it go to voicemail!"

The room erupted in laughter and shouts of agreement. Zanna craned her neck to see the woman Charlotte pointed at; she was poised and well dressed with beautiful blond hair and a twinkle in her eye.

"Hey, I told you that you could say no!" Patsy called out.

"Right," Charlotte answered from the pulpit laughingly.

Zanna pushed up the sleeve on her sweatshirt and rolled her wrist to look pointedly at her watch.

Eventually, the teasing fell away and Charlotte began what she called her testimony. For thirty minutes she explained how she had been raised in a Christian home, "given her life" to the Lord as a young child, but how she began to rebel during her second semester in college.

Rebel. Zanna had to stifle a snicker at Charlotte's idea of rebellion. A few nights of underage drinking, and what sounded like a normal college relationship with a man that wasn't a Christian.

Gasp! Oh tell me you didn't date a normal man, God forbid! Zanna rolled her eyes heavenward. Charlotte had no idea what rebellion and rejection truly looked like. Charlotte's parents were disappointed? Zanna shuddered mockingly.

Her own mother's face, flushed red with that throbbing, jagged vein standing on her temple, spit flying with each angry curse and scream, flashed in Zanna's memory. Her father's frighteningly cool, tight smile, words of hate and terror spoken over her in that deep, commanding voice.

No, Charlotte had no clue...

Charlotte ended the night on what Zanna assumed was supposed to be a cliffhanger:

"Once I finally gave in to temptation and became intimate with Jordan, there was no going back. I was so full of regret and shame that no matter what happened over the next year, no matter what any of my friends or family said, I clung with desperation to that relationship. In my mind, all could be redeemed if we stayed together. It didn't matter how much Jordan cheated or called me names; all that mattered to me was making the relationship last." Charlotte's voice cracked. "And through it all..."—her chest rose and fell as she gave a wobbly smile to the women waiting silently for her to finish—"through it all, the Lord was there. I thought I had wandered too far away, but He was there, mighty as ever, ready to shower me with all that He intended for me. But life had to get a lot worse before I would listen..."

Zanna snapped out of her reverie and watched the women talking and laughing together while they waited for breakfast. The sounds around her rose to a screeching hiss. *What am I doing here?*

The room began to spin as the screeching increased. The small clusters of women blurred and reddened.

Get away. Call a cab. Walk. Anything. Get out!

Zanna slammed her mug on the table, hot coffee slashing onto her hand, burning her fingers. Her chest tightened, her thoughts came in quick spurts with her rapid breaths.

The hiss rose around her, searing her behind the eyes with brilliant light.

Get out! Get out! Get out—

Zanna jumped when a hand gently landed on her shoulder.

The hissing immediately stopped.

"Oops, sorry." Judy, the woman that had checked them in the night before stood beside her, a hand still lightly resting on her arm. "I didn't mean to scare you. I just—" Judy leaned down until her eyes were level with Zanna's. "Are you Okay?"

Zanna looked away, uncomfortable with the woman's penetrating gaze. She pulled her arm away. "I'm fine."

To her dismay, Judy pulled out the chair next to her and sat down, arms folded on the table. She jutted her chin toward the women clustering together in the center of the room. "Not your thing, huh?"

Zanna snorted. "Not at all."

Judy's mouth curled up on one side, and she opened her mouth to answer, but was interrupted by Lydia and Charlotte.

"There you are." Lydia yawned and sat on Zanna's other side, crossing her arms much like Judy and laying her head on them.

Charlotte stood behind Lydia's chair and rubbed her younger sister's back. "All this time I thought the trip to Thailand had made Lydia a morning person. I almost couldn't get her up this morning." She looked laughingly between Judy and Zanna.

"At least you didn't sit on me and start singing to me about the sunshine this time." Lydia's muffled voice did little to hide her dry tone.

Zanna was left to wonder at her statement as a loud voice rose above the women and quieted them down for prayer.

Zanna waited in line when they were prompted to; she wanted to be sure she didn't waste meat again. The breakfast selection was what she'd expected: eggs, bacon, sausage, fried potatoes, yogurt, bagels, toast, and pastries. Feeling moody, she took only a bowl of yogurt and granola, her stomach cramping at the smell of bacon.

That's probably why I felt nauseated the minute I walked in here.

Her mother was frying bacon the morning Zanna told her that she was pregnant.

❖ ❖ ❖

Charlotte wished she could ease Zanna's discomfort. Truthfully, despite her years of rebellion, she had always found comfort in the presence of others that loved the Lord. Charlotte had experienced great love, acceptance and encouragement from believers, even during the times when a few brave friends confronted her and called out her sin. Zanna eyed everyone around her with great distrust, her back rigid, mouth set, muscle working in her jaw.

Lord, something made Zanna feel like she can't trust You or Your people. Would you break down her walls, even this weekend, Lord? Would You reveal Yourself to her in a personal, powerful way?

Charlotte took a shuddering break and rolled her wrist to check the time. Her stomach flipped. *Lord, I don't know if I can do this.*

Her brief testimony last night had created a stir of encouragement from the women in her church. Dozens of them had reached out to her and thanked her for her honesty.

Will they feel the same way by the end of the day?

The weeks of preparing to speak at the retreat, as well as countless sleepless nights praying for and worrying over Noah, had drained Charlotte. When Patsy asked her to speak, she wrote page after page in her journal of flowery, Scripture-filled anecdotes from her life as a stay-at-home mom. She had smiled in thankfulness over all that God had done in her life.

One night He made it painfully clear that she was not meant to speak on any of that, but instead on the darkest years of her life. Years that she had suppressed, stuffed down, smothered into silence. Years that crept into her mind, uninvited, unexpected, to torment her with screaming raging dreams that jolted her awake, trapped in a battle with twisted, sweaty sheets and a shame-filled soul. The nightmares had subsided when Charlotte married Sam and had disappeared completely with the birth of her daughters.

After Patsy's call, they returned, beckoning her to remember.

She fought the memories, choosing instead to speak on things that would be comforting and safe. Night after night the dreams came fierce and fast. Sam awoke with her one night and

The Heavens Are Telling

pulled her up to face him in a cross-legged position in their bed. Charlotte's sobs wracked her entire body, her tears hot and angry against Sam's bare chest. He held her close, prayed over her, his whispers filtering through her tangled hair, tickling her nose.

"You have to do this, Lotty," he spoke her nickname tenderly. "You cannot run from the Lord's purpose. I believe if you do this, you will finally be able to accept the peace that He has offered you in this all along."

"I-I-I can-can't do-do this," Charlotte felt ridiculous, her chest heaving in waves of aftershock from crying so hard. "I don't want to think about it."

"I know you don't." Sam set her away from him, patiently searching her eyes in the pale moonlight that filtered through their window. "But I believe God is showing you the way to never be tormented by this again. You need to follow His lead."

"He asks too much, Sam!" Charlotte slapped a hand on her knee, tired, frustrated. "First He asked me to nurse Noah, knowing I would fall in love with him. Then He made me hand Noah over, knowing my heart would be ripped out. When I finally felt a tiny dose"—she pinched her thumb and forefinger together—"of peace about that, Megan called to say Noah and his sister are gone, probably sold or something equally bad and…I just, I don't understand. He asks too much! He *takes* too much!"

Charlotte pressed her palms against her eyes, breathing deeply, willing her breaths to smooth out. They sat in silence for several minutes.

Sam cleared his throat and rested a gentle hand against her cheek. "Yes, Lotty, He does take sometimes. But He gives so much more than He takes."

When, at last, Judy called for the women to clear their plates and head to the chapel for morning worship, Charlotte rose shakily from her chair, determined to put this behind her. She might not be welcome by any of the women to sit with them at lunch, not after what she had to say, but she knew Sam was right.

You are indeed a God Who takes. But You give so much more. Please speak through me Lord, for whatever woman here that needs to know Your love and grace and mercy, would you set my fear behind and display Your glory?

Chapter Thirty-Seven

Canon Beach, Oregon

Ava's parents were out with friends from church. She signed into the computer, using the password that she'd figured out when her parents were gone months ago. Their address. *Clever, Dad*, she'd thought, rolling her eyes.

She hadn't really wanted to do anything wrong online, just wanted to check her sister, Jakobi's, blog. She both hated her sister being so far away and admired the work she was doing. Each time Jakobi shared stories from her adventures in the Peace Corps, Ava felt less lonely for her. At first she had only checked the blog and then would sign off. But her friends were talking about a funny conversation they all had online and she felt left out. After school, while her mom was out shopping, Ava set up her very own social account, complete with pictures that her friends had uploaded to their pages. She loved the times she could sneak on and share jokes and pictures with her friends, loved the freedom and inclusion she felt. And why shouldn't she? All of her friends were online, why couldn't she have fun, too?

When a boy named Toby started "liking" her posts, she was surprised. She had left her page open to anyone so she could meet more people, but she had to send Toby a friend request to see his page. His profile picture was too fuzzy to tell who it was.

But something about the kid in the hat and torn jeans, riding down a half-pipe on his skateboard, gave her butterflies.

He accepted her request and soon they shared messages every day. He said he'd watched her at school for a long time before his parents had moved to another town, forcing him to switch schools. She told him all about Jakobi and how her strict parents drove her crazy. He listened and told her how pretty she was.

He asked for a picture of her from the summer. "So I can look forward to our days to come on the beach," he'd written.

She sent him one of her picnicking with church friends.

"Don't you have one of you in your bathing suit?" he'd asked.

She didn't answer right away. Her stomach felt queasy at the thought of sending him a picture of her in her one piece. She wished she had a picture of the time Sarah let her borrow her bikini, and they'd tanned on a private beach in the back of Sarah's house. She'd asked Sarah about it at school and been excited when Sarah emailed her one that night.

Toby had been pleased. "Beautiful," he'd written. "You are stunning. I can't wait to get my arms around you this summer."

Ava had smiled. She even felt brave enough to write Jakobi and tell her about Toby, knowing her sister would understand how suffocating their parents could be. But Jakobi hadn't answered her and hadn't updated her blog in weeks. Ava was worried about her, but didn't know how to tell her parents that she had been checking Jakobi's blog without getting into trouble. She wasn't supposed to be online without them, and even then only for research for school.

She asked Toby what he thought she should do. He answered that he was sure Jakobi was fine.

"I'm sure she is," Ava wrote. "I just miss her so much. If my parents weren't such jerks they would take me to see her while she's gone. Two years is too long to go without seeing my sister!"

When he answered her next, her heart thundered with the possibilities that he arose.

The Heavens Are Telling

"My uncle does a lot of business near Cambodia," he wrote. "I've already asked him if he would be willing to take you with him the next time he goes. Would you be interested?"

Ava tapped her fingers against the desk. She was desperate to see Jakobi, but knew she could never afford a ticket, could never get a passport without her parents. She reluctantly told Toby her reservations.

"That's not a problem, Ava," Toby had assured her. "My uncle has loads of money, and he can get anything you need. You would only need to show up at PDX. Could you get a ride there?"

Ava excitedly asked around at school until she found a friend that had her own car and was allowed to drive into Portland on weekends to see her dad. "My mom loves that she no longer has to see my dad or his wife. She just gases up my car, and sends me away for the weekend. It would be no problem to take you," Ava's friend had told her.

Ava waited a day before she wrote Toby, excitement mounting. "I'm in. Just tell me when and where I should meet your uncle."

Toby wrote back two days later. "Excellent. My uncle isn't completely sure when he can go, but he'll let you know. He's still not sure that you're serious enough about me to take you on such a long trip."

She immediately wrote back that she loved Toby and wished there was a way she could prove it. He responded that there was.

Now Ava's heart pounded in her chest as she followed the instructions he had given her to turn on the webcam that came with the computer. She closed the curtains and checked the locks on the doors once more before she stripped down and posed, just as Toby had asked her to.

At first she'd felt insecure about sending Toby an intimate picture of herself. But after asking her friends at school, it seemed she was the only one that hadn't sent a nice photo of herself to her boyfriend. "That's how they know you really like them, Ava," Sarah had spoken to her with an air of maturity.

She had to take the photo a few times before she was satisfied that it was sexy enough. Her heart thundered as she clicked, 'Send'. She pulled her clothes back on in a rush and frantically erased the photos from the computer.

She felt sick for days. Her emotions raged between shame and fear that Toby wouldn't like what he saw. The next time she had a chance to check her email, there was a message from him.

"That's my girl," he wrote.

She sighed in relief.

Chapter Thirty-Eight

McCall, Idaho

Charlotte clenched her eyes shut and tried to steady her trembling heart. Public speaking was difficult enough without sharing personal sins and failures with a group of friends and strangers. Too emotional to sing, Charlotte raised a shaky hand toward the ceiling and let the voices around her and the lyrics of the last worship song wash over her.

Yes, Lord. You are holy and mighty. Thunder cracks around You. Lightning dances in Your throne room. You are surrounded by shimmering rainbows of life and color and Your name is Wonderful.

All too soon, the music faded and Charlotte stepped behind the podium. She held up her Bible. "I want to talk to you about a God who sees. And I want to share with you how He saw me and was gracious to me. I began to tell you last night about my years of rebellion. My relationship with a man that I had no business being with. Your encouragement last night and this morning touches me more than I can explain. I pray you will hold tight with me for the rest. It's not pretty."

Charlotte filled her lungs with air, grasping for confidence. She released her will and her pride and she opened the door to the darkest months of her life and held it for sixty women to walk through with her.

"The guilt of my choices piled up around me, and finally, I decided to change my behavior. I moved out of Jordan's apartment and changed jobs. I completely distanced myself from him and stuck to the changes. But I felt fragile, vulnerable. It was a constant battle with myself to stay away from the phone when I felt lonely. One night I invited my family over for dinner, and Jordan showed up unexpectedly at my door. I am so thankful my family was there, or I might have given in to my loneliness and picked right back up where I started. My Dad stepped between us and told me to stay in my apartment while he 'took out the trash'." Charlotte's smile wobbled. "I don't want to be offensive by telling you that part, but isn't that just the way fathers love their children...?"

"Tramp! You're trash! You're nothing! Who are you to spit in the face of God? Whore!"

Zanna shifted in her seat, getting hot all over as voices from her past converged upon her.

No, that wasn't the way all fathers behaved with their children.

Charlotte took a shuddering breath. The faces in the room were open, kind. Some nodded in understanding. She didn't want to tell the next part of the story. What would they think? Her stomach quivered. *Lord, please don't add a stomachache to this. Please calm my nerves. You asked me to do this; please give me Your peace.*

"My dad was able to get Jordan into a cab and on his way. He called my mom and sister back and we shared a pleasant evening. While Lydia picked out a movie for us to watch, I pulled my parents into the kitchen and promised them that Jordan had come on his own, that I hadn't spoken to him in weeks and had no intention of rekindling our relationship.

Understandably, they were skeptical. I had broken up with Jordan before, numerous times. I couldn't explain to my parents why it felt different that time. But I had gone to great lengths to remove him from my life: I changed jobs, changed classes, moved into a new apartment. I still don't know how he found out that I lived there."

Charlotte paused to take a sip of water from a bottle that had been placed on a shelf within the podium. She shrugged and met Zanna's skeptical gaze in the third row.

"I realize that it might sound silly how desperate I was to get away from him. I still don't completely understand how I became so attached to him other than that I was lonely at the time and he made me laugh...for a while. When we became intimate, I was so ashamed, so disappointed in my choices. I don't know, I guess I thought staying with him would cancel out the shame somehow. When I finally realized that I wanted my family back, my friends back, my happiness back, I knew I had to fight for all of it. I was true to my word; I never contacted Jordan again, even when I found out that I was pregnant."

Lydia sucked in the air around her. She felt like she'd been slapped. *Pregnant?* She narrowed her eyes at her sister, hurt and confusion pouring through her. How could her family have kept this from her? And...what had happened to the baby?

Charlotte chewed on her top lip for a moment, took another slow pull of water. Lydia could see her hands shaking and felt compassion for her older sister. Charlotte set down the bottle and gripped the sides of the small podium.

She cleared her throat, opened her mouth, and when no sound came out, she cleared it again. "To be honest, ladies, I don't want to tell you the rest of my story." She looked into their eyes, some confused and wide, like Lydia's, some expressionless, others open and caring, silently encouraging her to continue.

Patsy and Judy, sitting together in the front row, had prayed with Charlotte about this, and they smiled at her empathetically. Charlotte looked to the ceiling and blinked several times before she took a deep breath.

"I wanted to keep Jordan out of my life and was just as desperate to keep my parents in it. I couldn't afford a baby on my own. Lydia was in her last year at elementary school; it wouldn't have been fair to her to ask our parents for help. A friend of mine had given birth to a baby right after high school, and I knew her reliance on her parents for financial stability had caused numerous problems between them.

"My parents had finally begun to trust me again. Our relationships were mending. Classes were going well. My work schedule and wages were perfect for a college student; there was no way I could make any of that work with a baby to care for."

Charlotte stopped her torrent of excuses and stared. She took a deep breath. "During my time of rebellion, I became very self-focused. I was an expert at taking what I knew to be truth and twisting it into something that suited my needs. When I decided to change my life, I wish I could say it was because I had turned back to the Lord, but the truth was, I still didn't realize or acknowledge that I had turned away from Him in the first place." Charlotte's eyes drifted across the faces in front of her.

"I've heard it said that the most dangerous place for an unborn child is in the womb of an American woman," she whispered, her voice barely reaching the back of the room.

A series of small groans and gasps escaped from a few scattered women. Lydia heard the woman behind her whisper, "No!" her voice pinched.

Charlotte, no longer able to look anyone in the eye, fingered the pages of her notes on the podium. "I had gone through every scenario and the only one that made sense was to terminate my pregnancy."

Zanna's head snapped to attention. *What was Charlotte doing?* To admit something like that in any normal setting would get a few nods of understanding and even complacency, as if abortion liberated a woman, showed her as more dedicated to the rights of womanhood. But in a church setting? It was dangerous. People like these would never understand, would never accept such a thing.

Charlotte crinkled her nose in disgust. "I read everything I could about abortion, careful to avoid any source that would seek to challenge my reasoning."

Zanna hunched her shoulders and winced, waiting for the room to erupt with screams of outrage. Spittle would fly; accusations and fingers would rise above the din, firm in their indignation.

The room became very still.

Zanna shifted on the bench, heart pounding in fear for Charlotte, who continued to tell her story.

"I hated the pregnancy, hated the choice I was forced to make. As far as I was concerned, I didn't have a choice,"

The Heavens Are Telling

Charlotte continued, her voice soft, flat. "I needed to get my life back on track and a child would ruin everything. I had been raised in church; I knew all of the arguments for life and had proudly agreed with life over choice...until I was faced with that decision myself. Then the arguments for abortion became so terribly comfortable." She ran her fingers under her eyes.

"I called a clinic and made an appointment. I didn't allow myself to think about it, just made a mark on my calendar, arranged to have the day off of work, and did my best to stay busy."

Charlotte's tongue rested against her top lip, her eyes searched the ceiling again, glistening. "When I arrived at the clinic, there was a group of people outside."

Zanna's back went stiff. *Signs. Red faces. Marching. Shouting. Corded necks. Clenched fists.*

"Just a small group, sitting in a row along the walkway, heads down. Praying." Charlotte's voice squeaked. She drew in a breath to compose herself. "I tucked my chin, determined to walk on by."

Charlotte's flat, solemn face lit up; she flashed a wobbly, grateful smile at the front row, and she raised a shaky finger to point at Judy. A joyous, relieved sob escaped her throat. "That lady right there happened to be praying over the abortion clinic that day."

The room throbbed with something Zanna couldn't define. A charge in the air, a heavy—but magnificent—Presence.

"Judy caught my eye and I couldn't help but walk closer to where she sat with her Bible open in her lap, face open and calm. She watched me walk up and called out to me."

Zanna flinched. *Whore. Murderer. Slut.*

"'Hey kiddo,' she said, 'I haven't seen you in a while.'"

Charlotte laughed a little, brushed a hand across her eyes again. She shook her head appreciatively at Judy, placed a trembling hand over her heart. "That's it. She didn't look down on me or say cruel things. She just casually called me over and patted the place next to her on the cement."

Zanna pulled back in her seat. *What?*

Charlotte caught the astonishment on Zanna's face. Lydia had shared with her that Zanna was kicked out of her house when her parents discovered she'd had an abortion. Zanna's pinched, pale face spoke of a very different experience than Charlotte's.

Overwhelmed with compassion for the woman, and praying for God to reveal His loving nature to her, Charlotte turned her eyes from Zanna, so as not to single her out. She gestured to a beaming Judy again, and continued her story.

"Judy afforded me a chance to sit, to make it look like I was there for prayer. She knew better; she'd heard from my mom the kind of life I was living, and I'm sure the look on my face when I saw her communicated exactly why I was there. She spoke with me privately, and although I really can't remember what she said, I know that peace settled over me for the first time in a very long time. Judy wisely insisted that I get out of there. When she discovered I hadn't eaten yet—the clinic told me not to—she took me to lunch to ask me why I felt like I had no choice..."

The sights and smells of that hour remained sharp in Charlotte's memory. Judy had suggested a busy teahouse, a made-over home in an older neighborhood. They weaved through a maze of table displays and shabby chic hutches, covered in enough tea-themed merchandise to keep loose tea enthusiasts occupied and delighted while they waited for a table. The restaurant—complete with waitresses in lacy white starched aprons over black skirts—was like something from another time. A time when Charlotte would not have legally been able to do as she'd planned just an hour ago.

A cozy-wrapped teapot sat in the center of each table, and the menu boasted an assortment of loose-leaf teas, sumptuous sandwiches, and homemade casseroles. The dessert cart, set a few feet behind Judy, made Charlotte's stomach water, in spite of the heaviness in her heart. They ordered, chicken enchilada casserole and a salad for Judy, a Monte Cristo sandwich and wild rice soup for Charlotte, and Judy teasingly patted Charlotte's hand. "Right before we ordered, I panicked, realizing that I forgot to ask if your tummy was up to a meal. Should I assume you're doing just fine?"

Charlotte glanced around the small room; none of the other patrons looked familiar. She lowered her voice anyway. "I actually haven't dealt with nausea at all. I'm mostly just exhausted and hungry all the time."

"Do you know how far along you are?" Judy asked.

Charlotte considered her over a glass of ice water. "I think about two months." Charlotte lowered her eyes and fingered the cozy on the teapot.

Judy gently asked what had led Charlotte to the decision she'd made. Charlotte gave her the list of reasons. Her arguments for abortion fell flat once she spoke them aloud.

After their lunch, Judy ordered a chocolate cake for them to share. "I've heard it said that chocolate fixes everything." Judy had smiled sardonically as she forked a piece of the moist cake and held it in the air. "But that's not completely accurate, is it, Charlotte? The Bible says, 'Taste and see that the LORD is good.'"

Judy pointed the fork at her, straightforward and unashamed. "That right there is the only fix-all I can offer you. Whatever stress and confusion drove you to that clinic today, I can guarantee you, it will multiply tenfold if you go through with what you have planned."

Charlotte's soul awakened at the familiarity of that Scripture. It had been so long since she'd read her Bible that she wasn't entirely sure where it was. How had she gone from a woman that loved the Lord, that wanted to serve Him with all of her being, to a woman ready and willing to abort her baby?

Baby.

Her throat closed around that word.

The numbness Charlotte had embraced to get through what she wanted to accomplish began to thaw.

"I need to get out of here. I need to go home." Charlotte fumbled under the chair for her purse. Judy understood and offered to drive her.

Charlotte shook her head, eyes briefly meeting Judy's concerned stare. "No. But, thank you."

Judy reached in her purse for a small spiral notebook and held it out to Charlotte. "These are the verses that I pray when I sit outside the clinic. I want you to take them, read them, pray them."

Charlotte wiped her nose and nodded. She reached for the notebook. Charlotte didn't remember the drive to her apartment, only the cold darkness that enveloped her as she walked into the empty room.

Charlotte, shivering uncontrollably, walked toward the bathroom, tossed her keys onto a small table. Two steps into the hall, purse still looped over her shoulder, Charlotte fell back against the wall opposite of the wall heater and slid down it, her knees drawn up under her chin. The purse fell into the crook at her elbow and she yanked her arm free, instantly frustrated and angry. She choked on a sob, raking her hands back through her hair. She twisted her fingernails into the roots and pulled, a feral scream reverberating in her throat.

She hurt.

The horror of how close she had come to abortion—to murder—was more than she could bear. She kicked at the wall, catching her foot on the purse strap, spilling its contents across the hard wood. A tube of lip-gloss rolled across the small notebook and under the bathroom door.

Judy's notebook…

Zanna held her breath, stunned silent by the deafening quiet in the small chapel. She could almost hear the lip-gloss tube as it rolled across the floor, could see a dejected Charlotte scrunched in a cramped hallway, shivering uncontrollably.

Hadn't Zanna? It had taken Zanna weeks of practice straightening her spine and holding her torso rigid to stop the trembling. But if Charlotte had not had the abortion, why was she so upset?

Charlotte lifted a small spiral notebook, no bigger than the palm of her hand, between her thumb and forefingers, and shook it gently. She brought it down in front of her, grasped it with both hands, and flipped the top page.

Zanna slowly released the air captured in her lungs.

The Heavens Are Telling

Charlotte read aloud, tone soft, reverent. "'The earth is the LORD's, and all that it contains, the world, and those who dwell in it.' Psalm 24:1." Charlotte turned the notebook toward the women; the pages were filled with verse after verse in flowing, steady strokes.

"When I picked up Judy's notebook, I expected page after page of verses that we use to argue against abortion. Psalm 139 is a great example and she did have that. But, ladies, this book—and beyond that, God's Word—is packed with verses of love, forgiveness, and restoration. Verses about a compassionate Shepherd and everlasting God. These words were a balm to my grieving spirit, a reminder of the mighty God I had turned away from. A God who had never left my side, who embraced me with open arms the minute I pressed into Him. A God who cared so much about my unborn child that He orchestrated a way to save it."

Someone coughed when Charlotte paused.

"A God who cared so much about *me* that He saved me from myself." She set the notebook down.

"I miscarried two days later. I started bleeding and didn't stop and had to go to the hospital. I hadn't worked up the nerve to tell my parents about the baby yet, and I called my mom, terrified. To her credit, although she didn't completely understand, she rushed to me, got me to the hospital. She held me while I cried."

Tears of regret and sorrow still flowed freely, so many years later. Charlotte had told them the worst, and they had not thrown stones. She flashed grateful eyes across the small sea of faces.

"When Judy called me over that day, I was a strong and determined, albeit numb, woman ready to enact my right to eliminate a 'problem.' When my mom held me in that hospital and cared for me just two days later and in the weeks that followed, I was a grieving woman, shattered over the unexpected loss of her child. What a difference God can make in a heart."

Sniffs and coughs of sadness and disbelief peppered the room. Charlotte opened the notebook again, found a page with a blue scrap of paper taped to it. She read, "'And I will give them one heart, and put a new spirit within them. And I will take the heart of stone out of their flesh and give them a heart of flesh, that they may walk in My statutes and keep My ordinances and do them. Then they will be My people, and I shall be their God.' Ezekiel 11:19-20."

Charlotte glanced at the clock on the wall behind the faces before her, amazed that she'd done it, amazed further still by the kindness and understanding shining back at her from the women in her church.

Only one face glowered, gray and full of hate.

Zanna's.

Lord, please...Zanna needs You so.

"I don't know what you're dealing with today, ladies. I don't fully understand why God pressed upon me to share that story with you. I do know that we serve a God who restores the broken, Who seeks and saves the lost, Who is mighty and compassionate. Grace and righteousness balanced together in one perfect being. For a long time I battled with the miscarriage. I wondered if I was being punished for my sins for considering abortion. I had feelings of anger and resentment; why did He allow me to get pregnant, save the baby from abortion, only to take it anyway?"

She spread her hands, palms up, in front of her. "I don't know the answers. I don't know why. But, more than anything, I understand now that our days are numbered. Our days are determined. Time is in the hands of the Lord and nothing can happen without His approval. You are here on purpose. Your life may not be honoring, your life may not be all that He created it to be; but as long as you and I have breath, God is working. I was not to abort my baby because God had pre-determined its days. To end that life one second before He had planned would have been murder. Plain and simple."

Zanna bolted from her place on the edge of the pew, charged down the center aisle, face flushed, eyes hard, defying anyone to follow, and slammed through the back doors. The women glanced across the aisles at each other, unsure of whom—if anyone—should go after her.

Charlotte ended the session with prayer, then waited for the closing worship song before she slipped out the back door.

❖ ❖ ❖

"Where is it?"

Hot, angry tears flooded her eyes, ran down her face and into her mouth, salty. Bile burned in the back of her throat.

"Where is that stupid bench?" Zanna cursed and nuzzled further into her coat, fleetingly thankful that the chapel was chilly, forcing them to bring coats to worship.

Worship. Is that what they thought they were doing back there?

Zanna tripped over a tree root. She swiped at her eyes, shocked after trudging through a blanket of undisturbed snow. Swearing, she stomped on the offensive root, her heel smarting. A sob tore out into the frigid air. Desperate, she stopped and looked around. She'd gone at least thirty feet from the furthest cabin. The sun shone brightly on the white landscape, its brilliance reflected all around her, smarting her eyes. She raised a shaky hand to her forehead, her gaze finding only rolling hills dotted with majestic pines. A headache pinched between her eyes. Zanna dropped her palm down over her eyes, trying to absolve the tightness behind them.

"Zanna?"

Zanna dropped her hand, shoved it deep in her coat pocket and trudged on. "Go away, Charlotte. I don't want to hear your Jesus talk."

"Okay."

The snow continued to crunch behind Zanna. She whirled around. Charlotte's eyes widened in surprise, her cheeks pink and beautiful from the stinging cold. Her curly blond hair fell past her shoulders, shimmering with the sun and snow.

"I said go away!" Zanna screamed.

Charlotte stopped, and faced Zanna's rage, her stance unflinching. "I know."

Frustrated and weary, Zanna turned and marched on, rolling her eyes at the echo of shoes on the snow behind her.

"It wasn't like that for me, Charlotte." She wrapped her arms across her chest. It felt so heavy.

"I know that, too."

"How the *hell* would you know? No one knows." Zanna spun and lumbered back to Charlotte on the snow, wishing they were on pavement so that she could stand firm against Charlotte's reasoning and Bible thumping. As it was, the snow beneath her shifted, unstable.

Charlotte delivered Zanna's uncompromising stare back to her. "Because, Zanna, it is all over your face. You carry it in your slumped shoulders. It taints your eyes, hardens your mouth." Charlotte's coat crinkled as she pulled a gloved hand free from her pocket and placed it over her heart. "I know, Zanna. I know what regret and pain looks like."

Zanna shivered despite the heat creeping up her neck. She yanked a stocking cap free from her pocket, pulled it onto her head, nerves jumping, itching to rip her own hair out.

"You stood up there, high and mighty, pretending that you have an idea of what real women face." Zanna rolled her eyes heavenward, altered the pitch of her voice. "I had no choice. Baloney, Charlotte. You were a grown woman with a job and an apartment. You made your own bed to sleep in, to fool around in, you just didn't want to get caught." Zanna pounded her chest with a tight fist. "*I* had no choice."

Charlotte's eyes shimmered.

Was she crying? Zanna thought. "Don't you dare cry for me, princess. I turned out just fine." She made a dismissive slash with her hand and turned back around. *Where was that bench?*

Charlotte remained silent, quietly following after Zanna as she hiked further into the woods. Zanna ignored her. They circled around pine trees, over ridges and underneath pines where the earth was brown, protected from snowfall by the umbrella shape of the treetops. Zanna stopped beneath a tree, nose runny, cheeks and mouth stiff. She leaned, defeated, against the sticky bark on the trunk. Charlotte stopped just outside of the brown ring, respectfully keeping her distance.

The Heavens Are Telling

Zanna, resolve crumbling, glanced at Charlotte, and turned her back into the tree to face the other woman. "I only came here to feel close to my grandma."

Confusion passed over Charlotte's expression, but she remained silent. Zanna told her about the discovery of her gran's Bible, the note inside, the pursuit of the bench. Zanna, eyes trained on her boots, missed the flash of recognition in Charlotte's eyes.

"Zanna," she spoke, breathless, astonished. "I know exactly what you're talking about. Follow me."

Zanna pushed off of the trunk, unsure. Charlotte walked back toward camp. Zanna reluctantly followed, hoping it wasn't just a trick to get her back; although her frozen limbs wouldn't have put up too much of a fuss. The closer Charlotte led her to the camp, the more skeptical Zanna became. If it was close to camp, how could she have possibly missed it? Charlotte took Zanna around the edges of the property rather than through the middle, around the back of the chapel. Through a small cluster of trees, up a gentle slope and next to a large boulder, sat a small wooden bench. It stood at the top of a steep incline peppered with more trees and fallen trunks. A wide river surged at the base of the hill. Zanna's throat closed.

Gran.

Charlotte gripped Zanna's shoulder and turned back toward camp, leaving Zanna to her tangled thoughts.

Chapter Thirty-Nine

Thailand

Jakobi and Simon made their way through the throng of worshippers at the Tattoo Festival at Wat Bang Phra in Nakhon Pathom province outside of Bangkok. When Simon told her that they would meet a monk this time, Jakobi had agreed, imagining the tattoo festivals she'd heard of in the States: a mass of highly decorated individuals sharing their ink and maybe a drink or two. She had not expected the multitude of believers gathering to receive tattoos from Buddhist monks. Tattoos they believed would ward off evil spirits and protect them. Vireak explained that worshipers came for the protection offered with the sacred tattoos.

"They are in the shape of dragons and tigers and things that are mighty. Don't be alarmed when you see men charge and act crazy; they feel they are transformed into the animal of the tattoo they receive. Volunteers are all over to calm them down; just get out of the way."

"What is the purpose of the tattoos?" Simon had asked.

Vireak, somber, answered, "They believe it will protect them from all harm."

Simon scoffed, "And what happens when, inevitably, some are harmed in their life?"

"After they receive the tattoo, the followers are given a list to follow to live right. A contract, of sorts. If they follow it to the letter, combined with the tattoo, they will be protected." Vireak eyed the crowd.

"Well, that's a convenient way to blame the follower when the tattoo doesn't work," Simon observed.

"Exactly." Vireak wondered how he had ever believed in these things. But had he really?

Why would they pick here to make the exchange? Jakobi wondered when the men fell silent and Vireak left to meet with his contact. She always thought the exchange would take place in Cambodia, and was floored when they entered Thailand.

The air was charged with something she couldn't define. Anticipation? Or oppression?

Jakobi was immediately on edge, bracing herself, but unsure against what. Long lines snaked out of the doors of the temple, the vast courtyard hummed with row upon row of worshipers. Simon, obviously not as uncomfortable as she, walked just a step ahead of her, watching everything around them with observant eyes.

Simon stopped to take a few pictures of the rows of believers, working to blend in. He pointed the camera toward the temple, then crouched low in front of her. Jakobi stood watching the faces of those waiting for their tattoo. They were close enough to a monk giving the tattoos to see that he was smoking, his face grim and concentrated. He periodically reached back and took a long draw from a can of some sort of energy drink.

She leaned down to whisper in Simon's ear, her hand on his shoulder. "Where do you think the children are?"

He only shook his head and continued to train his camera around the courtyard, trying to spot anything that might give them a clue as to Noah and Maly's whereabouts.

No. Nothing.

"Are you going to get one?" Simon asked after a while, looking over his shoulder at her with a twinkle in his eye. He winked before turning back to the camera lens.

"What? A tattoo?" she snorted. "No. I somehow doubt letting a monk poke me with some ancient needle will be any more sanitary than getting a tattoo from some guy in a trailer back home."

She continued to watch the monk as he finished with one follower and waved him on. Another stepped forward, bowing to the monk reverently and presented his back for his tattoo. She shuddered when the same needle and inkpot was used, no doubt spreading deadly disease. She wished she could shout to everyone that only the Lord protects, that hope could be found in Him alone. *These worshipers would need a miracle to ward off AIDS after this day.*

Simon looked at her again, squinting into the sun. "I hear they do one in oil for women. It vanishes in a few days."

Jakobi felt immediate unease. She knew Simon was teasing her, trying to lighten both of their hearts as they waited anxiously for the children. But her spirit felt heavy.

Before she could answer, a low growl sounded behind her. Simon looked around her and bolted to his feet, grabbing Jakobi in a hug as a man came charging in their direction, writhing and snarling. Three other men in matching white t-shirts flew through the crowd to capture the man. Simon and Jakobi watched in disbelief as the scene began to play out again and again all over the area. Like popcorn exploding from the pressure of heat, the kernels of growling men popped up one after another and another.

Jakobi clung to Simon, watching in horrified fascination as the men continued to growl and contort their bodies. They stood as more young men in white t-shirts leapt toward the man closest to them and tackled him to the ground. Jakobi screamed, thinking they meant to hurt him, as the veins in their necks popped out and one put the growling man in a headlock. Another reached up and rubbed the growler's earlobe until he calmed down and his glazed eyes cleared. The one who held him in a headlock released him slowly and helped him up.

Jakobi rotated in Simon's arms to look up at him. "Whoa, Vireak wasn't exaggerating, was he," she said.

Simon shook his head in disbelief.

He squeezed her shoulder. "You okay now?"

Jakobi nodded. Simon released her and pretended to take more pictures, using the zoom feature to keep watch for Vireak.

Chaya had been unable to leave the country, no matter the bribe that was offered—more proof of the disjointed corruption of the system—and had agreed to wait at home. "We'll keep praying, Jakobi, my sister," Chaya had promised.

Simon rose from his place at Jakobi's feet and tucked the camera into its bag. He took Jakobi by the elbow and leaned to speak in her ear. "I see them," he said.

Anticipation shot through her. "Where?" She craned her neck, but couldn't make Vireak out among the throng of people, many that were monks.

"Just follow, Jakobi. Remember, when you see them—"

"I know," she interrupted, "pretend I've never met them. I'm just a new mom, excited to meet her kids." *That shouldn't be hard to do.*

Vireak had hoped to catch a moment with Maly alone so he could explain who he was and be sure she understood that she had to pretend to not know Jakobi. They could only pray that no matter what, it would work out and they could slip away with the children and get them to a Deliverance campus safely.

Jakobi craned her neck again. *Where were they? Wait. There.*

Vireak worked to walk causally, head down, a small bundle tucked in his arms. Jakobi didn't see Maly, but knew she must be right behind Vireak. She shook off her backpack ready to retrieve the Minnie from the large zippered pouch. She knew how the girl loved it and hoped it would ease the fear she must be experiencing.

Vireak stepped close to Jakobi and handed her the baby. Noah was sleeping, tucked into a frayed blanket, and Jakobi sighed in relief once he was in her arms. *Thank you, Lord. Thank you, oh thank you.* She rocked back and forth, murmuring over and over, tucking her face into his soft neck.

It took a minute to realize that Vireak and Simon were in deep discussion, their faces grim.

The Heavens Are Telling

She looked around for Maly, ready to hand Noah over to Simon so that she could embrace the frightened girl. She was not standing behind Vireak as Jakobi had expected.

"Simon, what's the matter?" She observed Vireak's empty gaze and looked around, panic clawing at her throat. "Vireak, where's Maly?"

Vireak and Simon exchanged looks.

"They only agreed to sell Noah."

Chapter Forty

McCall, Idaho

The bench was crusted over with a thick layer of snow. Zanna's boots and jeans hardened with a layer of ice crystals as she furiously brushed an arm back and forth across the bench. Hot tears spilled over and quickly froze against her cheeks. She threw her arms onto the bench, buried her face in them, exhausted, angry, frightened…lonely.

She was desperate for her gran's arms around her.

Desperate to change what had been.

Charlotte spoke of her miscarriage and weeks of mourning for her unborn child.

Zanna had spent years mourning the loss of her own life all because of a discarded clump of cells. *What if…?*

Moisture seeped through the knees of her jeans where she huddled in the snow. *He made me.*

"I had no choice," she spoke to the empty forest.

"Didn't you?"

Zanna recoiled at the question. She swiped at her eyes, pointed her face toward the wooden cross on the hill set diagonally from the bench.

Hatred boiled in her breast, spreading through her veins like liquid fire.

"You don't know me. You don't know what I've endured. You don't know!" She heaved with sobs, choked on the icy air.

"Don't I? Every step of the way, I have been with you."

Memories, long forgotten, fired through her mind, like bullets from an automatic rifle, shredding through her resolve, through every bit of reasoning she clung to…

"Father, no! Please don't make me do this. You don't understand!" A young voice echoed through her mind, encrusted with desperation.

She'd been on her knees, then too. Pleading, begging, hoping. Praying.

"No, Zanna"—that booming voice, the righteous glare—"perhaps *you* don't understand…"

Zanna clapped her hands over her ears, desperate to stop the flow. She drew in breath through her nose, snorting and shaking. She fought to control herself and focus.

"Breathe, Zanna, just breathe. Pull in the good. Take the good. Discard the rest. Don't think about it."

Lips tight, she released the air, lungs deflating. The memories remained…

Her father was at a church board meeting. If Zanna wanted a chance to speak with her mother, this was her shot. She pulled back the covers of her narrow bed, careful not to wake her younger sisters in their bunk beds across the room. The hardwood floors were cold and smooth beneath her bare feet.

Zanna padded quietly through the house to her parents' room. A light was on beneath the door, and she knocked quietly.

A sigh. "What is it?"

Zanna pushed the door open. Her mother, hair drawn into a long braid, just like Zanna's father liked, sat with her back against the headboard, reading beneath the lamplight. Small, dark eyes watched Zanna enter the room, her shaking hands clasped behind her back. Zanna's mother looked tired. Weary and worn.

She sighed again. "What is it, Zanna?"

The fifteen year old longed to climb onto the quilt-draped bed and be enveloped in her mother's arms. To sob and cry, to

The Heavens Are Telling

have her head stroked tenderly. To be told that everything would be all right.

Her mother arched a brow at her. "Well?"

Zanna licked her lips, rubbed the back of her leg with one foot. "Mama, I have a problem."

As Zanna explained about Mr. Jones, the way he made her uncomfortable on the car rides home after she babysat for the elder and his wife. How she did what she could to end the ride quickly, sometimes opening the car door in the driveway before he had completely stopped. But he was starting to take longer routes home, and he touched her knee a lot and her hair...

Her mother had sucked in a sharp breath, closed her eyes tight. "Zanna..." Only the word was spoken in annoyance, frustration. Not love and compassion for her daughter's fears. "That's just how Lloyd is. Now go back to bed before your father comes home and hears this nonsense."

Zanna rounded her eyes, knowing if she blinked the tears would overcome her. She nodded, afraid to speak past the sudden dryness of her throat. She managed to squeak out, "Yes, Mama. I'm sorry, Mama," before she turned and fled to her room.

She fell across her bed, desperate to hide beneath the covers, the pillow her only solace. She awoke hours later, unaware of when she had fallen asleep, to hushed whispers.

"It's nonsense. Absolute nonsense. That girl will say anything for attention!"

Zanna flinched.

"But, Robert, what if it's true?"

A strange, stifled noise. Zanna crept to the door, afraid.

Her father's voice was a low growl. "And even if it was true, Tabitha, then what? Lloyd Jones is the wealthiest, most influential member of our church, of the community. If we offend him, then what? You can say good-bye to your house, good-bye to our influence. Everything we have worked so hard for, gone."

There was a muffled bump, like a head hitting a wall, or a book falling from the bed. Then silence.

Zanna crawled back into bed. Defeated.

When Mr. Jones began to touch and kiss, Zanna knew better than to ask for help. After that night, her father had volunteered her to babysit for Lloyd even more than before. When Mr. Jones asked her to call him by his first name when they were alone and began to stop on back roads and behind dark buildings to treat her like his wife, Zanna knew better than to cry out. She'd been sold for her father's standing in the community.

When Gran started to ask Zanna what was wrong every time they went to her home for dinner, her father found other things for Zanna to do on Sunday afternoons....

Snow fell in fat clumps around her, sliding off of her slick coat in a graceful dance. Zanna pulled her frozen body onto the bench, stripped off the moist wool gloves and tucked her hands under her arms. She'd wanted to feel close to her gran, but it had been so long. The letter Gran wrote had been addressed to God; a God Gran loved and believed in. But no matter how much Zanna had cried out to Him as Gran had told her to, He remained silent, unmoving.

Jesus may have been a good man, may have died upon a cross, but He certainly felt no affection for her. It seemed He had been most pleased with her father.

Like the snow falling in heaps around her, blessings of wealth and popularity rained down on her father's church. He had found his voice, his purpose, his *angle*.

The fight against abortion.

His unflinching stand against a woman's right to choose became a beacon to people in the valley, calling them to become members of his church. Over and over, he would tell her mother in a singsong voice, "More memberships means more people tithing."

His face was often in the papers as he fought alongside congressmen to create stricter laws against family planning clinics. He organized marches and protests.

When a new clinic went in near their church, he had implored the members to raise funds to rent the building next door. Only Zanna, who became Lloyd's sounding board, knew that the building cost a great deal less than her father presented to the church.

Families had come together weekend after weekend to make the space into a pregnancy care facility, to offer support to women that found themselves with an unwanted pregnancy. The church offered counseling and adoption services. There were numerous babies adopted into church families as a result of the Life Clinic.

One morning her mother made a special breakfast of pancakes and bacon. A news anchor was coming to do a community in action piece on her father, and the family was in a rush to make the house just right.

The sizzling bacon was too much for Zanna's stomach. She'd been sick every morning for weeks, and now the aroma spread through the house, settling into her hair. She imagined that the fat liquefied, then turned to gas, coating everything in the house.

She felt like she had been coated in bacon grease and flew to the bathroom. Zanna needed to tell her parents about the pregnancy, figuring after the anchor had gone would be the best time. Her father was always in good spirits after an interview...

"Gran, I needed you. I needed your love, your arms. Why, if you wrote this, if you were so worried about me, why didn't you come to me?" She shivered, knowing it was time to go inside. But she had found the bench, sat upon the only reason for her presence in that place. She glared at the cross, felt nauseated and cold and numb and alive all at once. Something about the worship, about Charlotte's words and confession had stirred something inside of her. The same had happened when Lydia returned from her trip with light and life in her eyes.

Lydia claimed she had met the Lord in Thailand.

Zanna rubbed her nose and straightened her spine. "Well, I'm here. Gran prayed that I would come and meet You. Here I am. But where are *You*?" She jabbed a finger toward the cross. "Where have You *ever* been?" Furious tears blurred and cleared away again. She choked on them. She wrestled with the memories, desperate for a different story, a different outcome. She implored, haltingly, in a desperate whisper. "So here I am…if You are real…if-if You really care…show up." *I dare You.*

The sky continued to drift down in white fluffy clumps, muffling the air around her.

Zanna stared at the empty cross. Hope soared, then soured. *No, I didn't think so. Jesus is just as dead and useless as Gran.*

Chapter Forty-One

Charlotte entered the cafeteria and scanned the room for Lydia. She found her at a table near the windows, laughing with Michelle and Michelle's mother. Charlotte smiled, still in awe of the change in her sister.

"If anyone is in Christ, he is a new creation," she murmured. "The old has gone, the new has come. Oh, God, your transforming power in Lydia humbles me; You are so good."

As she made her way to the table, women repeatedly stopped her, some she knew, some she didn't. Each offered a hug of encouragement, a thank you, or their own stories of redemption. Charlotte was amazed. She had been terrified that no one would understand.

But of course, she thought, *of course God knew. Of course He asked me to step out in faith and share.* And of course He had been faithful.

But Zanna.

Charlotte knew, perhaps more than anyone in the camp, Zanna needed to know the love of a powerful God. She finally made her way to Lydia's table and leaned down to whisper in her ear.

"Have you seen Zanna; did she come back?"

"No! I haven't." Lydia stood quickly, pulling her sweatshirt down over her jeans. Lydia had gone from a woman that loved to show off her body to one that was anxious to be modest.

Charlotte absentmindedly rubbed her little sister's shoulder, proud.

"You don't think she's still sitting outside where it's cold, do you? It's been hours." Lydia's forehead pinched with worry.

Charlotte twisted her mouth, thinking. "She could be. You stay here with Michelle." Charlotte knew Lydia had been excited to spend time with her friend, who had only arrived an hour ago after working late the night before. "I will get some soup and a blanket and go see if she's okay. If I'm not back in thirty minutes, send a search party."

Lydia nodded, somber.

Charlotte lightly punched Lydia's arm. "I'm joking. She was at the prayer bench last time I saw her. I'm sure she's still there."

Charlotte approached the soup and salad bar. Remembering that Zanna was a vegetarian, she passed over the beef stew and dipped the ladle into tomato basil and filled a mug halfway. She wrapped a breadstick in a few napkins, making sure every bit was covered before she placed it in her coat pocket.

"Sneaking food out, are we?" Judy spoke accusingly behind her.

Charlotte spun, laughing. "You caught me."

Judy eyed the mug of soup. "You okay? I thought the morning went well."

"Oh, Judy, you were right. The women have been loving and gracious. But, Zanna…"

Recognition passed over Judy's expression.

"Right. I was hoping someone knew where she was." Judy reached for a mug and ladled broccoli cheese into it before handing it off to Charlotte.

"Not everyone likes tomato," she explained. "And this way you have an excuse to stay with her."

Charlotte flashed a grin at Judy. "Schemer."

Judy shrugged. "What can I say? I'm a real conspirator." Judy's eyes darkened, serious. "But, Charlotte, get her inside soon. I don't like that she's been in the cold this long."

"Aye, aye, captain." Charlotte, hands full, leaned forward and pressed a cheek against Judy's, thankful.

"You know you saved my life, right?" Charlotte pulled back to look into the woman's shimmering eyes.

"No, sweetie," Judy answered, cupping Charlotte's cheek with her soft, dry hand, "only God saves. I just listened. And fed you." She winked. "Praying for you both."

Charlotte backed out a side door. "Thanks."

※ ※ ※

Zanna's head turned slightly as Charlotte crunched closer through the snow. Snow clung to Charlotte's lashes and landed in the steaming mugs of soup.

"I brought some soup and a blanket." Charlotte stopped next to Zanna, held the mugs out for her to take, the blanket tucked precariously under her arm.

Zanna's nose was cherry red and dripping. She sniffed and reached hesitantly for the soup, her stomach cramping. She slipped her fingers through the mug handles, but was too stiff to support them. Charlotte dropped the blanket and reached to steady the soup. "Whoa."

"Sorry," Zanna shivered, voice faltering.

Charlotte stood over her, arms akimbo. Although they were the same age, a mothering look passed across her features as she assessed Zanna.

"That's it," Charlotte announced, setting the mugs of soup on the bench. "You're going to come inside and take a hot shower. Then you'll eat while we talk." Charlotte hooked an arm under Zanna's left shoulder and pulled her up. Charlotte left the mugs and draped the blanket around Zanna.

Something about the tender way that Charlotte wrapped an arm around Zanna's middle for support shattered her. As she'd longed to do with her mother years ago, Zanna tucked her face into Charlotte's neck and sobbed all the way back to the camp.

A soft, empathetic cry escaped Charlotte's throat as she tried desperately to bear up Zanna's defeated weight and hold her head tenderly. She stopped repeatedly to retrieve the blanket as it slipped off of the awkward pair and into the snow.

Zanna's doleful cries echoed through the center of camp, drawing half a dozen curious women from their cabins. Without hesitation, they assessed the situation and rallied around Zanna and Charlotte. One held the blanket around the frozen woman's shoulders; another ran to the dining hall for more soup, still more rushed ahead to open the chapel doors. Zanna was carefully led up the stairs and helped into the bathroom.

In a cloud of despair, years of pent up abuse and pain and disappointment poured out of Zanna. Blinded by grief, she barely noticed as the women, older than she, worked to slip off her boots and peel away her wet, frozen clothes. Charlotte, fully clothed, helped Zanna into the shower, and then backed out, closing the curtain behind her for privacy.

The hot water stung, sending shards of ice racing through Zanna's veins. She cried out in pain and grasped for the handles.

The water snapped off and Charlotte wrapped Zanna in a towel and helped her out of the shower. Still shivering and in pain, Zanna let herself be led to the bed and struggled to pull on warm sweats that were presented to her. Someone pushed a mug of piping tomato soup into her hands and she sipped it gingerly. The silky smooth blend of tomatoes and basil sprinkled with Parmesan was heavenly after her hours seated on the cold, hard bench.

She handed the mug back, only able to manage a few swallows. Warmth and exhaustion spread like a roaring fire to her fingers and toes. Loving, strong hands helped to guide Zanna down into her sleeping bag and blankets were settled over her. She heard soft whispers spoken around her, above her.

The air tingled, full and wonderful. A calloused hand, undeniably masculine, settled on her brow. She wasn't aware of any men at the camp, but supposed they could have called a doctor. She wasn't sick, just so very tired. So weary.

The room filled with the fragrance of wood smoke.

Snaps and pops—the crackling music produced by a roaring fire—lulled Zanna to sleep.

❋ ❋ ❋

She woke with a start, sweating profusely, and sat up. The wall next to her bed was bathed in soft, peach-colored light. Sunset already? Hadn't they just eaten breakfast? Zanna ran a hand over her face, pinched the bridge of her nose.

The day flooded over her in a rush.

Charlotte's story.

Gran's bench.

Her plea for God to reveal Himself.

His silence.

But how did she get in bed?

There was a faint rustling noise, then a quiet sip. Zanna craned her head toward the sound. She found Charlotte, seated by the window in a small wooden chair, a Bible spread open on her lap. Charlotte watched Zanna and smiled from behind a coffee mug. She swallowed and set the coffee on the windowsill.

"Hey there," she spoke softly. "How are you feeling? You satisfy your desire to be a human Popsicle?" She settled a hand on the Bible.

Zanna moved her legs beneath the blanket and wriggled her toes inside warm wool socks. They were still a little cold, despite how flushed the rest of her body felt. She pushed the heavy load of blankets off and scooted back out of the sleeping bag and against the wall, legs drawn up to her chest.

"Yeah...sorry about that." Zanna cleared her throat, still dazed and undecided if she was thankful that Charlotte had mothered her or annoyed. She sighed. Too much energy was required to be annoyed.

"Hey, uh..." Apparently too much energy was required to lay aside her pride and express gratitude. She leaned her head against the wall.

"It's okay, Zanna." Charlotte took another sip of coffee and held the cup out. "Do you want me to get you some? They have a pot downstairs."

"Yes. Thank you."

Charlotte returned minutes later. She passed a clunky brown mug to Zanna, then reached in the front pouch of her sweatshirt for sugar packets and creamer cups. She held them up. "What's your poison?"

Zanna held the mug for a moment, feeling pathetic and helpless. "I can do it." She hadn't meant to snap.

"Sure you can, I just didn't want you to have to balance it all. Here you go." Charlotte set the handful of cream and sugar on the bed and sat next to Zanna. Zanna set the mug in the crook of her arm and tore the sugar open with her teeth, then the creamer in the same fashion, glancing at Charlotte as she spilled a little on the bed. Charlotte considerately pretended not to notice while she sipped her own brew.

"Want to talk about it?" she asked.

Yes. "Not really." Zanna's tone was short.

Charlotte, undeterred, turned toward Zanna. "You sure? You said it wasn't the same for you. What did you mean?"

Zanna's throat closed. "I mean I wasn't some brat that made choices she claimed she didn't believe in, then decided to be a hypocrite and cover it up." *Why did she have to be so mean?*

Charlotte took in a sharp breath, surprised. Hurt. She pulled her lips in, eyes heavenward. "You're right, Zanna. You're absolutely right. That's exactly how it was for me, and that's one reason it's taken me so long to tell anyone. I was very ashamed." She tried to make eye contact, but Zanna continued to stare at the ceiling. "But I don't think that's all of it, is it?"

"You can't handle all of it, Charlotte. It's too ugly for your neat little world."

"Try me, Zanna."

Chapter Forty-Two

Boise, Idaho

The encounter with Zanna had both repulsed and exhilarated him. His power over her was intoxicating; the memories of her had tainted his dreams of Nataya, and he knew he was running out of time; he needed Nataya. He had to have her or go mad.

The project in the basement was proving lucrative; customers had come and gone the week before he'd been with Zanna, and although he hadn't had a customer since then, Gage's cash flow continued to increase.

Soon he could notify Ava that it was time.

He opened his social account and clicked on his messages with *her*, enlarging the attached picture of her posing nude in her living room. Her skin was creamy white, her hair strawberry blond. Her youthful figure aroused him. He smiled to himself, imagining the fun they could have on the way to meet his contacts. He re-read Ava's messages, checking for details about her hometown, Cannon Beach.

She had not come out and told him where she lived, believing, of course, that he already knew. But she hadn't been difficult to find; he knew she lived near the ocean, knew her school's mascot, knew her favorite place to get pizza. It had only taken a few words typed into a search engine before

Cannon Beach popped up. If Ava didn't cooperate and meet him at the airport when the time came, he could easily find her. She'd be as easy to overcome as Zanna had been. But he doubted it would come to that. Ava asked "Toby" in every exchange if it was time to leave for Cambodia. She was eager—desperate to see her sister.

Gage sat back and ran his fingers through his hair, agitated. His time with Zanna had stirred his appetite without satisfying his hunger. He thought one night of power and release would do it until he could be with Nataya, but he burned for more. He had spent hours on the floor in front of the trunk, but his hunger grew.

His stomach growled, his basic needs distracting his dark thoughts. A slow sneer worked across his lips.

He knew where he could satisfy both.

❖ ❖ ❖

"Hailey, honey, come down real quick and eat your lunch!" Hannah Watts waited for a moment and then cupped her hands around her mouth and called again for her daughter.

"Okay, Mama!" was the muffled response from the high play structure. Hannah smiled to herself and dropped her hands to her hips, watching expectantly for her four-year-old to pass by one of the bubbled windows.

A flash of purple whizzed by, then a thud as her daughter hit the top of the tube slide. Hailey emerged giggling, her blond hair a fuzzy halo from static electricity. Hannah laughed with her and scooped her up for a kiss as she walked back to their table. Haily wriggled out of her arms and climbed onto the bench, stuffing fries in her mouth.

Hannah laughed, "Slow down, Hailey, you have plenty of time to play. Chew. Then swallow."

The mother and daughter chattered about Hailey's morning at preschool.

The Heavens Are Telling

Hailey finished her lunch, and Hannah sent her back to play, hoping to wear her out enough for a nap so that she could get some housework done that afternoon. She cleared their food and looked around the crowded restaurant. It was practically full and Hannah sat, watching the little windows and mesh walls for Hailey sightings.

A weight of disquiet settled on her shoulders.

Her daughter appeared in a window, banging on it and calling out to her mother. Hannah smiled and waved. Hailey giggled and turned to play with another little girl. Hailey was fine. Still, Hannah's anxiety remained. The hair stood on the back of her neck, and it felt as if a shadow passed over her.

Hannah rubbed her arms and looked around. Mothers, some alone, some with friends, and a few fathers dotted the busy room. Some women read books, enjoying the quiet; some prodded their children to eat more. Kids of all ages ran to and fro, stuffing chicken nuggets in their mouths and heading off to play more. Some siblings fought. Children called loudly to each other, their voices echoing off the walls. It was a typical day in a fast food playground. But Hannah could not shake the foreboding that pressed upon her. She looked around again and noticed a man in the back corner by the slide, his back against the wall, turned toward the play structure, reading something on his phone.

Hannah frowned. Why did he give her a bad feeling? She turned away and watched Hailey a few minutes more before she glanced surreptitiously at him from beneath her lashes. The man sat in the same position, back against the wall, feet pointed toward the slide, reading on his phone. Hannah narrowed her eyes when he rotated slightly. No, he wasn't reading on his phone. He was taking video of the kids playing.

Hannah felt a shiver of anger and panic. She licked her lips and took a deep breath. *Calm down, Hannah. It is perfectly natural for parents to take video of their kids.*

But the more she watched him, the more her stomach churned. He wasn't with a child; she was sure of it. She stayed in place for a few minutes more, frantically connecting each child with a parent in the room, based on who she had seen eating at what table. Her heart pounded as it became clear that he was not with anyone and continued to record the children and watch them through his phone camera. In fact, he leaned forward slightly—eagerly—whenever a girl came down the slide.

What do I do?

Hannah bolted to her feet when she heard Hailey shriek. She met her daughter at the bottom of the slide. Hannah shifted her body, presenting her backside to the creep with the camera so that he couldn't record Hailey, before she scooped her child up and strode back to their table.

Hailey struggled, and trying to keep her voice calm, Hannah gently chided in her ear. "Sweetie, you need to trust Mama. We are going to put on your shoes; it's time to go."

Hailey cried out, unhappy that her play was interrupted. Normally Hannah would have given her a five-minute warning, but all she could think was to get out as fast as possible. She reached for Hailey's shoes, her hands shaking.

Hannah took a deep breath and forced a smile for her crying girl. "I know, sweetie, I know. Why don't we grab an ice cream on our way out?" Hannah suggested.

Hailey smiled at her through her tears and nodded. Hannah kissed the girl on her forehead before glancing once more at the man with the phone.

He was watching her, an undecipherable expression on his face. Hannah unconsciously curled her lips at him in disgust before she scooped Hailey up and strode to the food counter. She ordered the ice cream and, in a low voice, asked to speak to the manager. A young man, no older than twenty, came over.

"There is a man in the play area that is not with a child. He has been watching the kids and is recording them on his phone. You need to call the police," she whispered.

The young man licked his lips, obviously uncomfortable. "Yeah, sure. Okay. Can you show me which man?"

Hannah tried to describe the man by the slide without turning around. The manager looked over her shoulder, his brow furrowed. "Are you sure, lady? There is no man by the slide."

Hannah spun around to look through the windows.
He was gone.

❂ ❂ ❂

"Stupid wench," Gage muttered to himself. He had known the woman was watching him, had thought it was funny how she tried to hide her precious daughter.

Too bad it took you so long to figure out, lady. I got plenty of video of your little blondie to watch tonight, he thought, proud of himself.

He couldn't believe she tried to go to the manager. What was that little punk going to do? Gage snorted in disdain. *People are so stupid.*

He parked his car in the garage and strode through the door into the house. Lunch at the restaurant was the first time he'd left his house in days. He had worked at home most of the week, knowing he needed access to the trunk in the wake of his increasing anxiety and need for Nataya. When the trunk hadn't satiated his hunger, he had to find new material at the fast food restaurant.

But now that he had been outside and come in again, he could smell it.

The faint odor of decay.

He cursed and rushed into the basement. *How long had it been since he'd checked on them?* Gage clambered down the stairs, trying to remember. Three days? Maybe more? Not since that guy last week.

The stench hit him full force once he hit the bottom step. Gage coughed, angry.

He flipped on the light.

Glassy eyes stared back at him.

He swore and poked the lifeless body. *Now what am I going to do?*

Gage rushed to the other room and breathed in relief when she curled in on herself in fear at his presence. At least one was still alive.

Would that be enough?

Chapter Forty-Three

McCall, Idaho

"I can't eat meat," Zanna said.

Charlotte, confused, nodded slowly. "Okay."

"It started when he would stop for a burger on his way to take me home from babysitting."

Charlotte immediately felt sick. Her chest tightened. "Oh, Zanna…" she breathed.

Zanna didn't seem to hear her.

"My dad was the pastor of a large church in town. But it wasn't always so big. We struggled financially…until the Jones' came to our church. They had a lot of money…and a lot of kids. They had functions to go to—"

"Are you talking about Senator Jones?" Charlotte clamped her mouth shut. *What did it matter?*

Zanna looked askance at her. "They needed a babysitter and my dad offered them me." She sniffed, her mouth set in a hard line. "I babysat for the Jones' for two years…until I got pregnant."

Charlotte wanted to reach out and hold her hand or stroke her hair. But Zanna held her back so rigid and her knees so tight against her chest, she looked made of stone. Charlotte feared she would shatter her in this vulnerability. *Jesus, oh Jesus, how can I offer any comfort in this?* Charlotte's inner turmoil was palpable.

Zanna hesitated. *You haven't even heard it yet, princess.*

Once she'd begun, it was too much to stop. The floodgates were open and there would be no closing them until the raging waters, held at bay for so many years, were finally released.

"I told my mom first, then we told my dad. He was angry. I've never seen him so angry. He called Mr. Jones and set up a meeting. I think I spent that entire evening shaking in my bed. My mom had sent me to my room 'to rest' but I think she found it unbearable to look at me." Zanna held a deep breath.

"I will never forget what his knock sounded like..."

Tap-tap-tap.

Somehow she knew.

The light knocks on her door, where her father normally pounded, the light tap told Zanna exactly what Papa and Mr. Jones had worked out.

"It's really best this way," her father had said. "He'll pay for everything. He'll even pay for you to go to college next year."

Zanna, wizened from months of long car rides home, shook her head. "If you are going to send me away, why make me go to the clinic?" She asked in a strained whisper.

She had watched the awful videos that her father showed in Sunday school, knew the statistics. Her entire life her father had been against abortion, had screamed against it from the steps of the capital building, had shamed women entering the clinics, and now he wanted this for his daughter?

"No daughter of mine is going to have a bastard child. Lloyd can't afford a scandal; it's an election year. Our church can't afford for Lloyd to be out of a job. He's offered a good deal of money to get rid of the problem and will more than compensate for any inconvenience. This is non-negotiable, Zanna."

Her knees tingled from kneeling in desperation before him, her fists held his pant legs tight. "Let me call Gran, please. Before I do this, let me call Gran."

Her father exploded; his shoes and fists landed sharp and purposeful against her abdomen, as if he wanted to abort the baby himself.

"If you so much as think of talking to your grandmother or *anyone* about this you are gone from us forever. You are dead to us!"

Hours later, Zanna lay listening to the symphony of snores from a family asleep without a care. Her father had called the clinic, made the appointment for her. She had to whisper "yes" into the phone to let the secretary know that she agreed. The appointment was set for Monday, just after the weekend. Gran hadn't been to her father's church in years, Zanna hadn't seen her in just as long. Did she have the same number?

Zanna pushed back the covers, her stomach rolling in fear as she set bare feet on the cold floor and tiptoed into the hall toward the kitchen. She stepped gingerly, pain shooting through her sore body with every step.

With help from the small light left on over the oven, Zanna located her mother's address book. She fumbled for the page with Gran's name, wondering how she would ever explain. Maybe she could just call and ask to see her tomorrow. Gran sometimes met with her book club on Saturdays; maybe Zanna could ask to join.

"Just call her."

A calm assurance fell across her. She already had bruises across her body, how much worse would it be if he found out?

Zanna took a deep breath and lifted the phone from the receiver, the dial tone buzzed abrasively. *Could they hear it?*

She fumbled the numbers on the first try, placed a hand on the receiver to start again. She moved her arm and the light reflected on the family wall calendar. The next day was circled three times in red. A "protest day" at the clinic.

She went cold.

Her family was always expected to go together. They met with members of the church and stood outside the abortion clinic all day, marching, holding signs, screaming "murderer!" at women as they walked by.

Would they expect her to go? Of course her father would. And then he would expect her to abort her baby two days after.

She hung up the phone...

"The next morning, I snuck a call to the clinic while the family was outside loading up the car. Because my father had already called and given permission, it was no problem for me to change the appointment. Just as I'd thought, the family expected me to participate in the protest."

Charlotte sniffed, tears pouring down over her face.

Zanna twisted her mouth. "My mom made a big breakfast to keep us through until lunch. I still have no idea if she knew what my father's plan was. She just treated me like nothing was different.

"When we arrived at the clinic, a group from our church was already there. I waited until everyone was in place, and I made sure my dad was watching as I walked the line of them and entered the clinic. I'm sure they thought I was confronting the nurses or something. They would have understood what I was doing when I didn't return for a few hours."

Zanna spoke to herself. "A few hours. That was all it took for the procedure and recovery. I arranged for a cab that was wating for me when I was done. They were still protesting as I walked out. Slightly shaken and sore, my father was waiting near the doors, his face purple with anger. I walked straight to him and handed him the bill. Then I squared my shoulders and walked straight out in the middle of all of them..."

They'd crowded around her, outraged and offended. Necks corded, faces purple with fury.

"Whore!" her mother had screamed as she walked by, spitting on her.

"Murderer! Whore!" Her father had woven a sermon of fire and brimstone to heap on her as she walked past him, for the first time in her life she was brazen enough to meet his gaze.

"I had no choice," she told him, her voice inaudible above the screams. She felt bits of bread catch in her long hair as they threw their lunches at her. A mist passed over her as the crowd spit and yelled and screamed, her father the loudest of all.

She opened the door to the cab and slipped in, determined not to cry.

The driver twisted to look her over. "You okay, kid?" His face was aghast, obviously unsure if he wanted to take on the crowd surrounding his cab to shriek at his passenger.

Zanna watched her siblings push their way to the front of the crowd, their little faces twisted in rage and anger, over things they didn't understand. She looked away.

"Don't call me kid..."

"I took the cab to my parents' house and waited. When they got home, they kicked me out. Told me they didn't care where I went. I packed a small bag and asked my father for the money he owed me. From that moment on, every word I spoke to him, every action was retaliation. I finally saw him for the hypocrite he was and refused to cower before him. My mother must not have known about the plan my father and Lloyd worked out; she was surprised when my father went to their room and returned with a fat envelope."

Zanna set her empty coffee mug on the floor.

"I turned eighteen the next week. With the money, I rented a hotel room for a month while I went to the campus library and read as much as I could and talked with as many coeds as I could. Summer was approaching. Lloyd offered to pay for college, but I didn't graduate high school. I could sew and make clothes, but that wasn't enough to sustain me. I heard about places in other countries that let you volunteer in exchange for room and board. So I got my passport and spent the next five years doing that. The rest you know."

The room fell into heavy silence. The sun had set, and a small lamp near the end of the bed cast a weak glow into the room. Charlotte felt the oppression that followed Zanna's story. The room itself felt weighted down.

"Oh, Zanna, I wish you would have called your gran."

The words were enough to set Zanna on edge, tempting her to close up the gate and lock it tight again. But she heard the sadness and regret Charlotte felt *for* her. *With* her.

"Me too." Zanna whispered, admitting it aloud for the first time since it happened.

"Even more, Charlotte, I wish your God would have saved me like He did you. There was no Judy at my clinic. Instead, there was an unattached nurse, a stoic doctor. A cold table. A thin robe."

Though she knew it was impossible, Zanna had always thought she heard a baby screaming above the whooshing and sucking of the machine. Her entire body had reacted, tight and desperate to fight for the life within her. They had threatened to put her to sleep if she didn't calm down. She desperately tried to forget the videos she had seen. Eventually, shock held her still.

Charlotte spoke hesitantly, "I know this God I serve. He was there, Zanna. You only needed to call out."

Shame washed over Zanna. And anger. "I did cry out, I cried out then and I cried out just hours ago on that cold barren bench. Do you know why I came here?"

Zanna dug into her bag for Gran's Bible. She took out Gran's letter and shook it at Charlotte. "My Gran sat there and prayed for me. The date shows that it was just months before the abortion. She prayed that I would know the Lord. Instead, He allowed me to be raped, and then allowed me to get pregnant; He allowed them to force me into an abortion. And when I came here to ask Him to show Himself to me, He was silent. I almost froze to death waiting."

Charlotte faced her, hands spread open. "Zanna, please don't misunderstand me. What your parents allowed was *wrong*. What Lloyd did to you was *dead* wrong. There is no excuse for that and, oh, how I wish I would have known you, been a friend to you when this was happening. I know that in this world awful things happen. You've experienced that. You and I have joined the fight to rescue young girls from evil being done to them over and over. This world is so broken and lost. I believe it is from choosing our own way instead of the Creator's way.

"When Lloyd raped you, he did what *he* wanted, what was right to *him*. The same with your father and your mother. When I chose to get an abortion, it was right in my eyes. God stepped in and reminded me that it wasn't right in His eyes. And no matter what way I tried to swing it, I could never make it okay. But for the grace of God, Judy was there. Otherwise, I would have gone through with it, done it my way. I would have pushed through my hesitations and just hoped it would be okay one day. Didn't you?"

Zanna shrugged. "What's your point, Charlotte?"

"My point is you could have called your gran. You know she would have fought to protect you and your baby. She would have been by your side every step of the way."

"But he wouldn't have let that happen."

Charlotte opened her mouth and closed it. "Zanna, I'm sorry. You've shared something very painful with me, and I don't know how to respond; I want to fix it, want to be true to the God I believe in. I'm honestly not trying to bash you over the head with choices, I, myself made and almost carried out." She spread her hands again. "I want peace for you. I believe with everything in my being"—she pressed her hands against her chest—"that God is the only true Peace Giver. His ways and thoughts are far above my own, and yet He gives us His word to better understand who He is. I know if you cried out, He was immediately by your side. Maybe you just didn't see it. But I want you to feel free to talk without fear of judgment."

Charlotte patted her chest. "I believe God restores and renews. That He creates beauty from ashes, that He replaces hearts of stone with flesh that is like putty in His creative, giving hands. I just want you know, that God cares for you as an individual. That if you or I had been alone in our sinful nature, if everyone else but you had it together, Christ still would have sacrificed Himself on that cross for you. You are on purpose. You are precious to Him. You are fearfully and wonderfully made because You are made by Him and for Him. No matter what lies the ugliness of sin has told you, no matter what you've done or what has been done to you, don't doubt for a minute that the loving God portrayed in this book"—she held up her Bible—"is dead. He is alive. He didn't say these things once. He says them now, over and over. You can trust in the things He has established because He is forever. Every minute you are breathing has been determined and ordered by Him. You are precious. Every minute of your life means something to Him."

The next morning the women gathered in the chapel before the drive home. Judy and a woman with a guitar led the ladies in worship. Song after song, the women around Zanna raised their voices in adoration and love.

Zanna felt set apart from them, unsure of it all, but she couldn't forget Charlotte's words from the night before—couldn't deny their calming effect on her heart. The kind of calm she had only experienced with her gran so many years ago. After a while, women began to share, tears flowing, their own stories of survived abuse, adultery, abortions, and substance abuse. Zanna listened in awe.

So many of these "churched" women had stories to share that evoked not anger and wrath from self-righteous listeners, but groans of understanding, hugs of compassion. Tissues were passed, prayers were raised, songs were offered.

Zanna sat in awe, unable to form any defense or argument against what she witnessed. She witnessed abundant, forgiving love and marveled at it.

Maybe there was some truth to the things Charlotte had said.

Chapter Forty-Four

Thailand

When she realized that Maly was not a part of the deal, Jakobi's hopes plummeted into despair. She cried out in anguish; her voice drowned out by the pandemonium and discord of the tattoo festival around them.

"What do you mean they won't give us Maly?" she shouted at Vireak, fear coiling around her.

Simon squeezed her shoulder, turning her away. She shook him off, careful to hold Noah tight against her. She sobbed, pressing her face to the baby's soft head as Simon led her out of the courtyard, Vireak following them closely.

When they reached the street, she rounded on Vireak. "We cannot leave here without her!" she protested.

Vireak stared at her, his face white and hard. His throat constricted as he swallowed.

Simon set his mouth and gripped Jakobi's elbow, pushing her toward the truck. He spoke low, his firm tone breaking through her panic. "Jakobi, we have a job to do. Noah is not safe here; we have him in our possession, and we have to get him out of here. Pull yourself together and walk to the truck."

Jakobi sobered, ashamed and afraid that she had put the baby in danger and walked numbly beside Simon. Once in the truck, she unwound the blanket Noah had been swaddled in and laid him on her legs, checking him over. Vireak slid behind the steering wheel, and the engine roared to life.

As he maneuvered the truck through the busy streets, Vireak relayed in monotone all that he had learned from the monk that gave him Noah. "Once Dara sold the kids, Noah came straight to this *wat* and has been cared for by widows that have also dedicated their lives in service to Buddha. The check-ins and different *wats* were all part of an elaborate plan to shake us off."

"They didn't expect us to hang in with them and that charade for as long as we did; did they?" Simon asked.

Jakobi re-wrapped the baby and held him close, eyeing Vireak when he shook his head no. "What could they have possibly done with Maly?" Jakobi whispered.

Simon met her gaze, his eyes red. The answer was clear in his gaze.

Jakobi felt that she'd been punched in the stomach and she hunched over, a helpless wail escaping her lips. "No, Simon. No!"

Simon reached his arm around her, seeking to comfort her, though he felt hollow himself. Jakobi leaned into him, her throat burning. She cried until they arrived at a motel. They needed to rest a few hours and buy more formula before the drive to Cambodia.

Once they checked into the room, Simon used his phone to call Megan at Deliverance. "We should be there by tomorrow morning with Noah," he said woodenly. Simon's gaze flickered to where Jakobi lay on the bed with the sleeping baby. She watched him with glassy eyes and he turned away and spoke quietly to Megan. "No, we only have the boy."

Jakobi's eyes burned. A hot tear slipped down her cheek. She pulled Noah closer to her and curled her body around his small form.

Vireak borrowed clothes from Simon and slipped into the bathroom. He changed out of his robe and for the first time since he was a child. He pulled on shorts and a light t-shirt. The pretense finally over, he angrily shoved the orange robe into the

The Heavens Are Telling

trashcan and slumped to the floor, collapsing in exhaustion and defeat.

Vireak had felt an incredible fear for Maly since he'd first heard that Dara gave her to the *wat*. What Maly's grandmother thought was an act of love and protection had instead left the young girl vulnerable, available to be sold to a brothel. Still, Vireak and Simon—who also understood the danger Maly faced—had done all they could to play the game, hoping she would be safe when at last the farce was over. But in the end, all he had feared was true.

They had not been able to rescue her. In the fight of good versus evil, rescuer versus trafficker, the evil trafficker had won.

Vireak dropped his head into his hands, fingers digging into his scalp, his lips clamped together to hold back the shouts of rage that welled in his chest. He imagined the small, helpless girl in the clutches of someone that would use her body and see her as a toy and not a human being.

He punched the floor. *No. No, Lord, no.*

Vireak leaned his head back, eyes resting on the orange material spilling out of the trash. He sat motionless for several minutes before he rose purposefully, donned the robe over his clothes, and strode from the motel, not telling Simon or Jakobi of his plans.

❖ ❖ ❖

The *wat* was still writhing with activity.

Lines of devout men and women snaked through crowds of people. Those that bore the sacred prayers, written in ink or burned into their skin with oil were still jumping up and charging like mad men and women through the courtyard until they were overtaken and subdued. A chant still buzzed in monotone over a loudspeaker; holy water was sprayed over the worshippers.

But something had shifted. Earlier in the day, Vireak had walked through the *wat* unnoticed. He was just another monk in the vast array of activity. Now, although he still wore his orange robe, his head still shaved—although he appeared exactly the same as he had hours before—there was a shift in the atmosphere. As though he was a searchlight penetrating the darkness, eyes turned to watch him as he walked through the square. Dark, cold eyes turned toward him, followed his every step. Sweat broke out over Vireak's upper lip as the air closed in tight around him. He walked on.

He located the room where Noah was handed to him and barged in. The elderly monk sitting on the bed was the same that had given Vireak the baby. Despite the brightness of the sun outside, the room was bathed in languid lamplight. It did little to dissipate the shadows that draped the corners of the room.

"Where is the girl!?" Vireak demanded.

The monk's eyes flickered over him dismissively. "I don't know what you're talking about," he answered, turning away.

"Where is she!?" Vireak demanded again, striding across the room and yanking the man up by his robe. The droning prayer in the courtyard could be heard through the stone walls. It hummed in Vireak's head as he slammed the old monk into the wall, his fingers twisted in the smaller man's robe.

The monk rounded his eyes at Vireak, stuttering, sweat beading on his forehead. "I don't know!" he protested.

Vireak shook him again. "Wrong answer, old man." Years of pent up frustration, coupled with the weeks of travel and exhaustion, exploded behind Vireak's eyes. He pulled the man away from the wall and hurled him across the room. A dark, malevolent shadow settled around Vireak, filling the room. The man stumbled back onto the stone floor, and he scrambled away from Vireak in fear.

Vireak's lip curled in disdain over the man's weakness.

Kill him.

Vireak didn't stop to question the dark thought. He pulled the man up again, slowly—deliberately—and pressed his forearm against the man's throat, pushing him back into the wall. He gradually increased pressure, vengeance pounding a steady rhythm in his head as the man scrambled for air, fingers

The Heavens Are Telling

grasping Vireak's arm in desperation. The monk's eyes began to roll back in his head. The shadows shifted and there was flutter in Vireak's spirit. Vireak, horrified, realized what he was doing. He let go and the monk fell to the ground, gasping and coughing.

Vireak shook, ashamed and terrified of what he'd been about to do. "Jesus, oh Jesus," he whispered, dropping to the small bed in the corner, his head in his hands.

A terrible hiss echoed through the room, buzzing louder and louder. Vireak dropped his hands and looked up.

The old monk watched him with eyes wide, full of fear.

"What name did you say?" he asked, his face white.

Vireak hesitated. "Jesus," he answered. The hissing quieted slightly, but the shadows in the room pressed in.

The man trembled, his eyes darting around the room. "There is power in that name. Why?"

Vireak set his mouth.

The name of Jesus had been in his heart every night that he'd spent as a monk. First the name brought fear, as if Uncle Kosal would be able to hear it as it whispered through Vireak's mind. Then Jesus had become a curse; a name he could not forget or ignore, though he'd tried for years. At last, Vireak had realized that Jesus was the only balm to his bruised and broken heart. The only peace he would ever know. The Name that gave him hope as he spent so many nights in torment and darkness of strange *wats* as he pursued two innocent children. Children that were commodities to men like the one trembling before him. Who was this man that Vireak should tell him about Jesus?

The monk watched Vireak, his eyes empty, dark. Afraid.

"You're right, old man. There is power in the name of Jesus Christ..."

The hissing rose to a blood-curdling shriek as the shadows flew from the room.

Jakobi paced, chewing her thumb. Simon sat in a chair in the corner with Noah, feeding him a bottle of formula that Jakobi had brought. Noah watched Simon's face, eyes steady and stoic. Simon leaned down to whisper to him, "That's right, young man. You look people in the eye. You drink this bottle like a boss."

Simon winked at him, before glancing up at Jakobi. "Jakobi, you're making me dizzy, sit down."

She obliged, and sat on the edge of the bed, biting her fingernail. But within minutes her foot began to shake, then her knees began to bounce, and she was on her feet pacing again. Simon's mouth lifted in amusement, but Jakobi didn't notice.

"Where could he have gone, Simon?"

"I don't know, Jakobi, but Vireak is a grown man, and he can take care of himself. Maybe he went to get more formula. Maybe he's upset and needs some air. He will come back. There is no need to worry." Simon patted the chair next to his. "Come here and sit down."

Jakobi walked over, her eyes pained, her arms crossed, hands gripping her ribs. "I can't sit, Simon. I can't. I'm worried about Vireak." She licked her lips and took a deep breath. "I'm in agony over Maly. I can't even…" She shook her head, the words catching in her throat.

Simon sighed. "I know, Jakobi." Simon knew all too well. Numerous girls that Deliverance had rescued had first been sold when they were barely older than Maly. He knew stories of things that men did to little girls that turned him upside down and inside out. Imagining where Maly was and what could be happening to her ripped him apart. He closed his eyes, praying for the little girl.

"Simon," Jakobi whispered, "I don't understand. All this time we've been praying and following. Maly was safe in Deliverance in the prevention program. Why would God allow her to go with her grandparents, only to be trafficked?" Tears rolled down her face and dropped from her chin.

"I just don't understand," she repeated.

Noah finished the bottle and Simon offered him to Jakobi to burp him. She eagerly received the baby into her arms, her heart rejoicing in his rescue while her soul melted in despair over Maly's well-being.

Simon leaned forward, elbows on his knees, slowly rubbing his hands together. "I don't have the answers, Jakobi. I don't. I have dozens of verses flowing through my mind; such as ones where David asks the Lord to slay the wicked. But I think of the verses that say, 'For My thoughts are not your thoughts, nor are your ways My ways...for as the heavens are higher than the earth, so are my ways higher than your ways'."

Jakobi dipped her chin. "Simon, are you saying it is God's will for that little girl to be raped a dozen times a day for the rest of her life?" Her eyes shimmered in horror and pain, torn between her new commitment to the Lord and the ache of the dark world around them.

Simon closed his eyes, unable to look at her. "No, I'm not saying that at all. I know in my heart what's true: 'every good thing given and every perfect gift is from above, coming down from the Father of lights, with whom there is no variation or shifting shadow.' God is good and right and pure. The enemy, however, is opposite in every way and our world is his playground right now. Our fight is against him and him alone. I only know, Jakobi, that we have to trust the Lord and pray."

Jakobi looked at Noah, her nose red, her cheeks stained with tears. "And what if He doesn't deliver her, Simon? What if she's never okay?"

Simon met her gaze, his eyes bleak. "She might not be, Jakobi. But my only hope is in the Lord. If I praise Him when the sun is shining, shouldn't I also praise when a storm is swirling all around us? There is evil in this world, Jakobi. And evil will remain until Jesus returns."

Although she had surrendered her life to the Lord, and given her heart to Him, she knew she had to choose in the face of insurmountable wickedness if she would continue to believe when the Bible said that she served a good God.

"I am the Way, the Truth, and the Life..."

The gentle whisper sliced through Jakobi's heart, dividing her soul and her flesh. Her doubt and her faith stood firmly divided; there would be no middle road. She had to choose.

Either she would trust in the Lord or she wouldn't. Noah stirred in her arms, and she glanced down at him. He watched her face, and she drew him closer, drawing strength from his presence in her arms, in his soft skin, and his drumming heartbeat beneath her fingers.

Oh God, please help me to lean not on my own understanding. Where can we turn but to You? Oh Jesus, sweet Jesus…it hurts more than I can bear…

A light knock at the door made Jakobi start. Simon rose and looked through the peephole before he opened the door for Vireak. Once inside, he stripped off the orange robe, flinging it from him as if it was on fire. He slumped to the floor, covering his head with his arms.

Jakobi's heart filled with dread as the room shook with Vireak's mournful sobs. She sunk to the bed, overwhelmed with grief. Shakily, she set Noah down and turned away, her body wracked with sobs.

"Oh Jesus, Jesus, Jesus…" she whispered over and over.

A soft hand touched her shoulder and she turned to Simon, accepting his comfort. Her eyes widened in disbelief when she turned to find Maly standing before her, dirty and sullen.

"Lord God!" Jakobi cried out, reaching for Maly and enfolding her in her arms.

She looked over Maly's head to Simon, who leaned against the far wall, his arms raised high in praise, his face wet with joyous tears.

When at last Maly slept, curled in on herself, arms tucked tight around her worn Minnie Mouse doll, the three adults gathered in the bathroom whispering so she wouldn't hear.

Their faith was tested when Vireak told them that the monk had shaken in fear at the name of Jesus and opened the secret closet where he had hidden Maly. He had taken her from the beginning to be his own personal slave. All that they had feared for her had come true.

Vireak's lips curled in disgust. "He wanted to be free of the fear Jesus' name struck in his heart. He yanked her from the closet and begged me to take her and leave. All I could do was scoop her up and run."

Jakobi and Simon didn't speak, distraught and horrified that the weeks Maly had been in the *wat* in Thailand had been full of dark, twisted abuse.

Simon set his jaw, hands on his hips. All he could think about was asking Vireak to show him where the man's room was so that he could rip him to shreds with his bare hands. Bloodlust raged in his veins. He wanted vengeance.

Jakobi had never seen him angry and was afraid of the fire in his eyes. She placed a hand on his arm, imagining his thoughts, but not aware of how truly violent they were. "Let's leave. Maly needs Deliverance, she needs to be home. Let's just leave."

Simon and Vireak contemplated each other in silence before they both nodded slowly.

"You're right," Simon muttered. "Let's get them home."

Chapter Forty-Five

Boise, Idaho

Charlotte and Lydia dropped Zanna off at her home Sunday afternoon. They climbed from the car to stretch their legs and help her carry her things to the porch.

"Talk to you tomorrow?" Lydia asked.

"Oh, probably." Zanna rummaged in her bag for her keys. She located them and straightened. She paused, averting her eyes.

"Hey, uh, thanks, guys—both of you," she sighed, embarrassed.

"Not a problem, Zanna," Charlotte answered, tugging on Lydia's arm, wanting to give Zanna space. "Thanks for coming with us and putting up with our church's crazy antics." She winked.

Zanna laughed and opened the door, kicking her bag inside, and then walked back to the porch to retrieve her sleeping bag. She shut the door behind her and dropped the bag on the floor. She drank in the silence.

Zanna walked around her small bungalow, her elbows tucked into her ribs, hands clasped in front of her. Nothing had changed, and yet, somehow she saw everything differently. The edge of bitterness she had carried for years wavered. It wasn't gone. She was still afraid and angry and confused. But, somehow, also full of *hope*.

For the next week, Zanna read her gran's Bible. A lot of it confused her, but some truths emerged: God was after His people, unrelenting in His love for them.

She read story after story of His forgiveness and patience. It hurt to read sometimes. A lamp had been lit in her darkest memories and in her heart; she now saw her life in a very different light. Her own wrongdoings and intentions were suddenly clear. She felt remorse for her life choices, understood her responsibility for them.

Yes, she had been abused and mistreated, but…she did not have to make the decisions she had made, nor did she have to live the way she had for so many years. She could not lay the blame anywhere else for things she had done as an adult.

The letter came at the end of the week.

Dear Zanna,

Thank you for your sponsorship of Nataya. Nataya was rescued last fall and found to be in the early stages of pregnancy upon her rescue. She has shown a unique diligence in her studies and is a very talented seamstress. Because of your commitment to a monthly contribution, Nataya will be able to grow and heal in a safe place. She loves to sing and dance in her off time and is a very hard worker and an excellent student.

-Your Friends at Deliverance

Another letter was included in the folds of the formal one from Deliverance. Zanna bit her lip, hardly able to contain her smile as she read the words from Nataya, the girl she'd agreed to sponsor:

Dear friend,

Thank you for caring for me. I hope this letter finds you well.

I like to dance and sing, but I work hard.

I want to share with you that I have decided to keep my baby.

Zanna's head snapped back, surprised. Keep the baby? She read on.

The friends at Deliverance are busy teaching me how to care for the baby, how to earn a living on my own when I finish school. I hope to give my child a wonderful life. Mostly, I want my child to know how precious it is in the eyes of God. I have bad dreams about my life before, but God is helping to take those away. I see this baby as a gift and I feel strongly that I want to keep my baby, no matter where it came from.

Best wishes and thank you,

Nataya

A small card was attached to the letter, explaining that they would seek a sponsor for Nataya's child when he or she was born, and that they in no way expected Zanna to be the sponsor, but wanted to offer her the chance.

She folded the letter and slumped against the wall, allowing herself to sink down to the floor.

For so long Zanna had clung to the idea that her abortion was okay because she had been raped. The child in her womb couldn't possibly be anything but a monster, could it? She had no support and no way to keep the baby. No one would have wanted to adopt a baby born in such a way.

Precious in the eyes of God.

A young Thai girl that had been raped over and over by more men and in more horrific ways than Zanna could begin to imagine was pregnant. Yet, she saw a precious life in her womb as a result, one that deserved a chance at life. Even more, she wanted the baby, accepted it as a gift to her, in spite of the way it came to be.

Precious in the eyes of God.

Zanna covered her head with her arms.

"Oh, God, Oh, God..." she cried out the words over and over until her voice was hoarse. She curled onto her side, her legs drawn up against her chest and wept. She wept for the baby she'd thrown away in anger and revenge against her father, wept for the girl that had been abused and lost. Wept at the lost chance to reach out to her grandmother.

Wept for the years she'd lived her own way and rejected the God who created her. Wept for the grace He so clearly extended to her, through it all, to the end that He gave her the opportunity to support a young girl and her child. A girl that, despite great opposition in her young life, had chosen God. His goodness, His promises. The life He freely bestowed on any that would take it.

Zanna opened her hands, flat on her face on the kitchen floor.

"I'll take it, Lord. I'll take the life You offer me. I'll take the forgiveness You have offered me. I'll take life, Lord; I'll take it, and I'll give it back to You."

❖ ❖ ❖

Zanna spent a lot of time on the phone, looking for a new accountant. Tax season was just starting out and the standard response became, "We aren't taking new business clients until

The Heavens Are Telling

after the tax season." She called Charlotte and asked what she thought she should do.

"Zanna, if you think Mr. Easton raped you," she spoke quietly so that her children wouldn't hear, "I don't think it is wise to meet with him again."

"That's just it, Charlotte," Zanna said, "I'm not entirely sure. I've been very promiscuous in the past and that's not the first time I've been surprised when I woke up after a night at the bar. I'm wondering if I jumped to that conclusion because I'm so repulsed by him." She fingered the desk calendar in front of her, glancing toward the door to her office in the back of the store. "I think I just need to suck it up and have him finish out my taxes. Then I can start over fresh with a new accountant."

Charlotte made a noise in her throat as a loud shriek echoed in the background. "Oops, gotta go. Just promise me that you'll meet somewhere public, okay? Can you do that?"

Zanna agreed, already planning to ask Gage to meet her at a coffee shop to finish up her taxes. She had mailed him most everything he needed; the meeting should be brief. They rang off, Zanna laughing as Charlotte called out that her girls better be sitting quietly when she walked back into the kitchen before the line went dead.

When Zanna did meet with Gage, she suggested Remmy's, an old church-building-turned-coffee-house and restaurant. On the outside, Remmy's was a beautiful, white steeple church in the heart of charming downtown Eagle. On the inside, a large pastry case and espresso bar lined one side, fair trade products were displayed on the other. The building housed one large room decorated with local art. Patrons could choose mismatched chairs around worn tables to sit and enjoy a meal or relax in overstuffed chairs surrounding low coffee tables for inspired discussions. The coffee house had a heart for impoverished people and sold fair trade coffee, clothes, and jewelry that would help widowed women in poverty stricken countries support themselves and their families.

Zanna arrived twenty minutes early and chose a table in a private corner in the large, open room. She waited nervously, watching the front door, hoping Gage would come quickly and get the uncomfortable meeting over with. He finally arrived, five minutes early, looking around in disgust. Zanna wiped her palms on her jeans and gripped her shaky knees in an effort to still them as she rose to call him over to her table.

"This place stinks," he muttered, setting his satchel on the table and shedding his jacket.

Zanna tried not to bristle at his appraisal of her favorite place. "They roast their own coffee beans here," Zanna explained. She loved the robust, slightly smoky fragrance of Remmy's, loved how the rich aroma stayed on her skin and clothes for the rest of the day after she'd spent a few hours inside.

"Humph," he muttered. "Well, let's get this over with."

He gestured that she should be seated and lowered himself into his own chair, grimacing as if it were uncomfortable to do so. Zanna's blood boiled when he leaned across the table and spoke to her in a barely audible, condescending tone. "And this time, Zanna, let's be professional, shall we?"

She swallowed the bile that rose in her throat and did not respond to him.

They spent the next hour working on her taxes; him asking for certain papers, her digging through her box of files, handing the paper over and waiting while he punched the figures into his computer. The waitress brought Zanna a black coffee. She excused herself to doctor the rich drink at the cream and sugar counter.

"Zanna!" a voice called behind her. She turned to find Charlotte standing in line to order with a dark haired man that she could only assume was Sam.

Zanna smiled back, genuinely happy to see her in the midst of the tense meeting. "Charlotte, what are you doing here?"

Charlotte turned to Sam and spoke in his ear. He gave Charlotte a warm smile and nodded as she kissed his cheek and left him in line. She hugged Zanna when she got close enough and laughed when Zanna asked where the girls were.

"With their grandparents. We are officially on a date." She wiggled her hips playfully.

The Heavens Are Telling

Zanna smiled at Charlotte's little dance, noticing the extra care Charlotte had taken with her appearance. A touch more make-up, straight, dark jeans with heels, a peach colored layered top. "I like this shirt," Zanna said, reaching to finger the material on the shoulder.

Charlotte laughed, "Thank you. I like the layers. Camouflage, I call them. Three babies have been a bit hard on the ol' body."

"Says who?" Sam asked honestly, stepping beside Charlotte and handing her a number card.

Zanna liked Sam immediately.

"Are you here alone?" Charlotte asked as she introduced Sam to Zanna and they exchanged pleasantries.

Zanna's smile faltered. "Uh, no. I'm here doing my taxes with my accountant." She tried to communicate with her eyes that she was fine.

Charlotte's smile faded, but she didn't betray Zanna to Sam. She recovered quickly and made a joke about taxes and what it must be like to have a taxman. Zanna noticed that Sam surveyed the room, his face serious. Charlotte followed Zanna's eyes and slapped Sam playfully on the arm.

"Knock it off, you're on a date with your wife, not staking the place out," she teased. Charlotte turned to Zanna, her hand cupped around her mouth and whispered loudly, "He's always paranoid in public, checking everyone out."

Zanna snickered and said she better return to her taxes. Charlotte and Sam bid her good-bye and settled in at a table in the middle of the room to play card games. Zanna admired the way they laughed and talked together.

Gage was almost done cataloging her information when she shared her receipts from donations she'd made to Deliverance before Christmas.

"What's this place?" Gage asked, taking the papers from her, his brows arched in curiosity. Zanna explained about the work Deliverance did to rescue girls from slavery.

"Here," she said, wondering if the blank look on his face indicated that he didn't understand why she would pay them. She pulled the picture of Nataya, her belly adorably swollen with baby, and the letter from Deliverance about her progress and needs, out of her files and handed them to Gage. "This is one of the girls I support there."

Charlotte and Sam stopped by the table just then to say a quick good-bye.

"We're going to catch a movie before we head home," Charlotte said, leaning down to press her check against Zanna's in a reassuring gesture.

"You okay?" she whispered in Zanna's ear.

Zanna smiled, heart clenching at the care of her friend. She nodded. Charlotte pulled away and looped an arm through Sam's. Zanna noticed the way Sam watched Gage, feeling annoyed that Charlotte had shared her secret.

I guess I can't blame her, Zanna thought, *she's just worried about me and her husband* is *a cop*. Zanna bid them good-bye and turned back to Gage. He was studying the picture and letter she'd handed him, his hands shaking.

He looked like he'd seen a ghost.

✣ ✣ ✣

Instead of the movie, Sam drove Charlotte to his friend, Brett's house. "Charlotte, I'm sorry, but I have a hunch, and I can't let it go."

Charlotte wondered at Sam's behavior but didn't ask questions. Instead, she followed him into Brett's home and sat with his wife, Rayanne, in the kitchen, sharing a cup of coffee and book talk while the men went into Brett's office.

Brett was a detective with Internet Crimes Against Children. He knew Sam had an interest in someday becoming an ICAC detective and often invited him into his office at work to give him tips for working toward that goal. Sam had noticed a picture of a man in that office and asked Brett if he kept identical pictures in his files at home. Brett affirmed that he did.

"What's this about, Sam?" he asked, pulling a file from his desk and handing it to Sam.

"Might be nothing, Brett. Just something that's bothering me." Sam rifled through the files until he came to the picture he remembered. The name below the picture confirmed what the beady black eyes already had.

Gage Easton.

Sam held the picture up for Brett to see. "What's this guy's story?"

"Not sure yet," Brett answered, withdrawing his hand from his front pants pocket to retrieve the picture. He looked up at Sam over his glasses. "We're just watching him. We got a call from a fast food restaurant last week that some creep was watching kids in the play area and taking video of them. He was gone when we got there, but the manager let us look at their surveillance tapes. Fortunately, he parked right in front of the outside cameras, and we were able to trace him with his license plate. After we looked him up, we found out he's a person of interest with the detectives unit already for suspicion of money laundering. We found numerous social media accounts under his name. So far just sleazy stuff: liking pictures, stuff like that, but we're watching him."

Sam explained what Charlotte had shared about Zanna's earlier suspicion that he had slipped a drug in her drink and raped her. Brett scratched his chin. "Well, Sam, you know how it goes. Has she filed a complaint?"

Sam set his hands on his hips and hung his head. No.

"Then there's nothing I can do," Brett said, slipping Gage's picture back into his file.

Chapter Forty-Six

Gage barely made it through the rest of the meeting.

He had stared at the picture of Nataya, anger building inside of him. Relief flooding through him.

There she was, at a place called Deliverance—with a baby in her belly.

It had to be his. She couldn't have been with anyone else; she loved *him*.

His lip curled at the memory. That baby made her fat. He hated fat. There was a change in her face, a motherly softness that he couldn't wait to erase. The baby did it. He would just get rid of the baby.

He rushed home and shoved clothes into a bag. He raced around throwing things he would need on top of the pile on the bed.

Passport.

Credit Cards.

He paused, blood draining from his face. He had to have something to show *them* he meant business. That they needed him.

So they wouldn't kill him as soon as he arrived, uninvited, unannounced.

He ran to the computer. He booked a flight for two and called Zack, the TSA agent, to arrange the time. Next he opened the email from Ava. Frantic, angry, hopeful, he wrote her back, fingers fumbling all over the keys, his letters scattered, words disjointed. He pounded a fist into the desk and erased the message. He practiced his breathing, calmed his racing heart long enough to write a clear email:

"Meet my uncle at the airport tomorrow morning at 10:00 a.m. Do not be late or I will never talk to you again and my uncle will tell your parents. Be there." He clicked send and spent the night driving to the PDX airport, wringing the steering wheel in his hands, mumbling to himself.

"I'm coming for you, Nataya."

Finally, everything would be all right.

❖ ❖ ❖

Ava called Sarah at school and arranged a ride, thankful that the next morning was Saturday and her dad would be at a men's breakfast, her mom working in the church office.

She kissed them goodbye and waited until they drove away to call Sarah with the all clear and to retrieve her bag from under her bed. She had been waiting for what seemed like forever for Toby to tell her it was time. The day had finally come. The girls belted out music all the way to Portland, Ava feeling light and brave and adult. She was going to visit Jakobi! Her sister would be so surprised to see her. Ava snickered at how clever she was, how proud Jakobi would be when she heard that her sister had arranged her own way to get across the world.

Sarah pulled in front of PDX and told her to be careful, but to have fun. Ava leaned down to talk to her through the window. "Remember, I'll call my parents when I get to Cambodia. Don't say anything."

Sarah crossed her heart and blew Ava a kiss, beeping the horn as she sped away. Ava watched her go, and felt her first flutter of trepidation about the trip. *It's going to be fine, Ava, don't be a baby.* She straightened her shoulders and marched into the airport. She walked haltingly to the place Toby had told her to meet his uncle.

The Heavens Are Telling

A man was waiting and watching by the security checkpoint, dressed in a tropical shirt like Toby said his uncle would be. She walked close to him, her hands shaking, and asked, "Are you Toby's uncle?" She hoped he would say no.

The man faced her, eyes glazed, face mottled and perspiring. "Ava?" He looked her up and down, smiling appreciatively.

She lowered her lashes, uncomfortable. At least she could ditch him when she got to Cambodia. Jakobi would tell him to get lost. "Yes," she answered.

He reached to encircle her arm in his fat hand. "Toby said you were beautiful."

※ ※ ※

Hal and Molly returned to an empty house, wondering where Ava could have gone. When an hour went by with no word, they began to call her friends.

No one had heard from her.

They called the police, who said they would send a car over, but strongly recommended they call her friends and anyone else she could have been in contact with again.

"Hal, we should call Jakobi," Molly said, her voice trembling.

Hal shoved his hands in his pockets. "I don't have her number, Molly. Do you?"

He stood in the middle of the living room, his hands shoved deep in his pockets, his shoulders slumped. Molly mumbled something about a letter or email that Jakobi had sent and sat down at the computer.

Where did I go wrong, Lord? Hal prayed. *I tried so hard to raise them right, to be women that would follow after You. I protected them from the world as much as I could. Where did I go wrong?*

Molly found the email with Jakobi's information and dialed the long number, her trembling fingers slipped, making her start over twice. As the phone rang, Molly wondered what time it was in Cambodia, wondered if her daughter even had reception where she was. She was instantly ashamed that she hadn't tried to call her daughter before.

The line clicked, and Jakobi's soft "Hello?" made Molly's knees go week.

"Jakobi?" she whispered.

"Mom?" Jakobi drew back from the phone as if it were on fire.

They had finally arrived at the Deliverance dorms in Cambodia and she had just entered the room she had been assigned to for the duration of her time with the organization. Her eyes were gritty from crying, her chest tight. She waited for her mom to answer, thinking maybe she had hung up.

"Jakobi," her mother's voice was strained. "Your sister is missing, and we need to know if she's contacted you."

Jakobi already weary with despondency, felt as if her soul was sucked out of her body, like air escaping from a balloon. "Missing?" *No, Lord, too much; please, Lord. Not my sister.*

Molly explained that they had returned to an empty house and that none of her friends knew where she was. When her mother shared that they had seen Ava just hours before, Jakobi breathed a sigh of relief.

Get a grip, Jakobi. Not every missing kid is in danger. Ava is on the Oregon coast, safe and sound. Mom and Dad are just over-protective, remember?

Jakobi's mother was crying hysterically now, and Jakobi had to raise her voice over the panic. "Mom, have you checked her social account? Called her boyfriend?"

Molly was silent a moment. "What account? What boyfriend?"

Jakobi shook her head. She had assumed the account was a secret, but was still shocked by her parents' naïveté.

"Mom, call her friends back. Make them tell you about her boyfriend. Trust me, if I know about it, they know about it. They probably know her password. Call them again."

Her mother, distraught and overwhelmed, thanked Jakobi.

"Mom?" Jakobi said before Molly could hang up.

"Yes?"

"Please let me know when you find her, okay?"

The Heavens Are Telling

"I will, Jakobi, I promise."

Jakobi hung up, attributing the unease she felt to her distress over Maly, not believing that God would require her sister of her as well.

Please, God. Help them find her soon. Let her be making out with some kid in his car or smoking a cigarette or watching a violent movie...let it be one of the many things my parents were terrified of us doing. Please don't let her be in danger...please...

When Molly called Jakobi's friends back, Sarah finally gave her a different story. Molly's mouth went dry and her heart quivered in terror when Sarah confessed to dropping her off at the airport.

A policeman arrived while she was on the phone, and when Molly relayed the information, the officer's face turned to stone. "Ma'am, do you have the password to your daughter's account?" he asked, striding to the computer in the corner.

Hal wrapped his arm around Molly as she shook her head. "We didn't even know she had an account," she whispered, panic crawling at her throat.

"Freedom," Sarah called through the phone, having heard the conversation and just now understanding the weight of danger her friend might be in. "Her password is freedom." Molly's heart clenched and she whispered the password to the officer.

Another officer arrived to help sort through the computer. They found the messages exchanged between Ava and a boy named Toby, including the nude picture of her. Molly sat on the edge of the couch, staring out the window, thinking about Ava's strange behavior over breakfast. She had chosen to ignore Ava's pensive mood, chalking it up to teenage hormones. Instead of probing for a reason, she kissed her daughter good-bye shortly after 8 a.m.

An orange glow streaked across the room, blinding Molly where she sat. The sun was setting.

Chapter Forty-Seven

Sam backed the squad car into a space at the department, his palm flat on the steering wheel, turning it effortlessly. It had been a fairly quiet day, and he was ready to go home. He shut off the car and checked to be sure he hadn't left any trash for the next guy. He hated getting into a car at the beginning of his shift just to spend the next ten minutes cleaning out empty coffee cups and tossing gum wrappers. "Leave it cleaner for the next guy" was a policy he was on board with.

Sam ran into Brett as he walked up the sidewalk to the entrance. "Hey, Charlotte had a nice time with Rayanne the other—whoa, what's up, Brett?" he called as the detective rushed past him.

"You were right, Sam," Brett called out, not stopping as he rushed to his car.

"About what?" Sam called after him, confused.

"Gage Easton," Brett called, opening the driver door to his detective car.

Sam hesitated for one second before he rushed to catch up. "Make a space," he called, almost crushing Brett's hand as he cleared the passenger seat of files and papers. Brett turned on his siren and sped out of the parking lot, briefing Sam on the way.

"We got a call from officers in Cannon Beach, Oregon. A teenage girl went missing and when officers broke into her social media account, they found hundreds of emails between her and someone she thought was a boy her age. Mostly innocent until she says she wishes she could visit her sister in Cambodia and the "kid" says his uncle can take her."

Sam held onto the dash as Brett took a sharp turn onto the freeway, increasing his speed once he straightened out. "Oh, man," Sam breathed.

Brett nodded, face grim. "They traced this guy to a computer in Boise and—"

"Let me guess, it's Gage Easton?"

Brett tapped his finger against his nose. "You got it. To make matters more interesting, we heard a call go out for Boise PD that a home in the same area as Gage's neighborhood is emitting a foul, rotting smell. We thought that was worth checking into and it's his house. They're getting ready to break in any minute."

Sam scoffed, "Man, you know if he hurt the girl in Oregon this morning, there's no way she would be stinking up his house already."

"Right," Brett answered, pulling in front of a town home in an affluent neighborhood in Boise. "But if he made arrangements to meet this girl, there is no reason to believe she's the first."

They approached the house and explained to a Boise officer why they were there. The first officers on the scene had already broken down the door and a foul smell hit Sam as soon as he stepped onto the manicured lawn. He covered his nose, only sucking air through his mouth when it was necessary. He resisted the urge to gag. Whatever—whoever—it was, they'd been dead for a long time. He wanted to be respectful, but it was difficult to remain composed. Officers poured out of the house, walking away fast and choking on the strong stench.

Neighbors, curious by the line of police cars, stepped onto their porches and gagged as well, calling out to the officers.

"What is that?"

"Dear God is someone dead in there?"

Sam followed Brett toward the porch after speaking with an officer that had come out of the house.

Someone behind him answered the concerned neighbor's question: "Ma'am there are a *lot* of dead things in there."

The Heavens Are Telling

❖ ❖ ❖

He had told her to call him "Uncle." They sat in tense silence near the security gates for an hour, "Uncle" licking his lips nervously, eyes darting back and forth before he excused himself to go to the bathroom.

That was hours ago. Ava could only assume he wasn't coming back. She had wandered through the gift shop and terminal before she sat in a chair near the security gate, twisting the purity ring her father bought her for her fifteenth birthday around her finger. *What am I going to do?*

Ava had watched families come and go all day, some hugging good-bye, some hollering hello, others kissing so long and hard that she blushed and turned away. The longer she sat, waiting for "Uncle" to return, praying that he wouldn't, the more Ava realized how foolish she had been. Through the emails and the planning and the excitement of seeing Jakobi, she had ignored apprehension and reason, thinking only of how wonderful it would be to visit her sister. She wanted Toby to be real, wanted everything to work out just right.

Ava didn't know where "Uncle" had gone and was certain he would have returned by now if he was going to. She thought she could call a cab, but was too afraid to move; the weight of the danger she had put herself in pressed upon her from all sides. She felt glued to the chair, helpless to move.

She didn't know if she was more afraid of "Uncle" returning or of the looks that would be on her parents' faces. If they were angry at Jakobi about going to college and joining the Peace Corps, what would they think of her for sending a picture of herself to a boy online and agreeing to meet a stranger to take her out of the country?

Ava blushed, realizing what she'd done, ashamed of herself and sick inside.

Do you still love me, Lord? Even after all I've done?

"Ava!"

She sat up with a start and scanned the room. Her father rounded the corner, her mother and a police officer directly behind him. She stood, her knees shaking, her eyes on the floor, afraid to look in her father's face. Her eyes rounded when he went on his knees before her, his arms encircling her waist, his chest heaving with violent sobs of relief. Ava's mother stepped close and crushed Ava against her, weeping.

"Ava, oh darling, Ava, we were so scared, so very scared."

Overwhelmed, Ava burst into tears, ignoring the curious stares of travelers around her as she wailed and apologized over and over. Her suppressed fear of the last few hours melted into relief.

※ ※ ※

Sam stumbled into his house, inhaling the aroma of cookies, grateful that Charlotte had been in a baking mood that day. He wondered if he would ever get that awful stench out of his nose or skin or hair. Thankfully, he'd been able to leave his uniform at work for the dry cleaners to pick up. He called out for Charlotte, who answered from their bedroom. He followed her voice down the hall to their room, where she stood by their bed, folding laundry.

She flashed a triumphant smile at him as he shuffled in the door. "Proud of me? I decided to take your unexpected overtime and use the evening to not only fold but also put away the laundry. Can you believe it?" She lifted a pile of folded shirts and sauntered over to the dresser in the corner, making a show of putting the clean shirts away.

Sam, exhausted, leaned against the doorjamb and watched her appreciatively.

"Hey, Mister"—Charlotte playfully put a hand on her hip—"I'm expecting oohs and ahhs here." She walked across the room to kiss his cheek, but stopped short, sniffing at the air, her lips curled in disgust. "What is that smell?"

"Snakes," Sam answered.

"Snakes?" Charlotte fanned the air in front of her face, coughing.

The Heavens Are Telling

"Well, dead snakes," Sam answered. "I'll spare your nose and tell you while I shower." He walked to the master bathroom, shedding his clothes as he went. He turned on the water and tested it. "Girls go to sleep okay?" he asked.

"Yes." Charlotte's response was muffled. Sam laughed when he turned and saw the clean socks she had fastened around her face.

"Very funny," he said, climbing into the steamy shower, sighing in relief.

"So tell me about these snakes," Charlotte called out, leaning against the counter.

Sam told her about his concerns over Gage. She interrupted him, outraged that he hadn't told her about that earlier.

"Lotty, you know I can't always tell you stuff," he answered.

"Yeah, okay," she said.

He told her about the missing girl in Oregon and the call about the stink. When Charlotte gasped, Sam cringed.

"The girl is okay," Sam said quickly.

Charlotte exhaled, relieved.

Sam continued the story. "Turns out Gage had bribed a TSA agent in Portland to let him take a passenger through customs, no questions asked. The agent couldn't handle the guilt and confessed to his boss. He worked with the Portland police to catch Gage, so he wouldn't have made it through with her."

"Well, that's good," Charlotte said. "So what's the deal with the snakes, then?"

When Sam had used every last bit of the bar of soap, he finally snapped off the water, convinced that he would smell like rotting snakes for the rest of the night no matter what he did.

"Ah," he said, reaching for the towel. "Well, it turns out our Gage is a Jack-of-all-trades. He was breeding exotic snakes and laundering money through that venture. One of the walls in his basement was lined, floor to ceiling, with cages of snakes. Somewhere in the last few weeks, he stopped paying attention or lost interest in them. Most of them were dead." Sam shook his head, wrapping the towel around his waist. "I feel so bad for his neighbors," he commented.

Charlotte winced as he walked by, imagining it. "At least you smell better," she flirted, following him into their small walk-in closet while he pulled on sweatpants and a BSU sweatshirt.

"And," she added, "at least that creep Gage is off the street. Maybe now Zanna will feel validated about her concerns." She crossed her arms and noticed Sam watching her, his face unreadable.

"What?"

"Charlotte, they didn't catch him."

"What? But you said they were waiting for him, that the girl is safe." Charlotte protested.

"They were and she is," Sam said. "They found her waiting outside of the security check. But Gage apparently told her he was going to the bathroom and didn't come back. They found that he slipped onto a plane to Cambodia without her. He must have been tipped off somehow that they were watching for them, so he went through a different line away from the agent he had made arrangements with. Without the girl, he seemed like any other traveler."

Charlotte took a shuddering breath. "So can't they pick him up when he lands in Cambodia?" she asked.

"I think Portland PD is working on that, but I'm not sure how it will pan out."

Sam wrapped his arms around her. "You know better than anyone how that place works," he said, pulling her to him.

"Humph. Bribes speak louder than laws, I would imagine," she observed.

"And it looks like Gage had access to plenty of untraceable money," Sam said.

Charlotte leaned into Sam, absorbing his presence, pensive.

Sam, sensing a shift in her mood, drew back and looked in her eyes. "Are you thinking about Noah?" he asked.

Charlotte shrugged, ashamed of herself. "Don't get me wrong, Sam, I am grateful that girl was found safe and protected from what could have been. But I can't help but wonder about Noah." Charlotte's eyes misted over. "I thought that if I obeyed the Lord and bore my soul to the women at church that God would bless that." She swiped a hand across her eyes.

Sam took a deep breath. "He will bless it, Charlotte. I know He will."

"You do?" Charlotte sniffed.

Sam hooked his finger under her chin, drawing her eyes to his. "Yes, I do. I don't know what that will look like. This side of heaven we might not ever know the full extent of His purpose for you sharing your story. He's already done wondrous things. Think of Zanna and the change in her heart."

"I know. You're right." She sighed. "I'm so selfish, Sam. I want Noah here and I forget that life isn't about me. I keep dreaming of the day that Megan calls to say that Noah and his sister have been found and that we can go get him." She cocked her head to the side, searching Sam's eyes. "But how realistic is that? We haven't applied to adopt, haven't gone through the home visits or anything that would be required of us."

"Well, why don't we?" Sam suggested.

"What, apply to adopt?"

"Sure."

"But, Sam, Noah is missing—they might not ever find out where he or Maly went."

Sam thought for a moment. "Maybe the point is that God is calling us to step out in faith. What if they never find Noah and we give another child in need a home? What if they *do* find Noah and Maly in God's time and we are able to adopt both of them? Either way, I think we need to trust the Lord and walk this path until He tells us not to."

Charlotte weighed his words, absorbing them. Her heart felt a thrill at stepping forward to follow an unknown path in pursuit of something God might have planned from the beginning. She also felt a shiver of fear. Change was a frightening thing. She pulled her arms free from Sam's waist and grasped his hands, pulling him down to his knees on the floor.

There in the quiet of their room, in the stillness of the unknown, they rested in the promise that God knew the plans established for them and that He alone would lead them in His way. Sam and Charlotte offered their lives, their home, and their family to the Lord of Creation; to the God who hung the stars in the sky, and spoke the oceans into action; to the One that knew them intimately, every hair on their head, every thought, every intention of their heart. As they prayed and surrendered, Charlotte felt a charge in the air, a promise that she couldn't yet grasp. But she felt cloaked in peace.

"I love you, Mrs. Branson," Sam whispered, pressing a kiss to her forehead.

"I love you, too, Mr. Branson." Charlotte whispered back.

Three hours after they'd checked on the girls and tucked themselves into bed for the night, Charlotte's cell phone rang, startling her from a deep sleep. She fumbled for the phone, swiping a hand across the face before she held the device to her ear.

" 'Ello?" She cleared her throat and tried again. "Hello?"

The line crackled, then Megan's excited voice broke through. "Charlotte? I'm sorry to wake you, but I couldn't wait. I would have called you days ago, but we had to arrange medical check-ups and paperwork needed to be filed. I just needed to be sure it couldn't happen again and that I had him in my arms, and—"

Charlotte bolted upright in bed, grasping Sam's shoulder. "Wait! What? Megan, slow down, what are you saying?"

Charlotte could hear Megan's smile in her tone. "I have him, Charlotte. I have a safe, sleeping Noah right here in my arms."

Chapter Forty-Eight

Thailand

Gage fidgeted as the plane began its descent into Bangkok. He chewed his nails, wishing he had been able to get Ava on the plane with him.

He should have known Zack was a betrayer. Once Ava arrived, Gage led her to a chair and sat with her and watched carefully. Zack was acting real nervous. He kept touching his ear and talking to someone on the other end of the earpiece. Gage had been careful to avoid Zack's line of sight and was sure the agent never knew he was there. He still thought he could sneak Ava through, but she was taller than he'd expected, and wore a bright-colored t-shirt. She'd looked like she was going to be sick, and Gage didn't trust her to make it through security unnoticed.

Gage cursed, remembering. He'd waited for Zack to step away, and then told Ava he had to go to the bathroom. He bought a ticket on the first plane out and bought a new ticket in each airport he came to.

Idiots. They were probably scratching their heads wondering where he was.

The plane taxied in and he patted his pocket, as he'd done the entire flight, to be sure the money was there. Getting into the country, even if an alert had been issued, would be easy. Money talked.

And anyway, he thought, *I haven't done anything wrong. I didn't take her.*

He wasn't surprised when he was stopped and led into a small room. When the policeman walked in, Gage fell to his knees, terrified.

"Wait, I can explain why I'm here."

The officer smiled sardonically, but his eyes remained flat. "Oh, this should be good," he mocked.

Gage babbled about his discovery of Deliverance. "I know it sounds small, but they're taking all the girls. Your girls."

His Nataya. He just needed to get to Nataya.

The man squatted on the ground and tilted his head at Gage. "Do you honestly think we don't know about this…this little operation?" he asked, incredulous.

Gage's bowels quivered as he realized his mistake. "No-no-no, of course not," he stuttered. "I ju-just think that it's bigger than it seems, that you need to maybe do something. I could help, get on the inside; help bring it down. I could do that. I could help."

The man grimaced at him and raised himself up slowly, his stiff boots creaking. "No, Gage, I think you've done quite enough." He called for his officers and arranged for Gage to be removed from the airport. He relished in the fear that passed through Gage's eyes when he understood that the officers had been given instructions to put him in prison for suspicion of trafficking.

The officer left work and made his way home, into an expensive apartment in the heart of the city. He chuckled to his wife, telling her the story as they readied for an important banquet that night.

"Well," she asked, curiosity aroused, "how *do* you plan to stop Deliverance?"

He sneered, "My dear, these things take time, but are so simple. First, you create scandal—doubt. These organizations are built on the backs of their supporters. Without them, they have nothing."

"But how do you plan to do that?" she wondered, tucking a small beaded purse under her arm.

"Don't you worry, it's already begun. First, you create scandal, arouse suspicions. Trust me when I tell you, Deliverance won't be a problem for much longer."

❖ ❖ ❖

Jakobi sat in the shade of a tree, watching the preschool class play a game in the courtyard. They were so innocent and free, so happy. Maly stayed back a little and bounced a ball against the brick wall that surrounded the Deliverance grounds. She wasn't the vibrant girl that Jakobi had known before she left. She was quiet, reserved. Memories raged in her eyes, but she kept her lips clamped shut. Jakobi longed to take her pain away.

The wall was built to protect the children, to keep them from harm. The prevention program was created to keep children from being trafficked, to obliterate the need for a restoration program.

Jakobi watched the children squeal in delight as their teacher called them into a circle, watched as Maly reluctantly joined hands with two little girls.

Simon found Jakobi in the shade, her face somber and, understanding her thoughts, he silently sat beside her. Tears rolled down Jakobi's face.

"My sister called me. She told me everything. They discovered the kid she was talking to was some creep from Idaho. He talked her into sending him a picture of herself."

Simon closed his eyes in pain, and Jakobi saw that he understood what kind of picture she meant.

"Simon, she came so close to getting on a plane with him to come see me. I've been sitting here, watching these kids—these sweet, innocent children—play and laugh. I can't stop watching Maly, wishing we could have just got to her sooner, could have ripped her away from whatever horror was thrust upon her." Jakobi sniffed and rubbed a palm down her cheek.

"I feel such a heaviness, such a sense of responsibility. My sister was almost lost to us forever. By the grace of God alone she is safe. And while I'm praising God for protecting my sister, I'm trying to understand why He didn't protect Maly. I don't understand it."

Simon didn't answer. They sat side by side and watched the children hold hands and sing a Cambodian song together. He smiled at them, in spite of the emptiness he felt.

"It's overwhelming, Jakobi. This job, this life. It's a constant struggle between flesh and spirit. I have such murderous thoughts." Simon shook his head, once, as if he could rid his mind of the thoughts he spoke of. "I watch these children and hear stories of rescue, and I think of the story of the little boy on the beach throwing starfish back into the sea, one by one."

Jakobi tipped her mouth. "And a man walks up and asks why he's bothering to try, that there are too many starfish to save them all. 'It doesn't matter, little boy, leave it be.'"

Simon picked the story back up. "So the boy throws another starfish and answers, 'It mattered to that one.' That's how I feel. These kids are all worth it. The time Maly had with us before all of that might be enough to keep her spirit kicking while she's fighting through her trauma. She has hope to cling to deep in there somewhere. She will emerge again, restored. I know she will."

Jakobi narrowed her eyes, thinking. "You know what has always bothered me about that story, Simon? What are hundreds of starfish doing on the beach anyway?"

Simon shrugged. "What does it matter, Jakobi?"

"It matters. It matters because if we can find a way to keep the starfish safe in the ocean, they wouldn't need to be saved in the first place."

Simon was still confused. "Jakobi, that's why we have a prevention program."

"Then maybe I'm not talking about keeping the starfish off of the beach. Maybe it's the wave that swept them to shore that we need to work on."

The Heavens Are Telling

Simon, completely lost, sputtered. "What are you talking about?"

Jakobi, eyes shimmering, met his gaze. "Simon, as long as men lust after women and children and are willing to pay money to explore their dark desires, places like Deliverance will be necessary. Maybe we need to find a way to stop the demand for the sex trade. Is it possible that only then this awful reality will become untrue?"

Simon slipped an arm around her, understanding her thoughts, but feeling powerless to do anything about it. "It's possible, Jakobi. It's possible. In the meantime, let's just keep plucking the starfish free from the sand and set them back in the safety of the ocean."

"And what about the ones that are dying on the beach, Simon? What about Maly?"

Simon remained quiet for such a long time that Jakobi thought he wouldn't answer. And how could he? She turned back to the children, recognizing the song they sang and feeling tears prick her eyes all over again.

Simon heard the song too and nodded. "We'll just keep trusting and doing His work, Jakobi. His word says that, 'Weeping may endure for a night, but joy comes in the morning'. We will just trust and pray and keep at it, until the morning comes."

He squeezed her shoulder and they listened, tears flowing freely between them, as the children's voices—including little Maly's—rose above the courtyard and were carried on the wind.

"Jesus loves the little children..."

Epilogue

"Nataya, you're doing wonderful," Moree said as she dabbed a cold cloth across Nataya's forehead.

The laboring girl fought the overwhelming desire to kick her away. As soon as the contraction passed, Nataya felt a wave of remorse for her cranky thoughts. "I'm sorry, Moree, I'm so sorry…" she mumbled, thinking she had spoken her violent urges out loud.

Moree smiled and glanced at the nurse with a shrug.

Nataya's body tensed again. "Okay, girl, here we go," Moree said, grabbing Nataya's foot and helping to hold it steady. She ignored the pain in her shoulder as the girl bore down.

Nataya had been in labor for fifteen hours before she began to push over forty minutes ago. She had asked Moree if she would be in the labor room with her, if she would be the one to tell her whether it was a boy or a girl. Moree had enthusiastically agreed, amazed at the many ways God invited her to watch His restoring work in the Deliverance girls' lives.

The doctor shifted from her place at the end of the bed and smiled up at Nataya. "That's it, that's just right. I see the baby's head."

The contraction over, Nataya gave a low growl and fell back on the pillows, overwhelmed and exhausted. She turned to Moree and cried, "I can't do this anymore. I just want to go back to the house. We can do this tomorrow," she murmured through her frustrated tears.

Moree crinkled her eyes in a smile at the girl that was still so young. "Didn't you hear the doctor, Nataya? Your baby is almost here. One more push, just try one more." Moree brushed a hand across her forehead, reasoning with Nataya as if the force that would bring the baby into the world could be turned off.

Nataya strained upright as the contraction came upon her. With determination, she gritted her teeth and bore down. *I am making this the last one*, Nataya thought.

The baby arrived in a rush—pink and yowling in indignation. Nataya collapsed in relief. Moree followed with a camera as a nurse took the baby to a small bassinet. She snapped pictures like a proud aunt would and followed to take pictures of the swaddled newborn being placed into Nataya's arms.

Nataya reached out for the bundle—wrapped in a beautiful blanket that had been sent from Nataya's sponsor—and gasped softly when she looked into the liquid brown eyes of her baby. The blanket lit up from the flash of the camera, but the young mother barely noticed. A soft hand landed on Nataya's shoulder as Moree leaned close and whispered, "Nataya, your daughter is beautiful."

"Ooh," Nataya breathed, tucking her finger into the baby's closed fist. "A daughter. My sweet daughter."

"Do you know her name?" Moree asked.

Nataya glanced up at Moree, knowing she would understand. "Lawan."

Beautiful.

Moree smiled and nodded. Nataya laughed and leaned to press a kiss to her daughter's soft cheek.

Lord God, out of the ashes you have brought this beauty. I praise Your Holy name...

Author's Note

Thank you for reading *The Heavens Are Telling*. I hope you enjoyed the story. When I finished writing *The Earth is Full*, I had no idea what had happened to baby Noah and his sister, Maly. For months I agonized, wondering where they could have gone and—more importantly—how to save them. While listening to a piece on the radio about some holy places around the world that use orphaned or handicapped children to beg in the streets, to raise money for their temples, an idea formed: What if the children were in the most danger in a place that most of us would consider incredibly safe?

I chose monks and pastors to be the "bad guys" in this story because it is a painful reality in our world. The places we think are safe are often not what they appear. That is not to say that every monk or pastor is evil or corrupt. But as we see in the story, without the indwelling of the Holy Spirit to keep us in check, great evil can be found in any one of us.

Many of my readers believe that Charlotte is modeled after me in the books. And maybe in the beginning of *The Earth is Full* she was. There are moments in her history that are similar to mine. I, too, made poor decisions as a single twenty-something. I, too, found myself pregnant and in a very unhealthy relationship. But, unlike Charlotte, abortion was not something I considered. Still, I was amazed at how many people in my circle of influence, including the father, suggested it. That human life can so easily be dispatched because it is inconvenient is something that breaks my heart daily.

I did miscarry that child and have spent many years grieving the choices I made. The impact of that short life—and the overwhelming pressure from others to end it—changed me forever. The grace that God has shown me for decisions I made when I knew better, still overwhelms me. His grace is sufficient. He is more than capable of love and mercy regardless of our frail inadequacies. I stand forgiven and redeemed because of His blood and sacrifice. No matter what choices you have made in life, He is ready and willing to forgive, to restore, to make new.

When I learned that Destiny Rescue often receives pregnant girls into their care, I was astonished. Somehow I had never thought of the possibility. I was heartbroken when I was told that many Destiny Rescue girls have had abortion forced on them while in captivity. Isn't rape and abuse enough? How frail and mistreated human life has become, from abortion to slavery. The minute someone decides his or her desire is more precious than someone else's very life, true evil has been revealed. Destiny Rescue's commitment is to help these young girls keep their babies if that is their wish, and that makes me all the more endeared to this wonderful organization. I had to write Nataya's story and share this beautiful aspect of Destiny Rescue. Adoption is a wonderful thing, but enabling a woman to keep the baby she has carried and loved is nothing short of extraordinary.

I have had opportunities to meet volunteers and staff in the Destiny Rescue organization, and have discovered that they are simply people that have chosen to follow Christ, whatever the cost, to set captives free. They dare to reach into the darkness and pull young slaves into the light. If you haven't yet sponsored a child with this amazing ministry, I implore you to do so.

Thank you again for reading,

B.D. Riehl

Acknowledgements

As a single word does not alone make a novel, but rather numerous words and thoughts strung together, so an author does not work alone, but rather from the sidelines of influence, life, and love of others. There is no possible way to adequately thank those that have worked on this book with me. But I will try.

My Lord and my God: I write because You let me, and I long to honor You with my words. You and You alone know every moment that it took to write this story, every frustration, every excitement, every line of thought. I can never say enough to give You the praise You are worthy of. In this book, Lord, be glorified.

Richard Riehl: Thank you for your support, for reading my first book and being excited about this one, and for all of the moments in between. I love you.

My beautiful girls: Thank you for being patient with your mommy, even when she wasn't patient with you. Your antics and smiles are my sunshine. Thank you. Now for a summer of park fun!

Daddy: You helped me work out so many plots and scenes. Our coffee Saturdays are the highlight of my week, and I thank you for all of your help on this book.

Debbie Sloane, The Wonderful Editor: I am so grateful for the friendship that has formed from this working relationship. It doesn't feel like work; it oozes ministry and I am thankful to have you as a partner. You have braved the forest of pronouns, untangled vines of incomplete thoughts and squinted through pages of accidental italics, all with grace and wisdom. Thank you.

The rest of the NCC Publishing team: I am blessed to have you to go to with questions and ideas. You are gracious, fun, wise, and wonderful. Thank you for letting me be one of your authors.

Jeanelle Reider: Thank you for your wisdom, prayer, and influence. I cannot wait to see how the Lord guides your career as a writer, and I'm glad to have you in my life.

Luke and Susan Carter: You gave up your cushy retirement, your familiarity—everything you know—to move across the world and seek out the enslaved and bring them to light, freedom, and Christ. On top of that, you graciously took time to answer my questions. Thank you. I am inspired by you and thankful to be part of your church family. *Preah Yeasu Srolein Neak!*

To the women of Ustick Baptist Church: You have been a pillar of encouragement and love to me and many others. Thank you for showing one another the love of Jesus, the wonder that is the Body of Christ, and the fun that is church ladies unleashed at retreat. You're all amazing and I am blessed to fellowship with you.

Judy Ziemer: Thank you for being so hysterical and so real in one short weekend and for being the kind of woman that I knew would be there to help Charlotte in her darkest moment...you know, if she was real.

About the Author

B.D. Riehl lives in Idaho and drinks far more coffee than necessary to keep up with her husband, three daughters, and one crazy dog. When she is not writing, she likes to read books with her girls in their tree fort and sneak ice cream after they're in bed. More than anything, she wants to write books that honor the Lord and tell of His glorious deeds. She is the author of, *The Earth is Full*.

Follow B.D. Riehl:
Blog: `http://www.bdriehl.wordpress.com`
Facebook: `https://www.facebook.com/BDRiehl`

Would you like to receive notifications on free book giveaways, special discounts, or new book announcements from NCC Publishing? If so, you can "like" us on Facebook (NCC Publishing, L.L.C.), or send an email to:

specialoffers@nccpublishing.com

www.nccpublishing.com

If you enjoyed this book, you may enjoy some of the other publications available from NCC Publishing. The complete list of publications is available at:

www.nccpublishing.com/publications

Made in the USA
Charleston, SC
03 October 2014